HOMESICKNESS

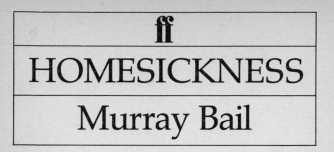

HOMESICKNESS

Murray Bail

faber and faber
LONDON · BOSTON

First published in Great Britain in 1980
by Macmillan London Limited
and simultaneously in Australia
by The Macmillan Company of Australia Pty
First published in this edition in 1986
by Faber and Faber Limited
3 Queen Square London WC1N 3AU

Printed in Great Britain by
Redwood Burn Limited
Trowbridge Wiltshire
All rights reserved

British Library Cataloguing in Publication Data

Bail, Murray
Homesickness
I. Title
823[F]   PR9619.3.B3
ISBN 0–571–13840–3

This novel was written with the assistance of an
Australia Council Literature Board Fellowship (1975–8)

To Margaret

1

Strange sensation then (August 26). To finally have the turbines cut, metallic whistle dying in the ear, and that drumming of the horizontal holding them to their seats like a hand, replaced by solid upright pressure, relative silence, of earth. They sat becalmed, benumbed. The hum and vibration remained within them, and would for some hours. For the time being they felt more like gazing than looking. Chins rested on hands.

Out there all around was concrete, colour of tarpaulins, stained with fuel. This canary-yellow tractor of obscene squatness came crawling towards them. It had a canvas canopy. The local people were going about their work; they took their time. The driver wore khaki and drove one hand.

Chins rested on hands. A majority of the party had flown long distance before; but it was always strange. The immediate end result was strange. Out there lay the beginnings of the foreign country known through hearsay (*heresy*) and photography, its name and persistent shape on the map. There was plenty to see; any minute now. Yet each one felt unable or reluctant to grasp the first impressions. It was as if their bodies had arrived—vaguely they were aware of that—but feelings for time and place were still back at the point of departure or at some point along their flight path; and who can say whether these ever catch up?

Strips of turf and grey, those browns: several dozen browns out there. Oblong cream patch to the left and the obligatory silver roof, and another, hooped. Blurred purple undulating beyond, creased, folded like dropped cloth, and tunnelling cumuli just above it. It's a clear day. Yet the fragments, static and commonplace, are stationed far apart. It's a mosaic—slabs broken, separated. Soon it would become a slowly moving fresco, clarifying, but with certain parts vague or completely missing; always be missing. Several pets, cats and a planter's dalmation, and someone's tortoise in the tail of the jet recorded similar sensations.

The Kaddoks, the couple in their fifties, sat near the back of the group. Here she drew in her breath: it shows the difficulty.

'It's a typical ordinary aerodrome,' she told him. 'Not very large. Some propeller-driven planes over there—hanger—some men coming here; native-looking—I can't see their faces—a dog—another dog.'

'Dogs?' said Kaddok, looking straight ahead. 'They shouldn't be here. What sort of dogs?'

These were cattle dogs with sandpaper noses, with dry skins, eczema (itching papules and vesicles) and the fleas; always jogging: in vast arcs like foxes.

'Brown grass to the right,' she went on, ignoring him. 'I don't see the airport lounge. Yes, I can.'

Behind them Dr Phillip North closed his book. During the flight he had looked up several times as Kaddok, a pale heavy man, felt his way down to the plane's lavatories, blessing each seat with his hand and occasionally someone's startled head. Kaddok wore dark glasses, an open-necked shirt, and a suit of some black thin linen material. Strapped across his chest in bandolier style a Pentax and a spare 75mm lens together looked like some ingenious directional-finding device, a magic eye; and the camera was enclosed in a black leather hood with button, the same as Kaddok's wrist-watch and his eyes. The V of his shirt showed a hive of silver hair bursting forth, yet he was thin on top.

Most of the long flight had been over water. About the only other time North looked up was when they had met land again, and then he followed the hypnotic doodles left by animals, the paths to water, and occasionally a straight yellow road, all part of the earth crust with the eroded beds and lengthy fissures, outcrops, lodes; old, old statements. Thorn trees spotted the land: blackheads on its jaundiced face. North recognized the Longonot volcano, that ancient sore, as the plane's shadow skated and fell into the crater's inkwell. In a dreamy state he waited for it to emerge—half

8

anxious. It had. He still remembers 'where'.

Now Mrs Kaddok smiled at North.

'We made it, touch wood'—her way of introducing herself. The others too began standing, slowly looking around, and put on expressions of unconcern and anticipation.

'No, he's alright,' Mrs Kaddok said, as North offered to help. 'Get a move on, Leon.'

Down on the tarmac the air was colder than the clear sky and the land had led them to believe. An aerodrome breeze, inevitable and international, scribbled at their faces; whiff of kerosene there seemed to be produced by distant artificial trees. With trousers and skirts rattling the group walked to the terminal, more or less duplicating the fuselage shape of their seat positions, even maintaining the aisle—though perhaps without knowing it—with the Kaddoks and Dr Phillip North taking up the rear.

The airport like any other was still neutral territory. Only outside the gates and heading towards the capital did they begin to spark up. The British-built bus had sliding windows and an incredibly long gear lever. Lining the road were typical airport trees resistant to the winds, obviously planted recently, but then the road turned sharply left into the foreign country itself, all exposed now, open for inspection. It was like a curtain pulled back on a foreign-produced film and they were driving into the scenery. It offered no resistance. The bent figures of women scratching at the earth didn't even look up. Occasionally a car passed. These were small English sedans, post-war, and crowded with joint families. In the bus some twisted in their seats to see, staring and switching from side to side, anxious not to miss anything.

From the front a young man assumed the role of lookout.

'A baobab tree, see, over there!'

He was right.

'The Traveller's Friend,' someone told them. 'You find tons of them up in our north.'

Dozens of the bloated baobab: bursting out, scattered like magnified pineapples.

'A bit of the old wattle there. Fancy. I would never have thought . . .'

Someone nodded: 'So it is, look!'

Behind the bus an elderly native had fallen from his bike, but no one noticed.

'Acacia,' a man told them. There is always one who knows the names of things.

Acacia melanoxylon. And to Leon Kaddok the landscape became coloured and jagged with their exclamations and he had to lean towards his wife, Gwen, to catch her running commentary.

The baobab tree (*Adansomia digitata*). Wattle. Then the lookout leaning forward down the front appeared to mutter to himself and blink before he swung around, pointing hoarsely, 'Gum Trees!' True: at a bend in the road, like the one at Rapallo, a superb specimen with the peeling trunk, the usual mess on the ground.

'Have we left home?' a wag called out. 'Everybody please check their tickets.' .

They had to laugh.

And they saw others at mid-distance, solitary old wool clippers under sail, and other eucalypts clustered on the grassy slopes, grazing gums.

'Eucalyptus globulus,' the man said, raising horse laughter. But he was being serious. It was Kaddok. He said it again, louder.

Eucalyptus globulus.

It could almost have been their own country: these sections with the gums briefly framed like a traditional oil painting by the slowly passing window. The colours were as brown and parched; that chaff-coloured grass. Ah, this dun-coloured realism. Any minute now the cry of a crow or a cockatoo; but no.

A tall figure in an ochre robe crossed ahead, sauntering, or rather floated among some cattle, and the cows were scruffy, with pre-historic pouch throats: drifting apparently aimless across the ground, kicking up dust. He was only a few yards from the bulky bus but ignored it, heading out into the stones and emptiness. They noticed his head partly shorn. His face was clay-dyed: jewelry glittered from his forehead. His gait had adapted to the jingling drift of cattle. Perhaps that had endowed him with the ancient stateliness. At any rate he silenced them; and they swung in their seats. The women sighed.

They noticed then other details.

This was an old, tangled land. It was complex, far more than they had realized. For there were thorn trees and oceans of swaying foreign grass, seeds flying off like spray, and at intervals the protruding thatched cone of a storage hut. And what was that species of tree, its blurred foliage isosceles triangle in shape, flat on top, unlike anything they had seen—growing everywhere here? (*Acacia senegal.*) Increasingly, the gums became incongruous. These were transplanted, surely: something from their past, their own country, and yet for that very reason worth mentioning on their postcards. Entering the capital the streets gradually became dense with rusty velocipedes, mechanical insects whirring, and early motor cyles British again, many fitted with chairs, Velocettes and Ariels, even a Panther, and silver scooters and hissing buses too were honking and dispersing the pedestrians, beggars on wooden skateboards. It was a scattered, low-skyline city. Their hotel was the tallest building, in pride of place.

Doug ('Howdy') Cathcart paddled backwards and for-wards alone doing his own private breast-stroke: appearing/disappearing, his metronomic head giving the impression he was treading on springs. Actually more decibels were produced by his wife in the deck chair, slapping oil into her thighs which shuddered something terrible: stubby woman of principle. On the lawn close by, Louisa Hofmann carelessly offered a comparison. She was slender, well-exercised, late in her thirties. Facing the sun, her head resolutely held to one side declared she wouldn't be going for a dip. Her husband sat up reading the latest *Time* and every now and then looked at the water. There were cane tables, and waiters in white jackets came around with colourful drinks. The pool area was protected from the elements by the L shape of the hotel, and on the two open sides by a powerful thorn hedge and a concrete wall; jutting from the wall a pergola converted into an aviary held tiny shivering black-and-white birds, though no one, not even Phillip North, had gone over to inspect them. They could hear over the wall the cries of fruit sellers and the blindmen.

Cathcart climbed or rather crawled out and fumbled red-eyed in a Qantas bag for his towel. He found his sunglasses and sank in the chair beside his wife. How many lengths had he done? It must have been a good seven.

'Did nine lengths, dear.'

A thud-bang and a spoilt double somersault/jack-knife: the way the board kept going like a tuning fork could easily get on some people's nerves.

Who kept doing that? The show-off in Hawaiian shorts.

At that point Shiela Standish came into the lawn at a half-trot, one hand shielding her eyes, but relaxed when she recognized the group. It had taken her several seconds. Strange how people alter when they shed their clothes. The men: it must be like them in a room just in their underpants, although here the thing wasn't hanging loose. Upstairs Shiela had a floral costume, a one-piece with bones. She'd brought it as always just in case. Shiela knew the longer she didn't put it on the more difficult it would be later. And yet she carried a cardigan and postcards to write. She chose a place next to the Cathcarts.

In the shade by the pergola someone plomped himself in the chair next to Phillip North. It was the diver patterned in tropical flowers. North had all along intended going for a walk, a stroll, to look around, and was dressed for it in an open shirt, cotton trousers and sandals, but the long flight and probably the events before it had made him tired.

'How's it going? Garry Atlas.'

Dr North shook the outstretched hand. It was dripping wet.

'This is the life, aye?' said Atlas, looking around. 'I'd say this is what it was all about. What do you reckon?'

Transparent globules hung all over his chest, caught the sunlight, and suddenly merged to piddle down between his legs. He was purple-lipped, shivering a bit. The silver watch on his wrist, of large diameter and sporting a black dial, leaked water. Staring at this North showed concern at the tiny white cloud forming under the glass. North noticed other signs of his ostentatious indifference to water. It seemed to be deliberate; it could be an affectation. A silver ring on one finger; and there jammed between his hip and saturated elastic he'd shoved his cigarettes and a box of matches! North began smiling, almost laughing.

'What are you reading?' Garry reached over.

And smiling North watched as he held the book in his wet hands.

'Shit!' said Garry, turning the pages: Goddard's *Method of Reaching Extreme Altitudes*. It was the 1919 edition.

'I haven't read this one,' he said, glancing at the pool. 'Was this what you were reading on the old plane?'

'Some light reading,' North nodded, seeing the joke.

But Atlas wasn't interested. He leaned forward and spoke out of the corner of his mouth.

'Listen, if you get browned off here, come over to us. There's a spare chair. You can meet some of the women. There's three of them.'

Dr North, who had a grey beard, gave a tired smile.

'No, I tell a lie,' said Garry putting his hand across his heart and looking up at the sky. 'There's only two-and-a-half. They're all dogs. But what the hell?'

Bending over, the neck and ears redden. Intestines appear in the forehead. Gazing at the young Adam's Apple, the neck of the racehorse, North saw a tremendous even suntan which wasn't coloured by blood-pressure: solar energy, solar myth. And as in his neck, veins ran wild on the back of his hand. Cigarettes were on his breath (non-filters).

'Have you tried that local brew they've got here yet?'

Before North could answer ('No') Atlas was on his feet.

'Jump!' he shouted. 'Now!' Grinning, nodding he made mock charges towards the girl on the diving board. 'Excuse me,' he said to North.

He sat down, shaking his head.

'There's one for you. She's a character.' The girl sat on

the end of the board and turned her back on him. 'Did you see one of her tits fall out before?'

'No,' said North.

He immediately regretted saying it. He wasn't interested.

'Only one,' Atlas explained. 'Her top slipped off. Phew, it almost knocked my eye out. Ver-ee nice! Sasha is her name. Sasha-somebody. She has a friend, an actress if you don't mind! And I thought it was her bloody mother.'

Only one swimmer now travelled the pool. It took a lap to see who this was: Hofmann, Kenneth Hofmann, without the glasses. And he was further altered by the Australian Crawl. It requires the mouth to regularly twist sideways for breathing, giving the swimmer the appearance of a sergeant shouting to men behind him. Hofmann's etherized wife still lay facing the sun, her mouth pulled slightly to one side (similar to her swimming husband's).

About then Kaddok came shuffling in, holding onto his wife. A number of people stopped in mid-sentence or lowered their voices. He had one hand slightly outstretched and his black suit was dusty. They'd been outside. As they passed she bowed slightly at North and smiled—energetic teeth! Kaddok's suit was buttoned up and one hand cupped his camera. Alongside the blue transparent pool he looked out of place.

Thud-bang again. Garry Atlas showed them how it was done. Most looked up: a reflex action. And sure enough he held them by staying under for an inordinate length of time, finally standing up ankle deep with a gasp and swaying, blowing his nose.

In the midst of such activity Shiela Standish had put on her cardigan and dated only one postcard. Doug had said 'Howdy' and commented briefly on the climate, the exchange rate he had managed to get at the hotel, and their holiday last year, a caravan tour around Tasmania. Nothing of course compared to this trip which he called the Big-Un.

Hello? Louisa Hofmann had sat up and leaned back on her elbows. Other eyes had turned to the glass door.

A man wearing a vivid blue suit and holding a silver

14

microphone had come through giving loud instructions over his shoulder in a language only Phillip North understood. He was stopped short. '*Merde! Allons!*' Small as it was the microphone wire had caught under the door. One of the waiters—they were all crowding the door now—silently sprang forward and freed it. Then came four young men each with a neat black moustache and carrying various bits of equipment, some of it heavy. One had the TV camera on his shoulder and trailed cables. A red-haired girl wearing a silk shirt and no brassière held a clipboard. Garry Atlas had been about to do another jack-knife but changed his mind.

For the first time Hofmann murmured something to his wife. Both sat up looking at the door.

The redhead acted all stuckup. She had her back to them while the man in blue strode over to the edge of the pool. They noticed then he had a pink unnaturally perfect complexion, and beautifully combed hair. His crew stumbled after him. At the chrome steps he stopped with his back to the camera, ran his tongue over his teeth several times, and slipped on a pair of rose-tinted spectacles. Oh là là! As he turned, a red light on the camera lit up. 'Raymond Canterel, *Antenne Deux, en extérieur*,' he said earnestly, almost worried. The rest of his spiel rose and fell among the chairs and tables: a never-ending sentence to them. Punctuation consisted chiefly of visual effects: a rhythmic shrugging of shoulders interspersed with a kind of hunching-up, look-up of surprise, and like a busker who simultaneously plays the drums, cymbals, bells and a mouth organ, threw in a wide range of calculated eyebrow movements and frowns, his hands describing sweeping arabesques and numerical symbols. '*Economie* . . . Briteesh Empire . . . *capitalisme* . . . *cuisine* . . . *Mélancolie* . . . *éléphants* . . . *le* noble *sauvage* . . . were some of the recognizable words.

In an adroit movement he turned unexpectedly to the nearest nest of chairs.

'Par-don,' he smiled. 'What are your *impressions d'Afrique?*'

Poor Shiela. She froze. Her grey eyes which were

normally magnified grew even larger staring at the microphone.

'Beg yours?' said Doug Cathcart, stepping in. A shade too loud.

His wife though understood perfectly.

'We've only just arrived,' she told them firmly, or rather the camera to the man's right. She gave the skirt of her bathing costume a few tugs.

But this didn't satisfy the Frenchman.

'First impressions, don't you find them interesting? Interesting, if perhaps dangerous?' Turning to the camera he rolled his eyes, '*Ah, ces Anglo-Saxons!*'

'Interesting! Oh, yes,' said Shiela, nodding.

'We've been told,' said Cathcart in his nasal voice, 'not to drink the ice here.'

'It's not exactly tidy,' agreed his wife. 'But we've only just arrived.'

The people . . . smell, she felt like saying. Or they smell different. And they don't talk. They stare or glance at us. Still, it's a holiday and interesting. We're on a holiday.

The TV crew had moved on.

No, not Kaddok! They all squinted as the crew surrounded him on the other side of the pool.

'My husband is blind,' explained his wife.

Profuse apologies! But Kaddok interrupted.

'Interesting country. Thorn trees, spoor and so on. The tall animals such as the giraffe. A colourful dark people. The women in their brightly coloured costumes—dyed from berries, I believe. Naked kiddies, Africa. I've always wanted to visit Africa. Livingstone's trek, remember? The Masai—very proud people. Burton and Speke. I've taken already, let me see, a number of subjects. Ektachrome X, I use,' tapping his camera. 'ASA Speed 64. I wouldn't use anything else.'

Looking straight ahead as he spoke Kaddok sweated. The camera's little light was off, saving valuable film, although the man in blue remained in front still holding out the microphone, *un diplomatiste*.

Garry Atlas who had trailed the crew stood beside the

redhead, and dripping water, spoke to her. It was his method usually to crack a small joke. But she turned her head away: hominivorous bitch, look and lighting up yet another Gauloise.

They moved on to Sasha and her friend, the actress; Garry began whistling.

Violet Hopper, recently Mrs: chiefly a taker of bit-parts in film, the distant aging sister in a period dress. Ibsen? Trollope? Her apparent trouble was: only occasionally could she go outside her own smooth surface, even there being interviewed. She lifted her chin, tilted her head and spoke. As for Sasha she could only hitch up her top and laugh across as her friend offered the answers. Sasha was no help, none. She was on the verge of collapse. North found himself smiling. Not even the *Rive Gauche* redhead could object. And matters were made even worse by Garry Atlas in the background there standing on his head, supporting the earth, waving his legs whenever Sasha looked up. Everyone had their mouths open, and some began laughing.

'Africa?' someone else answered. A tall wide-shouldered man in a wash-n-wear suit. 'Africa's got the ball at her feet. Good healthy climate. Not a bad diet when you look closely at it. Labour and natural resources: I think it's got a bloody good future.'

'Is he with us?' Louisa whispered. Her husband, Ken, was supposed to never forget a face.

'Was he on our plane?' asked another.

'I don't think I've seen that one,' said Ken Hofmann. He smiled. 'But he should be with us.'

'Nothing like the Aussie accent,' said Doug, pretty loud, nodding at the bloke. The stranger gave him the thumbs up.

Fancy being on television! Shiela, for one, had found it fascinating. That was always the thing about travel: the unexpected. The proof lay clearly on her lap. In all honesty she could say she hadn't had time 'till now' to write 'even a postcard.'

'I am with an interesting and rather nice group of

people,' she quickly began. But by then she saw most were getting up and going inside; and when the Cathcarts followed suit, with Doug yawning, she decided to gather up the postcards and finish them in her room.

Three tables had been pushed together, camouflaged by a loose-fitting cloth, more an iridescent blanket than 'table-cloth'; but away from their own country, in an unfamiliar dining room, even eating off an unstable surface seemed to be an adventure. They had dressed for dinner. The men appeared in patterned jackets and cotton trousers, their hair combed, and Cathcart and Ken Hofmann both came down in the same click-clicking white shoes. The women had put on special blouses, and skirts, some in long skirts or long dresses, and silk ribbons—Gwen Kaddok wore a shawl—and for some reason the wives entered with folded arms and solemn expressions. Skirts and dresses. Interesting . . . One is supported by the hips. The skirt is. Its weight must tug and remind that part of the body all day. In Africa: the grass skirt. Resting on the hips it creates a constant swish. Its removal eventually is in parts, two time-delaying motions: woman 'steps out of skirt.' The sensible floral dress was Mrs Cathcart's. Supported by the shoulders the dress is (eventually) lifted up over the hair, mechanical, elbow-jerking motion: those few seconds of blindness. Violet Hopper's dress had all lines, angles and energy aimed at the waistline: so narrow and brittle. As for the jeans worn by Sasha they traced the soft hourglass shape and other differences: how a woman's knees touch, as underlined in Life Classes. With Violet Hopper this could take place only beneath her dress. And Sasha had barged in ahead of her friend, swinging her leather bag.

At this stage the party kept to its original groups. Sitting with the Cathcarts suited Shiela. She could watch the others and appear to join in. Garry Atlas stuck with the girls. At the other end, Phillip North took his place with the Kaddoks without thinking; Gwen nodded acknowledging the habit. The Hofmanns sat together: he already gazed at a spot on the bare wall, drumming his fingers on his teeth.

Behind him was a mural showing ('depicting') a tribe of wrestlers rolling entwined in the sky above a tiny but widespread European-styled city. They were thick thighed, these coffee-coloured wrestlers—of course—and wore fur coats. Evidently it was the work of a well-known local surrealist. It was reproduced across the menu cover in full colour but unfortunately out of register, so that the menu or the dining room itself seemed to vibrate from the falls of the heavy men.

Two empty chairs: gradually they had an irritating effect. Just about everybody glanced at them and became distracted, some frowning and glancing at them again, as they tried to recall the missing pair, wondering where they were. There was fidgeting of forks. It had grown dark outside. Some who twisted in their seats seemed to think the waiters would arrive only when the group was complete— the anticipatory hunger of travellers.

Gerald Whitehead hurried in, and with him a younger man wearing an old US air force jacket, tropical style.

They quickly sat down. Gerald nodded at his neighbours, apologetic, and seeing the rest of the table looking at him with interest, put his head down. People naturally thought the two had been together but the younger one put out his hand and introduced himself. James Borelli. *Borelli.* Italian? He waved the fork like one. At the same time Gerald began spearing the bridge of his nose with his forefinger, to poke his glasses back. The odd thing about that hand, as Shiela and Mrs Cathcart observed, was that it had an additional small finger, a burden to that side which is connected to the brain's reasoning, non-creative sector.

But they quickly became accustomed to that and Gerald's nose-spearing (seven, eight times a minute), and turned to Borelli. He was a little over thirty but carried a walking stick. He hooked it over the neck of his chair. He had pleasant keen eyes. As he discussed with Gerald what they had seen outside he saw Louisa Hofmann watching, and gave an open slow smile.

Evidently Gerald Whitehead must have felt it. For then he looked up too.

Garry Atlas here took the opportunity.

'Say, you missed out being on television. We were all stars'—looking around—'weren't we?'

'There was a film here,' nodded Mrs Cathcart down the end.

'Yep.'

'Sixteen-mill,' Kaddok told them.

'French television,' others explained, several talking at once, and all looking at Borelli for his reaction.

'And I don't suppose we'll ever get to see it ourselves.'

Although he kept listening Gerald Whitehead remained staring at his hands.

'I went dry inside,' Shiela whispered to Mrs C. 'You were good. You told them exactly enough.'

'I wouldn't drink that if I were you,' Doug advised.

'Doug's right,' Mrs Cathcart turned to Borelli. 'You'll get the trots.'

'Never mind. We're not living long.'

'Don't you get constipated travelling?' Shiela asked, leaning forward. 'I find I do.'

'Thanks, chief,' said Doug to the waiter. Plates were now being served.

'I simply love the French language,' Louisa Hofmann was saying. 'I could just sit and listen to it all day.'

Her husband turned to her. 'You don't know a word of French.'

She was about to protest when the film crew trooped in and sat at the other long table, talking loudly.

For Borelli's benefit Garry Atlas pointed with his forehead, 'That's the crew there.'

It was the last mention of the film.

'I can't eat this,' Carthcart pushed his plate away. 'It's yams or something. How are you people finding it?' he called down the table.

'Right!' Atlas nodded with his mouth full. 'A T-bone anyday. But I'm wading through. When in Rome, you know . . .'

'I'll eat anything,' Sasha murmured to Violet. 'A horse or anything. Gosh, I'm hungry.'

'But you always are,' said her friend looking away.

Garry was going on, 'The beer's pissy too. It's not within a bull's roar of ours. Have you had any yet?'

'You're a vegetarian?' Mrs Kaddok asked.

North nodded.

'We too,' she smiled.

North cleared his throat. 'Yes, the diet of harmless beasts with slow reactions.'

'I hadn't thought of it that way.' And again Gwen showed her teeth. She turned, 'Did you hear that, Leon?'

North frowned. He hadn't exactly meant it like that.

'Elephants,' Kaddok confirmed, 'eat eight hundred to a thousand pounds of grass a day. They weigh up to seven and a half tons. Both sexes of the African elephant have tusks.'

'Eight and a half tons,' Dr North corrected gently.

'Our waiters,' Mrs Cathcart announced to the rest, 'if you look, have got bare feet.' And she made a clicking noise with her tongue.

The waiters too could understand English.

'Oh dear,' said Shiela, perplexed.

She'd asked for tea, they'd given her coffee. Shiela looked around and decided to drink it.

'Say, guess what?'

This was Garry Atlas again leaning forward with a quiz question; veins on his neck bulging. 'Guess what I saw on the end of the diving board?' He turned to everybody at the table. 'Someone had scratched on it with a knife, or something. "REMEMBER–DAWN–FRASER". It's there. And in brackets they've put A-U-S-T.'

'Austria?' Borelli suggested.

'She's our swimmer!' Cathcart cried out down the end.

'Right!' Garry nodded.

'Someone's been here before us,' giggled Sasha to Violet. Sshhh.

'One of the best,' said Doug. 'The 1960 Rome Olympics, remember?'

'The first woman to break sixty secs for the one hundred metres,' Kaddok said. 'Freestyle.'

The stranger they'd seen at the pool passed but didn't

21

stop at the table. He gave them the thumbs up.

North lit a small cigar and glanced at his watch.

There was a lull as they realized where they were; or how far they had gone away.

'Have you been overseas before?'

Sasha shook her head. 'This is the first time.'

Directly below lay the pool illuminated by Dutch underwater lamps, ultramarine slab sloping to dark cold at the deep end. The surface tilted with the shifting dining room fixtures and candles, fluid lights, and the board floated, an interesting twisted rectangle. The board and the surrounding tiles were still riddled with pools. Further out, the bordering lawn was soaked in shadow and suggestion, black but not completely, Reinhardt's black. And from the dining room they could see over the wall large silhouettes, evidence of new constructions, capital, and a hidden flashing light. There was no muffled racket from there now; no distant sibilance of wheels, not even the last truck or a bicycle bell. It was late but the window-wall also possessed pleasant editing properties. The entire continent felt empty.

'There aren't many lights,' Hofmann reflected as he folded his serviette, breaker of silences.

Does he mean neon?

'This is Africa,' Whitehead reminded him, almost rudely, looking down at his cup.

The Museum of Handicrafts: MUSEUM spelt MUSEU. Of handicrafts, arts'n local artifacts perhaps. These people were known for their woven baskets and the painted gourd; grass bags; jewelry as strapped to the forehead: and so on. Fabrics, but to a lesser extent.

Many other groups after sitting down to the English breakfast must have strolled the same three or four blocks to the Museum, for although they took up the full width of the footpath, talking and pointing things out to each other, often pausing for photographs, little notice was taken of them by the locals, the natives preferring the road. Doug Cathcart had a pair of powerful binoculars and now and then stopped, his bow-legged wife alongside, as he focused on a distant cyclist or a woman breast-feeding. The morning was clear and pleasant. Except for his shuffle and the way he leaned to hear his wife, Kaddok looked no different from anyone else. Most of the others wore special sunglasses too. As they turned into the square and saw the building, someone—it was Gerald Whitehead—let out a low whistle of disapproval.

Facing them the Museum dominated, overwhelmed the square. It was para-Palladian, ambitious in scope, hoping to gain kudos from one of the previous high points in Western civilization. It had the grey steps, the portentous columns, porticos and mock balconies; while the square in the foreground had been set aside as a piazza, concave à la Siena. Such was the Museum's presence (pressure) the roofs of the ramshackle shops lining the square had splintered upwards. On the short left side a collapsing lazaretto and a basket factory had trees and shafts of grass growing out of the cracks.

There were other things wrong. Gerald stood making sounds of unbelievability with his tongue.

1) Look, that proposed 'piazza' in the foreground was a dustbowl. It was paved with mud bricks but crowded with squatting apothecaries and vegetable dealers; skinny men flogged aphrodisiacs (displayed on folded blankets); outdoor butchers there to one side, a Club; rhythmic Malevich knife-grinder next cranking a large stone with one foot; what looked like rows of Medicine Men (their arcane jars, powders, animal skins); an elderly ocularist; Sirdarjis and drifting Somalis; the inevitable tellers of fortunes—at least two dozen of them under torn umbrellas; and there were canvas awnings, an acrobat suspended between nasal monotonous hawking. The function of the 'piazza' was neatly eclipsed.

2) The museum itself. Somehow its ratios were out. It was ungainly, oppressively so. Through an oversight or to fit into the square it had been made squat. A

23

good case of the Golden Rectangle ignored or mis-understood. Architects should sign their names on buildings, as they do in Argentina.

Gerald kept shaking his head, muttering. Was anyone else so aghast?

3) On the roof to one side had been grafted a cupola. Quite incongruous. It was pink, a huge Moscow breast, pierced by a tilting television aerial.
4) And flanking the entrance, two rusting pedestals held a half-ton pair of vulgar terrestrial condors—or were they crows?—cast in concrete. These were visible from a great distance. Dr North told Shiela they were African vultures.

They had climbed the steps and were approaching the main doors. From behind the pillars figures stirred. A beggar on crutches managed to stand up, other gangetic shapes moved and as both Louisa Hofmann and Violet felt it necessary to lift their hems, bones shot out, finger nails, yes, for baksheesh.

'Don't give them anything,' Doug Cathcart shouted, his mouth dry. Borelli had one hand in his pocket. 'Or you'll never get rid of them. They'll tag along!'

And Kaddok, raising his camera at one—a face swollen with ganglia—nicely caught the open mouth and milky stare of a native, blind.

Looking up then they could see that the sans-serif MUSEU OF HANDICRAFTS was 'printed' in neon pipes. MUSEU was not a misspelling or an example—as Sasha had assumed—of some local dialect. The M had long ago fallen off in a wind and as they passed underneath they were showered in sparks from the permanent short circuit.

Shiela attached herself to the Cathcarts as they moved inside and immediately began looking around for the Handicrafts. The unexpected bright lighting, circuits of flickering fluorescent, punctuated by duds and ceiling fans, and others about to expire, made her sneeze. She blew her nose. The Museum sounded completely empty. A few divisions of plywood broke up the cavernous space. Even from a distance these looked ricketty.

In a peeved voice Gerald asked whether it was open or finished yet.

There was after all a smell of fresh paint.

Doug Cathcart cleared his throat, a bit irritated.

Ah! a tall robed figure appeared. He had bare feet and so they hadn't heard him. Sasha and Violet exchanged glances, raising their eyebrows. He was a Masai, stone-faced, and smelling of cattle. Although he said nothing they all followed him. Now in the bright hall they could see heads and eyes of the museum staff in cubicles apparently waiting for their arrival. The guide stopped and looked on with them. An attendant—or was he curator?— in khaki shorts and bare feet busily wrapped some rope around a dented lawnmower. His cubicle was crowded with lawn-mowers. All appeared to be in original condition (the bottle-green duco) although the filigree of scratches and the mirror-finish of the flywheels indicated a long hard life. One still had the rare canvas grass-catcher, a British invention. Borelli speculated whether that model would have been pre-Suez. Along with the sturdy British motor cycle, the mowers (*By Appointment* . . . in gold transfer) held the lion's share of the export market. At the height of the Empire . . . Foreshadowing the Empire's decline, the BSA motor bikes and Moffatt & Richardson mowers of the 1950s developed stasis in their design and model range, proclaimed more a sturdy heaviness, as if the traditional arteries from Head Office had gradually and irreparably hardened.

With a leap backwards the mechanic/attendant started a two-stroke. Within the stone walls it kicked up a tremend-ous reverberating racket and the blue smoke made the ladies step back and press handkerchiefs to their nostrils. He started another, then a third—a small one with an unusual kick-starter. Then he turned to the one which clearly held pride of place, the large bowling green model in the foreground: heavy roller and perforated tractor seat! For all its size this seemed to be the quietest of them all, 'the Rolls

Royce of lawn-mowers'; but by then with what, four, five firing and vibrating together it was difficult to tell. 'For Chrissake!' Doug Cathcart shouted, 'Tell him to stop!' Turning and waving his arms at the guide he found the Masai and the Brown attendant standing open mouthed, watching the machines. The smoke—'carbon monoxide,' Gwen Kaddok repeated several times, choking—would hang in the hall for hours.

The next few exhibits were without attendants.

Under glass three English toothpaste tubes were at different stages of use: full, half full (thumb-dented tube, white worm protruding), and a fine example of a completely empty one, squeezed dry, corrugated, curled and scratched. Alongside lay a pair of false teeth and arrows pointing back to the toothpaste. The teeth alone were a source of wonder. The mechanic had left the mowers and with the Masai had both elbows on the cabinet. At intervals he looked up and Gwen Kaddok noticed him staring at her teeth. She gave a confused smile. He turned back to the display.

The next cabinet a few yards on held a compass and a French cigarette-rolling machine, but what attracted their guide's attention was nailed on the wall above it: a U-shaped magnet barnacled with small nails and hairpins. Visitors could apparently test its mysterious power for themselves. But when the guide touched a bottom pin the whole lot came away like bees and scattered over the floor.

Garry Atlas had missed this. With Violet Hopper and Sasha he had gone ahead, perhaps looking for the Handicrafts, and he called out, 'Hey, this is a beauty. Get a load of this!' The other came up to an early TV set standing in a slight puddle. To demonstrate its colour and moving qualities—because there is no television in Africa, the dark continent—the insides were filled with lime-green water and three brightly coloured fish darted about, this way and that, chased by a baby crocodile. 'Perpetual motion,' Phillip North nodded; he recognized the fish. About a dozen natives from the cubicles they hadn't yet reached were squatting in front, hands on their knees, watching. A striped sitringee had been placed on the floor for this purpose. Doug Cathcart stepped in front of the guide and in a loud voice asked where the Handicrafts were—'as you advertised?' There must have been a language problem. The Masai looked blankly at him, then back at the TV screen.

'Jee-zus,' said Garry through his teeth.

'Don't worry,' said Borelli with a wave of his hand.

Others began frowning and standing tiptoe looking around. That was what they had come here for: Handicrafts, local examples of. They moved forward again.

'A pantomimic guide,' North remarked to Gerald, 'is what I've always wanted when travelling. Though here it's a bit odd, to say the least.'

Gerald nodded but stopped. They'd bumped into their group crowding around another exhibit.

What was this? A fully grown lion fixed in a ferocious springing position by bricks and several wires. Facing it, scarcely a yard away, stood an old plate camera on a bandaged tripod, its legs splayed apart. Although an evocative scene, suggesting a range of possibilities—men found themselves grinning—the tall Masai went in among the wires and ignoring the lion stood stiffly in front of the camera. Garry, for one, began laughing outright. On closer examination it was noticed the lion's mane was moth-eaten, had not been properly preserved, and someone had stuck a cigarette in its mouth. The camera, a pre-war Linhoff, was clearly in mint condition, but Kaddok who was the last to leave, also shook his head in dismay when told of the wide aperture settings.

They scarely glanced in the next cubicle. A Kikuya in the Museum's khaki shorts demonstrated a wheelbarrow by lifting it, moving it forward, backwards, and repeating it.

Plywood walls at that point formed a sudden cul-de-sac—only a few yards deep. But natives, one brilliant tribal dress and a shaved head, stood in front of the important exhibit. It was lit by a powerful spotlight. Garry Atlas had to elbow his way through. 'Jesus,' he said and turned round, 'don't bother.' On a pedestal waist high for easy viewing stood a soda-water syphon. Admittedly, it possessed a compelling strangeness under a bright light in a museum but Mrs Cathcart reflected the mood of almost everybody as they tried to reverse in the narrow space. 'Most of this stuff,' she said aloud, 'we've got in the garage at home. It's garbage.'

It somehow made Shiela look concerned.

What in God's name, for instance, was the point in displaying a pair of pitted tubular steel chairs?

'An important invention of Europe,' James Borelli tried, 'on a par with the wheel.' He was leaning on his walking stick, telling Gerald. Was he being ironical? The rest had moved on. 'It was an early democratic breakthrough,' he said. 'A radical improvement—I mean on the feudal squat.'

Often Borelli threw out statements before he got to know people. Pursing his lips Gerald was about to disagree.

'Come of it,' Garry Atlas interrupted—this was bullshit. 'These natives had thrones, I bet.'

'You just want to be different,' Louisa smiled at Borelli.

But he repeated: 'No!' And using his hands extravagantly, he went on discussing the difference between a chair and a seat. 'For one thing, seat is an institutional term. It is commercial.'

'Oh? What about a dentist's chair?' Gerald argued.

For the first time, Mrs Hofmann turned and laughed outright. She lifted her chin and closed her eyes. 'I'm glad I amuse you, at least,' Borelli smiled.

Meanwhile their 'guide' was behind, still rapt in the empty soda syphon.

They passed two objects which had been combined: an early Singer sewing machine and an umbrella. To save space the umbrella had been opened, revealing its construction, and placed on the machine, but someone without thinking or to demonstrate the jabbering needle, had got it tangled and mutilated something terrible. This irrational massacre of the umbrella made some of them annoyed. It was another sign of real stupidity! To others, Shiela for one, the unexpected image caused a different

28

sensation: such a black indelible violation was almost thrilling.

Until then Shiela had taken a sincere, equal interest in everything. Her frown had remained generally constant, the same as when they had disembarked, when she had sat with them around the pool, and when she joined in at the dinner table.

'Cop this one!' Atlas called out. He'd managed to work his way to the front again like a journalist, always keen to be first.

'I wish he'd shut up,' said Louisa Hofmann. She'd found wet white paint on Ken's blazer and was rubbing at it with a handkerchief. 'It won't come off. I'm only making it worse.'

When the group reached Atlas there grinning with his arms folded ('Have a dekko!) they heard what seemed to be the hiss of a small foundation, and Mrs Cathcart first going abruptly terse, turned: 'This isn't necessary. This is disgusting,' she said, and glanced at her watch.

In the narrowest of cubicles, the attendant, only a boy, pointed to a porcelain urinal. Yanking on the chain, repeating paternosters in his own tongue, he'd watch, shaking his head. The Masai joined him and they muttered together, chuckling each time at the wonder of it: laughter bubbling from a collective cistern behind their teeth.

'So now we know what men do,' Violet offered drily, as they moved on.

'I've often wondered myself,' Sasha agreed. 'How funny. I feel sorry for them.'

'Now you know,' said Garry Atlas, as if slapping them on their backs.

'I don't think I've ever seen anything quite so ridiculous,' Mrs Cathcart kept saying. 'It's a disgrace.' For support, Doug kept quiet but made a show of frowning at his watch.

They passed a pair of German binoculars without testing their amazing powers. The old man twenty yards away apparently stood there at attention for this purpose.

It was about here that a nail tore Borelli's cotton jacket and as he twisted to free it, a partition somewhere behind them fell and—Jesus!—was followed by the sound else-

29

where of splintering glass. Not the soda-water syphon?

The Masai took no notice.

Moving quickly now they ignored a sidecar removed from its motor cycle, though Phillip North stopped as several natives watched a solemn chief wearing a bone through his nose try to sit in it while still clutching his spears.

All museums have teething troubles or problems of form. Here the exit seemed to be close, for they could hear the market crowd outside, but without warning they came upon the colour TV set again, and their tall 'guide' trod on Violet's foot as they U-turned. They had to keep walking.

No one spoke much now. The general mood was to get through it as quickly as possible. Most had their thoughts elsewhere as they shuffled along.

Hey. What dis?

The Masai and a group of his followers had pricked up their ears and gone off scouting ahead, a loping jog: close, definitely some sort of machinery making a subtle yet beckoning racket. Each one could hear it. Its familiarity may well have been obscured by the plywood avenues, well-known for acoustic properties, for when they reached the source each one pulled a face or shrugged. The clocks were the ordinary kind, not even antique, so of dubious provenance and tune, all ticking and telling a different time. About thirty different times. The overlapping ticks produced an obsessive almost intolerable density. A few wristlet watches, stripped of their bands, contributed, muffled crickets. Pendulum there of a Pisa-leaning grandfather, hell, swung among pale weeds. Faces had cracked and small hands were missing.

A wooden door flapped open, a cuckoo sprang out—but it sounded more like an outback crow. The effect on the natives however crowding the centre of the cubicle was a hopping on one foot, pointing and laughing, clapping hands. They were still waiting for the horologic bird to re-emerge, glancing at the false alarms produced by other chiming clocks, including one sick cuckoo on a spring which hadn't the strength to get back in, as the party led now by Cathcart moved off.

Ahead were the tall doors of the entrance. Perhaps they'd skipped a few exhibits? The museum suddenly seemed small under the cavernous roof. They looked back. Fledgling museum, an attempt. The assemblage, the policy of combing for items, would continue. Within sight of the doors it was felt they could linger and pay more attention to the remaining items. Only two or three left. An X-ray photograph of a grinning head tacked up and back-lit by a hair-raising electrolier attracted attention. It was a three-quarter side view of the skull; male. Estimates of his age ranged from 36 to 49. It was hard to tell. Garry Atlas cracked a few jokes which nobody got.

'A practised meat-eater, by the look,' North noted. 'Strong mandibles. He could be mid-West American or Australian.'

'Right,' nodded Hofmann leaning forward. 'Five fillings. Impacted third molar. Lower right five occlusal.'

Hofmann had barely spoken a word until then. Naturally they turned.

'You're a dentist?' Sasha cried.

'He won't bite though,' said Mrs Hofmann. And she went on, 'My husband is quite the most harmless creature. When anyone's hurt, he's the first to cry like a baby. Aren't you, Ken-dear?'

The last few words spoken partly through her teeth opened a silence as Hofmann remained gazing at a spot just above the cloudy negative, expressionless.

Shiela and Sasha, yards apart, glanced in unison at one Hofmann then the other. Both had smooth faces, not a hair out of place. It was Louisa who began blinking, biting with her mouth closed, and turned away. Tremours like spider's feet spread around her mouth. Shiela noticed and sympathized but could do nothing but stare. Shiela always looked concerned, aghast, even when surveying her own shoes.

'You're not one too, are you?' Violet turned to North.

Not a dentist, she meant; for she could tell he wasn't. But he had moved casually on and stood before a trestle table, hands clasped behind his back, with Borelli. And Sasha made a movement to ask him something, but stopped. Instead she watched him.

'There's a heavy piece of symbolism for you,' Borelli said, nodding at a plastic model of a DC3.

For display purposes it was mounted ('landing') on a piece of railway line.

'Ah, but it might be unintentional. We might be reading too much into it.'

Borelli tapped his walking stick. 'No! Both are what is left behind when a country is returned or left. Isn't that what the British always say? Don't complain, we've left you a beautiful network of railway tracks. Blah, blah. What a joke. Perhaps these people here have realized? Actually, I'm changing my tack. This piece of railway line here is an accident of irony.' Borelli scratched his head. 'But then why didn't they use a lump of wood?'

Both were uncertain and turned to the photograph curling above the table. It showed a chevron-legged man descending in a parachute. Trees stood in the background. Billowing in the countryside the quilted canopy resembled a phosphorous puff from a steam train. North turned to Borelli. 'Unintentional,' smiled the young man. 'We can't read anything into that.'

'The Dakota DC3 was the T-model Ford of airplanes,' Kaddok came between them 'It changed the face of the globe. Ten thousand nine hundred and twenty-six produced between 1934 and 1949. Statistically, it has the best safety record.'

But as he ran his hands over the model, one of the celluloid propellers fell off.

'Have you ever been in one?' Borelli asked North. They were waiting at the exit. 'They look like the world's dreariest plane.'

'In New Guinea several times. Oh, and out here in Africa.'

'When were you—'

'Ah-hah!' cried Gerald Whitehead. He turned with his back to the remaining cabinet. 'At last, what we've all been waiting for—a genuine Handicraft. The real article, in

32

every sense of the word.' Unsmiling he stepped to one side and waited with a bored expression. The rest bent over. Under glass a woman's glove was fitted to an artificial hand. Sky-blue and tight-fitting, it was a fine example of stitching, of intricate embroidery and fitting. By comparison the rod which held the slender hand vertical, like Buddha's benediction, was heavily rusted.

Garry couldn't stop himself.

'I wondered what you were driving at!' he yelled across at Gerald.

'Hand-made,' he nudged Hofmann, laughing. 'Get it?'

Gerald and Hofmann remained unsmiling.

'Careful,' North murmured.

The Masai who couldn't see into the cabinet gazed at him, and a group of youths behind the turnstiles, unable to enter, watched silently. One had taken Borelli's polished walking stick and was examining it.

Cathcart pushed through the turnstiles holding his binoculars onto his chest, followed by his wife. 'I had long gloves like that when I married,' she was telling Shiela and looking straight ahead, 'but they were apricot.'

Years ago: a Payneham (Sth. Aust.) church, JESUS SAVES lettered in lights on the board. 'The Reverend Glover,' she added, missing the casual connection. 'First thing out on the church steps, brushing off the confetti, Doug had wanted to know the footy scores.'

'Oh dear,' Shiela whispered still in the turnstiles.

'What's the hold-up?' called out Garry.

Doug came back and squatting down rattled the bars with both hands. 'It's jammed, wouldn't you know? We'll get you out.'

'What a place!'

It was enough for some to shake their heads, though the majority felt strangely vague, dreamy. In a foreign country, expect anything. Problems as such however have little meaning. Time was not a problem.

'We might have to leave you here,' Garry cracked, his way of cheering her up; but Shiela stared down at Cathcart's powerful hands gripping and shoving about her legs.

'It's stuck alright,' Doug said red in the face. He stood up and kicked it. 'Stupid!'

The natives stood back and watched.

'This is terrible . . . holding everyone up,' Shiela began to say.

Mrs Cathcart looked around. 'Here'—to Garry Atlas—'wake that one up.'

Their guide still had his forehead pressed to the glass, studying the hand-made glove. Atlas was about to tap his shoulder when Dr North spoke thick jumpy words quite casually to the Masai, rare pidgin, dark enough for the Masai to immediately nod and shrug. They conversed for half a minute more. Evidently this trouble occurred frequently. A negro in a loose-fitting boiler suit appeared carrying several big spanners.

'I am sorry,' Shiela mumbled to Mrs Cathcart.

'It's not your fault, dear. It's this place. I wonder if these people can do anything right.'

They were hungry, Sasha most of all, but watched patiently as the mechanic wielding the big spanners dismantled the turnstiles. The pipes suddenly fell on the cement floor, Habsburgian hoops from Shiela's dress. No! That dumb mechanic: squatting in the dusty shoes without socks or laces, infuriating thick lips; he allowed grease to brush against Shiela's hem and her pale elbow, look, as she stepped out. But by then Shiela was too engrossed in being free, out with them, and looked around blinking with the confusion.

'Well!' Whistles, sighs.

The sudden clarity of the square and hooded shops, with a litmus shadow encroaching from the end already along one vertical edge, folded, and the square's wide-openness and the hills beyond, made them adjust focus, squint, and reach for their sunglasses. They felt curiously dazed. It was similar yesterday stepping onto the wide white tarmac. The walls of the museum had reduced their field of vision to small portable objects, all within arm's reach. Outside on the steps, air currents and perspective operated on a natural grand scale. The air was unexpectedly cool. Louisa

Hofmann frowned with a headache. Borelli who didn't wear a watch asked for the time. The others smiled, surprised too, and looked at the sky.

Well, because the square had emptied. Vegetable leaves and other rubbish had been swept into green obelisks. An empty cart with wooden tyres stood to one side. A figure at the far end seemed to be going home. Sasha could eat a horse. 'At least walk in the sun,' Violet said testily. As for Mrs Cathcart, her brown shoes hurt.

The Museum receded behind them like a grey distorted head watching, and they met herds of goats being whistled and tongue-clicked into the square from all arteries, all directions, over-running the footpaths, bumping into them and irritating them, even outside the hotel, which they reached with relief.

In her curtained room Shiela suspended the pen over the postcards and wondered if she was enjoying herself. Somehow not properly, no. Not yet. It takes a time. It depends on the group. And they—those in the group—were merely faces at the moment, or fragments of dress, mannerisms (mysteries), though already some were emerging sharper and steadier than others. In the beginning certain people try to be remote, deliberately distant, withholding themselves; whereas she showed interest, really, and enjoyed company. But she never quite knew what to say, never knew if they would suddenly turn and stare. Some get on your nerves somewhat, talking loudly and across, all the confidence in the world. James B—. Having a walking stick irritated her as soon as she saw it. How old could he be? He didn't seem to need it. Mrs Cathcart was a help but not enough to be a friend, not yet. It wasn't a bad group; no stinkers, yet. Gradually the group would become equal and then the less interesting ones would recede. Those at the far end of the table, the Doctor with the beard, kindly, and the big blind man ('Fancy a—') and his wife, Mrs Kaddok, attracted her for some reason, perhaps because she hadn't spoken to them yet. She'd been busy watching them. She couldn't help wondering.

Ha! These additional foreign stamps she stuck on the cards for the noisy children of her friends made her nod. Distant pleasure! Shiela was given to pondering. Her magnified eyes seemed specially suited for it. She could imagine: the little ones arguing over her stamps from Africa.

The afternoon light angled in. Violet sat on the edge of the bed naked, filing her nails: calcium powder drifted onto her moist Tasmania, to the carpet floor. How many men had shoved themselves into her? Small slack breasts seemed like scars. But across her creased belly the filtered sunlight laid a small pavonine triangle, and with her bowed head, engrossed, a beautiful sight. Sasha who was generous and given to shouts (suddenly here: 'Don't move') told her so. Placing her hand on the coloured strip she pointed like a child. After washing underclothes Sasha's hands were soft, pleasantly wrinkled.

In another room with the curtains drawn, Room 411, Phillip North dozed. This was his holiday. He was almost relieved at his weariness.

Doug Cathcart worked a special nylon string between his back molars, working it like a rifle cord, and succeeded in removing particles of the soggy lunch. His wife had kicked her shoes off. 'Is there anything you want to say to Reg and Kath?' She too wrote postcards; usually the same sentence to one and all, just to let them know. Doug shook his head.

Borelli and his walking stick had gone out somewhere.

Gerald Whitehead squatted with a type of dysentery. Perspiring, trembling, he cursed at the bathroom mirror facing him: he couldn't avoid his glaring red head. Poking his glasses back on his nose he returned with distaste to the empty yet claustrophobic MUSEU OF HANDICRAFTS and the broken fences and the craters in the roads, the over-crowded buses, smells of rotting vegetables, grunting beggars, and all those mindless goats, their bulging eyes. Africa! He could think of nothing worse.

The group moved within a certain loosely defined shape, elastic yet definite protoplasm formed by the individuals themselves. One might suddenly branch off—Borelli!—and make a narrow inroad, stretching the group's perimeter before returning. It was at its most stable and rectangular seated at the table for meals; at its most ideal yet unnatural compressed in the hotel lift, transported vertically, themselves vertical with one always cracking a joke.

Room-service woke Dr North by mistake. The African beer was for Mister Atlas—he's across the hall.

The boy waited in the doorway as Garry drank from the bottle and pulled a face. Pressing his stomach with his hand he read the label. 'Chr-rist Almighty.' Then he called out: 'Hang on a sec. Send us up two more.' He held up his fingers like Churchill. 'OK?'

The Kaddoks were preparing to go out. Leon checked the Pentax on the table the way a priest absently blesses a child.

With the pen still in her hand Shiela went and stood near the bathroom. She could hear Louisa Hofmann brushing her teeth. Then the running water stopped.

'What are you doing?'

Hofmann's muffled reply.

'Stop it.'

Hofmann murmured something.

'I've told you. Get away.'

'Bitch!'

'I don't want to. Stop, you're making me sick. Stop it, please.'

A scuffle through the wall, and Shiela squatted on the floor, listening. She stared at the spot. They were on the floor. He was on top; her gown had opened past her thighs. There was kicking, rhythmic hissing through teeth, and increasing. Shiela's mouth and eyes remained wide open. She was about to cry out. A foot kept scraping against the wall.

Finished?

Louisa Hofmann was crying.

Outside, clusters of bell-ringing cyclists leaned into the yellow afternoon shadows. The spokeless wheels were elongated to a point several lengths behind each machine, like the stretch in an hour-glass or anamorphotic ink portraits, and indeed some shadows tangled and bled into others. On the edge of town smoke from cooking fires: shacks and warmth must be beckoning them, the workers. They pedalled in a westerly direction.

'Lagophthalmus,' Dr North muttered, as if he was a general practitioner. 'At least I know that.' Rubbing his eyes he pulled the curtains back and looked out a while. On his knee lay Harry Ricardo's *The High-Speed Internal Combustion Engine* where the benefits of hemispherical heads are exhaustively discussed. He sighed.

At seven he washed and went down to the dining room and took a seat, without thinking, near Atlas and his two girls. Shiela sat in her usual position, hands clasped on her lap. Although her head made constant sparrow movements she kept it bowed like Gerald's, three along, but for different reasons. Giving her neck a tap, Doug said: 'We've said grace.' It was a joke, meant to spark Shiela up. She hurriedly smiled but then stopped. Directly opposite sat the Hofmanns, side by side.

Changing the subject Mrs Cathcart asked aloud, 'Is it one we're waiting for again?'

What's his name, Borelli: in the army jacket. And they moved their tongues around in their mouths which were filling with saliva.

The Hofmanns sat neatly ironed, as smooth as before. Again he had his arms folded and gazed at a spot on the facing wall. They barely spoke. But then they hadn't much before. At least Louisa glanced about, more animated, as if she was anxious to join in. Perhaps that was the only sign: when she found Shiela staring she smiled. Shiela reddened and looked down at the handkerchief ball in her hands.

At last: Borelli came in. Doug had started drumming the table.

'I am sorry; no excuses; terribly late again.'

He sat beside Shiela: 'Hello!'

'You're looking pale,' Louisa Hofmann observed unexpectedly.

'Oh I've been out.'

38

And the wind was still in his jacket and hair. Before Shiela could begin to say something or even smile Garry Atlas shouted from the other end, 'You missed out on a little party. Didn't he?'

Violet Hopper shrugged a shoulder.

'A few beers, and we had the pool to ourselves. Very nice.'

Before knocking he'd looked through the hole and seen Violet's little tits. And then what happened: the friend had entered starkers too. He wouldn't mind getting his hands on either pair. He couldn't stay bent down, and with the tray of glasses in one hand, had suddenly knocked and entered.

'Bazaars and alleyways, open sewers, gangs on street corners, wild tribesmen wearing lion skins—I'm not kidding; you should have seen them—and terrible lepers, naked babies, huge women—really beautiful women—in bright costumes,' Borelli told Louisa; and even Shiela began smiling as Borelli stretched his arms, exaggerating. 'All this is true. You don't believe me? That's why I'm late. I got completely lost.'

'Why were they beautiful?' Louisa smiled.

'You mean, the women I saw?'

'I photographed some goats,' Kaddok was telling North. 'Have you seen their goats? It's the staple diet here. All colours. Interesting patterns.'

'Say, that looks very nice,' North leaned towards Kaddok's wife. 'Where did you get that? Today?'

The long native dress had drawn glances and only polite comment from the other women: swirling bandanna browns with magenta; swollen as if she sat over an updraught. It didn't suit her. Had others noticed the waiters had been rude—bumping against her and talking loudly in their language?

Placing a finger on North's arm Sasha made herself small, 'What are you a doctor of, doctor?'

'Ah, zoology et cetera.'

Violet laughed. 'Et cetera?' But Sasha remained looking at North.

'Is that why you came here? For the wild animals?'

'I'm afraid not,' North coughed, but glanced kindly enough. Sasha seemed interested.

Clapping his hands Garry had the waiters running around him.

'This is on me. Try the beer.'

'Count me out,' said Doug firmly.

'And me,' spluttered Whitehead. For the moment he was aptly named. He shouldn't have been at the table. In Africa glycerine is added to beer to preserve it.

'My wife died last month, as a matter of fact,' North nodded. He kept nodding. 'Ah, she was in zoology too. Along with me. We researched together and so forth. We travelled. For the time being, I've lost much of my appetite for zoology.'

'Ohh.'

'I am sorry,' Gwen put in, listening.

As James Borelli observed with approval they were at last making as much racket as the French crew, the Latins toasting at the next table.

It was true. Largely it was the beer, but it was also their growing familiarity. Garry burst out laughing for no reason at all, and slapped the table. Shiela kept glancing from one speaker to the next. And later, near midnight, when the last-to-leave eventually all squeezed into the mirrored lift and it took off but shuddered and slowly settled between floors 3 and 4, it produced laughter and endless wisecracks, and Sasha squashed between Hofmann and Garry Atlas got the silly hiccups. It was North who'd remarked, 'This should have been in the Museum we saw today.'

'I think it was,' said someone over the din.

The pygmies were located in the equatorial forests north of the capital, on the other side of the hills. The usual practice was to set out early taking a lunch packed by the hotel; but there had been a misunderstanding or carelessness, for some hadn't been woken. Irritatingly, half the places at the early breakfast were empty. It was well after seven thirty before they got moving. The tourist bus was new and painted black and white to simulate a zebra—strange sitting inside it. The road soon petered out into a 'road', and then a track: broken, dusty, blocked with goats and cattle, and they found their young driver wearing a government cap had a policy of swerving violently towards any stray dog and playing chicken with the birds. So the bus skated and shuddered: a good thing it was Made in Germany. To reach the pygmies would be long and tiring. But it would be worth it.

'The little fellahs?' Doug Cathcart had nodded, keen. They were the sort of things you read about. He had his binoculars with him.

There had always been a pygmy in the agricultural shows. The burlap flap pulled aside: half-naked, bulging belly, glaring on a low stool. Usually he held a tasselled spear or three bone-tipped arrows . . . But the agricultural side-show and that kind of circus act are on the decline in Australia. The caravan life don't appeal no more. Civil liberties, Invasions of Privacies (pulling back the flap!), Racial Laws, Trade Description Acts and the combined fingers of the libs and the churches have left their mark.

Early on, questions had been raised (of a semantic nature).

'Surely they mean "colony".'

'You're thinking of lepers.'

'It definitely says here "Pygmy Collection".'

Kaddok spoke up but obscured the point: 'From the Latin, *pygmaeus*. Less than 57 inches high—150cm. Pygmoids of course are slightly taller. Sing songs and mime. Have little concern for the afterlife.'

'The little fellahs,' Doug nodded again.

Shiela asked about the poisoned arrows.

Doug shook his head. 'Not anymore. Not these days. You'll probably find they get fed by the government, a bit like the aborigines.'

As they drove Phillip North sat in a pleasant daze, gazing at the shuddering grass and blurred thorn trees passing, sudden ancient gulleys and rounded eroded hills, recalling other times in other lands. Occasionally, smoke marked a

41

village among the trees, and mud and thatch huts, as baked as the land itself, appeared on hills. Their driver had another policy: throwing the bus into neutral down the slightest and even steepest hills. But while others spoke out about this and hung onto the seat rail in front North settled back contented, in pleasant limbo. Behind the mountains they saw large slowly flying birds and the silent forest beginning. The soil turned black and rotting leaves on the side made them shiver. Changing down to bottom gear, adagio, the bus took a melodic path in and out of the sun, in a sense duplicating their own zebra pattern, but gradually more black than light: until the sun now was thatched out overhead and behind them. They were in a tunnel of leaves and roots, tangled, dripping and rotting. The wheels slipped on the mulch and stopped.

Silence in the forest: broken by, what, an occasional rotten branch or falling inedible fruit.

In the Bermuda shorts and long white socks, Doug stamped the ground, a cone-shaped footballer warming up. 'Shhh,' his wife said. The forest felt like a library or a great art gallery. Those who made comments whispered them. ('Watch out for leeches.' 'What?') But following the driver along a thin path Garry Atlas let out the Tarzan cry: 'Oh oi, oh oi-oi-oi- . . . oi-oi-oi-oi . . . '

'Shut up!' Sasha hissed as it reverberated. 'Shut up! You're not funny.' And all but the driver agreed. They frowned and glanced around as he walked on unperturbed.

The smooth vertical trunks on either side, forming the path, were like large green pipes, rows of them, and there was one species of tree that occasionally grew hair like a human leg. The further they went in the closer the trees grew, and the trees multiplied and were divided by immense shadows and long shafts of light. They were forced to go Indian file and increasingly squeeze through sideways. Difficult for Leon Kaddok: one hand gripped the back of Gwen's belt, the other cupping the loaded camera. The driver seemed to know the path, but sometimes one of them slipped glancing behind. Following Louisa, Borelli smiled: she shouldn't have worn such fine high-heeled sandals. She also carried a snake-skin handbag. Monkeys shrieked and jumped high from branch to branch, more like sliding shadows; but the group had become used to them and watched intently for the pygmies, even one, male or female.

'I shouldn't be here,' North muttered. 'Nothing,' he said to Sasha. 'I'm just talking rubbish to myself.'

The driver waited as they stopped before a large tree growing in their path. Borelli pointed with his stick. Cut deep, still wet:

JACK O'TOOLE

WORLD AXE CHAMPION

(AUSTRALIA)

'Someone,' Atlas whispered, rolling his eyes left and right, 'has been here before us.'

They laughed: a relief. It was like finding an empty cigarette pack in a remote picnic ground. For almost the first time Shiela looked around—and she saw a multi-coloured bird swoop between the trunks.

'I'm disappointed,' Sasha pouted. 'I thought we were really off the beaten track.'

'She's never satisfied,' her friend Violet observed to the rest.

As he waited, perspiration collected on the driver's forehead and nose.

'He was real credit,' Cathcart told Sasha. 'I saw Jack O'Toole once clean up a Canadian, a Swede, the lot, in one afternoon. And a smarty-pants Californian who'd come all the way over. Nobody could get near him.'

Royal Easter Show, that was: Sydney, 1956? O'Toole in the white singlet. White dungarees. White sandshoes. Arms like hams! Short back and sides. The Swede remember had a ginger crewcut and chopped in a ridiculous check shirt. Had a short fast swing; but it couldn't last. O'Toole won. In Australia for a time he was a household name.

'But who would have? . . .'

'I knew a bloke at work who knew Jack,' Cathcart went on. 'He said he was a corker fellah. He didn't have a swelled head at all.'

With his ear against the trunk the way a safecracker opens a door Kaddok traced the block letters with his fingertips. 'It's still fresh,' he told them. 'This will be legible for another hundred years.'

'That's a good one,' Borelli laughed. 'Australia, in the heart of Africa. We have stumbled upon a particularly insidious imperialism. This is taking national pride to extreme lengths. Who would have thought, doctor?'

'But carving messages on trees was a tradition among our explorers,' North argued.

Borelli laughed. 'You're right! Agreed!'

'Don't they talk a lot of rot?' Mrs Cathcart commented.

Doug nodded. He raised his binoculars and panned slowly through the trees. Stepping back Kaddok took a few quick pictures.

'Such a marvellous strong tree,' Louisa turned as they began moving. 'It's a pity.'

After crossing a bridge made out of vines the path widened and they came upon a crude trilith fashioned from tree trunks, and Gerald near the driver immediately put on his pained expression. In a clearing stood a low white building in the strict Bauhaus or shoebox style, in this instance horizontal. Straight right-angled paths and lawns of mown couch were between it and the towering devouring jungle.

The driver spat and pointed to the glass door.

'I don't see the pygmies. There's nobody here.'

'It looks more like a bush hospital . . . They've got them locked up.'

'Well let's see the little fellahs.'

'Why on earth don't they design in their own ethnic style?' Gerald complained. 'Such as it is.'

North agreed. 'The Bauhaus is a curse. The dreary disease has spread even to here. It's like one of your imperialisms,' he said to Borelli. 'The colonization of style, I think it is called.'

The Collection of Pygmies housed inside was immediately superior to yesterday's . . . museum. A sense of purpose, of clarity, showed in the smooth tiled floors, the straight lines and natural light streaming through the carefully placed windows. The pygmies were clean and placed with considerable ingenuity, often in some historical context. There were no attendants. None were needed. Each exhibit spoke for itself and in the midst of that primordial silence, the green forest always in the corner of one eye, each statement was somehow amplified or underscored, increasingly, as they shuffled and clacked with their various footwear on the stone floor. Neatly printed labels—unlike the Museum of Handicrafts—jogged the memory. In short, a surprisingly fine example of imaginative scholar-curatorship.

Old, short men; though not all old. Occasionally, middle-aged men had the resolve and distant gaze of the very old!

On low white boxes and striking familiar poses they exhibited all their old *baraka*. Quite a few wore ceremonial (purple) robes. Some had the pith helmet. But by far the majority used the pin-striped suit buttoned up, and a television-blue shirt. Where did they find all these suits? It explained the shape of the building: there were long avenues of them. The sebaceous figures held spectacles or important pieces of paper, and stared thoughtfully as if they were being photographed (Karsh of Ottawa), or they gazed at a mythical point just above the horizon: resolve and optimism which know no boundaries. Others, again the majority, seemed to lean forward with promises; or were they breaking promises? It was hard to tell. In either case, an outstretched finger or a possible handshake occasionally brushed their clothing as they walked past. And this overall impression of appealing to reason or of hectoring was further heightened by figures well known for their oratory: the arm held high conducting an invisible orchestra or ordering another round. Winnie! Feet planted well apart, gold watch-chain exposed, glaring magenta face (but this is cruel: not drinking again?). Good on you, Winnie! 'Never has so much . . .' Never mind Gallipoli, the Lusitania, the little invasion of Russia, his switch to the gold standard ('25), the *British Gazette*, smashing strikes and Dresden, and that 'half naked fakir'. Magnificent orator. Others too had their excesses preserved, indeed highlighted. And yet these trademarks, once so endearing, appeared now in isolation as ridiculous appendages: the furled umbrella there, a cane, several spotted ties (one bow), the pince nez, her corgi bitches, the General's golf clubs, another's rocking chair, yachting caps and bowler hats, snuff, cold pipes and coronas, toothbrush moustaches.

'There's Bob!'

The eyebrows, double-breasted suit draped with ribbons; one eyebrow raised.

'They shouldn't have him like that.'

'That's how he was.'

'I thought he was a big man.'

A few were still alive. Ha, ha. Scratched recordings hidden somewhere kept repeating the same old newspeak. There were combed acephalous faces which still managed to nod and wave from imaginery balconies. The president spoke into an embossed dictaphone, leaning back in his chair, forming a cathedral with his fingers. A few exhausted ones, imagine, vibrated over memoirs. Almost inevitably a monarch wearing a tiara sat on a white lavatory, so bringing her eyes down to their level. And what was the Boy Scout leader doing there?

Various backers, anonymous lackeys and lickboots, party advisors hovered in the background. The marvellous detail of each one kept comments to the monosyllable, or a gesture, a nod or frown, an arm suddenly pointing to a minor figure amazingly well portrayed.

At the end of this long corridor a small drawing room decorated with a marble mantlepiece and maroon wallpaper held a collection of apparently essential accessories. They were spread out on an oak table. Items such as hair oil, cuff-links and loudspeakers were represented with real examples, but others were shown by photographs or abstractly. Close and careful inspection showed each item was either glued or bolted down on the good table to prevent theft. Here were expensive fountain pens, the striped tie, after-shave lotions, a selection of chevrons,

epaulets, 'omelets', a cemetery of uniforms, monogrammed Swiss handkerchiefs, aperitifs, toothpaste, medals, the
ball-bearing navels, red carpet (sample of), editorial
writers, the flags and bunting, panegyrics, brass bands,
national anthems, Constitutions and proclamations,
Vernacular Republics, Workers' Parties (haw, haw!),
opening ceremonies and an ominous oubliette (blueprint
of), black shoe polish, several ways of kissing babies,
television make up, black limousines and a typical firm
handshake.

The group had split around the table. Even those not
interested found themselves bending over, studying the
paraphernalia. Each object clearly had a personal touch
and seemed to belong to the one man; and the combination
somehow formed a distant yet ideal figure.

'The only thing missing,' said Borelli as they filed out, 'is
a reliable deodorant, and the candidate's blonde wife,
preferably with two new babies. It's all a joke, isn't it?'

'Our Sir Robert was a good man,' said Mrs Cathcart
firmly.

No one else quite knew what to say. As they walked to the
final room, their feeling of bafflement and annoyance
increased. It showed in Mrs Cathcart: fuming, looking
grim. All along she hadn't wanted to come. On one side a
series of windows revealed the jungle, the vines and teeming
density, less than an arm's length away. Some slowly
flapping butterflies resembled tropical fish. Shiela who'd
glanced, looked again. She thought she had seen a dark
face.

At the end of this room a group of silent African school
children looked up at the wall, moving their heads left and
right, and filed out.

'I say, isn't he that man from the hotel?' Sasha whispered.

A man looking up at the wall turned.

'Howdy!' Doug ambled over; you could always go up to a
fellow Australian. 'What d'you make of this?' he nodded,
putting knowledge into his disgust.

The others were reading the message on the wall. It was
neatly hand-lettered.

THE LANGUAGE HAS BEEN TWISTED TO
DESCRIBE THESE TYPES. TO ACCOMODATE
THEM? PERHAPS WE HAVE BEEN TOO
LAVISH.

Large neat lettering, no spelling errors, followed:

> Your psychopaths and·aristocrats, knights, preten-
> ders and upstarts, padishah, sahib, arch-dukes, their
> genitures, governor-general, king and queen, con-
> sorts, generalissimo and admirals, plutocrats, British
> prime minister

It ran in upper and lower, apparently jumbled. The
words were not listed alphabetically but to the rhythm of
drums, calypsocane. This became increasingly apparent
as Gwen read out the words to her husband. All together
now:

> ministers, The President, rhetorical reverends, Pope,
> demagogues, chancellors, ordinary members, ham-
> strung burghers, whip, hospodars and sycophants,
> obeisant encomiast, the High Commissioner, duce,
> orators of note, monomaniacs, viceroy, vicar viscounts,
> legal tenders, governor and Colonial Secretaries with
> plenipotentiaries, panders, the chinless wonders, de-
> puties, the Speaker, rigid premier

It soon became choked in general terms and abuse. Most
of them stopped reading the rest.

> you lymphatic despots, lick-boots, dictator and cunc-
> tators, head prefects, idiot pierrots, *banya*, cryptoneur-
> ous imperialists, usurpers and back stabbers, bandogs,
> buggers, swine, yellow pettifoggers, major-domo, pink
> mad prince charming, old boy, smiling margrave,
> cacique, placebo, man, Jack the Ripper, Führer,
> bloody parvenu, mutillids, silver Order of Thistles,
> that ridiculous, mamamouchi, the lackeys, all griffins,

halichondroids, koobsburners, satrap, mawworms, cadaveric committees, colonialists, blue-eyed boys, seignior, pilgarlics, fanakalo, all acrita, heresiarch, pygmies!

'It was only words. I wouldn't get too steamed up,' said Atlas outside.

'Why,' Sasha's friend complained, 'do they always have to bring politics into it? We came for a holiday.'

'I thought it was a pretty poor show,' nodded Doug gravely.

They were relieved to be outside, standing and looking around, but they remained close to the building, the jungle pressing in on all sides. The clearing was small, a square of lawn. Birds could be heard chattering which didn't help. It felt like standing on a new postage stamp of a strange alien country: one that is proud of its silent white architecture. When Phillip North went out along one serrated edge and tugged at a few leaves and kicked at a vine Shiela wished he wouldn't. The slightest pull could bring the whole forest forward and over them.

To photograph the building Kaddok had fitted a special wide-angle lens and even then had to lean back and half disappear into the jungle, his elbows supported by his loyal wife. While Atlas remained with the rest Borelli moved out onto the lawn and leaning on his walking stick surveyed the architecture.

'It's not as bad as you think, Gerald. In fact, I'd say it's quite a radical design. Straight lines are anathema to these people, remember. Their experience is mainly coned or rounded.'

Gerald shrugged. 'You'll probably find it's designed by an American.'

Hofmann looked at his watch as Louisa wiped her forehead.

'This is ridiculous,' Mrs Cathcart hissed. 'All the way—'

Sasha called out. 'Come on. This is giving us the creeps. Where's our driver?'

North was talking to him in the corner. He turned:

'For an extra few shillings he says he'll take us back a different way. Agreed?'

Achchha, seated in the bus again it was good to take the weight off the feet, to sit back; and there was the prospect of further scenes unfolding, and at the end at dusk the hotel with its now-familiar entrance foyer, its chairs and mustard carpet upstairs, a hot shower.

Borelli put his chin between the Hofmanns and cleared his throat, 'Didn't you feel, well, I mean, a bit small in there?'

Louisa looked at him and laughed.

Hofmann didn't turn from the window. 'It was almost as bad as the place yesterday, whatever it was called.'

Across the aisle Garry was telling Violet, 'I'm sorry, but Africa just isn't my scene.'

'The Museum of Handicrafts yesterday? I liked that.' Borelli stared at Louisa. 'But didn't you?'

'I certainly did not!' she laughed again.

'If they want foreign exchange,' Ken Hofmann said (another long sentence for him), 'they're sure going about it the wrong way.'

'Today's, you'd have to admit, was extremely well done. And it's had its effect. We are a shade different from when we arrived. The damage is done. There's a little worm inside our heads.' He laughed. 'And there's nothing we can do about it.'

But here Hofmann swung around with the rest to see the galloping giraffes and Borelli looked closely at her. 'Then what is it you're interested in?' he asked. Louisa looked out the other side and frowned. 'You're making our holiday sound very complicated,' she smiled.

Borelli nodded and leaned back in his own seat.

They were speeding across a dun-coloured plain, across the afternoon. The Mimosa trees and piles of boulders broke the horizon. Spasmodic cultivation at mid-distance: sweet potatoes chiefly, some maize. Such right-angled patches here were distinctly unnatural, man-made. Over to the right a distant village. 'Leon,' Mrs Kaddok suddenly pointed, 'would like to take his photographs. Do you mind?'

Garry Atlas immediately gave two loud sharp claps to the driver. He slowed down and turned. 'Ah!' Shiela cried. Stock pigeons flew up from the verge and one hit the windscreen. The bus went on to the village.

'But they're beau-tiful!' Sasha whispered as they stepped out. 'Look at her.'

The village women had remained squatting around their cooking fires: smooth dark bodies, their shaved heads. A young girl was pregnant. Violet Hopper and Louisa Hofmann both had their sunglasses resting up on their hair and didn't say anything but gave them an interested smile. Bold as brass then Mrs Cathcart went up and casually stood beside a group. Pale-skinned and holding the handbag she suddenly appeared to be burdened with superfluous weights—the extra pale-blue cardigan, sunglasses, gold watch—and by her flesh which spread out and fell beyond her basic skull, camouflage. It was further aggravated or even symbolized by her hair: uplifted, distinctly cal-iological. It tilted like a frail tower. By comparison, the shaven heads of the village women were close to the original: sculptural, flowing into their bodies. Yet Mrs Cathcart stood around unaware. Some of the others became awkward. They found their shoes clattered on the white ground.

Louisa watched Borelli gazing at a young girl. She had a brightly coloured greegree high on one arm, and wide solemn lips. Seeing Borelli she cupped her hand over her mouth.

'I could stay here a few years,' Garry Atlas told North. Nudge, nudge. 'What d'you reckon?'

North suddenly cleared his throat loudly. Cathcart was peering inside the nearest round hut: travel broadens the mind. And Mrs Cathcart began pulling faces. There must have been a smell nearby. Or was it the dirt? Cross-eyed goats watched; dogs with sores trotted in and out among shards. Holding up money and pointing, Hofmann tried to buy a woman's necklace, but she kept laughing and glancing at her friends. 'Good, good, that's it, good,' Kaddok kept saying, shooting close up: women, balloon-bellied children, goats, their cooking pots and huts. Rapidly reloading in the shade he fumbled, such was his eagerness.

On the ground lay large squashed insects. A dry wind rolled brittle carcasses among the huts. Bending down North smoothed the dust and inspected like a geomancer: *locusta migratoria*. Wide pronotum, or dorsal selerite, yellow and black (gregarious phase). Characterized by short horns. Locust, originally from LOBSTER? Could be. A plague here: been? gone? In many countries used for food. Balance; revenge.

'Take it off, someone! Quickly!' Sasha screamed, both hands over her ears.

'Who did that?' Violet demanded. Garry lifted a long locust from Sasha's shoulder and stamped on it. The old women of the village were all laughing: toothless, with jewelry jingling. Their dogs began barking and ran around in circles. It seemed to the group they were liked, or had been accepted, and at such short notice.

The Cathcarts came back to the bus, satisfied. Doug beamed a bit to show their approval. These people were alright. Some of the women stood up, breasts swinging, and children crowded around the metal door, staring. The driver started the engine.

Mrs Cathcart bent down before getting in.

'And what's this little tacker's name?'

The boy pointed to himself:

'Oxford University Press.'

'She means your name,' Doug put in, encouraging.

The boy nodded.

'Oxford University Press.'

'That's nice. Doug, give him a coin. What would you like to be, dear, when you grow up?'

The boy looked up at Mrs Cathcart. The driver began revving the four-cylinder engine.

'A tourist.'

2

Heavy stone: bevelled edges. If not bevelled, the edges blended into the cement-coloured (overcast) sky. The downpipes of houses, the edges of elms and the poles, the outline of a man's nose and forehead blur with the air, a type of barnacle or optical protoplasm—opposite to the startling clarity of the Southern Hemisphere. There was a heavy steadiness. Untidy stateliness. Even the air seemed old.

Permanence (stone), ancient power of seats and establishments, stone fingertips and pigeon shit: grey, all weighed down and rained upon.

Order, order! Time had worn channels in the city, but smoothed the faces of the English. In a bus which suffered from respiratory problems the group gradually approached the centre, channelled by the houses and bevelled hedges which immediately closed in behind (the jungle in Africa, the maze at Hampton Court); yet once at the centre there was no 'centre'. It was somewhere else. Rolls/Bentleys blurred past all a-glitter, tall cabs knocked on diesel—immensely practical; and Jaguars, dark Daimlers with the gold line hand-painted along the side (patience: handed down), and small Triumphs, labouring Hillmans, Morgans and many Morrises—miles of Oxfords and Minors, like those rows of trimmed houses. Yet at the same time London offered to them an instant gaiety. Not only with its little window-boxes and the double-deckers the colour of geraniums, but in the language; theirs again. Messages were everywhere. And there was gaiety, subtle and yet explicit, in the acceptance of civic channels, resulting in a pedestrian smoothness. Such helpful hand-signals and zebra-crossings painted without Africa's wild undulations, the Bobby's nylon sleeves of special iridescent dye; immensely practical.

Possibilities and maybes, perhaps, actually: almost a gaiety.

Let us stick to the facts. The hotel was a converted wing of the British Museum, in that WC2 district of public lavatories and map shops. Pedestrian pairs consulted maps, many wearing the nylon parka and glasses, looking up like stunned mullets at street signs. Americans sat on steps. Outside the hotel a Cockney sold dying flowers.

Like the rest of the museum their wing was well known for the quality of its echo, its long avenues of linoleum. Fitted with coiled heaters and the cream iron bed the rooms resembled more a hospital, the Platonic idea of a hospital, and evidently to dispel such a ridiculous impression, each room had been given a colourful Mughal miniature from the Museum's reserve collection—though somehow the one over Shiela's bed was an erotic gouache (Nepalese?) showing a Tantric couple locked in intercourse, the man leaning back on an elbow pulling on a brass hookah. The bathroom furniture was all-white, hair-cracked, vitreous. The coil heaters must have been old too, for they were prone to a kind of throat-clearing, without any warning. In certain rooms it verged on the obscene. At first Shiela stood back alarmed, for her radiator had vibrated and complained as she spread a towel on it to dry. Sasha and Violet, sharing a room, couldn't help sitting down and laughing at theirs. The Cathcarts were a bit peeved. This hotel had baths, but no showers. Already Gerald had left in high spirits, setting out for the National Gallery; in London his face and walk were transformed.

There existed a pleasant feeling of freedom, of this vast city offering itself. It was all there, waiting. They could go where they liked, where they chose. While the rest of London was working they could stand and watch, and it felt luxurious. A shoal of Japanese had also assembled in the foyer, their leader holding up a metal flag. Doug who was going to Australia House nudged his wife. Those little Japs: you had to laugh. Their leader adjusted a tiny TV set fixed to his lapel which instantly showed, out of the corner of his eye, when one in the group strayed.

The stipple effect blurring London increased the minute they stepped out and walked. They immediately proceeded to lose themselves among the columns and grey type of a vast newspaper, interrupted by half-remembered photographs (Piccadilly Circus!). A foot occasionally slipped into the gutter, tilting their vision; and as in a newspaper they glanced ahead, anticipating, while still 'reading' something close at hand. They skipped most advertisements. They came upon the solid façades of places usually found on the front page, the source of editorials and powerful headlines: Number 10 and 11, the old Foreign Office, House of Commons, grubby Buckingham Palace (to Borelli, 'eyesaw Buckingham Palace') . . .

Further along were the bronze doors of the city, the old bowler hat and awfully discreet countenance of the waiting chauffeurs (board meetings take place alongside the footpath), which gradually suggested the apparent tranquil sea and attendant tidal actions of stock market quotations, produced daily, and big deals (floats), announcements across tables. The theatre section: linguistic electroliers, sentences of critics! And some when they went on further turned into new areas and noticed how the layout and language altered sharply. Fonts switched to *sans* bold: small traders dropping their aitches. Page numbers were sometimes written in chalk. They entered the Classified Section, small types flogging trusses and stockings, uniforms, exploded armchairs, tangled coat-hangers, and shop-soiled blankets where you have to read between the lines. Sex shops; mail order only. And leaves rustled like loose pages. Speakers' Corner, Hyde Park. A Wolseley accelerated out of Scotland Yard. Gee, it was good. The sun came out. The Kaddoks stopped and checked the directory, *London A-to-Z*—doesn't it resemble a proof-reader's handbook? Of course, some turned back to the retail advertisements for there was Boots, *Aquascutum* (in italics) for raincoats and elastic-sided boots, look, Libertys, Simpsons of Picaddilly; Sasha had pointed to Selfridges and steered Violet in. The others simply drifted like lost sheep, stopping at random. They became tired—blinking their eyes. A grey sludge underfoot felt like pulped newsprint and words, discarded sentences, shades of opinion and history. To them it was a further blurring of distinctions. London was the home of the semi-colon; also a grand depository of facts. The Cathcarts found their way to Australia House where it was easy. They could sit down beneath the chandeliers and Brangwyns, and leaf through their own newspapers, amid the sounds and brown appearances of their own people.

In St James that afternoon several world records were shattered. Arriving early the Hofmanns sat in seats which had apparently been reserved for Arabs. Nothing was said of course but the adroit auctioneer with the carrot-coloured shoes and the Etonian's tie clearly accepted Hofmann's occasional nodding with disdain. Before long they were surrounded by silent white-robed Arabs who had filed in, and Louisa put her sunglasses back on. The musk-perfumed playboy seated beside her kept losing his chappal and looked at her sideways as he bent forward, brushing her ankle, her knee, sending her mind back to other places: filmy odalisque? Hofmann meanwhile looked around at the oils hanging one above the other, some falling out of their frames, and parallel sunbeams from the skylight bathed the cool chinless wonder at the lectern in a nimbus much favoured by the Dutch Old Masters.

First to go was an early cornucopia, oil in canvas, about three yards long, and so darkly varnished or neglected it was almost monochrome. Bidding began slowly. The auctioneer murmured the platitude: 'Really, the gilt frame alone is worth *that* . . .' It then passed the previous record as Louisa's neighbour kept idly raising his finger, but he remained gazing at her for too long and it went to a Bangladeshi businessman seated in front.

Hofmann wanted a major stripe painting, long and horizontal, American, c. 1964. This too would have been a good three yards long, though it was barely eighteen inches high. Again it was almost monochrome: grey strips stained into duck. So it seemed to blur like a sentence or London's traffic which could be heard faintly outside. Hofmann wanted it and Louisa watched as he joined in: his face now a petulant boy's. He frowned as he kept nodding—short, stubborn nods. Transparent bulbs of perspiration popped out above his lip. All his attention concentrated on the Old Boy but when the five figures passed the world record set by a similar work he seemed to falter. His eyes slid off the lectern, down, and to the right. He seemed hurt. Louisa turned to see her neighbour raise his jewelled finger again. She placed her hand on him, restraining him—and flushed. *What was that?* The Arab grinned. Louisa moved her leg from his.

There was a teeming stillness. They remained at its centre.

'Hon,' Ken was whispering, 'it's ours. I got it. Isn't she a beauty? It's for you. I bought it almost for you.'

A dealer with superbly combed hair swung around.

'Do you mind? We happen to be working. Or some of us are trying to.' But then seeing the Arabs he suddenly smiled, 'Excuse me . . .'

Outside on the footpath Hofmann kept thudding his gloved hands and shaking his head at the barely legible name in brass of the venerable auction house. He could visualize how the recently won picture would fit into his collection. It was Louisa's turn to be silent. Almost to himself Hofmann nodded, 'Very good. Yes, very good. I'd say it's easily the best one in Australia. There'll be nothing like it. Hey, listen, come with me.'

He took her arm.

Even on Old Bond Street they stood out as a fine-looking pair. Both were trim and radiated that good health and well-earned time on their hands. Both had wollen coats, buttoned to their chins.

Although Louisa didn't want another Cartier bag he walked in and bought her a new one of special grey lizard skin. It was quite out of the ordinary. At a certain angle in daylight it had been noticed that the tesselated skin reproduced—quite by chance—the pattern of a ten pound note. It was like a poor but distinct photograph. The late Charles Darwin, coughed the manager, would undoubtedly have been pleased. Quite unusual, what? Hence, its premium price. The Natural History Museum had expressed an interest . . .

Hofmann asked for the contents of Louisa's old bag to be tipped into the new one, and to Louisa he proposed they return to the hotel and have a drink. 'Would you like that? Are you quite positive?'

Louisa turned her head.

'Or what would you like to do?'

She stood on the footpath wondering. Feeling as vague as London's outlines she went along with him.

Shiela Standish had gone out to Wimbledon, the first to reach the Sports Pages, and was on her way back, the black cab slicing through the houses. An aunt lived at Wimbledon and whenever in London Shiela always liked to go there first. How many centre-court finals had they seen together? Throughout the nineteen-sixties the longest sighs and woman-shrieks heard on the tennis broadcasts came from those two in the best seats. A good men's singles would leave them exhausted but chattering. Her aunt had skinny legs and a brown neck. Lately she had grown abruptly old, and for two seasons running Shiela had missed Wimbledon, though she always looked forward to seeing her aunt. This time when the driver found the street she suddenly directed him on to 'Wimbledon', the courts just around the corner.

There was no tennis but lines of tourist buses were queued outside. Outside the Players' Entrance a Cockney entrepreneur gave tanned Americans a yellow racket with broken strings to hold, and ran back and—'Hold it, luv. Gotcha'— took their photographs. Nearby a partner had set up a small tent displaying Famous Tennis Balls plus other artifacts of the game: chlorophyl-stained canvas shoes, a Czech sunvisor, early athletic supports and some frilled knickers all worn at some time by the Great. It was the smallest museum Shiela was ever likely to see. The holiday crowd waited patiently in line, and Shiela walked a little around the stadium walls. In the wet grass she noticed several lost balls, resting like cannon shot, and was startled to see the stadium's concrete marred by graffiti, most of it obscene—BALLS TO TENNIS—in a variety of chalks and sprayed colours. Among the limericks, the lonely confessions and phone numbers, one message stood out. It had been sprayed through a template, repeated all over, professionally.

AUSTRALIANS ACE

That wasn't dirty. It was often true. Shiela smiled a little at the recognition. 'Australia' otherwise tended to disappear in such a vast place as London.

Behind her, a man's voice broke in.

'What d'you know? . . .'

Shiela's eyes and forehead went haywire. She turned.

'Africa, right? Just the day before yesterday. Well isn't this something? What was our crummy hotel?'

'The Safari International . . .' Shiela frowned, confused.

'Bugger me,' the tall man went on, 'this is something to write home about.'

His wide hairy wrists and a man's knuckle bone.

Thank goodness: they were walking back to the crowd. Around forty, he was tall with worn straight features. He asked her name.

'And where do you come from, Shiela?'

'In Sydney.'

'Sydney or the bush,' he roared. 'Aye, Shiela?'

Shiela smiled.

'Listen, what are you doing now? Could you do with a cup of tea or something? There'd have to be a place around here.'

Glancing, Shiela thought he might be a country man originally, or even now; and so perhaps they could have talked. But she consulted her watch more out of habit.

'I can't. I'm afraid I can't.'

'Alrighty. No problems.'

Keeping his cigarette in his mouth he squinted exaggeratedly through the smoke as he wrote down her hotel. 'Good on you. I'll be in touch, Shiela. Be good.'

His name was Hammersly, Frank Hammersly.

Shiela went along to her aunt and was still biting her lip,

confused, when she returned to the hotel. She took little notice of the scenery. It was growing dark. The man—Frank Hammersly. Certainly he had the gift of the gab. Not that it . . . He was a tall figure of a man, solid timber. In the big suit his face and shoulders consisted almost entirely of straight lines. His shoes were dark tan, crinkled brogue. These had made her think he was from the country, originally. She should have asked him! He would have said. He could certainly talk. He'd be phoning and she'd have to say. He said he'd phone. And she didn't know.

The driver wore the cloth cap. Fat creased his neck: horizontal cuts of a knife. He was a heavy man, but not as solid as Frank Hammersly. As they crossed the river he twisted, 'That's where the coppers caught Christie, the pervert-murderer. Right about . . . there.'

Steering with one hand he pointed. Then he began shaking his head.

'He was a shocker. How many women was it he carved up? I must have passed him that day. I had a job out here. It was when we had our fogs. That wasn't all that long ago. I still have the foreigners getting in asking to see the house. Number 10 . . .'

Shiela tilted her head to be polite.

A travel firm ran a tour over Christie's house, Christ, every Monday night. They have his cupboards open, the old bath, and on the mantlepiece his National Health eye-glasses. Some of the floorboards are up for you to see. It's for the Irish and the Scots who come down. You get a few tourists—Frogs. Americans have heard about him.

Shicla fumbled for change.

'I've only been told about it,' he said over his shoulder. 'I haven't been in myself.'

To make matters worse, Shiela wasn't familiar with the currency yet. Here you had to give the drivers a full tip: but the handful she shoved through, not counting the African coins, was probably far too much.

The Hofmanns were there in the lounge listening to Gerald Whitehead who still wore his raincoat. They nodded when Shiela hurried up; Gerald kept talking.

'I didn't believe it at first. But it was everywhere I went.'

'Oh what a pity.'

'Why, what's wrong?' Shiela asked.

'Let's have a drink,' Hofmann smiled. 'At least our day wasn't bad.'

Nation, island, capital city of facts. The black-and-white half-tones had moved indoors. Someone had noted this year was the 156th anniversary of Niepce's invention of photography, and the only time the anniversary would match the camera's most popular (Number 1) aperture setting, f5.6. And that wasn't all! The retrograde of 56, it was pointed out, was 65—sixty-five years ago Oscar Barnck in Germany built the first 35 mm camera! Photography—who said it?— is the folk art of the industrial age. The great museums of London were taken up with appropriate celebratory exhibitions.

At the National Gallery, X-ray photographs of the Renaissance paintings replaced the originals. From a distance they looked almost the same. The enlarged X-ray prints were fitted into the ornate frames. This was the work of the forensic experts in the gallery's basement. Explanatory paragraphs and cotton arrows pointed out the struggling artists' 'real' intentions, ghost-like here, and their appalling early errors in composition and perspective. Nothing is as it appears. Photography's efficiency had stripped away illusion. These Renaissance masters, it was revealed, were racked by the same doubts and timidity experienced by the average Sunday afternoon amateur.

The gallery was crowded. Parties of photographers strolled around as if they owned the place. In addition to their expensive dangling equipment—the gallery's NO CAMERAS rule had been temporarily waived—they wore expressions of triumph and understanding. Groups stood talking together, their backs to the 'paintings', introducing themselves and inspecting each other's gear. Photography had come a long way.

As Gerald fought his way out, other buses pulled into the curb, including one constant double-decker painted yellow like a film box, disgorging more photographers, enthusiasts having flown in from America and Japan, each one instinctively glancing up at the sky. Many a German's snap included the ears of Gerald's enraged head.

The National Portrait Gallery, around the corner, attracted similar crowds. Here they'd put on an important historical show. The rooms had been made specially dark and oil portraits of pioneer photographers hung in place of the usual. Oil paintings of photographers? To some this was an ironical sommersault. It was a cause for serious contemplation. Oil paintings of . . . Others though, the photographers, saw it as the supreme belated compliment. As the excellent catalogue in a footnote challenged: when before had a photographer been enclosed in gold leaf and an artificial convolvulus border? And here were more than forty. They had been tracked down and unearthed from the most unlikely of places. Many had scarcely seen the light of day before.

There were fine realistic renderings of Daguerre, Talbot, Lartigue, Rejlander and Julie Cameron, et cetera; a mysterious oval portrait of Mangin; and what appeared to be a child's drawing on graph paper of Lewis Carroll. From America came a rare blurred portrait of Marey descending stairs and in charcoal a Cherokee's sketch of Brady. There was a small group of 20th-century works where a painter has employed a photograph (Salvador Dali, Andy Warhol), closing with a stunning tongue-in-cheek canvas after the French aristocrat Picabia, *Portrait of Camera*, (c. 1917).

But was photography 'art'?

A brave attempt to sort this one out was made at the big Hayward Gallery, across the river. Posters and banners announced the continuous conceptual 'event': a series of boxing matches between artists and photographers. Big names had flown in from Europe and across the Atlantic. So far, the artists had won every round, though each fight was recorded on video tape—a point the photography faction claimed as an overall victory. A number of photographers were accused of cheating. A disciple of crazy Eadweard Muybridge insisted on wrestling with his opponents, naked.

Shoot-outs between trigger-happy Polaroid teams took place at dusk.

Gerald didn't bother crossing the river. He'd returned to the hotel, bewildered.

'What about the Tate Gallery?' Hofmann asked, being sympathetic. The Tate had a fine collection of stripe paintings. He'd been planning to go.

'Don't bother. I was told that instead of the *paintings*—can you imagine?—they've tracked down the actual subject or place. And these were carefully photographed—understand?—so a person could see what the scene *really* was like. So at the Tate there's nothing but colour slides of French canals, hay stacks and lily ponds, apples, yellow chairs, and ballet dancers; God knows what else. For this they flew one photographer to Tahiti, so I was told.' And Gerald hung his hands between his legs. 'I don't know what the world's coming to.'

Shiela felt sorry for him; she hated seeing people upset. Gerald drained his dry sherry and ordered another.

'So that's what's on at the Tate?' Hofmann said.

Borelli who had joined them looked down at the carpet, toeing a crown.

'Impressionism, Cubism, Surrealism, Futurism, Abstract Expressionism and Tourism are all related. I doubt now whether one can do without the other.'

Oh and Commercialism, never one to be left out: two multinationals, Kodak and the Kraft Corporation, had joined forces to sponsor a European food photographic competition, 'SAY CHEESE!'

Hofmann turned to Borelli.

'If it's tourism they're after, they're going about it the wrong way. I must say I'm surprised at the British letting this happen. They're normally better than anyone with museums. As I say, I'm surprised.'

'I completely agree,' said Gerald, putting it mildly.

But Kaddok had bumped into his chair, followed by Gwen.

'Ah, hello there,' said Kaddok in his monotone. His fingers followed the edge of the bar. 'My wife and I have just been to the National Gallery. It was the finest exhibition I've ever seen.'

As Kaddok spelt out the highlights they sat quietly, politely. Gritting his teeth Gerald looked towards the door.

'Leon just loves his camera,' Gwen whispered to Shiela.

'Tell you what'—Garry Atlas had sat down—'have you been to the Imperial War Museum? I'd always wanted to have a squiz there. What I've always wanted to see was a real Spitfire. I've never seen a Spitty. But all they had up was aerial photographs, whacking great things, of bomb damage—mainly World War Two. Chrrrist, you should see Hiroshima. Not a shack standing. They also had about six different camera guns.'

They had a photographic history of camouflage; a discussion on the picture-plane; selection of re-touched press photographs with captions to show the art of propaganda; nineteen-forties newsreels.

'Hey, and you should have seen this incredible bloody picture of a bullet hitting an apple. Amazing. You've got to hand it to the Yanks.'

'Gwen, make a note. Where was that?'

The rest were intrigued, but subdued.

Since they had arrived, this famous city London seemed to have become one vast montage. And already there was something dated in the sight, or even the thought, of such well-documented factography. Unlike painting, photography wasn't timeless. It depended on death. The curiously dated clothing in photographs of former Prime Ministers standing in Downing Street reminded them of the past and their own fleeting presence. Photography: melancholia.

In the hollow-sounding halls of London University a seminar chaired by an Austrian discussed *The Difference Between Photography and Philosophy*: 'Vell I vould have thought, yes, vun is logical vhile the other is negative.'

Commiserating with Gerald, Borelli suggested that the armies of photographers tend to come from countries similarly bent on golf: America and Japan, for example. These people photograph to indicate their freedom, to remind themselves and others of the work which enabled the leisure. With his photograph a photographer likes to feel superior to the viewer. Familiar scenes—Borelli went on— are given meaning or context by the photographer placing the partner, usually a wife, in the foreground. Later this proves not merely 'I was there' but 'I saw'.

'I say,' Kaddok objected, as Louisa gaily laughed.

Mrs Cathcart stumped over to the news-stand to see the postcards. At least Doug joined in, nodding, 'This is right, this is right.'

Garry Atlas ordered another round, and cold ones, not that warm piddle.

Remembering Wimbledon, Shiela told them how she'd bumped into that Australian man they'd seen in Africa, and reddened.

'Then London isn't entirely grey,' smiled Borelli, not unkindly. 'Alas, for some of us, as you have heard, it is.' He placed his hand on his heart in mourning; and even Gerald, a grey one, had to laugh.

Nothing appeared to concern Borelli. He was loose with time. Yet as Louisa Hofmann watched he fell silent and gazed down at the floor.

Glancing at his watch Hofmann took Louisa's elbow.

As they were leaving, Cathcart cleared his throat and told Garry about the photos he'd seen at Australia House. These were on special Masonite stands in the foyer, quite an interesting group: shots of old fencing posts, bleached shearing-shed walls, and a selection of eccentric gates taken all over the ruddy outback.

'Christ! That sounds alright,' Garry nodded sagely.

Cathcart smacked his lips. 'And tell you what. It makes you appreciate the old place.'

They dressed up that night for the theatre, though some had other tickets by mistake. At the Opera the Kaddoks shared a box with Louisa, sat quietly behind her, and in the dark the crumpled arm of Borelli's jacket kept shifting, occasion-ally brushing hers. Louisa wasn't sure what to say. Talking in the group at the hotel she thought he might have looked across and posed one of his questions again, or even acknowledged her. He didn't seem to notice her. Then why should he? So Louisa began stretching her neck concentrating on the stage, so that no one knew her thoughts. Neatly clasped, her hands formed a T across the programme.

'What beautiful scenery,' she whispered out of the blue.

Borelli sat up. 'Shall we have a drink?' He turned to the Kaddoks too. 'I'm having one.'

In the loges opposite Louisa saw other people seated motionless, intently watching the opera. Shirt-fronts and pale irregular faces showed as patches of light; jewelry and spectacles glittered in the dark; here and there equidistant mauve stars (contact lenses?) shone similar to the eyes of foxes when caught in a spotlight. Louisa no longer looked at the heavy soprano, now tiptoeing with the strain. One hand rested on her cheek. She bit her top lip. For the audience, of which she was part, this was entertainment at the end of a long day. Fashions had changed but in the darkened hall the scene would have been the same as on any night seventy or a hundred years ago. Men and women then had dressed up and sat in these seats through each act, engrossed, a night out. They had since gone; had died. This audience too, these men and women, would gradually be replaced. They sat now engrossed, some leaning forward, oblivious.

This faceless replacement of life and pleasure caught and held Louisa. She felt isolated and irrelevant; a childless body draped in fine clothing briefly bumping around. Even pleasure seemed futile. When the lights came on she suddenly wanted to be alone. The Kaddoks said something and stumbled out.

Louisa wanted to turn away.

'Isn't it odd when you look at it,' Borelli was murmuring. Slumped in his seat he waved one hand: 'That a place like this has been specially built to be filled with polite people, strangers sitting next to each other, to witness some entertainment or other performed by other people? And see how it's been built: deliberately ornate, almost grotesque. It has to be ornate. No one wants to come to a bare hall. This decoration says: you are out having a good time. You are,

66

for the evening, in a separate remote world. Or feelings to that effect.'

The tall walls were fluted, balustraded, spiral-columned, draped with royal velvet and lungeing caryatids. The ceiling was pastel cupola, inside of a lemon, gesso, adorned with little lights.

Borelli remained slumped.

'I wonder if other cultures have these elaborate, set-aside places? It all seems strange. Do you feel that? I wouldn't, myself, have come here if I wasn't travelling.'

Louisa glanced at him. His speculations had wandered up and down and around her, searching. Vaguely they were similar to what she had been thinking, though not exactly.

'Partly, that's why we travel. Tourism compresses time and events.' He laughed at himself. 'In a sense we actually live longer. At least that's what a tourist somehow feels.'

'You have so many theories.' And she was about to add, 'What good do they do?' But when she looked at him, he was still slumped.

'You were tired before; you look pale.'

He sat up. 'You're right.'

Her foot knocked over the gin-and-tonic. It was enough: she began crying, a little. She couldn't stop herself.

Borelli was leaning close to her.

'I am sorry. I didn't mean . . . '

'It's not your fault. But I don't know.'

The night, the emptiness, the distance. Her size.

His hand took her arm.

'Shhh. You should be happy. Imagine yourself. You're on holiday. Isn't that what they say?'

'It was my husband's idea. It was to go away together. I don't mind but it was his idea. We haven't been getting on.'

'Then, Louisa, you're not having a good time?'

'I am really!' She suddenly smiled.

The Kaddoks had returned.

Taking out a small round mirror Louisa began checking her face and telling Borelli about the stripe painting Ken had bought at Christie's. He nodded, watching her. Part of

Gwen's burlap shawl came between them. Smiling in the dark, Gwen asked if one of them could change seats so Leon could photograph the last act.

Such a cold afternoon, Tuesday, as expected. A river of a wind to boot. It soaked into their ears, chill brains, and down their open necks, cleft chins and cleavages. It soon found gulleys in their trousers; entered regions where it shouldn't. They were crossing the Thames: which of the London bridges? It was possible to walk across all nine in a day. North had undertaken to guide them. He had a map and a pair of sturdy shoes. The cold certainly livened the man up. Among many other things he noted English tramps were attracted to bridges and invariably wore neckties (usually red). And it seemed that much of the population was either lost or establishing its location: so Sasha and Violet began laughing whenever they saw a couple bent over a map in a small sedan, or another policeman pointing for a squinting pedestrian. A colonel consulted a khaki compass. Taxi drivers shouted across at confused drivers. Almost from birth, North had an unusual knack for folding maps. People would bring them to him to fold. It was his love of maps, of globes and atlases, which had years ago led him, in a roundabout way, into the world of Zoology. So many maps had he pored over in his time that he dressed, without fully realizing, in the gentle pastels of cartography: yellow corduroy trousers (6000–9000 feet above sea level), the jacket of darkly woven maroon (Antarctic Tundra), shirt of Viyella peach (less than 1 inch of rainfall per annum), and the red fleck in his woollen tie looked like International Boundaries or 'population over 500 persons per square mile.'

They sat down in ye olde tea shoppe and Sasha's nose was shining. Violet lit up a cigarette.

'Colleague of mine in Sydney,' North was telling them, 'collected railway stations. He claimed to have the finest collection, I think it was, in the Southern Hemisphere. Of course, Jack had travelled a good deal in his youth. For example, he still has the old Dresden station, and some of those in Japan, before they were destroyed. You'd find with Jack that he'd always angle a conversation around to bring out his "collection". Nothing would stop him then.'

North laughed softly. His shoulders shook. Sasha and her friend were both interested.

'In his collection he has the world's hottest station, the longest and the widest. There is one somewhere or other that's circular. He often mentions Mussolini's station at Rome. Do you know that one? Huge marble mausoleum. He even has one of the mock one stashed away, built in Germany for the concentration camps . . . But I must say, others sound extremely attractive. Up in the Himalayas, a tiny one which smells of fresh tea leaves; coffee-smelling ones in Brazil too. My favourite is the Zanzibar station. According to Jack, it's always hot and has a permanent aroma of cloves.'

Sipping his tea, North pulled a face.

'Reminds me. He'd spent years, home, trying to duplicate railway station tea and coffee, but could never quite achieve this elusive watery-ness. Let me think. What else did he have? That famous New York station located under the skyscraper, and a Mexican one inside a cathedral. Flinders Street, Amritsar, Edinburgh and Rangoon. In the Philippines the station built completely out of cane—cane walls, cane seats. There was a nightmarish one somewhere . . . I forget now . . . but it was completely rusty. The platform, benches, even the ticket office, according to him, were all made from old railway track. Passengers would always come away with orange hands. But he's like any collector. It's the rarities he's most proud about. He has one where the trains are always early, Latin American stations suspended by cables, and one near the Arctic Circle where the platform is made from blocks of ice, and replaced every night—a transluscent station. A good collection. But I've been talking too much. Excuse me.'

'No, go on! He sounds terribly interesting.'

'Oddballs are, aren't they?' Violet added, inhaling; and a

sliding shadow of a double decker engulfed her arms, face and throat.

North coughed. 'Well, he prefers Leftish governments everywhere, because they appear to have more time for railway stations. His favourite painter of course is the Belgian man, Delvaux; and there's apparently a German collagist who liked to use train tickets in his art. With books he'll talk only about those which have a climactic chapter in railway stations. You know, *Anna Karenin*, *To the Finland Station*, and so on. The ones he holds high though are a little Czech book, *A Close Watch on the Trains* and an English one—John Wain—called *A Smaller Sky*. Both are novels set entirely inside railway stations. I can only tell you all that because he forced me to read them.'

Violet pulled a face. 'Fancy living with such a man. How obsessive.'

'I think it would be funny,' Sasha laughed.

Looking at North she noticed he'd let one of his cuffs unravel. A thread was hanging down.

'He is obsessive, but then I've told you only the railway station side of him. I imagine he's what the newspapers call Incurable Romantic. He is a harmless, gentle character. Such people are antidotes; I sometimes think we'd go mad without them. Jack actually is extremely intelligent. In any case, collecting appears to be a central human characteristic. We are, ah, part Bower Bird.'

'Is he a good friend of yours?' Sasha asked.

'I used to see a good deal of him!'

'I'd love to meet him.'

'Sasha, what for?'

North smiled: lines spreading out from his eyes, sinusoidal projections. 'If you like, but he's my age. He's old enough to be your grandfather. Shall we move? I think we should.'

Again and again: bent figures consulting maps. On the second last bridge they saw the Kaddoks approaching, Kaddok holding his wife's elbow, at a jog.

'Hello,' Sasha waved. 'We've just been—'

'Leon's left his light meter on a train. Does anyone know

the Lost Property Office? We can't get a taxi at this hour.'

As they spoke a ferry-load of tourists below tilted up and photographed them: five talking on a London bridge.

North said, 'It used to be over there. It's not far, but it's complicated.' He turned to the others. 'Shall we drop the last bridge?'

'I'll come with you,' said Sasha.

It was an old brown station made redundant by inflation. Sasha leaned against North, 'I bet your friend what's-his-name doesn't have this one.'

North stroked his beard. 'I don't remember it being like this myself.'

It resembled the small out-of-the-way museum, run by a dedicated amateur. The Found Objects, as the sign pointed inside, were behind the counter, placed at easy intervals on tables and shelves, labelled, clearly visible. There were also pigeon holes; as the attendant explained to North, these were for lost pigeons. And you'd be surprised how many they get, some with foreign words on their feet.

While the Kaddoks were busy filling out a form, the attendant motioned the others to come behind the counter.

'A lot of these Found Objects have been here for donkey's years.' He pointed to a white bicycle wheel with hand-pump attached. 'Before my time,' he nodded, reading the red tape attached to it. '1913. Some of this stuff could be quite valuable.'

Early coins corroded with patino; dead letters now with several rare stamps; Victorian toys; dusty bottles of port; a 1913 edition of *À la Recherche du Temps Perdu* (vol. I) in a Woolworths bag.

The collection of lost luggage alone offered a valuable insight into changing attitudes, the gradual democratiz-ation of travel. The attendant here complained bitterly of lack of staff. A *catalogue raisonné* was badly needed. Sociol-ogists had recently discovered the cache and pub-lished important findings. At one end of the scale was the monogrammed carpet bag of 'REES JEFFERIES' left on a channel train one morning in the twenties; at the other more recent end were the unclaimed canvas bags with flap, grubby and open, the kind favoured and discarded by the international army of hirsute stowaways, bus travellers, hitch-hikers and bodgies.

In between were steamer trunks and enamelled tin productions, the inevitable Gladstone, and portmanteaux of silk-coated cardboard (port, short for *porter*—where have they gone? *Manteau*, the French for loose upper garment worn by women). There were cardboard valises, Argentine stitched leather or the classic papier-mâché model . . . plastic, vinyl, Taiwanese imitation leather . . . a floppy bag like a coarse pillow with rope handles . . . the ravages of inflation again. All were heavy with invisible possessions. Rusty locks, secret numbers, belts, string and leather straps prevented yawning! The sides and fronts were nostalgic collages of customs crayon and shipping line labels: those ships long broken up or (some) angled deep in Davy's locker. It was enough to make any aging man ponder. The attendant had an enormous honest jaw, the bottom lip of which had rolled out with the gravity of the situation, exposing his stumps, his gums, and a spot of gold on the left. His eyes were small and red. He was more like a cemetery attendant.

He pointed to heavy ports fitted with little nylon wheels: favoured by elderly folk, young ladies and Boston Brahmins. They laughed when North picked up a Brisbane kitbag. How did that get there?

By far the most fascinating odd-lot, a perspex case, home-made, revealed three or four tins of kippers 'swimming' among a man's soiled shirts and underclothing.

Violet, the actress, tried on a top hat and did a brief vaudeville shuffle.

North smiled but like the attendant looked on subdued.

'That there's a burglar's torch,' he said to North. 'At least that's what we think. No one is going to claim a lot of this stuff. But we can't throw it away.'

He tilted a motor cyclist's helmet to show a hairline crack.

'Found near a railway intersection, 1963. So it was sent here. Out the back we have bags of fruit and sides of lamb.

All rotting into nothing. We can't throw anything out. It's like abortion. I ask our staff: who has the right?'

Other found objects included a small meteorite the size of a basketball and a mountaineer's ice axe with IRVINE burnt into the handle.

At least here, unlike a museum, you could pick up an item and turn it over (though it would take three men to lift the meteorite). Each object appeared to be close, indeed intimately entwined, in the daily lives of ordinary people. So here the recent wide distance between artist and bewildered spectator was dramatically narrowed, if not entirely bridged. These objects were strange, yet compellingly 'real.'

'Something like eight hundred and twenty umbrellas,' the attendant was saying, blowing his nose.

Both Gwen and Leon Kaddok touched his elbow.

'We've filled out the forms.'

'Just a minute.'

He scratched his elbow.

'I've lost track of what I was saying.'

He turned to North: man approaching his own age. At least he appeared to be taking genuine interest.

'This is nothing unusual,' scratching his elbow. 'I'm told asbestos miners suffer from some variety of lung disease. Imagine here every day surrounded by lost property and trying to sort it out! Of course it must affect a man. I find now I'm continually losing things: telephone numbers, a pocket knife, my wallet. I lose track of time and memory. The place acts like a drain. I keep losing staff. I couldn't even tell you, if you asked me now, my wife's birthday.'

To help out North ventured, 'We're not getting any younger,' But he looked troubled. He had just lost a wife; the loss had spread and remained like a white stain.

Standing on one foot Kaddok hovered anxiously for his light meter, and although he couldn't see them could hear Sasha and Violet whispering and laughing.

'Whyte, the man before me,' the Attendant recalled, 'in the end used to "lose" things on trains to see if they'd come back as found objects. This is his raincoat, poor fellow.

Excuse me, what were we saying?'

North had stopped listening.

Was time composed of broken fragments, some lost, some occasionally coming close, before drifting into dots? Perhaps with age the fragments become widely spaced: arms and feet plunge through and grab trying to hold onto things.

Softer giggling behind the canary cages and tangle of walking sticks. It was Sasha: 'I lost mine six years ago in St Kilda, you know when—that New Year's Eve. I remember I could hear a clock striking. I must have had too much to drink. God, he was a creep.'

Her best friend gave a harsh laugh.

'Look around, baby, you might find it here.'

'They can have it!'

'Good riddance, eh Sasha?'

They both laughed.

North had pursed his lips but couldn't help smiling. They said something else.

'You can talk!'

But the Kaddoks raised their voices, pointing.

The attendant had their forms at arm's length.

'First, let me show these people the rest. Do you have a photograph of this light meter of yours? Well, then—'

'But this is ridiculous.'

'I know exactly what it looks like,' Kaddok said.

'Leon, let me handle this.'

The attendant had turned and pushed open a metal door. He winked at North, 'Have a dekko here.' And as they walked through Sasha whispered, 'Have you seen the parrots? Just back there?'

North shook his head.

Taking up the rear Kaddok kept mumbling.

Here a girdered annex housed an entire English railway station, presumably one of those lost in the savage rationalizations back in the sixties. Each component, each heavy piece of equipment, had been placed more or less but not quite in its original operating position—ticket box, platform, bench-seats, the Roman clock, refreshment room—

and so the proportions and angles were subtly wrong, peculiarly cramped, and everything of course was unstable, not bolted down, making them hesitate and step back. And it all had a fine covering of dust.

The attendant shook Kaddok's pincer-grip from his elbow.

'Your collector-friend,' said Violet, 'what would he think of this?'

'Very interesting,' North nodded. 'I'll have to tell him.'

The rusting tilted mass had lodged in North's mind. Similarly, yet miles away, Kaddok decided to take a photograph: an image to pass around would prove they had been there.

'We don't shout it about; no one has yet claimed it. I don't show this to every Tom, Dick and Harry.' The attendant jangled his keys. 'Foreign tourists are alright.'

'Whew, I found that very spooky,' Sasha whispered, 'didn't you?'

North bent down to inspect the parrots: North African wax-bills, gray parrots (*Psittacus enthacias*), a stuffed racket-tailed among them, eclectus, and a galah from Western New South Wales. The cage was clean and they had plenty of water.

Almost back at the entrance the Kaddoks stopped. First Gwen, then Leon, pointed to a shelf of photographic equipment. The attendant swung around.

'Go on then, take the whole lot. You walk in; you're never satisfied. Go on! I hope you're satisfied. Now you can get out, all of you.'

Cars, lights, buses, electric messages, pedestrians crossed and abruptly flashed or thundered before them: overlapping montage. Otherwise, the street outside was dark.

'Are you alright?' they peered at the Kaddoks.

'I got frightened!' Sasha laughed.

'It's after eight!'

At their table in the hotel they found only the Cathcarts left, having a second cup.

'Howdy,' said Doug.

Sitting heavily down and perspiring Kaddok related

their experience. The man had no right to do that; Kaddok quoted verbatim the relevant sections from the Public Service Act.

'This is right,' Doug nodded, nasal. 'The old poms, you know, can get a bit uppitty. We found this.'

North sat quietly reading his palms.

As Cathcart spoke he shook out a tablet from a bottle beside him. 'D'you have any H_2O?' he asked the waitress going past. Along with Enterovioform he took the small quinine tablet before and after each meal to counteract the condition of London's underground pipes. It was pretty obvious. Work it out: 'Some of the pipes here'd be hundreds of years old. The insides must be half flaking. You can't tell me the place is clean.'

'Their toilets aren't exactly,' Mrs Cathcart had said, filing her nails. 'We take our own soap.'

If there was something she—they—hated it was untidiness. And that was the trouble, the further away from home. Some of these countries could do with a good scrub. And the dreadful smells. Take Africa! It said a lot about a place, its progress and hope.

Ah, according to a recent survey by the Department of the Environment, London has fewer flies than any other region in England. The newspapers had written it up. Frinstance: average London household in summer can muster up only 0.9 of a fly per day. In East Anglia the figure is 5.7. That's the largest in the country. Compare that to East Africa! (What about Alice Springs?) Method of counting is simple enough: clarity of vision, concentration, patience. All over the country men sat in rooms with a pencil, a paper, and ticked off the flies as they saw them. Many flies, the report admitted, look alike. Nevertheless, industry would put the results to good use, especially the aerosol syndicates.

Other news (in brief): 20 INJURED IN EXPLOSION IN SODA SIPHON FACTORY. 'More than twenty people were taken to hospital suffering from shock and burns . . . Windows were shattered some distance from the explosion.' The newspapers published aerial shots of the devastated plant and the squinting foreman, L. Wyndham, 42, with a Band-Aided nose. BABY THROWN IN SEA MUM HELD. Blankets were rushed to the scene. Groucho, the London Zoo's much-loved hippo, shown as a proud father (photograph caption: *Cigar, Groucho?*). JOBLESS RISE. Same as home: no difference; only remoteness in the nouns. This English news didn't much matter. It was distant and fragmented. Australia? The word was not to be found, not even in the bloody shares pages, Garry Atlas pointed out. It might well not have existed. Only at Australia House and among themselves did it have a shape, grown naturally into the faces and voices, and in the familiar pages of their own newspapers. But here? 'DEAD' UNDERGRADUATE SPEAKS. Interesting, esoteric. The billiard table, essential in understanding the resilience and stability of the Empire, is making a comeback. Unknown, irrelevant laws being passed by parliament. A cold snap is expected.

'Smile?' Sasha suddenly got it into her head.

Bending down she had to whisper it before North looked up, thousands of miles away.

'That's better,' Sasha beamed, hitching her strap. 'Remember you're with us.'

With the curtains drawn and the bottle-shaped lamp switched on but occasionally flickering, Shiela remained enclosed in her room. It had become warm, a personal humidity, immediately noticeable to those who had popped in to see if she was alright. She appeared jerkier than usual, a shade, and to Mrs Cathcart who called, her eyes slid off her face more, off the architrave and light switch.

But that could have been due to Mrs Cathcart's sturdy presence, legs apart, in the centre of the room.

'I'm doing some catching up,' Shiela mumbled: postcards fanned out there by the phone. And she immediately looked concerned. 'That serves to remind me,' said Mrs Cathcart. Postcards and the sky-blue airletters; she and Doug had gallivanted around so much she'd hardly written to anybody, and she should.

Shiela remained suspended, in a sense, by the angles of

the room, a cube filled with rubbish. And then it was as if she was being sieved, for she was activated first by the stuttering lamp, then without warning the throat-clearing radiator pipes and—at distant regular intervals of a railway schedule—a slight volcanic tremor beginning from the floor through the soles of her feet, as if one of the underground lines ran directly below her room (quite possible). Taken separately the vibrations were pleasant; a combination of all three was rare and even then not unpleasant. They blurred the emptiness of the room. Shiela had placed her belongings to her liking, not windswept like the two across the hall. She'd seen them before returning from somewhere. The young full-breasted one, Sasha, was always horsing around but not badly—casually—and Shiela had to smile. Facing each other the three understood. There were no men watching. Approaching her door, Sasha began wobbling her behind, and putting her tongue in her cheek, dangled her key below her throat, dropped it down.

Professing to be shocked, Violet elbowed her, laughing, 'You're a tart.'

'That a gun yah got there honey,' said Sasha, 'or yah jest happy to see mah?'

They were still shoving and collapsing as they tried to unlock the door; they were having a good time. Shiela smiled.

The others all had tickets to Ascot and were in high spirits, even Gerald who had decided to go along for the ride, as he put it, and Phillip North who had never before been to a horse race. At breakfast Shiela enjoyed the table's anticipatory nerves, a form of contagious jokiness, but shook her head. Again she'd decided to stay in. Lucky for her. The Queen's dark horses came seventh, second, last. Garry was up seventy quid before it rained and the mud larks came in. He lost his shirt. As he kept shaking his head, he'd been 'taken to the cleaners'. Fair enough, it was the heavy track, but look at the stupid fucking way English jockeys ride high in the saddle. It even looked wrong: 'emotional cripples, afraid to be seen being intimate with a horse,' Borelli suggested. They laughed at the leisurely race-callers. One would hardly know there was a race on.

Comparisons were unavoidable and were made constantly. It became at least a definition, or one measurement of experience.

To Gerald, the side view of the straining horses was inseparable from those elongated bay geldings depicted in 19th century English paintings. Craning his neck he found himself enjoying the spectacle far more than he'd expected. But Kaddok who disliked being out of things ploughed in: 'Their legs in those paintings are wrong. That's the trouble with art.'

Gerald reddened. Normally, he quickly began shouting in arguments.

'I've taken photographs here'—Kaddok tapped the telephoto lens—'that can prove to you, anyone else if you're interested, that a horse's legs are all in the air. I believe that's one of the troubles with art,' Kaddok concluded. 'It misses the real truth.'

'You mean,' said Gerald harshly, 'you mean we suffer from a form of visual blindness.'

'That's right.'

They were a weary yet still vocal group.

'At least we've been to Ascot!' said Doug notching it up.

Only Ken Hofmann who'd won sat as usual with his arms folded, gazing at the ceiling molding.

'Tell you what,' said Garry suddenly; and because his mouth was full began clicking his fingers. 'I saw our friend from Africa, what's-his-name. You know, from the hotel.'

'I saw PHAR LAP and THE MELBOURNE CUP some larrikin had carved on the rails,' North put in.

'You don't believe me?' he turned to Sasha. She was the one laughing most at him.

'Frank Newman?' Doug pronounced.

'I think it is Hammersly,' said Shiela simply. She reddened.

Leaning across refilling her glass Garry Atlas made Violet laugh about something. He then lit her cigarette with his Zippo, snapping it shut, and dropping it in his side pocket. He adjusted himself on his seat.

'What's bitten you?'

Sasha was smiling at Violet. Most of the other women were now watching Violet. She blew smoke and turned to Garry.

'I'm allowed to smoke, aren't I?'

'Well? . . .' Sasha raised her eyebrows.

Seated next to her Phillip North listened politely to Kaddok's views on the light sensitivity of silver nitrate.

So Garry thought he'd crack a joke. 'God, she's old enough. How old are you, Violet?'

The stomach punch wasn't hard and while he fell forward with an exaggerated coughing fit, Violet met Sasha's gaze.

'Darling, you remember all my cigarette commercials? I'm a regular chimney.'

'Yes, you know what you're doing,' Sasha smiled.

Down the end Doug's hoarse whisper: 'I knew I'd seen her somewhere before.'

For Shiela again it was something other people often spoke about. She had somehow never looked at much television.

Returning to her room Shiela seized a couple of post-cards. She scribbled:

Harrods is just the same—lovely atmosphere— weather a bit chilly—some rain. Must be going. Tomorrow we go to the country to see

She walked around. She began brushing her skirt. She picked up her passport and sat down: the earnest, startled photograph. Turning the pages, one for each country, she tilted her head at some of the entry stamps. It was almost filled.

It was dark outside, the city rumbling with movements. Through the gap in the curtains Shiela could make out the opposite wall fifteen yards away, dizzy with the heavy fire escape, and facing her a lighted window, like her own. So much for their curtains: a silhouette moved across. It came back and stopped. She was soon recognizable with her hair pulled up, now falling down, small breasts rather like Shiela's own. One arm kept banging her hip, a signal. Hurry: impatience, nervousness. A man, he came in from the right pulling his shirt over his head, and look there projecting from his hips the urgent something, pointing up. Shiela could see it. Abruptly the shadows merged and the thing seemed to hoist the other up, their faces joined. Her leg wrapped around his thigh. Swaying and hopping they hurriedly left the window. Shiela waited but nothing more happened. The light went out.

'God, I hate tourists,' said Gerald. 'They've made a mess of everything. Nothing is real anymore. They obscure anything that was there. They stand around, droves of them, clicking with their blasted cameras. Most of them don't know what they're gawking at.'

They'd exchanged their raincoats for a plastic token each, its polished colour and the ritual enough to remind North of early visits to Africa, of dust and diminishing herds of elephants. But instead they were in the old world. Trays of glass in the roof again reproduced a kind of standard cathedral light, drawing their heads up. Along two walls quasi-Egyptian frescoes illustrated The March of Progress, dwelling on those instruments of Victorian expansion, the sextant and steam-engine, and the marble floor was inlaid with abstract symbols, a mosaic of large equations.

'I've had a rotten time,' Gerald admitted, opening the museum guide book. 'London has changed since I was here last. It's an anti-climax.'

'Where are we?' North asked.

'This way,' he pointed.

The psychologists, neurologists and psychiatrists, quacks, and even the chiropodists continue to argue the left indicates the past and individual characteristic, the right the future.

Right: they clattered along the travertine, Gerald poking his hornrims back on his nose. It was a museum without

space problems, either through design or judicious arrangement of objects.

'I usually go to places where there are no tourists—places that haven't been spoilt. But it's getting to the stage now where even the size of a city or a country is no longer a defence. You know how mobs pour in and stand around, taking up room, and asking the most ludicrous basic questions. They've ruined a place like Venice. It's their prerogative, but the authenticity of a culture soon becomes hard to locate. The local people themselves become altered. And of course the prices go up. Yet the tourist is still pandered to. That's what irritates me. This week I've had a kind of bilious attack from it all. Several times I thought I might be physically ill; I've had splitting headaches. I used to love London. And the rest of the world's going down the drain like this.'

'I say.'

'Well, this is your Science Museum,' said Gerald bitterly.

To reach the main hall they apparently had to first enter this plywood offshoot, a prefabricated antechamber. The world's first museum in Alexandria was a Science Museum. North pulled back a purple curtain. Gerald following bumped into him. Their eyes had to get used to the dark. A system of holograms littered the black air with the century's most far-reaching equations, giving a distinct impression of the elegance and excitement of discovery. 'Written' as if with chalk in mid-air the equations were three-dimensional and suspended like stars; the room, a kind of cloud-chamber, represented the illimitable universe of signs and knowledge. They could pass through this accumulated, human knowledge; or rather, the knowledge could pass through them. Indeed that was the whole idea. But Phillip North couldn't or chose not to. In the dark, his feet on the floor, it had become suddenly like standing on the edge of space; there were no walls; only endlessness and shifting relativity: a rebuilding in nothingness. Towards something: what? Did these exquisite figures exist merely in mid-air? The edifice of knowledge, of mathematics was transparent. There was then a shrinking sensation of smallness, accompanied by pride, faint hope, a glimmer. 'Whoops!' Was he leaning forward? Vertigo: he clutched at Gerald's elbow. They were both perpendicular. He touched the side-wall, painted black. 'Surprising,' he muttered. He reached out and passed his hand through Ramañujam's nearby formulate, (1.10)–(1.13). 'Well, it's remarkable. Though I don't understand it,' he said aloud. Over there among the alpha particles floated the first scribbles on quantum and calculus. Numbers in prime condition; set theories. At waist level Wiener's slender calligraphy demonstrated cybernetics; in its wake a new measurement of quarks. Structure of DNA as if etched in acid. Of course! Formulae of nucleotides! Glowing symbols: produced a distinct resonance. Alone, they stood watching. In the corner, far away, the periodic table of chemical elements lay angled or propped in mid-air, a plank, a symphonic score.

But then Gerald in the dark had to maintain science wasn't 'natural' and added, 'What's-his-name, James Borelli, should be here. He's a complete atheist; so he says.'

North's zoology was flesh. The noun embraced all that was furry, including termites and shit. Here stood the spotless clarity of metals. Gerald squinted at North and began shuffling.

'We're just the poor misunderstood laymen. Come on, we haven't got a chance.'

'Yes, I suppose.'

As Gerald inched his way forward, $E = mc^2$ appeared stencilled on his neck, and across his cheeks and teeth when he turned: Phillip North found it all so interesting he was laughing.

The next room was dark, another antechamber.

Gerald groaned: 'No, not photography!'

From early engravings and oil paintings a second system of holography reproduced a roomful of half-tone heads-and-shoulders of the big-wigs in science (there's Leibnitz, goldilocks Newton) up to the present day, using photographs, though finishing early with Dr Gabor himself (balding, spectacled, naturally pleased). It was like standing among a crowd of gazing ghosts, a room full. They do their work early but live to a ripe age. That was why North spent time trying unsuccessfully to identify most of them. Outside in the main hall Gerald sighed, 'I frankly find this rather dreary.'

'Really? Not the first room? You didn't find that interesting?'

Gerald shook his head. 'I don't know why you bother. I'm like most people on this. Science leaves me cold. And actually I think it's over-rated.'

'To tell the truth,' Phillip North admitted, 'I've switched subjects. In a sense, I have. I'd like to avoid my old field for the time being. Let it lie fallow, you know. This interests me, a new area. It's adjacent but almost the opposite to zoology: what our American friends, I think, call a "whole new ball game". Dreadful expression.'

'Isn't it a bit late in the day?' Gerald asked, matter of fact.

'I can't pretend I properly understand. But I'll look at anything,' said North. And in this place his eyes were keen, darting ahead.

'Can you imagine: every time I've been to London I've never been to the Science Museum? It was a form of blindness.'

Whitehead looked glum. Before them stood an assortment of brains, not run-of-the-mill brains, the Great Brains, preserved in jars sealed with stainless-steel lids and clips, labelled and bathed in crepuscular light. Chief among them was the brain of Einstein. On the floor in front of it the linoleum was conspicuously worn. Such a small brain! Except for a slight protuberance in the frontal lobe— noticeable only by crouching down—it could have been any of those ranged on either side: the rocket engineer's from the Ukraine, or that of the brilliant French biochemist with the IQ of 149 who died at twenty-three. Perhaps it weighed more? There was no way of telling. Since they all looked alike the instinct was to read the label, then peer inside the jar. And then and only then did the grey matter of the half dozen or so mathematicians appear to be teeming with blurred numerals and symbols, jostling to be multiplied. And that Cambridge astronomer (the knight): his resembled a soft meteor. Three sad brains from child prodigies: small cantaloupes, not tremendous cabbages.

'No great poets, no artists, oh no'—Gerald complained. 'It's what I was saying before.'

'I don't see a zoologist either,' said North glancing around. 'Well, we've always been in the shade.'

A fine reconstruction there of a great English brain, possibly the greatest (Sir Isaac again), consisted of plasticine and putty; effective, almost believeable. This was for the layman and schoolchildren: it had been placed alongside the brain of a male elephant, four times larger than Newton's, but as a long chart of its deficiencies showed, hopelessly inadequate.

Some of these brains could still work.

By the window some had been set up to take a small (?) electric shock. If administered in the right place the amazing trapped organ shuddered, proving that the brain is a 'convoluted mass of nervous system'. Speech had not yet been reproduced; but one, look, made some coloured lights wink like a pair of eyes. Another submerged in its bath of formalin produced bubbles (thoughts?). North stood back as Gerald tried a few switches. Simple sums could be answered: the potential stirrings of science. What if you connected them to loud-speakers? Would they scream?

North cleared his throat. Science raised a myriad of questions, no answers.

They turned their attention to a spasmodic *chess game* between the brains of a French-American master—no names, please!—and what purported to be (there in writing) Leonardo da Vinci's. Both were well preserved. They trailed coloured wires. The first, not a scientific brain in the dictionary sense, had a scientific turn of mind, and had retained much of its old elegance and daring. The second had never played before, but was doing well, having castled early. A grey-faced attendant sat in a chair keeping his eye on them. He operated the clock.

Gerald turned to North really bored.

Entering the room from the wrong end came a group of South Americans who, all talking at once, gathered around the game. Others drifted over to the jars and called out to their friends.

Gerald and Phillip North had to push their way out. North wore a vague distant expression. He would have stayed and drifted, taken a table in the cafeteria, and then continued in the afternoon, the sharp edges of metals an alternative to the imprecision and roundness of flesh; but Gerald still pulling faces and muttering didn't stop in the next room.

'There's your cause. Right here,' he pointed, then dropped his arm. His voice rose. 'To think that a great museum should glorify this and make it "interesting". What a marvel of technology, they say. No mention of the ruination it's causing. It's a symptom and typical. This is a vulgar specious age. Look at it: the great leveller, mob-generator, the lowerer of values. I'm sorry. You stay if you want to. It makes me sick.'

Partially (patiently) re-assembled: fragments of Sir Frank Whittle's first jet engine, the one that disintegrated, almost decapitating him. Alongside with its own oil-tray was a centrifugal monster from a transatlantic air liner, in superb working condition.

. . . . . . Tuesday. It's Thursday. Hold your horses. That was . . . several Sundays had stretched and passed. The trouble or the pleasure was that each and every morning smacked of 'Sunday': open-endedness tinged with possibilities or emptiness. It was corrected once they stepped outside. It was in the morning. Good, a Friday. The day leaked and dripped as they finished their toast. Outside the streets flowed with arriving office workers, five, six abreast, passing between each other like counter-marching bands, and more emerging from underground, abruptly halted and dammed by lights, spilling into the gutters, before moving again; amid the purpose, smoke and vibration of the big city awakening; trucks, vans, post and hand-barrows delivering for the day; policemen orchestrating. It took place outside as they remained chatting over breakfast: the clink of forks and crockery sounded pleasant. Looking up from the stained cloth Phillip North apparently felt sorry for Gerald—his contorted forehead. He offered him a second cup. It was enough for Whitehead to blink with gratitude. It was the usual table. At the end Doug Cathcart went briefly cross-eyed as he swallowed a pill, his insurance policy; and Garry had to lean back, one hand behind his head, to blow smoke rings.

A new side to Violet emerged as they settled at ten in the minibus. It had been laid on by one of the genealogical societies.

Violet sat next to Garry Atlas but took no notice of him.

'The stars,' she turned, 'the stars say this is an auspicious day for travel.'

'Thank God for that,' Hofmann murmured.

'Is anyone here a Libra?' Violet went on.

'Don't tell me!' Borelli put his hand over his eyes, 'Not stars, please.'

Sasha breathed into North's ear, 'Violet's quite batty. She's into astrology as well as this other business.'

'I'm always fetching Kiwis, bloody Aussies and Maple-leafs,' the driver spoke up. He had a hoarse voice. The last year had seen a boom: from the colonial back-blocks folk want to know their origins, and test the old soil. They came in droves. Life would make better sense after tracing the roots; not only place, county and such: but had forebears sprung from the thighs of convicts or vice-admirals? Among the genealogical societies were warring factions and inter-national advertising campaigns, though it was generally conceded Lady Pamela Hunt-Gibbons was the most re-liable. Her leaflets were passed around, printed on lemon dunny paper.

* PEDIGREES COMPILED AND SCRIVENED
* COATS OF ARMS RESEARCHED AND PAINTED
* FAMILY TREES
* TOUPEES

It is, I imagine, impossible to gauge the exact number of people who, in this age of increased leisure opportunities, have discovered

*the fascination of tracing their family history, but clearly the
number is increasing at an astonishing rate! Not many other
intellectual pursuits whip up such enthusiasm, which so easily
gives a sense of achievement, and joy at sharing one's knowledge!
An added pleasure is the meeting of others of similar temperament
but of different background, of making friends outside one's own
occupational group or even—let us say it—social class, of experiencing the pleasure of communication and exchange of ideas. But I
am being read here by the converted . . .*

Green leaves, grass, pale green water, long weeds in the
streams, and if they'd squatted down, moss on the under-
sides of posts and stones. That of the trees: a bright
shimmering green. It caused them repeatedly to exclaim
and point, though not all. It was so soft on the eyes, the
colour of slow holidays. As they passed, apples fell off trees.
To complete the picture Lady Pamela's cottage appeared
at the end of a lane. It was thatched.

'This is a corker,' said Doug, really pleased. 'This is
something to write home about.'

It could have been straight off a calendar or a postcard.

'Chrysanthemums there,' Mrs Cathcart pointed with
her chin.

Already Kaddok had jumped out and began moving in
the garden, treading on the odd flower bed, to find the best
angle. And Violet who had tiptoed ahead to find Lady
Pamela instead found herself lost in the maze of waist-high
lavender hedges which always steered her away from the
mullioned windows. Here was the topiary art at its finest.
When viewed from above, the precisely cut hedges actually
formed the exceedingly complicated coat-of-arms and
motto (*Nosce te*) of Lady Pamela's family; though Violet on
the ground wasn't to know. After laughing at herself she
began flushing. With the others watching she realized how
confused she must have looked.

'This way. Come along. Is that you Violet Hopper?' a
woman called.

In a room with low oak rafters they found a white-haired
lady seated before an easel. Camel hair brushes and a jar of

grey water were at her elbow. Against the window stood a rack of Derwent pencils, complete, like coloured organ pipes. She wore nylon sleeves over her cardigan and being a lady she didn't turn or stop painting as they crowded in. This was an experience. Cream antimacassars on all the armchairs; and Gerald examined the porcelain on the walls, English plates, English dogs and cups mainly, though all of a very high quality, and a group of early steel engravings of tall African and New Zealand waterfalls. Piles of manila folders tied with pink ribbons lay on the floor, as in a solicitor's office. Over the fireplace *Wills and Their Whereabouts* (the 4th edition) and *Wills and Where to Find Them* were separated by *Cooper's Creek* and the Everyman's *Origins of the Species*. She blew her nose.

'Pamela Hunt-Gibbons. How d'you do? Sit down. Don't all stand around.'

Squinting at her picture she rattled the brush in a jar.

Doug cleared his throat. 'Do you get any leaks with the thatch?'

Lady Pamela appeared not to hear. Again she rattled the brush which allowed some of them to glance around at the ceiling. She painted nothing but waterfalls; had, what, for the last thirty-something years. Stacks leaned behind the sofa, watercolours. Never having been out of England, she had not seen a major waterfall, relied on hearsay and imagination, and as the latter grew weaker took to rendering substitutes. Merely the same thing, she said to herself, but on a smaller scale. She persisted, the last vorticist. Rainwater overflowing from a gutter, water swirling down a bath hole, the brief turmoil of a lavatory flush were some of her subjects. The large stomach testified to her years spent at the easel. She had blue eyes and untidy white hair. And her nose which was red and thin kept leaking (*Self-Portrait with Two Waterfalls*), but she seemed decent enough. She wasn't stuck up.

'I loathe ponds and stagnation of any kind. The clash of the sperm and the ovum is like the spin of the earth. Feel it now. It's kept us all going. I am seventy-six. Fit as a fiddle. There's nothing stagnant about Natural Selection or the way roots of trees surge through the soil like fingers. It's my greatest regret I have never stood outdoors in a monsoon. That must be an electrical experience. I am told steps and alleyways and rocks become one gushing torrent.' She dabbed at her nose with a tissue. 'And the intermingling of molecules. Who is Borelli here, James Borelli?'

Leaning against the mantlepiece: he raised his walking stick. She must have seen its shadow on the wall.

'Bor-elli,' she repeated. 'I am afraid you are the odd man out. I could find nothing on you after an awfully long search. Seems your people never set foot on our island.'

'Flying visits,' Borelli smiled. 'We come from far away.'

'Italians,' Mrs Cathcart whispered.

'He's alright,' Doug said.

'I think it was grain elevators, passenger lifts, feather merchants. In that order. Rise then a crash. A great catch for the Australian migration boom.' He bowed slightly.

'Haw-haw'—Garry Atlas.

It was an indication of how accustomed to each other they had become that they allowed, even enjoyed, the others to hear their past. They waited quietly as Lady Pamela selected another brush.

Atlas: 'Scots, originally. They were glassblowers of Glasgow. In 1726 David Edward courted and married a Bartholomew of Edinburgh—above him, so to speak. They were small distillers.' Atlas grinned and looked around. 'In 1790 Clarence Atlas was shipped out to Van Dieman's Land.' They all laughed with Garry. 'For manslaughter,' Lady Pamela went on. 'After Tasmania, I suppose you know the rest. You have a rough past.'

The Cathcarts were a common enough name from the Renfrew's district and the River Cart. 'As the second syllable implies: cleaners, washers. Which is perhaps why you chose the occupation of Customs Officer. Your people scarcely left that county. Many are still there today; yet here you are. I suppose you have red hands.'

Doug nodded gravely.

'I am doing this alphabetically and I'm summarizing. I have typed sheets for each of you. You can take them home.

I'm told some like to frame them.'

People had often looked twice at Hofmann's smooth lips which were strange, and his complexion. Now it was explained.

'Your English extraction began with the German invasion and plunder of A.D. 400. One awful mix-up then. Which makes it extremely difficult for us. By the early sixteenth century you had intermingled to such an extent the name had almost expired. I thought I was tracing a ghost. But several of your Hofmanns were found hiding in London: Golders Green traders. Some went to America. I almost lost you again. But the males were apparently determined. The strain survived. One on the Isle of Wight married and migrated to Australia prior to the Great War, just like that. We don't know why. Two children. One of course is your great-grandfather Walter. A broken line, but surviving. Do you have any children yet?' Hofmann shook his head. 'Louisa, your side,' she said over her shoulder, 'were Hollisters from Middlesex.'

'Goodness!' Louisa giggled.

'Do you know what Hollister means?' Borelli frowned. 'Tell me!'

'I don't think so,' said Borelli, catching her husband's eye.

'Violet,' said the lady raising her voice, 'knows hers. Don't you, dear? Violet and I have corresponded.'

'No, tell us,' they shouted. 'We want to hear.'

A small ballet leap from Violet made them begin clapping.

'Leaper, dancer. Court musicians. Welsh and part-French—that was the "Butcher" side.' More laughter. She curtsied. 'One Hopper died in the Battle of Waterloo—perhaps speared by a Butcher? I am also related to the Captain of a Wool Clipper. Some Hoppers have achieved fame, I believe, in America.' Violet held her chin high and switched to a Cockney accent. 'I think now I'm the only Hopper left treading the boards.'

Lady Pamela gave a laugh like water running over

bricks. 'And don't forget, Violet, your great-great grand-mother.'

'Molly was a suffragette. She was in the clink several times.'

'A suffragette?' Garry repeated.

'Yeah, watch it, ocker,' Sasha called out.

'So, Violet, how many silly husbands have you gone through?'

'Oh it's about four. So far.'

'She has life!' said Lady Pamela firmly, while Mrs Cathcart drew in deep through her nostrils.

Kaddok, Leon. From a line of heavy Swedes (Vikings in horned helmets?), stubborn nomadic tribe. Survivors some-how of the Battle of Hastings. Subsequently turned to the land, the Church and the Work Ethic before one, Eric, became entangled in the Wheelwrights—daughters of long flaxen hair. Leon was the name given to their second. The boy grew to love the spoked wheels, flanges and artificial thunder of the period: went on to invent that humidifier with the thermostat soon used by all the Midlands cotton mills, the only Kaddok (so far) to make a name. In the cotton world he was world-famous. This Leon married in the nick of time Anne, nee Bewley (Bewley: 'beautiful place,' Durham). Then middle-aged he quickly lost his fortune in some other venture in North America. In 1874, he suicided. His only son married an Eastman, returned to England (Lancs.) in his twenties. And it was their son who went first to humid Calcutta, then landed in Melbourne, the year of Federation. Through the generations the Kaddoks were wracked with late marriages and atcknia: produced slender threads like loose cotton. With the remaining Kaddoks childless the name would return to darkness, and Leon Kaddok was busy taking many photographs.

The others listened quietly as the story and its prospective dead end unfolded. Kaddok showed no concern seated in one of the armchairs, looking straight ahead. Only Gwen on the floral arm fidgeted and had her mouth open, which attracted attention.

In the silence Lady Pamela went in close to the painting, almost touching it with her nose. She then spat on her handkerchief and rubbed at a spot with her little finger.

'Phillip-Spenser-North.'

'Doctor,' Sasha put in.

'Realah? Oh that is interesting. Atavism is a mystery and yet perfectly understandable. His is a distinguished name in land reform, science, medicine and so forth. The strain is extremely well defined. Harks way back—clean as a whistle. You are a descendant of the Earl of Guilford. Quite a few Norths eventually are, but usually they are collateral. I knew your great-uncle, Edmund—'

A murmur of respect and surprise spread, forcing North to scratch his neck. Tilting his big head Gerald looked at him afresh.

Gurgle-flush, the laugh of a London landlady as Lady Pamela remembered: 'Edmund was a gentleman, but quite mad! The things I could tell you about that man!'

She put her brush down and for the first time turned around.

She certainly had blue eyes, startlingly blue. Tributaries ran down from them, a type of erosion more commonly found in white skins transferred to the tropics, among old India hands, and another channel or sluice had formed below her nose. It was a small face: lids, cheeks and chin had sagged but combined in their intensity, visually to counter-balance the rising stomach.

She had her eyes fixed on Gerald Whitehead.

'I can tell you're a North! I have a snapshot of old Edmund on a pony somewhere, if you're interested. Most of the family served in the colonies, you know, but came back here to distinguish themselves.'

A rattle of crockery interrupted these opinions and all turned in their seats, except her, as an elderly man, coatless, but wearing a Guard's tie, wheeled in a traymobile. Cheery chap.

'Hello! How's the name-wallah, what?'

Lady Pamela was smoothing her skirt.

'Oh shut up, Reggie.' She turned to the women. 'My

husband's a bit daft, like the rest of his family. At some stage they had a touch of the sun. Notice his patronymic name indicating descent.'

Sir Reginald stood there beaming.

'Pammy's ancestors are Flemish; she may have told you. That's why she has the runny nose all the time.'

At that Garry Atlas let out a laugh and a piece of scone dropped out of his mouth.

'Oh, fuck off, Reggie!'

She looked at her watch. 'I've got another busload at twelve!'

'Lovely tea,' said Mrs Cathcart putting her cup away. It was a matter of quickly thinking of something proper to say, to fill in. The others looked surprised and suddenly unsure too.

Lady Pamela consulted a sheath of papers and returned to her painting.

'Two to go. Am I right?'

Violet glanced around. 'I think three.'

God, this was an idyllic place! Swallows twittered in the trees; transluscent shifting leaves superimposed on the browner green of sloping tilled fields.

Lady Pamela blew her nose, shuffled the papers.

'I have Shiela Standish nicely mapped out. The line is strong; you find this with rural families. More conservative, slow movers. I found a surprise here somewhere. Ahem . . . Gloucester, Lancashire people, that's you, with some Scottish blood introduced one night early in the nineteenth century. Standish, incidentally, the name explains: strong enclosure/pasture.'

'I know,' Shiela spoke up though perhaps missing the point. 'We were always on the land. My father never tired of telling me.'

'Hugh Standish pulled up his roots by the Cotswolds— marvellous rich land—and settled in New Holland in the mid-1800s. Am I right?'

Shiela nodded but looked alarmed.

'It was a family quarrel, not unusual in those times. Hugh Standish was a blue-chip Tory, a sporting man, and so forth, with many tenants. One of the family married a Bartholomew, well-known Chartist. When the so-called "reforms" were pushed through, Hugh resisted, at least he tried to, and when he failed simply sold up. He never spoke to the family again. He left his wife. He was one of those rare men who can put pride before property.'

Garry Atlas sat up, 'This Bartholomew . . .'

'That is correct. He was one of yours from Edinburgh. That was the surprise. Perhaps you both knew?'

Garry grinned at Shiela. She had turned the other way, reddening. The others gazed at them as if they were newly-weds.

'I'll be damned.'

Violet gave a snort. 'Isn't that nice?'

'Jesus. Well how about that?' Garry shook his head.

'I don't know,' Shiela mumbled. 'We seem poles apart . . .'

Garry gave a laugh; not unfriendly.

'A little bit of incest wouldn't hurt, eh Shiel?' he cracked, rocking on his balls. Shiela became confused and could only smile all the time.

Lady Pamela wiped her mouth with a tissue. 'Listen, that's taboo. Enough of that. It comes as a terrible shock,' she told them, 'when one sees it on the genealogical line in black-and-white. One immediately double checks, but then sits back stunned by the immensity of the act. A genealogical tree reads like an epic novel, occasionally relieved by slapstick and so on. With the information spread out before one, all one needs is imagination. Love and imagination. A tragedy leaps out from the page. When I was younger I used to burst into tears. Besides,' she added, 'an incest incident only makes it more difficult for us in the trade.'

Leaning back, head to one side, she contemplated the picture. She selected a smaller brush and took up Sasha.

'The Wicks descend or plummet from a pedigree of Picts and Celts. You are blessed with a backlog of barmaids, heavy-breathing and insistent innkeepers—I know the type. I see filial traces in your eyelashes and slightly plump fingers. I noticed as you were drinking your tea before. The

Wicks then became all mixed up with Irish horse dealers and peat diggers, and one married Boardman's eldest daughter. Edward Boardman, you may know, has a footnote in history as the first man in Dublin to own a bicycle with pump-up tyres. This daughter, Joyce Boardman, one night went down Great Brunswick Street riding no hands and smoking. If I were a man I would be attracted to such a free spirit! A little Irish blood is a fine thing. Where am I now?'

As she bent down to find another page Sasha glanced at Violet. Her friend had one hand over her mouth.

'How the present is intricately controlled by the past. The depth of your neckline this morning is a result of some action several generations ago, perhaps geared to that performance of Joyce Boardman on the bicycle. She became a mother with six children.

'We are now in the year 1900. A group of Wicks is still alive in Rhodesia. One was mauled by a mad lion. But your side suddenly concentrated, for no rhyme or reason, on the Isle of Man: the tree surgeon, Patrick Frederick Wick. It was he who landed a contract with the Government of Queensland, sailed out, and was almost immediately bitten by a mad snake, and died.'

'A Taipan,' Kaddok interrupted, 'the most venomous snake in the world.'

'I thought—'

'We've also got the deadliest spider.'

'The black *funnel-web*?'

'Right.'

'Here we only read about your man-eating sharks,' Lady Pamela said primly. 'I must say they sound fascinating.'

Now they all wanted to tell her about their distant, empty country: sudden brown and wide light, the dry sticks and undergrowth, hot rocks and straw-coloured grass. The long undulating edge of Australia is stroked by blue, exploding white at regular intervals.

'We shouldn't be there. Do you ever feel that?' Borelli said to North. 'I mean, notice the way the country batters our faces and arms. I don't only mean the climate. We don't belong. We feel hopeless there, doomed.'

'The average Australian,' said North 'hasn't even seen a kangaroo.'

Lady Pamela picked it up. 'A *beautiful* word . . . Isn't that a beautiful word?'

'It's aboriginal,' Kaddok told her.

Abruptly she pulled herself together. She turned to Gerald. His face seemed to ring a bell. Already he was fidgeting.

'So you're Whitehead? Funny . . .' She looked down at her papers again. 'Well you must be the last then.'

And Gerald began looking first at the floor, then up at the ceiling.

'It seems Gerald Whitehead, you come from silent stonemason stock and the ancient art of gargoyle-carving. The gargoyle side is difficult to prove. We're talking about the sixteenth century, in Yorkshire. I don't know why such marvellous craftsmen should have been anonymous. A cousin was the Bishop of Something. I have added two and two together.'

Hence his hereditary red ears, bushy eyebrows. And the grey flecking Gerald's wiry hair in the small English room seemed like a shower of stone-dust.

'You have a soft job but I imagine you still have the wide fingernails. This stoney side, I should say, was not called Whitehead, not then. They were Bredins and Rowntrees. Out of the blue, for no apparent reason, both produced a flock of missionaries and nun-nurses. They dutifully trotted off spreading the word to the coloureds in China and Africa . . . some of our colonies.'

'We were in Africa,' Sasha said, 'a few weeks ago.'

The old woman paused and put down her brush.

'The Victoria Falls! . . .'

She went misty at the thought.

Gerald had to clear his throat.

'At any rate, of the Rowntrees saving souls in China, one was a young Mary—no doubt another virgin. An atavistic quirk occurred: around 1890 outside Canton she was struck by a shocking case of leucosis. Poor girl. Imagine. She must

97

have felt singled out by God. In that vulnerable state she succumbed to a fifty-year-old tea planter. His name was Whitehead. Nicely ironical, what?'

'I didn't know all this,' Gerald admitted.

'Their two sons were educated in England. Harold, I discovered, was known at Oxford for his collection of bookplates and early Bibles. The other young Whitehead married a descendant of John Hunter. You remember he was the man in the 18th century who wanted to be frozen alive and thawed each century?'

Even Gerald laughed.

'Is he on my side?' he asked interested.

'Christ, we could have told you that,' Garry shouted.

But Gerald was listening to her: 'No, you're from Harold. After Oxford he worked for a very good marmalade outfit and then a big tea company. In the early 1900s he was sent to Australia as their head taster. Whiteheads have sprouted in the Antipodes ever since. There must be a good many now.'

Like a tea-taster about to reject, Gerald twisted slightly and pulled a face.

'I never see my relations. I go out of my way not to. I dislike everything about my uncles and their know-all children. To see them together depresses me. One of my uncles, for example, cracks his knuckles. Another pinches the girls. They all think he's terribly funny, the black sheep. We all have vaguely similar features. A roomful with the joker and the latest new baby is terrible. At least I find it so. For the same reason I hate airport departure lounges and railway platforms. People gathered together with their similar features and awkward faults: reminds me of death or something. I can't help it I'm afraid.'

A twenty-second silence. Lady Pamela sat facing the easel. Looking down at his hands Gerald reddened; so he rocked on his heels, almost violently.

'I feel sorry for you,' said Mrs Cathcart loud and clear. 'Families are all you've got. You wait,' she added menacingly, 'when you get older.'

'Fair go,' Doug shuffled. 'He's alright.'

'I know what you mean,' said Louisa. 'Most of us don't like our cousins.'

Everybody turned. Now there was another speech.

Lady Pamela seemed to be engrossed in her brushes tray, poking in it and rattling. Now twisting around and still without looking at them she gave them the brush-off: 'Are you all satisfied? I hope you have enjoyed it as much as I have. You know all about each other now, the warts and all. I have supplied your backgrounds. They in turn tell you about your foregrounds. Understand? Savvy? Splendid. Marvellous then. Bye-bye. Have a safe journey. Violet? Where are you, dear? Send me a postcard.'

'I will!'

Of the Niagara Falls.

As they waved entering the bus ('There's a character'— Mrs Cathcart. 'I didn't like her'—Gwen Kaddok) another pulled up and a group of tall long-jaws fell out, and stood blinking in anoraks; Kiwis, by the look. Bye!

So James Borelli visited his uncle; said to be a legendary uncle: clacketty-clack, tap-tap (footprints, swinging stick). A difference evidently exists between seeing an uncle at home and one in a distant foreign place. There is the feeling of paying homage: tourist versus knowing expatriate. Hector Vincent Frank had been trapped in the fast-moving days of 1939: now viewed in speckled black-and-white, rolling smoke of shattered oil refineries. But why remain in his Soho room, unheated, ever since? He was sixty-four, with his own teeth, was skinny, as sharp angled (in knees, elbows and nose) as the letters L and K: unfolding, he snapped and cracked like a carpenter's rule. Various rumours had reached home but Uncle Hector had never married. He shaved with a leather strap and razor: always a bad sign.

Borelli climbed some stairs above a sandwich shop.

Almost immediately he had to talk louder than normal. At about the same height across the narrow street came the throb and vibration of a strip joint, rising, falling, and another soon started up through the side wall, accompanied by foot-stamping and cat-calls. If one stopped, its opposite started. As well, the uncle's face and arms in the small room were bathed in an unsavoury puce from the flickering neon opposite, FREDDIES—THIS IS THE SHOW! 'I imagine it's what hell must be like,' was his uncle's comment.

His uncle was in bed.

Borelli hooked his walking stick over a chair.

'I've got one of them too. Let me see. It's almost identical, if I'm not mistaken. That's interesting . . . But how are you now?'

Borelli sat down. 'Not bad.'

'I see. A stoic. Then how is my beautiful seester? When did she come here last? Six years or more. How is your mother?'

The Australian accent had remained. Words unexpectedly flattened fell away in mid-air. But to Borelli they leaped out, waving. Barely discernible, the nasal twang had remained, a wind from the desert, to blur an English clip.

Such vocal adjustments are needed to reduce the bloody velocity of words in the wide spaces and emptiness of Orstraliah. Words would otherwise travel too far. A similar speech blur evolved in the United States of America. By contrast it seems that the British enunciate clearly in order to penetrate the humidity and hedges, the moist walls and alleyways, as well as the countless words used by previous citizens . . .

'A distinct possibility,' his uncle nodded. 'I've been travelling along a similar trail myself. I can't say on that evidence great minds think alike, but wc're not light years apart. It's always interesting to discover someone thinking along similar lines. But of course we have a drop of the same blood.'

Indeed: the small face opposite seemed to be loosely draped over Borelli's mother's, like a mask here and there wrinkled and out of shape. Under the eyes and throat it was slack. A subtle yet major force lay in the shared bone of their foreheads, its breadth and slope. Those family shadows around his eyes made the old boy alert, an eagle's head; while with Borelli's mother it appeared more as a wistful bruising. Other smaller clues showed as the minutes passed.

His uncle had Borelli's nose in profile. And at the back of his head were a few once-dark curls.

'How long have you been in bed?'

'For years.'

'I mean today.'

'This is my desk,' the emerite yawned. 'I'm up to my neck. The more I unearth the more complex it gets. You think you're close—zoosh—you're further away. There is always another side. It's a matter of cutting through and hanging on. No shenanigans, no holidays. It's all go.'

Some girlie magazines lay on the bed, true, but they were among the *Anatomy of Melancholy* and a new Arabic dictionary embossed with ivory demilunes. Ironically, a magnifying glass protruded from a red paperback of Dunne's *New Theory of Vision*. There were the *Koran* with notebooks and scraps of green paper, and by the pillow a pair of brass binoculars.

Borelli picked up the *Arabian Nights* and put it down.

'I'm with a group. It reminds me of Africa, this. We went there first. It's not a bad group. We haven't resorted to cannibalism yet.'

'And where does this group go to next?'

'I think America.'

'Much-maligned America,' his uncle commented.

Borelli paced the room. Without his stick he limped a bit.

'We wear sunglasses and cameras. I suppose we look like any other group. But who knows what we think? I was going to ask you: what should a person see in London if he could see only one thing?'

At the window he paused and—Good Lord! Jesus!—naked woman opposite. Combing her hair. She had small white breasts. The window box empty of geraniums made her legs short and thick. And in the window above a redhead passed wearing nothing but a black brassière. Seeing him she stopped, legs apart, and waved. Borelli drew back. But others had seen him, including huge-breasted twins sharing one window, and the laughing West Indian hot mama one down and two along. The surface of the small building became alive with soft caryatids: waving, beckoning, mocking. Come on, come on.

'I don't understand it,' his uncle was saying. 'If you people stayed in the one place you would see more, a million times more. The biggest, the smallest, the worst, the best, the tallest, the most expensive. Such questions come from remoteness and emptiness. Then when you do see something extreme or rare you think you've *experienced* it. Which of course is not the case; quite the opposite. Incidentally, Karl Marx and Casanova de Seingalt lived in that street you see. Not together, of course.'

Returning to the chair Borelli still glanced at the window.

His uncle kept shaking his head. 'Cocky over-fed country. You've produced lantern jaws and generalizations. Tourists are a natural follow on. You people are very demanding.'

'Travelling,' Borelli waved his arms, 'there is the time factor to consider. We, ah travellers, operate in a condensed unreal time. For us, even time is summarized.'

Not bad: but as he glanced for a reaction he shook his head and began laughing. It didn't matter.

Like Marat in the bath his uncle rested his head back in the pillows.

'See if my socks are under the bed. There's something seriously wrong if they're not.'

And from a nail in the wall he lifted a greatcoat, surplus from one of the Armed Forces. Its outline remained on the wall, a lighter grey, as if the wall had been sprayed around it. His pyjama top was Garibaldi red and as he fitted a tie, added a scarf, and finally a beret, his appearance altered from bedridden pensioner in the bare room to bulky livewire with penetrating stare and the clear skin of a child.

Outside he was recognized by the stall-holders who waved and called out, and many girls in fur coats. To them all he introduced his nephew, twisting Borelli's head to point out the vague resemblance, and showing how they had both used the same walking stick without knowing it.

Borelli pointed across his uncle's chin.

'What?'

Funny: a truck there waiting at the lights carried in its back two sets of traffic lights. And that young woman with a crippled leg. Attractive; but see how the leg had pulled down one side of her mouth; already a deep crease had established, by remote action.

His uncle nodded, and Borelli kept his head cocked listening.

'One thing I've decided, after my years of study, is that we behave differently with women. You'll say everyone knows that. But it's a strange thing, isn't it? With women we subtract or multiply our faults.'

Borelli shrugged knowingly, 'So?'

An iron ball passed through an empty building and a tall wall fell in a complete straight edge, as in World War Two.

'Don't be stupid! Think of the change in your behaviour. By measuring it—measuring the falsity—you define your own character. Sometimes the results aren't very pleasant. I'm saying, if you care to, you'll learn more about yourself from women, than from men. It doesn't hurt,' he added, 'to spend a lot of time with them.'

New districts, new intersections.

The bus emptied. They waited under an umbrella shop and caught another.

All the time which is through light and shade Borelli listened, sometimes putting in a question. He wondered where they were going. In times of world crisis English sales of fishing rods rise. Compare the English deck-chair with the French wrought-iron seat. Gentle and accommodating is the canvas type, tracing the shape of national character; the other, the hard seat, makes the sitter aware of himself: wrought-iron provokes, is histrionic. The American bar stool implies can't-stay, gotta-go: like the fabricated vertical American cities. Conquering, looting armies destroy musical instruments but preserve mirrors. London proves that strange evolution of towns: human expansion is instinctively westward, leaving the east in poverty, dying on the vine. Could it be that our physiognomy is formed mainly during sleep? The frowns, smiles and hopes formed by dreams leave their mark. There is a reason for everything.

Looking over a long wall Borelli saw rows of faded submarines stored end-to-end for salvage and scrap, suburban submarines. His uncle signalled and they left the bus; followed the submarine wall for several hundred metres; a hag pushed a wicker pram filled with vegetables and a wheel fell off; but they didn't know.

'What sort of passport do you have?' Borelli decided to ask.

'What's that?'

'I imagine you must be fairly English now. I mean, you've never returned home, have you?'

'I've told you, I don't believe in maps, unnatural boundaries, rubbish of that sort. I think street directories are suspect. The travelling I do is all up here' – tapping his forehead.

'You can say that because you've already been everywhere.'

They had turned into a small church. KARATE and KUNG FU master classes were advertised on the services board. Although protected with rusty mesh many of the stained glass windows were broken.

Old Hector led him around the back where weeds came up to their knees. Here was a forgotten cemetery. One of those Victorian tombs for a merchant and his spouse had marble elbows growing out from each headstone, clasping hands in mid-air.

Borelli turned. 'Eternal love personified. You're saying I should find a woman?'

Leaning on his stick his uncle had one foot in a grave. He said nothing.

Another headstone consisted of a massive saxophone carved in the most exact detail. Pigeon droppings over the years had dribbled and solidified into a substance like Rosso wax, altering the instrument's centre of gravity, like the saxophone found at Hiroshima.

'I need a hobby. Is that it?'

'You're nervous. Why else would you be busy making a fool of yourself? For all your travelling about, the fancy hotel rooms, at the end is death. Travelling is postponing it.'

Borelli poked around some more, whistling.

'Well, I don't know. This isn't so . . .'

His uncle followed as he left the cracked headstone of a parricide. All along, the largest tomb had been obscured by the octopus-oak, and now it could be seen against the side fence; indeed it was like stumbling upon the source of the Nile.

Here was a large tent, as grey and weathered as the paling fence, a traveller's tent. Nothing about it moved the way tents move; for it was concrete, solid through. It was as tall as a man. Carved to be partly opened, its 'flap' revealed nothing but black impenetrable stone. So it exerted a force through its density, a silence, overwhelming. Where it peaked at the front someone had fixed a Moslem star.

At his shoulder Borelli's uncle breathed, 'This is Burton's tomb. As you know, the translator of *The Perfumed Garden*.'

Walking slowly around, Borelli tapped it with his knuckles.

'It's like a stone bird.'

'Something like that,' Hector nodded, 'It's immovable yet it's a monument to a great traveller. That's the paradox; one that you won't forget. Think about it.'

'From you,' Borelli turned, 'who dismisses tourists.'

Tight smile there from his uncle. 'I've always said "traveller" never "tourist". Burton explored literatures and languages, religions, fauna, rivers and women, and other things we don't know about. It's an object lesson. In those days they didn't have fancy sunglasses. And all you can say is "terrific" and "fantastic".'

Often Borelli had trouble matching words to sensations, especially when travelling. When the words came out he often felt stupid. The words sounded dead.

'I often get excited, or hasty.'

'It could be a form of tiredness.'

'I know what you mean,' said Borelli. 'I mean taking

photographs gives the impression of getting around the problem. I suppose it's one of its apparent advantages. Mechanical literacy: ideal for travelling.' Borelli stood back from the tent and shook his head. 'But this would test them out. A photograph, especially in black-and-white, would simply look like a real tent.'

His uncle began grinning. He didn't know much about photography.

'I'm afraid I need a piss,' said Borelli pulling a face.

'Richard Burton was broadminded.'

They were pissing down one corner of the tent, one on either side.

'We're like dogs,' Borelli called across. 'It means we'll be back here one day.'

His friend shook his head.

'Few people know about this place.'

But Borelli noticed some words appearing on the concrete surface: his piss seemed to act as a catalyst. They grew in focus and stopped.

CAPT. COOK

BURKE AND WILLS

CRAP ALL OVER BURTON

And to one side, smaller (a footnote): AUSTRALIAN DESERT BOOTS

Borelli looked across at his uncle.

'What's the matter?'

'Nothing. Doesn't matter. You right?'

They left. In the long time it took to zig-zag into central London they didn't talk much, each one left to his own thoughts; though after Borelli mentioned the mystery of women, dismissed as a simplicity by his uncle, the psychology of uniforms was briefly discussed. As for his uncle he wondered how certain Moslems could bear to have themselves buried in ornate but unidentified graves; to be buried nameless. Neutron stars sighted in outer space have a tremendous density. According to reports a tablespoon of the material would weigh several thousand tons. Borelli mentioned it. The memory of Burton's tent must have reminded him.

On their visit to a stately home Doug and his wife had been unable to penetrate the ivy. They'd fronted up to where you'd expect a door, and parted the leaves. Mrs Cathcart stepped back and hoisted her bust to be as venerable as the house. 'Yoo-who?' she called out. Doug ran his tongue over his teeth. Some of these places have the front door round the back. They walked all around, which took a time, deliberately talking loudly. Mrs Cathcart remained grim—respectful. Even slowly panning his German binoculars, as she waited at his elbow, Doug couldn't locate an opening or even a clue, and after several more circuits they lost their sense of front and back. The 'house' was a featureless mound at least two storeys high, shaped like a loaf, teeming, dripping, literally shivering with the leaves in the slight breeze. Sharp corners and cornices, the manorial straight lines, had long been strangled. The sole human touches were the silver television aerial at one end, and smoke from an invisible chimney. Six bumps along the top or the 'roof' could have been eaves or mansard roofs; it was difficult to tell. But it was also true that the victorious vines had grown as deformed and as stagnant as the mansion underneath. Close up they were arthritic, hairy and mad: they'd turned in on themselves, devouring and twisting. With nowhere else to go it was a pyrrhic victory.

Out of decency Doug had invited the Kaddoks, but they weren't much help. As soon as a full view of the house had appeared Kaddok had rammed his tripod into the marshy lawn of the foreground and Gwen had to steer him along the paths which were overgrown. Already he had tripped over an ornate hitching post. Faint traces of a superb piece of English landscape gardening could still be perceived, like an old wreck in low tide.

It was Kaddok's idea to shoot the house from various angles and he kept chattering and tripping over the borders. 'How many rooms would she have? Multi-windowed

Georgian, I suppose?' Gwen shaded her eyes and searched.

'Aye? Only one? That figures,' Kaddok told her; and as he reloaded and puff-cleaned the camera eye he rattled on about some medieval window tax, and how the nobles got around it by bricking up their windows. 'The old aristocracy mightn't be as stupid as they look,' he shouted.

It hadn't been Doug's idea in the first place. Any old building, even the tallest and most revered cathedrals, left him cold: seen one, seen 'em all. He'd clomped around them stone-faced. Nothing ever happened. They were old walls. It was an obligation though. He'd be the first to admit, if you were in England you had to see them. For one thing you'd get people asking back home.It was the first thing they asked.

He checked the guide book. It was recommended alright, there in black-and-white.

Around the back they wandered among a collection of baroque bird baths and solariums, randomly placed—there must have been a hundred or more—and wild roses roughly the size of prize cabbages (Chelsea Flower Show, '27), arbours, and false gates frozen on oxidized hinges, slatted wooden garden seats, and stone benches stippled with moss held layers of rotting leaves. Overall it was distinguished and calm. The ground was soft underfoot, mulch and moss. Doug kept sinking into heaps of dead leaves. Towards the bottom of this garden they heard voices, and as they ducked under a tilting pergola, Mrs Cathcart who had good eyesight squeezed Doug's arm. The length of a cricket pitch away, no more, a party of nudists played badminton and leap-frog. Others sat in deck chairs or played draughts alongside a graciously stagnant pool—the ornamental cherub in the middle spat out green fluid as if it was being sick. The nudists mostly late in years were red-faced, heavy in frame, and seemed to be quite oblivious of the politics of the world. Doug had lifted his binoculars but was pulled sharply back—yanked—by his wife, and they beat a retreat back to London, she holding an expression even more grim and determined.

Yet they were curiously satisfied. Even this had been an

experience. It was something to tell people about; that was the thing about travel.

At the hotel Violet had gone out somewhere with Sasha and by late afternoon had not returned. Putting the cigarette in his mouth, balancing four Brandy 'n Dry cans in his big hands, Garry managed to knock on door number XIV. He walked straight in.

'How's it going, Shiela? Good on you. Say, this is a view-and-a-half you've got here.' He moved back from the window and ripped open one of the cans. 'Where do you keep the glasses?' He cleared a space on the bedside table. 'That was a real bombshell the other day, eh? What do you reckon? Who would have thought we were'—pressing his stomach with his hand he gave a belch—'related? That's what I call a real bloody coincidence.'

Blinking, bumping into the edges of things, Shiela didn't know where to sit, let alone where to look or what to say. Now he leaned back on both elbows, daks bulging at the balls. The first four buttons of his shirt were undone: a canyon, Simpsons Desert in colour. She could only balance at the other end near the pillow. These rooms were small. She wore no shoes.

He raised his glass.

'Yep, I got the shock of my life.'

'I was surprised,' Shiela admitted, distant. 'It is an interesting little snippet, isn't it?'

He slapped his chest.

'The odds must have been a thousand to one. It's something to write home about.'

'Oh I have,' Shiela said.

'Yeah, I'm a sucker for postcards,' Garry said. He sat up to pour another two drinks. 'Jesus, Shiela! Hang on a sec. You've got thousands of the buggers here. You're not intending to send all them?'

For added effect he held his mouth open and bulged his eyes. Shiela couldn't help smiling. Here she could tell someone about herself.

'People have come to expect it of me. I'm always travelling. When there's no postcard I think they must begin to worry. And there are their little ones: the children like them.'

'Always on the go? Come off it.'

'No, I like to be moving. When I get back from this I'll join another tour. I have my eye on Persia next.'

'You're kidding!'

'I don't stay home much, not anymore. My uncle calls me Perpetual Motion.'

Garry slapped his knee.

'Ha, ha. That's a good one. He sounds a card.'

'Uncle Milton,' Shiela frowned. 'He is a card.'

Garry sat up. 'How many times, frinstance, have you been here?'

'England?'

Shiela shrugged.

It began to worry Garry. 'But listen, you haven't told me why. I mean why are you always on the go?'

Days were brown and dry in the wooden house; the tin roof and windmill creaked together in the heat; floating kah-kah of the crows, close and far off; and in the distance, low hills, paddocks and shimmer.

'I don't know, I must be used to it now; I prefer it. I like a group and mixing. There's the sights and the interesting people you meet. I like being with people.'

Her glass leaned as she looked at her ankles. Shiela had smooth straight legs.

'That's right, your family are on the land.'

She nodded.

Suddenly Garry laughed. He shook his head. 'I've known some funny shielas in my time.'

'Oh my uncle always says that.'

'Ah we're related alright. No worries, Shiela. You're as nutty as a bloody fruitcake.'

Her shoulders gave a jump.

'I don't know why I should tell you this.'

Moving beside her he slowly filled her glass.

'We're celebrating. Drink up.'

And leaning across to casually stub out his cigarette his arm brushed against her. He kissed her cheek.

'There,' he said kindly. He patted her knee. 'Give us a look at you. Show me with the specs off. I'll see how related we look. Jeepers! That's incredible. Listen, I'm not kidding. Have you ever considered contact lenses? What's up?'

She seemed to be trembling.

But Atlas took her glasses. He looked around the room. 'Jesus, these are like milk bottles.'

Shiela remained looking at the floor.

'Get a load of this. They don't suit me, that's for sure.' Groping his way back, he called out: 'Shiela?' (Silly bugger.) 'Shiela, don't leave me. Shiela! You're hiding,' he whined. 'Where are you?'

As he advanced like Leon Kaddok she looked up ready to smile. She had decided. He deliberately bumped into a chair and tripped over the bed.

True: without the twin reflecting discs she was fresh-faced, long, a dish.

Now less than a yard away and squinting, hands outstretched and fluttering, a conductor asking for quiet, he whined again, 'Shiela? You're hiding. Where are you?'

Her specs balanced on his nose: all for her. Crossing her legs she leaned back laughing.

Then he touched her, 'Ahhhhhh!' and she let out a cry as his hands searched her shoulders, her arched throat, and as she fell back and squirmed, ran over her breasts, one at a time, slowing down, suddenly breaking a button.

'Ah-haaaa! Got you . . .'

He sat down and took off the glasses.

Shiela returned to her embarrassed self, fidgeting next to him. She smoothed her skirt.

'Hey, don't put 'em back. You look alright like that. I told you you did. Anyway, that's what I think.'

'I never know what,' Shiela confessed.

She went to the mirror and tried with glasses and without, turning her head left and right, and frowned. 'It could be these frames . . .' But she suddenly turned: 'Ugly face!'

But after studying the Tantric miniature above the bed Garry had reclined and picked up some of her postcards. At least a certain familiarity had grown between them.

Shiela had her glasses back on.

'All the grog's gone?' he asked, though he already knew. He looked at his watch. 'Christ, I should go.'

She was blinking so much Atlas almost missed the smile. He was moving fast anyway. 'Eggs and bacon, gin and tonic—thick and thin. That's us, Shiel. What do you reckon?' At the door he gave the brotherly slap: whack!

Small out-of-the-way museums often contain a wealth of bits and pieces, bric-à-brac, well worth the detour. An amateur has happened upon some object, or the broad subject, and before long his nose develops into a classifying mania (that pale Dane with the *catalogue raisonné* of Sardine Tin labels; what's his name?). And sheds are tacked onto garages; annexes onto houses; disused warehouses, odeons and empty churches are seized and converted. The overwhelming desire is to be definitive, to corner the subject. Even without achieving this, results can be impressive: a lifetime's work, one man's preoccupation, arrayed. It cannot be ignored. And what had seemed like junk in the early days in turn becomes valuable, sought after by others. Almost inevitably these collectors acquire an inflated idea of their collection's worth, a kind of blindness. A small town, a city, or the collector's distraught widow is 'left' the entire collection and the attendant problems of housing, preservation, lighting, insurance and security, for these donors invariably insert the clause, 'said items to remain intact, under the one roof, for the benefit of one and all' (the Patrick Hill collection, in New Orleans, of shovels and spades. There is a Moustache Museum in Prague). More often than not a poorly painted sign on the edge of a town points to these museums, and the custodian is a man without a tie, interrupted from his lunch or sleep.

In the guide book, the Corrugated Iron Museum seemed like a colloquialism for the building itself, its shape, colour and size; and who could tell what interesting things were arranged inside? In fact, when at last they found it in the hinterland of east Yorkshire, it had the appearance of a familiar *shed*, low and long, traditionally unpainted, its roof and walls of galvanized iron. It stood astride a moor, both in silhouette: the moor like a grey sandhill a half mile back, and the single sick ghost gum, *Eucalyptus panciflora*, near the front doors, which were also of corrugated iron, seemed to have been planted there for shade; CLICK! Kaddok took that picture. Built appropriately from corrugated iron the one-and-a-half-million dollar (*dollars?*) museum housed a superb collection of corrugated iron: history of, uses, abuses. Many items were steeped in unusual history or possessed special significance. Admission was by silver coin.

'Mr Cecil Lang,' the spokesman explained, a young man in an open-necked shirt and straight-combed hair. 'Mr Cecil Lang spent his early years in the goldfields of hum, Western Australia. Made his fortune; where, incidentally, he became good friends with Herbert Hoover, there as an engineer.'

'What, the American president?' Hofmann asked.

Kaddok of course knew. 'He was in Kalgoorlie in the early 1900s.'

'That's something,' Ken Hofmann told his wife. 'I didn't know that.'

But Louisa, her arms folded, was glancing at Borelli.

'Hoover was there twice,' Kaddok added, 'for long periods.'

They stood at the end of a long room as functional and as atmospheric as a shearing shed. It had plain iron walls. On rough tables, scattered, as if waiting to be classified, various objects were illuminated by beams of natural light, and from a distance most of the things also appeared to be grey. A few other people were sauntering around the end tables.

The conductor waved his hand.

'Cecil Lang was rather influenced by the hum, pioneering landscape down there. Out on the Nullarbor Plain, and so forth. Are you Australians? Then you would understand. He always said—you'll excuse me—it put muscles in his shit. Ha, ha. Yes, he said that.'

Glancing at Mrs Cathcart he reddened. He'd sunburn easily.

'He was another Rhodes, a plain man but a dynamo personality. He created this Trust, a kind of monument, hum. The site he chose personally. It is slightly out of the way, perhaps inconvenient, but that is part of the point. It's like Australia. I'm his grandson.'

'What's your name?'

'Wayne.'

'Go on, Wayne,' said Mrs Cathcart.

'So, I say, what impressed Cecil Lang was the rough-and-ready, the getting of things done. Such a practical, plain life purged him. He was extremely impressed, terribly impressed. The museum is a memorial to that, ah hum, quality of life.'

'Hear, hear,' said Doug.

So they moved forward.

A Plaster of Paris globe identified the most heavily concentrated areas of corrugated iron in the world. Clusters of the tin-like substance protruded here and there, miniature cities, almost entirely in the Southern Hemisphere. It had been employed widely along the coast of China and throughout East Africa as well as isolated regions of South America. New Zealand had an extremely high ratio too. But Australia, New Holland, Van Dieman's Land: that white continent had become grey with bits of the metal, even the so-called 'Dead Centre' (spotted all over with corrugated iron, ultimately a sign of life), further significant concentrations along the northern towns and cities, with heavy deposits in Lang's western goldfields.

At the first table on which lay a piece of galvanized iron the guide pirouetted, Oxbridge-modulated:

'He paid a fortune for some of these rare pieces; and of course when they knew it was Cecil Lang buying they held out and quadrupled the prices, the sods. It is almost impossible to acquire fine examples these days. The Australian Government, like so many other countries, won't allow its heritage to be removed. We understand that. In any case, we now have most of what we want. Do you wish to buy your catalogues or shall we get them later?'

They were all staring at the table. Shiela stood close to Garry but he had his arm around Violet's waist.

'I have it on the garage and side-fence at our place,' said Doug. 'It does a good job. But it's heavier than this.'

'Fourteen-gauge,' Kaddok told him.

'But what is this?' Gerald Whitehead asked.

Yes! an irregularly shaped sheet painted silver, it had small striations and a row of rivet holes along three edges: an unusual example of the material.

Wayne gave a chuckle.

'It makes you wonder, eh? I should say, even here we tend to forget its uses were not restricted to elementary shelter—roofing and such. In fact, what we have here is a section of the fuselage of the first Qantas aircraft—'

'The Avro 504K, 1920,' Kaddok told them, and quickly shot off two pictures (but only caught the guide's neck and combed head).

'A ruddy good airline,' Doug put in.

'So this illustrates very effectively what struck Mr Lang: the way corrugated iron is *adapted*, yes adapted is the word, down there for a whole variety of hum, tasks. There's a self-help quality about the stuff.' Garry Atlas shrugged and the young guide gave a cough. 'Sadly missing, one feels, in our present day and age.'

A sepia photograph showed nine workmen in shorts, navy singlets and boots standing on a sheet placed between two beer barrels. the single sheet had a slight dip—only about four inches.

'The importance of the corrugations,' Wayne pointed unnecessarily. 'When any flat surface is hammered into a bulge, like the monocoque construction of racing cars and aeroplanes, and the ordinary egg, its strength, its rigidity, is multiplied something like fivefold. How much would all these working men weigh? God knows. Certainly its durability must be a factor which has contributed to corrugated iron's popularity.'

'I love these old photographs,' Louisa whispered to Borelli, 'don't you?'

Alongside, Kaddok misunderstood. 'The early photographers are our archaeologists.'

'A galvanized iron aeroplane . . . ' Borelli still seemed to be turning the idea over in his mind. To Louisa he said, 'It's machismo, isn't it? It's too strong and plain. Corrugated iron must be boring to you.'

He watched her closely, poker-faced. He raised his eyebrows. Slowly smiling she turned her head: provided a profile.

'And observe the picture frame,' the guide was saying. 'See the soldered corners? It was bought at an auction in Brisbane in the 1950s. Again it illustrates the practical, no-nonsense nature of the people who lived with corrugated iron. A grazier's wife wanted a picture framed, perhaps an old calendar, and they used the most familiar material at hand.'

Garry Atlas lit a cigarette and as he shut the Zippo winked at Shiela. Others too had noticed: either she had a new lipstick or more of the old, much more. It didn't suit her.

As they went towards the next long table, Violet and others looked up at the roof and frowned.

'It's not raining, is it?' asked Mrs Cathcart (who hadn't looked up). 'It never lets up. It was lovely this morning.'

And glancing at them all, beaming, the young man unable to contain himself began slapping himself and laughing. A thin load of gravel seemed to be pouring onto the roof, soothing them.

'It's a tape,' he explained. 'Pretty good, eh? Quite the most marvellous sound.'

The 'rain' turned heavy and he had to raise his voice, almost shouting. He soldiered on.

'I must say I have never slept under a tin roof—to my shame—but I believe it is absolutely first-rate. Am I right?'

Some of them nodded, watching him.

'When Cecil Lang returned to England, he replaced a perfectly sound thatch with corrugated iron so he could lie in bed when it rained. "Antipodean drumming", he called it. For him, it undoubtedly produced a flood of memories!'

'Mmmmm . . .' one or two nodded, imagining.

'Where is that?' asked Gerald.

'Oh a marvellous little cottage in the Lake District. All hell broke loose. The National Trust ordered the thatch to be replaced.'

'The bastards,' said Garry.

'Some of our finest homes have—'

The guide held up a lily-white hand.

'Look, I couldn't agree with you more. Our museum illustrates the point. The Roofing Section is one of the very best endowed.'

Against the wall, a row of evenly spaced vertical sheets demonstrated the power of rust and/or the fighting qualities of galvanized iron: beginning with glittering argentine (brand new sheet); turning to dull grey after twelve months; one showing orange freckles; the next slaked with beer-coloured streaks; and so on to overall russet, darkness spreading; until the last was a scaley brown, crusted with disease, with a hidden powerful lamp showing it riddled with pinholes of light.

'Mechanical. Dreary,' Gerald turned.

'Rustic charm,' North murmured to Borelli.

'The Hindus say everything has a life of its own. That must include corrugated iron.'

Only Hofmann had gone up close to the sheets, touching one with a finger. 'These are like modern American paintings. Louisa, isn't this one like that Olitski we missed?'

The guide cleared his throat.

'In the Oxford dictionary, you'll find "Corrosive" is the word before "Corrugated". Is that a coincidence? We think not. The association is true to life.'

Samples here taken from city and country; seaside and snow; the rain forest and below sea-level; and in pride of place, sand-blasted and pale outback. Neatly labelled, dated.

Sasha asked a question.

He shook his head. 'I haven't been yet. It certainly is hum, one of my ambitions to go after Austria and, oddly enough, Yugoslavia.' Pointing for the benefit of the others he smiled, 'Still on roofing'.

A roughly cut rectangle of faded red stood on the table at 45°, 'PLEASE TOUCH' neatly lettered beside it.

'Youch!' Sasha squealed.

The guide looked around at them all, smiling.

Garry and the others who had laughed crowded forward.

TAKEN FROM KALGOORLIE, SUMMER 1932, the documentation explained:

> A TYPICAL IRON ROOF. THE TEMPERATURE HAS BEEN
> PRESERVED FROM THE MOMENT OF REMOVAL AND
> MAINTAINED TO THIS DAY (DAY AND NIGHT) BY MEANS
> OF ELECTRICITY AND A THERMOSTAT; A GLIMPSE OF
> THE CONDITIONS UNDER WHICH OTHER PEOPLE EXIST.

'Well, you should touch;' cried Sasha, sucking her little finger. 'It's like an iron.' Looking hurt at Phillip North, who was gently amused, she grabbed his hand.

'Cecil Lang worked under such conditions,' the young man commented. 'Very rough indeed.'

'Come off it.'

'Yes.'

And they told him, several talking at once.

'When I had Glenys,' said Mrs Cathcart, 'it was a hundred-and-seven. Remember, Doug?'

'It's not iron,' Kaddok suddenly corrected. Again, slightly misunderstanding: 'To be exact, it's mild steel.'

'I believe you're right,' the guide turned. 'Even the name has a charming incongruity.'

'He's a real smart bastard,' Garry said. 'You've only got to look at him.'

'Sshhhh,' said Violet.

Here were large photographs of familiar buildings. The guide discreetly stepped aside. Spanning a broad spectrum of architectual styles, each building had a corrugated iron roof. Factories and barns, warehouses with Architects' Society citation ('Rarely has the material been used with such . . .'), tram sheds, tractor garage, the country racetrack grandstand, abattoirs (the original bloodshed), were each represented. Again, the idea was to underline the metal's outstanding flexibility, how it can 'get a job done.' God, here a cathedral had a fine belfry, turrets and many ogivals of stained glass—with a corrugated iron roof. A marriage of the old world and the pragmatic new; but the rusting iron somehow didn't seem properly God-like. Abo humpies flung out to the edges of towns by some centrifugal force had it collaged with flattened kero tins ('The poor things'—Sasha). Views of more than one State parliament house: first, the stately granite façade, and next to it a bird's-eye view revealing the iron roof! University libraries and conservatories were the same. The group looked on silently.

But the houses, the gracious old spacious homesteads: the iron blended in. The diminishing straight lines of the corrugations sharpened the roof's perspective, even falsified it in some cases, flattening a roof, making it shallow, giving it clarity; and hooped it formed long verandahs, the stone walls there pierced with French windows for the westerly. At the sight of those verandahs: their ohhs and ahhs.

'I tell you what, they make the English places we've seen look pretty sick.'

Gerald snorted. 'I'd better dry up,' he said to North.

'Oh,' said Shiela, so matter-of-fact, 'they've got our place.'

And they all stopped.

She pointed: large low homestead, stone, shaded and stately. It was the grandest of them all.

Garry whistled, 'Ver-ee nice.'

'But Shiela, that's lovely.'

They turned to the guide: they wanted to show him. He should see. But he'd already come over, instinctively.

'What d'you think of this?' Garry asked, jutting his jaw.

The young man studied the photograph and nodded. 'So you're a grazier's daughter? It looks a nice little place. You call them homesteads, I believe. That's a fine piece of roofing.'

'Jesus!' Garry groaned.

'Family property?' Wayne asked.

'I have a manager. And I have my uncle living there.'

'How lovely,' Sasha sighed.

Garry turned to them showing his familiarity, 'She's never there though. Are you Shiela?'

He shouldn't have said that. She fumbled.

'I'm fond of it, but it's quiet.'

'I'll have it,' said Violet, grim; and they laughed. Shiela looked around, characteristically startled.

'We should continue . . .'

They moved on, altered somewhat. They relaxed, talking among themselves more. It felt good to have Shiela in their midst. Garry acted familiar, like an old family friend, and others wanted to ask her questions. The guide had to stop several times in mid-sentence to have their attention.

'Uh-hum. As I say. Now, how did this marvellously dextrous metal handle the vast historical forces of the day, eh?'

'Dear,' Mrs Cathcart broke in, never one for fancy ideas, 'what's he on about?'

Corrugated iron had given them a peculiar relaxation, superiority even. Young Wayne had to use a firm hand.

'I mean, of course, the Second World War,' he said almost shouting, and pointed at a table. 'How did it help stop the world becoming engulfed in fascism?'

Good question. It took a second for the example before them made sense.

'In the defence of Australia, corrugated iron played a vital role. Thousands of square yards—of roofing—were painted thus in these camouflage tones, painted by the leading artists of the day. Many a roof was signed. A sheet like this'—a corner of an enormous olive-green and brown abstract—'is worth a considerable sum in its own right. They are of course parts of an artificial landscape. Collectors and certain unscrupulous dealers have had sheets ripped off old buildings, mainly from the Darwin area, and gilt-framed. This one is signed "R.D., 1943." Our curator thinks it is either Drysdale or Roy Dalgarno.'

'I don't know Dalgarno,' said Hofmann interested. 'Drysdale painted *The Drover's Wife*.'

The young man smiled, 'That's right . . .'

Suddenly he bent forward and swore. 'For Pete's sake. Who would have done this? A vandal's been here.'

'Don't look at us,' Garry held up both hands.

'It has been done today,' said Wayne, smoothing it with his fingers. 'I can tell.'

It glittered, now that he mentioned it. Along the LH corner freshly scratched in caps: BHP'S TOUGH AS NAILS.

Borelli began laughing.

When Gwen read it out for her husband, he said, 'Ah yes, that's our steel company, the third biggest in the Southern Hemisphere. They make the corrugated iron.'

'I bought BHP when they were under $5.00,' Cathcart told North, hitching up his daks. And he briefly rolled back his lips to expose both rows of teeth, satisfied. North said nothing.

'I'll say this,' Garry joined in, 'it's a bloody good company. By any standards.'

Talking seriously with Louisa, Hofmann remained in front of the painted sheet, perhaps deciding whether they'd acquire one.

Their guide resumed but kept staring at the few visitors drifting down the end of the museum. A family in identical tan duffle-coats climbed in and out of the corrugated-iron caravan; but they were English. Interesting fact (he resumed): sheets were dropped by aeroplanes during the war to foil enemy radar. Lethal unless done over water. Interesting fact (lesser known): estimates suggest the Antipodes has more sheets of corrugated iron *than Merino rams*. And what other nation—pointing to glass case—has corrugated-iron buildings proudly printed on one of their banknotes? Research showed: no other.

They then saw one horribly twisted and torn sheet, knotted into a ball; it was like a neurotic's handkerchief: a roofing sheet found outside a northern town after a devastating cyclone. 'It illustrates again, if illustration is needed, the extraordinary dexterity of the metal.'

The guide went on quickly.

'Now here is a curious specimen, hum, rather macabre I would have thought.'

Those in front craned towards the sheet lying flat on the table, and some angled their heads horizontally to fathom it out. Except for several dents along the leading edge it could have been unused.

They turned to him.

He pointed. 'Along the bottom there. The dried blood. And you can see bits of hair. The sheet was loose and it killed a cyclist, a Tasmanian postman.'

Garry gave a slow whistle.

Now they stared again at the sheet.

'A working-man with five children. It decapitated him. A windy day in Hobart,' he added.

'The poor devil.'

And a sad clicking sound came from several tongues.

Bending down, the guide read the sentence beneath the caption, KILLER SHEET! 'An act of God. A Mr Clem Emery, uninsured, was struck while riding his red bike. Out of the blue, from nowhere. Father of five little ones. Uncommited religious views. March 31st, 1968.'

'Galvanized iron obviously isn't perfect,' North murmured to Gerald.

It was quite a relief then to pause at the unpainted water tank, its cylindrical surface, striated, and cold to touch. It had the usual cone-top and a tight brass tap. You can play tunes down its sides to test its level.

Doug raised the enamel mug.

'Good old rain water. You can't beat it. We've got one of these tanks at home.'

'Do you really?' the Englishman said, but glanced away.

'You're quiet,' said Louisa to Borelli. Ken had wandered off, hands behind his back.

'I'm stunned; I don't know why. It'll pass.'

'I remember we used to have a tank at home,' Violet was telling Shiela. They had scarcely spoken before. 'It was under a trellis and water spiders used to come out of the tap.'

And Sasha had joined North and Gerald Whitehead, glancing at one then the other. For the first time Gerald was shaking with laughter. It reddened his ears and face. 'All we need next' (North had said, rocking on his heels) 'are some red ants and a few thousand flies.'

No! Abrupt crash behind the tank and then tin clattering like notes on a wild xylophone. They found Kaddok on all fours, the clumsy tourist, his camera swinging on its strap.

'For Pete's sake! Why doesn't someone look after him?'

Leaving Gwen to lift Kaddok to his feet, the guide collected the corrugated-iron knives and forks scattered around the concrete floor, lifted the trestle table up. He stood up, red in the face, and 'set' the table.

'Come on then. I was about to go through this next anyway. Is he alright? Removed from civilization, it was necessary to make-do. Small comforts require ingenuity. A stubborn, down-to-earth people grew. We saw it reflected in your architecture. A miner, hum, made this cutlery set from corrugated iron as a silver anniversary present for his wife.'

North picked up one of the forks.

'I think we now know,' the guide suddenly laughed, 'what Oscar Wilde meant in *The Importance of Being Earnest*. Marvellous play. Ha, ha. Cecily says to Algernon: "I don't think you will require neckties. Uncle Jack is sending you to Australia."'

'Fair go,' said Garry quietly. 'We're not the backwoods, you know.'

Shuffling of feet; silence.

'That's right', pouted Doug.

'I don't know,' said Borelli. 'What about a corrugated-iron necktie?'

Garry put down a knife and turned. 'You're not knocking the place, are you? What's wrong with Australia?'

Here Shiela suddenly reddened as a tall man came up to the table. Doug called out, 'Well, look who's here? Howdy. You came just at the right time.'

'What's the trouble?' And seeing Shiela, Hammersly smacked his forehead with his palm, an exaggerated gesture.

He said something to Doug and came over.

'Improving the old mind? It's Shiela, isn't it? Whoopsie, hold that smile. That's it. I could sight you a mile off. I'm not so hot on names, that's all.'

Their young English guide had to clap and clear his throat. The group·had fragmented. Factions had developed; some interested, others not. Frowning, he seemed to be wondering if his delivery was at fault. Seizing the initiative, he asked loudly and informally, 'Anyone musical here?'

No one responded. They watched him.

Muttering to himself he bent down to pick up the next exhibit. It was secured to the table by a chain which he had to unlock. After considerable rattling he held it up, a grey home-made violin.

'Mr Lang brought this back. It was his first acquisition. Not exactly in the Stradivarius class, you might say, but it has rather a good hum, tone.'

Resting it under his chin he held up his hand:

'Quiet.'

He played a few notes.

> *And he sat as he watched*
> *and waited till his*
> *billy boiled*
> *who'll come a . . .*

'Very good!' they clapped.

'The construction is certainly quite remarkable,' said North leaning forward.

Sasha laughed—for no reason at all.

Others smiled a bit and nodded, out of respect or embarrassment.

Now it was *God Save the Queen*, and Kaddok involuntarily came to attention.

The violin's stubborn appearance had made some of

them want to laugh; perhaps it was nervous admiration of it.

But something worried Doug. Keeping his eyes on the guide he said to Hammersly out of the corner of his mouth 'What d'you make of this place?'

'I think it's a bloody disgrace. It should be pulled down.'

'I thought so,' said Doug looking around at the walls.

They were joined by Garry Atlas and Violet. Only two or three tables remained.

'This way,' Wayne was calling, stretching his neck: ostrich, emu. Wet patches had spread under his arms, a litmus test. He was rushing it, losing his calm.

'An outside dunny?' Garry laughed. 'I thought it was, from back there.'

Somehow this put him in a better mood. He kept grinning, looking at the others. And they smiled too, recognizing it, a kind of fond respect.

But it was Mrs Cathcart who asked, 'What is this here for?'

The guide frowned. He pointed to the tin roof which appeared to have been loosened by a wind, and the dunny's dented corrugated sides in a mixture of green and faded brick-red, in places peeling. It had a wooden door held by a piece of fencing wire hooked on a nail.

'When it arrived, we thought it a Guard's box'—the young Englishman began hiccupping at the thought— 'until we opened the door. We had never, hum, seen one of your dunnies before. Of course, we think it absolutely first rate.'

God, this bloke spoke through his nose.

'So we think we know where the term "rude shelter" originated.'

'Corrugated iron *sheet*,' Garry called out.

'Ha, ha, ha. I say, that's very good. I must take a note of that.' And shaking his head, keeping his mouth open as if he had something caught in his eye, he pulled out a notebook: 'Corrugated iron sheet . . .'

'Ah, we're a rough people,' North decided. 'As rough as bags.'

And Kaddok made continuous sorties on the edge of the group or suddenly in the front, and they watched as he suddenly fumbled and found a flash-bulb, and aimed inside the dunny.

'We're stuck with it,' Violet shrugged. 'It has its advantages.'

'What has?'

'Our rustic charm,' Borelli answered. 'We have the rest of the world often laughing and that isn't easy.'

'If the Greek civilization can be measured by their ionic columns lying around, ours is by the corrugated iron,' Gerald Whitehead put in.

'Aye, steady on. What are you getting at?'

And Mrs Cathcart spoke up. 'At least we don't have airs. Not like other countries.'

'That's right,' said Hammersly with Garry alongside. 'Listen, we've got nothing to be ashamed of. A lot of this talk is hogwash. It's time people realized. At least we get things done.'

'That's what this museum is saying,' Gerald put in. 'We get things done—come what may.'

'What's wrong with that?'

'We're not fools. We don't mess around,' Borelli said to Louisa with a face so serious she began laughing.

Their guide hadn't been listening. He'd found scratched on the side of the dunny: AUST.—WORLD'S BIGGEST IRON ORE RESERVES.

Yahoos! Bloody larrikins!

He hurried them past the large country Holy Bible fitted with a protective corrugated-iron cover and brass lock; past selected ochre photographs of windswept sheets tangling the foreground of stunning desert landscapes; past a remarkable cut-out policeman painted blue to fool motorists in some one-cop town over the Great Divide.

Standing before the last exhibit he glanced at his watch before talking. They looked up and automatically frowned. Ten large black-and-white photos: close-ups of corrugated-iron sheets? Horizontal, trimmed to the same size, they were hard to tell apart.

'It fits. It makes perfect enough sense,' said he. 'One thinks of these as photographs of corrugated iron sheets. In fact'—and here a slight smile appeared as he turned to look at them—'these are close-ups of Australian foreheads, taken at random. We believe it must be the loneliness and harsh seasons you have, the glare and the flies, the distance from help and the rest of the world that makes a man—and goodness me, ladies too: that one is a Darwin typist, aged twenty-two—perpetually frown. The furrowed forehead. Cecil Lang came back wearing one after only seven years. By now it has probably established in the antipodean genes. Corrugated iron therefore matches the Australian psyche. So there you are.'

He nodded at them, neat. There was no time to discuss this assertion.

Pushing out, frowning, they met an iron sky, the colour of old roofing iron, dripping wet; and some began bellowing and hissing. It was that English weather again. All along it must have been drizzling in that part of England.

'I think to see the world. That was it.'

'Christ, there's nothing wrong with that.'

'What about yourself?'

'The old itchy feet: last year it was Bali. I tell you, that's worth seeing.'

Beautiful fuckun' beaches.

'Yes, I felt like a good break.'

'We'd heard about England and places. I thought: darn it all, we'll go and have a squiz. Everyone else we knew had. We'll see what all the fuss is about.'

Long-service leave.

'The children were off our hands. Glenys, the eldest, was married last June.'

'And I had a bit of cash up my sleeve . . .'

Fair enough.

Gerald turned to Borelli, 'To have the feeling you could never get away when you wanted would be unbearable. I think I'd go mad. I always feel I want to go away. And yet lately I've had nightmares about dying and being buried under a stone in a foreign country. I don't understand it.'

'What we've seen,' said Doug putting down his glass, 'makes you realize how ruddy lucky we are.'

'By now I have been to most countries at some stage, except Tibet. But I find there is always something fresh to see, something I've missed.'

Yes, that's true.

'Perpetual Motion, eh Shiela?'

The disloyalty of some; of men.

Always there comes a let-down. It's done casually, easily, suddenly a shock.

Kaddok told them: 'The Eiffel Tower was completed in 1888. And the same man did the Statue of Liberty too.'

'We could get to see that . . .'

Yes.

'I'd prefer the Niagara Falls. I hear they're fantastic.'

'It was chiefly Leon.' And they turned to Gwen. 'He wanted to take his photographs. As you know. And we liked the idea of a group. We think we have a nice group here.'

Garry put in, 'Listen, don't ever go to Singapore. I was sick as a dog.'

'I'd heard it was spotless . . .'

'Not in my book, it wasn't.'

'Yes, I must say a lot of the most unusual places are terribly filthy. Remember Africa on the nose?'

'I think we could have skipped that. I didn't feel at all at home there.'

Garry belched.

'Get your hand off me!'

'One thing,' Garry went on, overfilling another glass, 'I didn't come for their beer. Have you ever tasted such pissy muck? I'd heard about it but never believed it.'

Violet pulled a face. 'Ho-hum. You keep saying that.'

'Piss off!'

Louisa smiled widely, a ballerina's mouth. 'It's one of my favourite things in the world, travel. I'm not conscious of time. You meet all sorts of people.'

'Being away, especially in a large city like this,' Borelli suggested, 'don't you feel you can do things you would otherwise not do? We feel anonymous or separate,' he said aloud. 'Sometimes I feel no harm could come; I could do anything.'

Louisa watched him over her glass.

'By that I mean—'

'I'm myself wherever I am,' said Mrs Cathcart, clearly and firmly. For she always suspected the worst.

They were not conscious of time. They looked and felt separate from the main population, to one side. Their chairs formed a closed circle, regularly punctured by a darting waiter with a club-foot who could lift six glasses with the blue fingers of one hand.

'I haven't been to good theatre for years,' Violet was explaining.

Beside her, Ken Hofmann gazed at the spot near the ceiling, fingers tapping his lips. Yet he readily answered.

'The tax man pays for mine.'

'Ken! You were keen to see the paintings and the museums.'

'Yes, but there were other reasons, if you care to recall. Weren't there?' To the others he explained, 'My wife has a poor memory or chooses not to remember. There are other reasons for coming all this way, tax being one, but I would not like to embarrass Louisa. Would I, wife?'

'Here's the Professor! Sit down. We were talking about you. We know all about you.'

Ha, ha.

'No we weren't,' Sasha quickly told him. 'Where have you been? You can sit here.'

As far as safety records go, the colourful South American

airline, P——— ———N——— ——— ('no names, please!'), again topped the list on the casualties-per-kilometer scale. Their figures were really horrendous. It was the seventh year in a row. P——— ———N——— ——— made attempts to suppress the data. Failing that they cited the peculiar weather conditions over the Andes, the beautiful afternoon light, the incidence of condors, and the low standard of mosquito netting in several stopover towns. These may have contributed but it was generally acknowledged that other factors, known in the trade as 'invisibles', distorted the picture.

P——— ———N——— ——— had begun as a jungle carrier—stones for metropolitan museums, tropical fish, a little cocaine—when nobody had ever seen a vapour trail, when the very idea of jet-propulsion and the 'sound-barrier' made people burst out laughing. Indeed, around then P——— ———N——— ——— achieved early and steady profitability with a charter service to find the lost explorer, Colonel Fawcett. Today its business connections are more obscure. Its major shareholders are difficult to trace. Astonishingly for a commercial airline its routes are pragmatic and can alter from hour to hour at the whim of the management or pilots. Those mid-air collisions which had boosted the year's figures occurred when a P——— ———N——— ——— Douglas had joined the flight path of another airline. And those who take an instinctive suspicious interest in the Central Intelligence Agency point to the inordinate number of mid-air explosions. A wild, still unsubstantiated rumour had it that last year's wreckage near the Bolivian border showed the fuselage full of strapped-in soldiers, *American soldiers*.

Flying for such an airline somehow made the pilots extremely attractive to women, and they could be seen wearing silk scarves and Polaroid sunglasses, and practised that careless swagger like the Battle of Britain pilots. This clique in the airline's work-force scorned passenger nervousness as 'bourgeois'. But the crash figures were serious; of course they were. The subsequent fall in market share and the airline's growing unprofitability prompted the Public

Relations Department to act. The real lolly was in the Atlantic run.

At breakfast Gwen Kaddok said (in her steady, vegetarian's voice, almost forgotten): 'Before you go.' She thought they might all be interested . . . 'There's an event here at the hotel this morning.'

That was the thing about travel: you could decide on impulse to turn left instead of right, or stop dead, the real inhabitants hurrying past or bumping into them. Conscious of this their faces had settled, smoothed: flâneurs, travellers, dilettanti.

'As well, the stars tell me to stay indoors today,' Gwen mused, unsmiling. With her arms crossed she used her fingertips to lift the shawl on both shoulders.

'You follow the stars too?' Violet leaned forward. 'What are you?'

'I can see you're a Scorpio,' was Gwen's answer. 'Am I right?'

Then she told them only what she had heard from the receptionist: the 150-year-old man had been flown in from a mountainous village in Ecuador. The idea here being the aura of his astonishing longevity would perhaps rub off onto P——N——Airlines, offsetting its sudden-death reputation, a bold and imaginative stroke on the part of the Public Relations Department. The press conference would begin at eleven sharp. Expected to attend were representatives from the *British Medical Journal* and other such organs, as well as radio and television.

'It is my theory,' said Gwen who was never original, 'preservation has us all interested. We'd all like to live long.'

'Too right!'

'"Preservation?"' Shiela queried. She knitted her brow.

Cut out meat and sugar. Eat roughage! Cold baths and secret exercises, oils and ointments: spend years to live another day.

'A hundred and fifty? That's incredible. Is that right?'

'It'll be an experience,' Doug nodded. 'I'd like to see him.'

And when they returned to the dining room before

eleven, they found twenty to thirty metal chairs facing a dais, as in a Fabian Society lecture or an anti-vivisectionists' meeting. On the dais were two chairs, a card table and a cliche carafe of water. The group filled the first two rows on either side of Gwen Kaddok. She placed her hands on her lap.

The others were not so patient.

'It's twenty past,' Gerald whispered.

Twisting in their seats they found the seats behind them empty.

'I find her a bit spooky,' Sasha nodded towards Gwen Kaddok. 'Don't you? She hardly says a word.'

'What?' North started. He had been . . . miles away.

But then a very old man shuffled in from the left supported by the Public Relations Director, and they became quiet. To climb onto the dais he lifted his vibrating front leg twice as high. Realizing his mistake, he stopped and tried again, better. They stared at his head. It was all dark holes and cracks, an old rock, with a few bursts of thin hair protruding. He wore a burlap shirt and rope sandals. Calm man: it had much to do with his slowness. He took no notice of them or the surroundings. When he sat down he emitted an ancient sigh like life escaping a perished air cushion. 'Wow!' they all heard Gwen murmur.

The airline's representative remained standing. 'Ladies and gentlemen of the press . . .' and flashed them a smile.

Excellent teeth! A pencil moustache, crumpled cream suit and floral tie.

'We're behind schedule . . .'

He glanced at the old man and shook his head.

'In the lift, José Ruiz Carpio believed he was back in our Douglas jet. I had to correct him. He's never been out of his village before. Most of what he sees he cannot believe. But when one thinks about it, to be taken in a lift is an intercontinental flight on a reduced scale: acceleration, the smooth ride, gentle touchdown. I speak here only of our airline. What do you say? . . . To hell with the rest. But you want to hear from José Ruiz. Hey, señor! Did you have a pleasant flight?'

The old man had his head on his chest.

'The old man's weary. Excuse me.'

From his side pocket he took out a small syringe. Shiela turned her head as he lifted the old arm, and gave an injection.

He spoke of José Ruiz's 'astronomical age', of his village in the Province of Loja in Ecuador, its valleys of mists and steady temperatures. The average age up there is 114.6. And it's rising. One theory was the complete absence of wristwatches and clocks. It was suggested the body becomes conscious of ticking, our metabolism embeds itself into that mechanical, artificial Time. In José Ruiz's village the sound of time was replaced by the never-ending rattle of mountain water, which could very well drag the soul of a body along with it, as the heart pumps blood through the veins.

All this was very interesting.

They glanced at the figure beside him. He was sparking up.

Dr North asked, 'How do we know he is, in fact, 150 years old?'

A good point. (For example, he could have been ninety or a hundred.)

'Ah, an oversight! It is all here.'

He handed around Xerox copies of the original birth certificate.

'As you will notice, today is his birthday. We have a little party planned for tonight, to show what life is all about. He may have lived long, but he's missed a lot. Then we'll fly him home. Won't we, José Ruiz?'

The old man threw up his arms and let out a hoarse cry. Kaddok had crept up on all fours below the table and slowly raised his head fitted with camera.

Calming him by hissing a sentence in Spanish and vibrating one hand, the PR man turned to them and shook his head. 'He's alright. He thought it was a machine gun. His experience of the media is zero.'

He then held his smile for five or six seconds as Kaddok took another photograph. Excellent teeth!

Beside him the figure sat mumbling.

'Amigo! How old do you say you are?' Garry Atlas called out, getting into the spirit.

The PR man translated.

The old man had a surprisingly deep voice: 'One hundred and forty-nine and seven fortnights.'

'What does modern science say about this?' Gerald asked North. 'Eh?'

The PR man was explaining or apologizing. 'His village doesn't have English or electricity . . .'

He smiled to encourage further questions, and the witness helped himself to his cigarettes, putting one behind his ear and stuffing a handful into his shirt pocket.

'Any ailments?' Cathcart called out, a seasoned journo.

This old man frowned—a deeper transformation—and cupped his ear.

'Ailments! *Le duele algo!*' shouted the Public Relations manager into the labyrinth of the ear.

The other one shrugged and coughed something. He blew out shafts of smoke and studied the cigarette.

'He says, none. He feels like a baby. That's a lie. He's hard of hearing and has weak legs. You should see his legs. Perhaps you would like to photograph them? He suffers from shortage of breath. He is as creaky as hell. In the air cargo business he is the equivalent of a very fragile heirloom: an old oil portrait on crumbling canvas held in a loose frame with broken glass.'

Gwen writing in a small notebook looked up. 'How have you lived so long?'

But that's an impossible quest—

The deep voice: 'When I wake up each morning I have to remember myself, and all that has happened, before I can continue. Otherwise, I am no longer sure who I am. Understand? I would be lost.'

They nodded, respectful. For a while, no one spoke.

It was Borelli who asked, 'What have you learnt, overall.'

'There is no such thing as truth,' came the answer. 'And things are not always as they appear. Catholics live longer than heathens. I can't live without tobacco. The geese fly in winter. Dying is harder than you think.'

A terrible coughing, deep down and fundamental, cut him short and an arm not seen before came out of his shirt and slapped his chest. The airline representative stared at him before allowing the next question. Obviously he was pleased at how things were progressing.

'Sir?'

Louisa had a question.

'Please ask him what is there about Europe that interests him.'

He caught the word 'Europe'. Wiping his eyes he turned to his manager.

'Where you are now,' the PR man explained. 'Eur-ope.'

He looked around the room and nodded. He shrugged as he spoke.

'Oh, he tells me the night sky is different here. There are fewer stars. He says the air is smaller. And here the moon is warmer than the sun.' He questioned in Spanish and returned to them. 'By that he means, the nights are warm.'

They all smiled and nodded.

The old man who took no notice of them lit up another cigarette and went on. 'And the bath water here. Where I come from it falls straight down the hole.'

Garry Atlas laughed.

'He must live right on the Equator,' North murmured.

The PR man finished by asking a few questions about the flight: the food, the amount of leg-room, the quality of the hostesses. But José Ruiz had tired. As they watched a kind of vagueness drifted across his features. He became distracted. Smiling at them, the PR man kept talking. Suddenly, the old man leaned across the card table as if he had just noticed Gwen's neatly crossed legs. A confused or surprised expression over-ran his face. It ran all over. He tried to speak— while the other one still produced statistics—and his big tongue protruded. Sasha cried out and others pointed. His arms conducted distant orchestras, knocking over the carafe and glasses. His head hit the table.

The airlines representative bent down and lifted the 150-year-old eyelids. He then tested his pulse. 'Damn!' he frowned, stubbing out his cigarette.

3

Dozing, flipping magazines and whispering, they traversed the ocean as the albatross or the crow, held aloft by the Third Law, action/reaction, Boyle's expansion of gases, Mach's wind-tunnel tests of Hargrave's surfaces, just the right degree of dihedral—the age of refinement!—radar noise, crackling wireless, screech and the known strengths of titanium and magnesium. Ancient navigators had creaked their way across here in wooden ships, across the expanse, their tracks erased by the next swell, or stopping dead. Ocean of plain great depth, of substance and extent, ruffled pewter, occasional crest and a tramp plowing on course, scratching the surface. Seated in comfort amid Latin pastels they could sense the despair of the enormity, became vague (so tiring), and turned to daydreaming. They looked away. Some took to drinks, cracking silly jokes. Visually their indicator of progress was the suprematist shadow below containing them, rollercoasting the troughs at 650mph (plus). Even so it offered little comparison. Those who woke after a doze and looked down found the same haliographic grey, scarcely any change; endless. They wondered and looked away.

Deep canyons beneath and weed, currents and contranatent migrations of fish underneath, invisible whales; and lying deep, wrecks split on their sides and the slippery streets of Atlantis. They passed over the Cape Verde Basin, so called—fracture zones, ridges. They crossed Cancer's dotted line. The colours lightened: green by mid-afternoon; a few distant white islands to the north-east.

Then they took to the windows and pointed. Editions of *Time*, of *The Economist*, and the single *Stern* (monopolized by Hofmann, noticed by Louisa), in the airline hard-covers were shoved to one side; closing the thriller, *The Double*

Helix, Phillip North placed it on the seat beside him. All along Garry and Violet Hopper had two air hostesses in the seats facing them, Garry shouting drinks and more than once ordered out of the stainless-steel kitchen. Now they shared windows, touching heads. At the sight of land Violet produced an ostentatious wolf whistle normally used by strong males. She'd had one too many. Mrs Cathcart nudged Doug. Looking down to where she pointed he immediately began grinning. Almost everyone—Shiela, Gwen Kaddok—began grinning.

A submarine from the navy of a small land-locked Latin American nation had surfaced after an exercise and lay long and lethal, matt-black in the water. White bodies dived off her conning tower and churned the surface. Others were draped over the bow, sunbaking. They were near the Equator. The water would have been warm.

The plane banked and descended and those at the windows turned to each other laughing. 'Hubba hubba, ding ding!' Violet cried out. This was P—— ——N————Airlines, Flight 2213. Alerted by Gwen, Kaddok switched to the starboard side and waited with his telephoto lens.

Borelli whispered to Louisa, 'I don't think you should look. Quick, close your eyes.'

And Garry gave a harsh laugh.

Look at that! Down there!

From the water men waved—one doing the backstroke. A large number there were mulattoes. On the cigar-deck they rolled over or stood up, shielding their eyes, and as the airliner passed low overhead, engulfing them in shade, one able seaman began dancing and pointing his cock up at the plane. The jet must have screeched: for then the crew all put their hands to their ears and the red-haired bosun poised on the conning tower dived off, belly-flopping. Bodies, heh heh, diving in all directions.

'Christ, that was funny,' Garry yelled, wiping his eyes. He turned to the others, 'Jesus, we were close!'

They'd seen a wristlet watch, identification discs and rows of teeth flashing, the pale divided buttocks and big balls swinging. (P—— ——N—— ——Airlines, Flight No. 2213.)

They were still talking about it, already embroidering it, when they sighted land, and slowly passed over what clearly was impenetrable jungle, as Amazonian as languages and cancer, the substance myths, and anacondas down there, occasional lonely smoke. At late afternoon they touched down at Quito, behind time.

'Quito,' Louisa repeated, 'what a lovely name.'

'Oh, yairs,' said Violet swaying and rolling her eyes. 'Quito.' And trying to light a Benson & Hedges she dropped Garry's lighter.

The Indian sweeping the terminal floor bent to pick it up. He had small eyes and wide cheekbones.

'Give it back!' Violet cried out. 'Here! Thank you.'

The Indian watched as she lit the cigarette. Drawing in she spoke the words of one of her television commercials. 'The right taste . . . the right length . . . yes, sir-ree!' And with her actress tongue she made a sound like a horse galloping.

She looked around the airport lounge.

'So this is what they call Quito?'

North cleared his throat.

'Violet,' Sasha said in a low voice.

The customs officers had stopped and were watching her. Garry grabbed her elbow. 'Come off it. Come on.'

She shook free. 'You piss off!'

'What's eating her, for chrissake?'

'All this is your bloody fault,' Sasha hissed. She took Violet's arm. 'You don't know her. You know *nothing*. Excuse,' she raised her chin at the customs officer. 'Do you have a washroom?'

He shrugged. The customs officers were eating bananas.

'*Donde están los retretes?*' Gerald asked.

A captain pointed at a door, and tipped everything out of Borelli's bag.

Red-eyed and vague Garry stood around muttering. He turned to Phillip North; but North was talking to Hofmann and Gerald Whitehead.

At the counter, Louisa remarked to Borelli, 'It's quite cool for the Equator . . .'

'We're at nine thousand feet,' came Kaddok's explanation from behind. 'The second-highest capital in the world.'

She looked at Borelli.

A kind of casualness as always smoothed his face, as if he had only just woken up or had recently been ill. Taking no notice of his belongings scattered over the counter, he nodded: 'You were right before. Quito is a nice-sounding name. It must be the Q. I've always thought it has the most beckoning shape in the alphabet. It has essentially a feminine quality. What do you think? We say "Q" or "Queen" and have to make a kissing shape with our lips. I imagine Q would make any word beautiful, visually and orally.'

Beside them Doug added, 'Qantas, Circular Quay.'

'What about *quim*?' Hofmann enquired; and Louisa went quiet. She had wanted to talk to Borelli alone.

Her husband and Borelli remained gazing at each other; Hofmann smiling.

'If you like,' said Borelli. 'I wouldn't quibble.'

'What do you say?' Hofmann asked. 'We're discussing *quim*.'

But Louisa remained watching Borelli's mouth. Whenever he experimented, usually aloud, he pursed his lips. Sometimes he closed an eye. It was as if he forever dwelt on the letter Q.

'Oh *quim*,' Louisa answered, 'is not a word I normally use. But I think it's nice. It's not derogatory. Anyway,' she glared at him, 'you should know.'

Borelli now closed one eye. 'Q is conception, a pierced womb. It reminds me of that. I probably connect it with Queen.'

'Oh, isn't he nice!' Louisa cried, turning to her husband. 'Why can't you be like that?'

Borelli quickly turned back to the counter. They were shovelling his clothes back in.

More place names begin with Q-U in Latin America

than anywhere else in the world. Arab countries follow next—include Moslem Afghanistan. But the Arab place names do not always employ the U. So you find Qishn, Qom, Qasr Amij, Qafor on the map: those shrouded names. Many are quadrilateral words. And of course, *Qu'ran* itself. There are also a surprising number of Q-names in the Isle of Man telephone directory.

'It's all very interesting,' Borelli turned from the counter. 'Perhaps it is why in Latin America earthquakes are so prevalent. What comes first: the word or the event?'

'Ha, ha, yes. The chicken or the egg theory,' Kaddok nodded from behind.

This left a bit of a vacuum. It wasn't what Borelli had meant.

'Leon knows a great deal,' said Gwen anxiously, looking first at the Hofmanns and then Borelli.

He sure did; but it had been a long flight. Now he was explaining how Ecuador got its name from the Equator, which was a local landmark, and his listeners gazed around the terminal. These buildings are all the same, an esperanto of lines, as if composed by the one cost-efficient architect (nice contract), though Quito's possessed the odour of roasted coffee and sulphur. Standing among their luggage they soon tired of the posters on the wall proclaiming the jaguar, the tapir, the tree-dwelling kinkajou (with pre-hensile tail), the various macaws, and the montage of cooking pots. Gringos, come to Ecuador! But can their infrastructure handle the influx, especially the touchy blue-hairs from the north, those Brahmins with the hearing aids and the astonishingly shaped spectacle frames? It's a poor country. Population: only 6,000,000. More than a liberal sprinkling of *zambos* and quadroons there. Soccer, bullfights and horse-races.

'I say, what's the hold-up?' Gerald called out.

It's an agricultural economy: bananas, coffee. The large estates owned by city-dwellers, the mestizos, operate in a time-zone of slowness, of decay, few mechanical shapes and sounds. The stillness or stealth had infected the capital. They grow the carludovica tree, its fibres used for Panama

Hats—forests of hats, of shadows and shade. The Indian leaning on his broom had accumulated half a dozen banana skins in his sweepings.

What is a comparison?

'After London, I thought we'd seen the last of queues.'

Garry put his elbows on the counter, looking anxious, glancing at the door for Violet, while one of the officers tested his After Shave with his finger, staring at him. They wore pistols. The one with the stained collar and mournful eyes picked up a pair of lace panties with a ruler. Shoving his sunglasses onto his forehead Garry tried grinning, man-to-man. The officer cut him short. 'We're a decent people,' he said in a husky voice. 'Understand?' Sure! But to show indignation—because you had to—Garry stared down at the floor and slowly shook his head. Born to a different order the customs officers took this as repentance. They beamed.

The rest of the group had noticed the large clock on the wall. It had broken down. To avoid confusing travellers who had already crossed several time-zones its hands had been obliterated by tape and bandages, so that Time looked impoverished, or as Borelli declared, sick and disabled, time with time on its hands.

It reminded Shiela: 'I don't know what day it is.' And the others smiled, similarly vague.

'God, this is a dump,' Garry said, joining them with Violet. His hands trembled which made him more unsettled. He put them in his pocket but then immediately scratched his neck. The customs officers in their flashy uniforms had looked more like army generals.

The capital of Ecuador lay in the hollow of a hand, one side climbing a slope, adobe houses in layers mercifully all prevented from slipping by churches, damned by churches or walls of churches and sudden plazas—horizontal breathing spaces. It is the size of Adelaide, the size Adelaide was, and like that religious town its streets are laid out in graph-paper pattern. Order, order! In Quito they persisted over a terrain of gullies and jagged *quebradas*. It was as if the Spanish were determined to exert their will on the unstable elements, regardless, like the Jesuits drumming Revelations into the ears of stoned Indians. The slope with the houses, with the ravines, was the volcano Mount Pichincha. It erupted in the year 1666, year of the Great Fire of London and Newton's theory of colours. But there were other volcanoes. They are the tourist attraction. Quito is encircled. Volcanic amphitheatre! The white towers of the churches were outlined against their dark cones and thunder-clouds: a reminder of fire and boiling water, constantly pointed to with the surpliced arm from Quito's pulpits. Even in the plazas, palms with the pineapple trunks erupted jagged fronds, which then drooped in suspended semi-circles, like sparking dark metal from a distance: eruptions of a decorative sort.

And they noticed the architecture of Catholics was volcanic in essence (known elsewhere as feast or Baroque). It gushed almost in desperation here, what with the swarming doors and porticoes carved in wood, the multi-layered plinths for the many (so many!) optimistic winged statues and seven-sided fountains, Plaza Independencia, and the quadrant-shaped lawns, quadrangles of lapilla, Good Lord, green cupolas and belfries capped with intricate weather-vanes, so many palaces, so many cloisters, walls set with hypnotic bricks, quoining and famous bells, all commissioned and urged on by mad Jesuits, one eye on the weather (i.e. the volcanoes). While the buildings and columns swarmed and flickered the citizens were peaceful.

To sleep and copulate at the foot of volcanoes, to be surrounded: in Ecuador they cheer themselves with sad music.

Old Yank tanks—Hudsons, de Sotos—left behind by expatriates who'd long ago fled, hissed and sometimes shot out steam. Such saloons suggested the nineteen-forties and the *Saturday Evening Post*, as if the recent past still lay ahead. The houses in the Spanish style had iron-grilled doorways and secluded gardens.

Their hotel was the Atahuallpa, near the river, and the desk clerk stared first at the cigarette ash on Hofmann's lapels and then the dandruff on Kaddok's dark shoulders,

and when they weren't looking glanced behind at Pichincha.

Mrs Cathcart wrote after tea,
  Who would have thought. Your father and I
  are on the Equator *wearing cardigans*. This is
  because—I am told—our hotel is situated
  higher than Kosciusko—hard to believe.
  Wonderful views—The food is spicy. Cobbled streets.

It must have been the jet lag. Already Doug was in bed
without cleaning his teeth . . .

Violet hadn't come down for tea, but first thing in the
morning she was seated characteristically in the front of the
bus in sunglasses and a kangaroo pelisse for their first
outing. A few seats behind, Garry sat moodily and then
moved further back to sit with Shiela. She had a Baedeker
on her lap from a previous visit.

'Aren't you cold?' Louisa cried out. 'Look at him!'

Advancing down the aisle Borelli had on his cotton ex-
Air Force jacket.

'But isn't this the tropics?'

'Yes and no,' North replied. They were usually cheerful,
setting out.

For some reason, North was seated alongside Doug
Cathcart. As the bus began moving they both held onto the
seat rail in front.

'Did you get a good shut-eye?' Doug put in. He had the
window seat.

'I can't complain.'

Several times he had woken and looked at his watch.
With the curtains wide open he could distinguish the dark
shape of Pichincha against the lighter sky, and he thought
about his lost wife.

The clapped-out Pegaso gathered speed down the cobbled street, its tall bulk and the powerful horn-scattering
pedestrians, women yanking their children or heavy baskets
aside, for as in Africa these people preferred not walking on
the footpaths.

Odd words flashed into view and swung back; words

disconnected from images. NIETO PINTORA! CALLE de la RHONDA   PALACIO de ☞   ESPAÑA CANI.

Fragments of. Amid impassive faces pausing from their tasks a few feet through the glass. Someone spat and brown juice ran unnoticed down the window at Sasha's shoulder. By then the bus broke into sudden white space, one of the plazas, and the hunched driver, elbows splayed, dropped the clutch, the cylinders fired, and the crowd at a bus stop all rose from a stone bench, then slowly sat down again, mistaking the turismo bus for the municipal one. Look, women washing by a river—that's straight out of *National Geographic*. The windows kept juddering down, which made them laugh, and two or three ashtrays fell off the back of the seats. Never mind.

On the edge of town squatters' shacks appeared as picturesque landslides of tin, cardboard and hessian; and Mrs Cathcart made that single clicking sound with her tongue. Lotta Indians there. Sasha turned and smiled broadly at the others: see the Indian woman wearing a bowler hat? And another.

Violet Hopper lit up a cigarette.

'If you watch out,' Dr North announced, 'you might see a monkey or two.'

They darted their heads, the way the iguana does, at the slightest movement.

Around the next corner was a light forest of balsa trees; a file of Indians wielded mattocks like helots. So this is where balsa comes from? What is it used for now? The bus kept turning. A silken camanchaca wreathed through gullies of straw grass and covered the road, fumes of dry ice or fog sculpture, and as the cursing driver changed down and sounded the horn, someone pointed above to the clear sunshine: Scottish pines and various crops of grain quilted the tops of mountains. Gorgeous, breath-taking, amazing were the words used.

'He's taking us the long way round,' said Gerald. 'The Equator is only fifteen miles from the city.'

'This is like a museum of crops and trees,' said North. 'We can sit back and enjoy ourselves.'

'Yairs,' said Doug, the way he talked on the phone. 'Yairs, it opens your eyes.'

Well, he'd been using his binoculars; and Kaddok had clambered down the back to photograph the receding view.

Pointing to a plantation Phillip North said to Cathcart, 'I think you'll find that's where your tablets come from!'

'What? Where?'

'Those are cinchona trees.'

'Ar, the old quinine tablets. Go on, eh?'

They were used to each other but were essentially strangers, speaking in fragmentary bursts, comments mainly, thrown down like cards. Half-listening, the other person would respond by nodding and then going off on a tangent with some piece of knowledge, an anecdote just remembered, unrelated but taken from his own experience; a kind of ready balancing act. It was the talk of nomads.

Something had reminded Doug about *cloves*.

Yes on television the other day he'd seen a film documentary about cloves. Very interesting. These are grown in Zanzibar. Hang on—Tanzania? Anyway, Africa somewhere. Funny looking tree. They pick them by hand and dry them on the footpaths . . . Apparently a multi-million dollar industry.

North could hear other comments around the bus. Brief, broken observations. 'That's a . . .'

'Look at the . . .'

And Doug again, speaking in Ecuador, 'Bloke in Melbourne, good friend of mine, has a . . .'

North nodded.

The bus slowed down and stopped at a boom gate painted like a goal post. A carabineer in an overcoat poked his head in, then spoke to the driver. He waited near the door and used a twig to clear something stuck in his teeth, pulling a variety of faces.

Without turning the driver yelled some Spanish back at them.

Gerald went down and asked with histrionic hand movements a series of questions. The driver merely shrugged.

Poking his glasses back on his nose, Gerald translated. 'He's after baksheesh. Not the driver, but his charming friend out there. I'm pretty sure he doesn't have any authority.'

'Of course he hasn't!'

'It doesn't matter. We can afford it,' said Borelli towards the back.

Irritation swept through the bus. It was like tiredness on an empty stomach.

'That's not the point. It's the principle!'

'Yes, it's people like you,' Gwen turned with surprising venom, 'who keep the beggars and that on the streets. You encourage them.'

'I hate being fleeced.'

'Right, I don't think we should.'

'Tell him, no!'

'Well I doubt whether we'll get in,' said Borelli simply. 'Isn't it a fact of life here, a custom?'

The driver had his elbows on the steering wheel taking no notice of the debate. Gerald asked him something else.

'He says twenty sucres. What's that? Two each. Alright?'

'We don't have to have much choice.'

'This happened last time I came here,' Shiela smiled at Garry. 'I can get yours.'

Garry wasn't happy. 'They're rotten crooks. No wonder the whole show's falling apart.'

A few yards in, the bus stopped.

Doug rubbed his hands and looked around. 'It's good to stretch the legs.'

There were stone benches and kiosks. Families had spread cotton rugs on the ground. It was a favourite picnic spot.

'Why the barbed-wire fence and everything?' asked Sasha.

'Because it is our most important asset,' an Ecuadorian answered. He'd been standing nearby, watching. He had dark combed hair; good English.

They ignored him and strolled over to the Equator.

It was a metal rail a foot or so off the ground. It wandered in a fairly straight line over the bare ground of the valley and up the other hill, as far as the eye could see, clearly indicating the divisions of the hemispheres. It appeared to be of stainless steel. Either that, or it shone from people constantly touching.

Resting one foot on it Garry said, 'Two beers, please.'

It made a few laugh. But they were more conscious of the shape of the earth. It seemed to begin here, spreading in a massive curve of great weight on either side.

Neatly illustrating the point, concrete chairs had been set up several inches apart, and a man and his wife were sharing a thermos of cocoa, the man naturally in the Northern Hemisphere, a Panama hat on his knees, his spouse to one side seated in the Southern Hemisphere.

Slippery dips had been set up. Children and even adults could slide from the Northern to the Southern Hemisphere in a matter of seconds.

Kaddok tripped over the Equator.

He'd been manoeuvring to take some colour slides, and now visualizing his own position, legs tangled in the Equator rail, he called out for someone to quickly photograph him. Irrefutable proof, this would be, that he had seen the Equator.

'Notice. There are no shadows here at noon.' That Ecuadorian remained at their elbow. 'No one can bear living without his shadow. People come here for the picnic, sure, but all attempts to populate the region have failed.'

A little mirror had been nailed to a post, and Louisa Hofmann automatically touched the back of her head. She smiled when Borelli observed she had her face in each hemisphere.

'If only that could last!' Standing behind her, Violet gave a harsh yet understanding laugh.

A special mailbox stood on the other side. If people had letters they could post them here for fun. (A circular postmark divided by a horizontal dotted line: EQUATOR, ECUADOR.)

'Ladies and gentleman, this way,' Borelli called out.

The local man agreed. 'We have scientists coming every

day from all over the world. To observe. It proves the hypothesis.'

Louisa joined Borelli. 'Is this what you wanted us to see?'

He nodded but turned. 'Phillip, now have a good look at this.'

A tall plastic curtain formed a kind of opaque 'box' across the Equator. Borelli pulled it aside. There stood a standard white bath on cast-iron paws. It had the wire tray for soap and a brick-coloured plug on a chain. Out in the open, positioned longways to the Equator, it looked out of place, ridiculous even. On closer inspection they noticed the heavy bath was mounted on two short pieces of tram line. These intersected the Equator at right angles. The bath could be pushed with an easy movement of the hand into the Northern Hemisphere, or the Southern (where it rested now), or smack on the Equator itself.

'Excuse, excuse.'

The local man pushed his way to the front, enveloping them in the dense perfume of his hair oil.

'These shouldn't be here,' he clicked his tongue.

He held up a snorkel and mask. A square hand-lettered card on string fell down.

'*Niños*,' he muttered, looking around.

He must have had poor eyesight, squinting at the card, holding it at arm's length. Even those standing behind could read:

THE GREAT BARRIER REEF

Gwen whispered it to her husband.

'What does it mean?' the busybody from Ecuador asked. From the beginning his fastidious frown irritated them.

'It's the longest coral reef in the world,' Kaddok told him. 'One thousand two hundred and fifty miles long. One of nature's miracles.'

'But I don't understand.'

He threw the rubbery gear to one side.

'Excuse me, continue with the demonstration. *Por aquí. Por allá.*'

'Right. Now let's see,' said Borelli.

This was an outdoor laboratory. Doubting Thomases, empiricists, the last remaining vorticists evidently came here in droves. Bathwater let out in the Southern Hemisphere spins out clockwise, like Time. See?

'Just like home,' Sasha agreed.

Filling the bath up again, Borelli pushed it across into the Northern Hemisphere. Here it ran out . . . anti-clockwise.

They cheered. The old man in London had been dead right.

'Very good.'

'Do it again!' Sasha laughed.

'Ah-ah,' said Borelli. 'We now come to the important experiment. Am I right, doctor?'

North had his arms folded. 'Cut the cackle.'

Setting the bath carefully astride the Equator, Borelli yanked the plug like a man starting a lawnmover, and for good measure imitated a trumpet fanfare. With hands on each other's shoulders, they watched . . . The water fell straight down the hole. No vortex.

Borelli gave a bow.

'Again!' cried Sasha.

'Americano?' the local man asked. No one took any notice and when they turned he had disappeared.

'Watch him!'—Kaddok almost fell in aiming his Pentax at the performing plughole.

'Very interesting. Most unusual.'

Even Shiela put on her most thoughtful expression, although she had seen it before.

'It makes sense when you think about it,' argued Hofmann.

'Well worth the trip,' said Doug slapping his stomach and turning away. 'It broadens your knowledge.'

They wandered along the Equator for a while, hands behind their backs, tagged by half a dozen hawkers in ponchos offering souvenir corkscrews and spiralling brooches. There were paperweights from a local rock crystal which showed at the flick of the wrist the site in a paradoxical snowstorm. While Violet bargained for a key-ring with a marvellous miniature bath plug on a coilspring, solid silver, señora, the others looked on amused, or like Mrs Cathcart made a bee-line for a nearby kiosk. There she bought a handful of postcards which illustrated in colour this phenomenon of water running down the hole, without a swirl.

It was a fine spot. Thrust up by such volcanic forces the mountains opposite were green-black, in shadow. Only their own small plateau with the kiosks seemed to be illuminated. The largest mountain directly ahead had been laced with a recent line of shining poles and wires, like the raised knee held down in Lilliput. There was a thin sharp wind.

Hofmann had returned alone to the bath. Pushing aside the curtains, positioning himself, he began pissing down the plughole, hands on hips, a type of luxuriousness.

'Hell-o!'

Hofmann splashed his shoes. 'Excuse me,' he fumbled.

'Ah, I thought it was one of the Indians. You know the dunny's by the gate?'

'But I thought I'd have a go at this. It was here.'

Frank Hammersly gave a laugh. 'Fair enough.'

Wide in the shoulders, and easy. Strong as a bull. Fit as a fiddle.

Hofmann finished. 'That feels better.'

'We must have a similar ticket . . .'

'Possibly. We're taking it easy, of course. A leisurely sort of cruise. You're on business? Are you making any money?'

When he wanted to, Hofmann could speak like a friendly dentist.

'Winning a few, losing a few,' came the platitude. Putting a foot up on the bath, Hammersly felt for his cigarettes.

The bus sounded its horn.

Hofmann zipped up.

'Okay,' Hammersly waved. 'I'll see you.' He took his foot off the bath. He was looked around for the snorkel and mask as Hofmann ran to the bus.

Landmarks vaguely remembered or briefly seen but forgotten re-appeared and fell into place, supplying the key to other sections. Nondescript yet memorable street corners (why?); the main plaza with its fountains; colonnades, oppressive palace of the Archbishop; the wide shaded street with the villas of the eminent quinologists; a palm tree from a certain regular angle—established and grew as facts. A kind of sadness then grew out of the familiarity, the dusty façades of buildings. That repetitious '48 Buick with its wheels off, the female fenders painted with land-reform slogans, scarcely rated a glance now. It was fixture, embedded in the ground near the leather shop and cigarette advertisement. Other entire suburbs and smaller plazas remained a blank. These they would never see. Normally they took the narrow street to the main plaza on the right. From there they radiated after strolling the arcades. The plaza provided authority. In an alleyway behind it some had come across an Indian market, congested and noisy, but obviously safe.

Within such brief boundaries the confidence they had acquired was unstable. It was merely awareness of their freedom of movement. Wandering singly or in groups their curiosity lured them into corners and strange culs-de-sac where the racket of the market or the plaza could suddenly no longer be heard. The cluster of craft shops facing the hotel, the faded yellow words on a building, the Archbishop's palace, the street lights strung on dark wires between the buildings, and the porous nose of the nervous desk-clerk were evocative of the city, the spread of buildings, called 'Quito'. In fact, they knew very little.

Those like Borelli who preferred the local people to museums and religious carvings—although Gerald Whitehead tried to explain they were one and the same—searched the faces which zoomed in and went passing, for a clue. Somehow they were different from Australians, from the English. They were close, but far away. Their intentions were smooth. The women avoided his gaze. When Borelli entered an alleyway (once) ragged boys began throwing stones: waving, he ambled back. What did that mean? Why should they? Several blocks away Phillip North bending over some parrots in rusty cages lost his wallet containing travellers' cheques and the image of his dead wife seated on a garden chair.

'Bad luck, but that's one of the things about travel,' said Garry.

And he told them how he and Ken Hofmann had dumped the women and went looking for a cockfight, and for the first time saw a man dead in the street. Yeah? People had stood around and stared.

'What'd you do?'

'We thought it was the cockfight.'

'He was dead alright,' said Hofmann. 'We turned back.'

And for kicks they both had their shoes shined.

'Ever had that done?' Garry lifted his foot up by the ankle. 'How about that? It was really funny. This little codger must have spent ten minutes rubbing away. Didn't he, Ken?'

What some people do for a crust.

Nodding; comparing notes.

'We got lost,' said Sasha, 'and we had to get a taxi. Hey, how much is twenty sucres? I thought so.' She turned to Violet. 'We was done.'

Families squatted on the pavement, some leaning against the poles, eating tinned pet foods. The major brands competed here: Mighty Dog, Kal Kan, Jo-Bo, Perk, Puss 'n Boots, Chug Wagon and Wag. A mother, no oil-painting, but wearing a marvellous woollen shawl, dropped dobs of Wam into her son's stained mouth.

'They have nice looking coins,' Shiela remarked.

Doug had spread them out on the table. 'What did you get at the bank? Thirty-eight to the dollar?' He pointed to the coins. 'Fifty-three. You know the leather shop? There's a young fella there in a red shirt.'

Gerald picked up one of the coins, then another sprouting cactus and terraced temples. He cleared his throat. 'These are Centavos.'

'What?'

'He's given you Mexican money.'

Everybody laughed.

Cathcart was now emptying his pockets, comparing coins.

'Give them to some of the beggars.'

'I'll buy some,' Shiela said. 'I take them back for children I know. It's something of a habit.' She turned. 'They're little blighters now. If I don't, they'll only ask.'

'I almost forgot,' Sasha cried out. Swinging around, her breasts tangled, and her voice came from under the table.

'It's for you . . .'

She planted a Panama on North's head.

'Aw, shucks,' he mumbled, gauging the rim with both thumbs. 'Aw, shucks . . .' He put it back on. He put on an act.

Leaning back they laughed with him.

'It suits you,' Sasha decided, her nipples rising. She stood in front of him. 'You look lazy and seedy.'

He said, 'I thought everyone knew that.'

Sasha sat down beside him.

The hotel as meeting place: the firm knowledge of its location. How it stood in their minds, at the back, waiting. It was theirs. Friendly were the dimensions and shadows of the mellow foyer and its miniature-pillared news-stand displaying postcards and street-maps, *Ecuadorian Made Easy*, Bibles, and leather-bound manuals for American cars out of production decades ago. There were the wide-elbowed chairs and low tables. There was the aroma of that universal floor polish favoured by hotels, and the creaking wooden lift, the familiar state of their scattered clothes, and the window where the outside and ordinary world could be looked down upon—here like some social realist painting seen from a distance.

North thought of going to the zoo in the morning. Would Sasha like . . .

'But I thought you'd given up animals?' said Sasha, and she met Violet's eye.

'Ah, that's true. But perhaps I could try out this hat, you see.'.

When Sasha turned she was smiling.

'But we have that museum tomorrow.'

'I think that's in the afternoon.'

With a kind of dull anger Doug and Mrs Cathcart picked up and examined each of the Mexican coins again.

'Where's Louisa?'

Violet turned to James Borelli.

'I haven't seen her. She must be up in her room.'

'Someone bang on their door!'

'Louisa's nice, isn't she?' Shiela ventured. She looked anxious but the others seemed to agree.

They were still discussing Louisa when Gwen Kaddok returned with a brown paper bag. 'I'll show you,' she said, 'what I found.'

Normally Gwen remained to one side, what with Leon; and so they wondered. Putting her hand in the bag she felt around, then pulled out by its hair a charcoal-grey head. It was a man's, slightly larger than a cricket ball.

'No!'

'But that's awful!'

'I've always read about these. Let's see.'

'Gwen, give us a look. Where'd you get it? How much was it?'

'Careful with it, please. Careful.'

And Gwen herself remained gazing at it as others turned it over. They tested it with tips of their fingers.

'The poor man. Imagine.'

He had tiny nostrils.

It was difficult, no matter how hard they stared, to estimate his age.

'Take it off the table,' Mrs Cathcart shouted. 'For goodness sake. I think I'm going to be sick.'

And here Shiela surprised almost everyone by suddenly laughing. Not only was it unexpected: her eyes seemed to be blazing. The laughter came from deep in her throat, a-bubbling. Could it have been embarrassment? Its unsteady nature made some of them glance at her.

'The shrunken head,' Kaddok rattled off over it all, 'called *tsantsa*. War trophies of the Jivaro indians. They're head hunters. Upper Amazon.'

'Perhaps it's where our head-waiter comes from!' Borelli cracked.

'What? Oh stop it!' Sasha laughed.

They were all having a good time.

North passed the head back to Gwen. 'I think it demonstrates very much the dangers of psychoanalysis.'

This made Borelli laugh and Shiela returned to gazing open-mouthed, but Gerald leaned across, 'These days you'll find they are made from goat skin and horse hair. It's a racket for the tourist trade.'

'What?' Doug swung around.

Gerald shook his head. 'It doesn't matter.'

'Only a hundred and thirty sucres,' Gwen was saying.

'What's the matter?' Mrs Cathcart asked.

'I don't like this city,' Doug announced. He shifted in his seat. 'Everyone's either crackers or they're getting at you. I'm not stupid.'

It was the stillness, a kind of aerial brooding over all. Them sad natives singing the *yarabí* in the street outside. Some could be heard from the bar. What an atmosphere, unnatural, even inside. It was ragged. People kept brushing their shoulders for no apparent reason at all. Darkness had descended on the houses stacked in cubes, filled the hollows and the holes, merging with the mountain normally to their left, so obliterating all perspective and sense of direction, making even the source of sounds ambiguous. Only a few holes pierced the dark, some in vague clusters like the Milky Way. The land had become sky.

Curious too how the barman with the sliding wet-nut eyes was drenched below the hairline: a forehead of crystal until he wiped. For it wasn't hot here on the Equator. It was mild. And he wouldn't talk, not even *gracias*. At latitude zero there existed that all-pervading stillness. Pores and pulse expanded, ebbed and contracted, overflowing in the inexperienced. Most in the party had gone to bed with itchy skins.

At the bar Garry Atlas splashed his drink on a pair of

crocodile-skin shoes: the South American racing driver, Ricardo Monzan. 'I know you,' Garry moved his cigarette to his mouth. 'Christ, put it here. This is something. Hey, Hammersly,' he called out. 'Come here. Meet the great Ricardo Monzan.'

Monzan wore the stereotyped gym shoes and the slender red overalls (fireproof) favoured by the international stars. FIRESTONE was embroidered across one breast. And yet he was a pear-shaped man, going bald.

'Christ, what a—'

Monzan held up his hand. 'If you don't mind. I have a father and a brother called Jesus. My father is living in Buenos Aires.'

So he speaks English.

He nodded at the barman. 'And my good friend there. His name too is Jesus.'

Garry winked at Frank Hammersly, 'Fair enough—'

'I remember,' Hammersly put in, 'Jack Brabham thrashing you in the—what was it?—American Grand Prix. How did that feel?'

'The South African . . .'

'Brabham's Australian! He was World Champion.'

Emptying his glass Monzan placed it on the bar.

'Everyone knows that.' Hammersly persisted (veins bulging in his neck). 'How long have you been driving?'

Monzan displayed the calm, the experience, typical of racing drivers, glancing first at the other bourbon drinkers and then up at the wall where he'd noticed a crocodile-shaped vertical crack.

But Monzan's tanned hand alongside the glass trembled. He had to hold on.

Garry scratched the place on his neck normally reserved for problems.

'Are you here for races or what?'

Monzan blinked.

'On the way somewhere or sort of a little holiday then?'

The South American pointed to their empty glasses. This made him better though no more understandable.

'Alright, I'll be a slob,' said Hammersly recovering nicely, 'another beer.'

'Say,' Garry turned, taking the opportunity, 'I was going to ask. What is it you do for a crust?'

From his wallet Hammersly drew out a card the size of a matchbox:

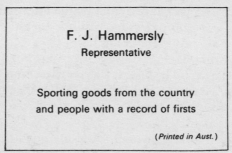

F. J. Hammersly

Representative

Sporting goods from the country
and people with a record of firsts

(*Printed in Aust.*)

'It's mainly public relations,' Hammersly explained. 'Living out of the old suitcase. I travel the globe.'

Garry nodded. He added two and two.

'Growth areas. Population explosion and the increased leisure time. The ball's at our feet, if only we knew it. We're selling tons of bloody tennis rackets and jock-straps. We've just introduced a new type of crash-helmet. I should tell Monzan, but that character doesn't seem to know what day it is.' Hammersly laughed. 'He's pissed, look.'

Monzan had their drinks in each hand but an athletic-looking Latin held onto his elbow. He became free as the other one used a moist handkerchief to demonstrate a bullfighter's pass.

'An old friend,' Monzan explained. 'The forecasters tell us it will happen. It has been confirmed. So be it.'

Garry glanced at Hammersly.

'They're all matadors in the corner. Some not so good. Not any more. Like me they're no longer young. So is the barman. You've heard of the great Porfino Paz?'

They hadn't heard of the great Porfino Paz.

'His nerves are gone—shot to pieces. His last corrida was bad, very bad.' Monzan gave a high laugh in his cups. 'Each of us has a difficult season this year. It is not getting easier. So here we stand in its direct path. The slightest tremor is a terror for me, ever since a boy. But the waiting will strengthen me. We are a group. Thirteen. It is a test. Such preparations are needed for the coming season.'

Garry must have looked puzzled.

'Ah, you have not experienced an earthquake before? I assumed that is why you too are here.'

'Jesus,' Garry breathed.

It was getting late.

Now that you looked at Monzan's smooth face, sweat there had moistened the nose and the dark tufts sprouting from his ears wilted like the winter grass on the pampas. A faint tremor along his lower lip was constantly erased by his tongue, but always began afresh.

'And that's what you're staying here for?'

'It is shock treatment,' Monzan admitted.

'You're mad!'

'Who are you? You have experienced, what, nothing. Understand? Nothing. So you might say it is lucky. *Que suerte*? Suffer through nature and pain. Emerge strong.'

'We have bushfires . . .' Hammersly tried to tell him.

'Live dangerously! Go to your perimeters.' He stamped his braking foot down onto the floorboards. 'We are on top of a fragile seismologic line. It runs under this floor. The earth will open up. It's almost intolerable to be standing here. Who's going to fall in?'

'Not me.' Garry murmured, but he frowned.

For the time, volcanoes were completely forgotten. They can erupt in another year. Praise God, there is the trusted statue strategically located throughout Quito, the Virgin of Quinche—protectress against earthquakes.

Hammersly belched. 'No one gives a fuck about Australia.'

Swaying, red in the face, Garry stared at Monzan.

Well, there are many types of phobias: acro, claustro, agora and zoö. Why, some people are known to be afraid of midnight and the pattern of Persian carpets. In the elevators of the world's tourist hotels there is no number 13.

'Come on,' said Hammersly. 'They're crackers. You believe in Santa Claus? That's the trouble with these little countries.'

But Garry was stumbling towards the corner. He had never met a bullfighter and here at least a dozen stood in ill-fitting suits, and one was lying on the floor, drunk.

In Room 217, opposing flesh sent an ornate wooden bed creaking alive on the floorboards. These picturesque hotels erected at the turn of the century: parpen walls of monastic measurement, but the tongue and groove of the floor worn thin and cracked. A line of dust like wavering string, sand in the hourglass, fell onto Shiela's pillow. Lying still, alert, Shiela duplicated Louisa Hofmann almost exactly; though she, Shiela, lay motionless—legs, mouth and eyes all open, mouth dry, imagining, in drift, while Louisa attempted twists and a kick, the gown above her waist, and she tried shoving to force Hofmann's elbows back. But he was strong; he always was. And she was his. The lamps had been left on as if she was being violated before a crowd. All she could do was subside, and hiss as the dowels in the joints sang. For different reasons she and Shiela bit their bottom lips. Louisa twisted her face away; Shiela began shaking. 'Come on!' That was a Hofmann instruction. Shiela lying below almost caught the murmur. His hand had reached up to her breast as he shoved in, both now swollen beyond control. Louisa began crying.

Always crying.

'Shut up.' She heard Hofmann's voice.

Enjoy yourself.

With her right hand Shiela switched off the bed lamp, and a few lines of yellow seeped through from above and ruled her body, a grid. She touched her cheek.

'I'm bored,' came Louisa's voice clearly. 'It's you.'

'Don't tell me.'

Close to Shiela's head another voice whispered: 'Oy, where's your light? For Chrissake. Shiela, you there?'

She sat up.

'Hello. It's me.'

Shiela saw Hammersley, rectangular and tall His tie was undone.

'Should always lock the door, Shiel,' he said, giving his tweeds a hitch. 'You can get any perv coming in.' And he added, incongruous, 'How are you?'

Here Shiela had difficulty finding words. She glanced around the room.

Hammersly made himself at home now. 'It's like mine, exactly. Same mirror, same bathroom.'

'What must be the time?' Shiela whispered.

'Never mind,' he said. 'Live dangerously.' He sat on the edge of bed. 'I flew in yesterday.'

'I was about to fall asleep. What do you want? I heard at the table someone had seen you.'

'Following you, Shiel. My word of honour. All around the world.'

Shiela looked at him startled.

'You're all hot! Open your window.'

'I look like the Wreck of the Hesperas,' she managed, confused again. Her movements became clumsy, or they seemed to be, but her body was soft. She should quickly ask him something, make a comment, anything. She tried to think,

'Leave your glasses,' he said quietly. 'Not that you don't look good with them. In fact, I'd say the opposite. Definitely.'

Then what was he moving for? What was his idea? His face was near. He'd been drinking, and his suit smelt of cigarettes, but he spoke confidently, persistently, all the time watching her.

And before she knew it her pyjama top ('It's like a bloke's,' came his breath) had been slowly removed. She shuddered at the touch of his hands, rough hands, and caught her eyes and mouth in the mirror; but almost cried out as Hammersly with a shove removed her arms. 'So there we are . . .' his hoarse voice. Her breasts beckoned. In the mirror she could see his shoulder and the back of his head. She began breathing, almost heaving, through her mouth, when the door opened in her eye's corner, and the voice of Garry Atlas filled the room.

'Saw the light. Anybody home? *Hey* . . .'

Hammersly stood up; cleared his throat.

'We-elll. Bugger me.' Atlas acted all surprised. '*Excuse me!* I'll leave the room!'

But he turned from Hammersly to Shiela, slowly lifting his chin. Facing the wall Shiela appeared to be making almost imperceptible shaking movements of her head. So he began smiling at Hammersly, casual-like, 'Well you're a cunning bastard.'

And then his mouth moved without saying anything. He swayed, drunk.

'What happened,' Hammersly asked lighting a cigarette, 'with your bullfighters?'

'They were all yacking in some other lingo. They were pissed out of their minds on Tequila. Anyway, I wanted to see my old friend, Shiela here. I come up and what do I find? You here. So that's why you snuck off early? You're a shady bastard, aren't you? God's gift to bloody women.'

'Just a minute,' said Hammersly.

But Atlas turned to Shiela, swaying. 'Do you want him here?'

'Now just a minute,' said Hammersly. He put up his hand.

'Listen, you're not with us, you're not in our party. We're a group. Understand? You've got a bloody cheek.'

Atlas took a step forward.

'Shhh. Stop it!'

They turned to Shiela. Her head was still turned.

'Please go. Both of you.'

She went into the bathroom and closed the door.

Hammersly and Garry Atlas stood looking at each other.

'Mmmmm . . .' Hammersly looked concerned.

'You're in the shit, fella,' said Garry casually. 'Caught in the act. How's the missus back home? Kids alright? Better luck next time.'

'You're a prick. What'd you barge in for?'

Atlas jerked his head towards the bathroom. 'I know,

she's not bad. She's not as square as she looks. How did you go?'

Hammersly shrugged, being modest.

'Come on!'

In both side pockets he had a cold Heineken. 'Hey. I almost forgot!' He snapped them open, spraying the mirror. Positioning the chair he put his feet up. Hammersly sat on the bed. They raised their cans.

'Better luck next time.'

Atlas guffawed.

'You're a bastard.'

Garry let out a small belch. 'Shiel,' he twisted on the chair, 'would you like a snort? Come on out.'

'We won't bite,' Hammersly winked at Garry.

No answer.

'She will,' Garry predicted. 'Shiela's alright. She's just a bit shy.'

Travel broadens the mind. Along the passage Gwen Kaddok moved her lips as she dreamed of that large circular contraption of notches, hieroglyphics and saplings, invented nearby by some Mayan priest, which made it easy to recall events up to 300 years past (crop failures? marriages? plagues?); an insomniac in Room 219 sighed and closed Burton's *Anatomy of Melancholy*, dissatisfied.

The museum attracts the missionary or Ancient Mariner types, one-eyed with zeal. 'Yes but, but . . .' the guide interrupts, scarcely able to let another speaker finish. They hold on, won't let go: with moist eyes, the pincer grip of the thumb and fingers, or with peripatetic rhetoric. Some astonishingly do it by affecting *boredom*, thereby giving the object in question superior status. 'Formerly it adorned,' said he, with a bored look, 'the tomb of . . .'

'They become involved, obsessive. In the end they can never properly share it.'

Phillip North had long experience of them. He smiled at the very idea. 'Such harmless people are important to us.

We should be pleased.' At the zoo he and Sasha had followed the keeper with the stained bucket and leonine features—a burnt-out case—and watched another inside an aviary, barefooted and with sparrow's hands speaking non-stop to the eagles.

And you know there is the obese Irish curator of the Potato Museum in Reykjavik—the world authority; in C. that pan-chewing Bengali docent all day under the sun who simultaneously spits out sideways a stream of betel juice (Scandinavian tourists step back, 'Tuberculosis!') while pointing a lingam-tipped pole at details in the remarkable erotic sculptures; in the Vatican, what about that clattering cicerone with the permanent smile retailing amazing miracles? Dozens of them (cicerones with permanent smiles). Keepers of the facts, the inventory of civilization, the interesting flotsam manufactured and subsequently preserved.

In lower Quito was the MUSEO DE PIERNAS, and the only way to reach it was by foot. Stone bridges, cobbled alleyways, new districts had to be crossed—itself an experience. They arrived pleasantly puffed.

On the steps a group of twenty to thirty lazzaronis lounged in descending order, and abruptly stopped talking. Around them squatted a few shoe-shine boys who should have been at school, as Mrs Cathcart observed, and began banging their brushes, rattling tins (Kiwi polish, Export Quality), pointing to the group's feet, '*Zapatos sucios!*'

It must have sounded an alarm, for the museum director came bursting through the swing doors, a short man on mahogany crutches, shouting in Italian, switching to Spanish: both sufficiently theatrical. He had one leg missing. Significantly, his remaining tan shoe was highly polished. The empty trouser hung like those deflated windsocks at country aerodromes, partially raised here above the knee with safety pins, exposing clear daylight.

But his crutches; they had seen nothing like these on their travels. The instinct was to comment, show a keen interest. After all, this was a Museum of Legs: it licensed them, so to speak. As the man stood there Doug Cathcart squatted down, wife looking over his shoulder, and tapped with his knuckles the left side crutch.

'Very interesting,' he said, ponderous, slightly nasal. He looked up at the others. 'Take a good look at this.'

He was recommending it.

Both crutches were carved in the manner of one of Quito's baroque cloisters, the dark wood twisted with myths and figures, expounding the doctrines of Catholicism. A neat, nay natty man, the director. Little fella, he wore a ballooning red shirt.

So keen and natural was he that the Australians adopted their relaxed, normal manner. They stood around as if they had met years before. And by casually avoiding his face they announced to him their acceptance.

'Ag-ost-in-elli,' he pronounced his name. And beamed at every one of them.

'We have them living next door,' Mrs C. stepped back: this one had been eating garlic too.

'What is an Italian doing here running a museum?' Gerald asked.

The Italian had an electric-bell laugh.

'*Running a museum?*' He waved a crutch. 'You can be funny! Ha, ha!' He had to stop and wipe his eyes. 'I must remember that. The director of the Museo de Piernas is . . . *Scusi*. Why me? you ask. It is because of the shape of my country, Italy, and think of our history of tight trousers. Also, I was a Roman Catholic. I was a natural.'

On the steps Louisa looked pale and red-eyed, and seemed to take an excessive interest; beside her, standing in a kind of alliance, Shiela concentrated more than usual, and glanced occasionally in Atlas' direction. Squatting, Kaddok was busy trying to focus on the crutches. Everyone found the Italian interesting. The man's energy gave the impression of unbounded optimism.

Hofmann, his hands in his pockets, nodded: 'What about your other leg there?'

'On my own initiative,' said the director glancing at the space, 'I had it removed. To draw attention to the contents of the museum. It was well worth it.'

'He's pulling our leg!' Garry whispered.

Only Louisa turned and tried to smile.

As they watched, the Italian propelled himself up the steps—remarkably agile. He turned. 'Without question, ladies and gentlemen, this is the most significant museum you'll ever see—and I mean anywhere. *Meraviglioso*! You ask, why a Leg Museo? Why so significant? Because,' out of habit he panned their faces, eyes bulging, 'because your leg is fundamental. Not only to tourism. It is at the heart of all that is human. The quintessence!'

Raising a point of order Gerald cleared his throat. But Agostinelli had turned to usher them through, ladies first.

'Fundamental,' he kept on inside, 'was that glorious moment when *homo sapiens* first straightened his legs, lifted his face from the earth, separating himself from the apes and monkeys. The leg is the key to our evolution. We know now that man stands upright'—the Italian's voice rose in sympathy, cracking at falsetto—'in order to speak his thoughts, to propel words. Think of that. The straightened leg has promoted language, which is the supreme faculty of man! You see? You see? We never forget this. When man worships, the knee is bent—we return to earth. Such is our acknowledgement. The homage role of the knee before gods and kings . . . occasionally women. Custom dictates that we touch and kiss feet. Shoes are removed in mosques and other temples. Christ *walked* on water. He didn't crawl on water . . .'

Switching to etymology: the great word 'knew' came originally from 'knee'. But he threw that in as an aside (a footnote), in a fading voice. Only those in front—the Hofmanns, Gerald Whitehead, Borelli—caught the gist of it.

Silence. Some frowning among them; and pursing of the lips.

They passed wax and plaster casts of legs in genuflexion, a Bourdon etching speckled with rust, 'The Child Jesus Treading Sin Underfoot.' On the wall and under glass were famous examples of Achilles' Heels.

The Italian hobbled along. 'The foot has twenty-six

bones, thirty-three joints. An amazing engineering feat, ahem, by any standards.'

Unusual for a guide, he went ahead ignoring individual exhibits. Positioned on either side the items seemed like the small towns and things which support the broad path of history. He had studied the entire subject. He knew it backwards.

'Human locomotion,' he was saying, almost talking to himself, 'left-right, one leg before the other. Man keeps going—forward! We are brave. It is all we have. Understand. History is nothing if not a record of man's movements. Crucial messages were once delivered by runners. Wars were fought on foot, and always will be. The coward runs. Migrations! Refugees! Much has been written lately on the stirrup's influence on history. What about the invention of the horse-shoe nail?'

A pause to let that sink in.

They had just passed a bronze replica of Rodin's masterpiece, 'The Walking Man', and someone pressed a button on a counter and a life-size leg constructed by a Quito engineer of plastics suddenly came to life on a table, walking backwards and forwards, whirring, creaking, illustrating the miracle of tendons, muscle and fetlock. As they watched, it stopped. Then it began tapping to a 78 disc,

> Gee, but it's great after bein' out late,
> Walkin' my baby back . . .

Agostinelli, their guide, had turned the corner, and they could hear him pontificating (which went so well with 'Agostinelli') about the stirrup in history. Invented in the eighth century it revolutionized the early horse wars. Men could shoot from the saddle. It literally altered the map of Europe, of Asia. And doesn't the leg fit into the stirrup?

Resting on his crutches he lit a cigarette and kept it in his mouth squinting, like a Frenchman.

On a surgeon's table: an amputation kit, and a surgical saw used in the First World War. A vivid description of gangrene. Various jodhpurs, puttees and khaki trousers were tacked on the wall.

'Take the Industrial Revolution! It could not have occurred without the full co-operation of thousands of legs. Those pale thin legs of the . . . downtrodden.'

Borelli nodded: they understood each together. He nodded at Borelli's walking stick.

Splints and artificial limbs keep a man going: chiefly of varnished wood, though the trend these days is to plastic and aluminium—so a small sign with many spelling errors noted. A fine example of an antique peg-leg was found to be, when they bent down, riddled with white ants. They were like maggots. Alongside it a Chinese model carved in pure ivory had millions of human hairs glued to its calf, for authenticity's sake. And the guide, still going on about the storming of the Winter Palace and the tommies wading into the sea at Dunkirk, reached out and stubbed his cigarette into a large circular ashtray which happened to be an elephant's ankle. Civilization and its contents.

'Any questions at this juncture? *Mi lasci passare, per piacere.*'

For they were crowding around barrels of insuetude shoes, the girls holding up greaves and clogs, delicately embroidered slippers, and exclaiming at the sabots from Normandy, boots and bootees (and jackboots), the ballroom pumps and moist galoshes, rope sandals, stilettoes, the inevitable blue thongs (one missing), Wellingtons and moccasins, English plimsols, a pair of Viet Cong sandals crafted from a Michelin tyre. Most were down at the heel and dusty, stained with sweat inside.

Agostinelli enjoyed their keen interest. There were comments and grimaces the way determined bargain hunters crowd the opening of a store's annual Fire Sale. When Borelli went up and asked about Italy, Agostinelli only nodded, his eyes on the others.

'The History of Footwear has been inserted at this point to provide light relief. It always works. These are cast-offs from the Bally Shoe Museum, in Switzerland. Do you know it?'

Borelli shook his head. 'We haven't been to Switzerland.'

'The first measurements of distance were naturally made by the legs,' the monopede remembered his job. 'There is a universal harmony. When we run each step is about equal to our height.'

They trailed after him again, glancing to the left and right, as Agostinelli talked with his red back to them: difficult to get a word in edgeways. Fully warmed to the subject now he managed sometimes to fling an arm out as he heaved on the crutches, his tenor's voice bouncing off the ceiling, walls and exhibits and back to them.

Arranged in a glass cabinet were examples of elastic garters and stockings through the ages. A misty photograph showed a man's hand on a woman's slender knee; Sasha couldn't help laughing.

'Madame,' Agostinelli came tripping back, 'permit me to be frank. Allow me to point out the obvious. Above the knee, your legs spread out and meet at the top—pointing to what?' His voice had gone hoarse. He stared at Sasha. 'Your legs,' he persisted, gently, 'point upwards to what?' Glancing at Violet, Sasha reddened; North sauntered over to the collection of walking sticks. 'Straight up,' the Italian yelled, 'to the most mysterious sacred centre of the body, your essence! To the centre of life itself. That is why we—I speak not only of myself—are drawn to a woman's legs. We know what awaits at the top. *Scusi* . . .' He bent down. 'Ah, you have possibly the finest ankles I have encountered. They are museum quality.'

'What's he on about?' Hofmann asked. He couldn't hear at the back.

Sasha was looking around for North, but he was discussing with Gerald the selection of table legs, mainly South American. Violet told her, 'You've got a great future. These Italians; but he is a world authority.'

'He's made good points,' said Borelli. 'I think he's pretty good, don't you think?'

He had asked Shiela, but she could only blink.

Nearby, Louisa said, 'Oh, he makes it sound mechanical.

He's very theoretical. It's not as simple. I don't believe anything is,' she added.

'For a man on crutches,' Borelli admitted, 'he certainly is agile.'

'I think so, yes.' said Shiela suddenly.

Agostinelli had sketched the leg's importance in evolution, in religion, in art. Wall posters showed how it figured in axioms and wise slogans handed down over the ages.

> BEST LEG FORWARD
> ONE STEP AHEAD
> 'Feet of clay!'
> YOU'RE PULLING MY LEG!
> I CAN'T STAND IT

Such evidence supported Agostinelli's overall view. Returning to history he switched from orthopaedics to metaphysics, to hold their interest.

'Which country,' he turned to them, 'do you come from?'

'Ah!' said he respectfully. 'A nation of travellers. You've never been afraid of using your legs. I understand Australian tourists are all over the globe. What are the figures? You must rank with the Americans and the Japanese. Why is this? Your country looks beautiful!'

'Too right it is,' said Doug.

But Agostinelli now mentioned the 'feats' of the early explorers, the boy scouts who trudged across the interior waste, in the end leaving a dying horse or camels. 'On foot, on foot. One leg following the next. That is how your continent was opened up. From South to North, East to West. The despair!'

He knew more about the early explorers than they.

As well as the megacephalic Burke and skinny Wills, and Eyre, Leichhardt, Voss, he broadened his canvas with other noteworthies, Richard Burton and Speke; and of course Polo from Venice; naturally he emphasized South America first with Cortez, then Col. Fawcett, and Humboldt, and Charles Darwin; and then those loyal waders who struggled towards the North and South Poles on wicker snow shoes. Wasn't Mount Everest conquered on foot? These were some of the glorious episodes of man. It gave the colour and tragedy to maps.

Speaking of endurance, of pushing on further: several in the party were standing on one leg or resting against pillars. Expressions were distant; Sasha banged her buttocks with her handbag. At least Borelli had a walking stick. He could lean on it. In an informal aside Agostinelli mentioned a cousin living in the outback at Alice Springs for *dodici* years running the Sand Museum, which sparked some of them up. No one had heard of it.

A photograph of a leg said to be the hairiest in the Southern Hemisphere. Famous legs standing to attention. The co-ordinated kick of a line of can-can girls. Interesting X-rays revealing hairline fractures and the infrastructure of talipes.

'Do you get many visitors here?' Garry asked casually.

The director appeared not to hear. Garry remained bent over a showcase devoted to 'Athlete's Foot (*tinea inter-digitalis!*) examples of.' Someone had scratched into the glass with a diamond pencil: HERB ELIOT RON CLARKE WALTER LINDRUM (AUST.) WORLD RECORD BREAKERS. It was extremely effective. Like the subtitles at the beginning of films it was impossible to see the water skis, the medley of soiled basketball shoes and football boots, the cricketer's pads, Polaroid shots of twisted ankles, without registering the names of those athletes and recalling their feats. Straightening up, Garry tugged his ear lobe and looked around. The rest of the museum seemed empty. He turned to show Shiela but decided not to. She was listening earnestly to Phillip North.

Legs of sprinters leaving the blocks; a jockey's calf alongside that of a horse: ha-ha.

The cantilevered action of the mahogony crutches had driven Agostinelli ahead and his high voice from behind a corner caused here and there a glance, a smirk. It had been his style all along. Again he returned to the primordial function of man's legs: we keep going, one leg following the other, day after day, don't stop. They support the weight of the body. Legs tire before the arms. 'Feel them now,' he urged unnecessarily. Inherent here is the persistence of man: the inbuilt momentum. In the end it is all we have. Our brittle legs.

A blankness had washed the facial expressions; it had ironed their movements; and the brows of the older ones became corrugated as they felt the dull weight on their legs. Even North who had spent much of his life scrambling over rocks felt the strain. Interestingly, it made some—Mrs Cathcart, Violet and Gerald Whitehead—gradually bad-tempered. There appeared to be a subtle gradient here, and the floorboards felt as hard as iron. When they stopped and stood patiently the aching became a hunger, a soaking acidity. Certainly they were aware of themselves, of their bodies' perimeters in weight, endurance and such. It was exactly as Agostinelli had said. They continued, one leg trailing the other, out of habit.

It was all very well for him: he had his blessed crutches.

Waiting for the stragglers—the Cathcarts, Borelli and Violet Hopper—the upholstered leather shoulders enveloped his armpits. Most of them would have given anything then for a pair of crutches; and yet as museums went this was by no means a large one. The director seemed to be aware of their tiredness. He gave them a long encouraging smile. 'I have a headache coming on', Violet told him.

'A lot of these museums become the same,' Gerald was saying, complaining.

'We are almost there, almost there. Ladies and gentlemen, please observe here this interesting graphic case.' For the first time he pointed to one of the exhibits. They'd been standing beside it, and perhaps out of tiredness, had taken little notice. On the podium stood a life-size figure in a simple black dress, one arm outstretched like a window mannequin. They noticed then the face perspired under the spotlight, and an eyelid moved as a moth flew near. The woman—the figure—frowned slightly. She had grey hair pulled into a bun, a thin face. The director stepped in front of them.

He pointed to her legs.

Varicose veins.

Sounds of surprise and sympathy broke out as if their tongues had slipped sucking jubes. They shook their heads and stepped back for others to see.

These veins were like the roots of banyan trees which become part of stone walls and wrap around the trunks of other trees. It seemed as if her bulging tired soul was about to burst out from her limbs and leak.

'What is your name, *señorita*?' he asked for their benefit, and looked down at the floor.

A toneless voice: 'Freda.'

As she spoke Kaddok who had fitted a flash took several pictures. There was some shuffling in the group at this, but Freda didn't seem to mind.

'Freda, how old are you?'

She told them.

'How long have you been on your feet, as a waitress?'

'*Treinta siete años.*'

'In Mexico City,' he explained to them.

They looked at her legs again.

'The remarkable thing is,' he said in a low voice, 'is that these are not just any old varicose veins.' He ran his hands over them. 'You are perhaps not familiar with the region, but these duplicate the main rivers of Mexico. Below the knee there'—he pointed with his finger—'is the entire network of the western reaches of the Rio Saldo.' Agostinelli began moving away. 'It is quite a find. Thank you, Freda. A real discovery. I don't quite know what to make of it yet.'

It didn't make much sense to any one of them, either. The legs were a blank statement, that was all.

Still it seemed necessary for some to declare a position. 'I wouldn't like to be in her sh—' But it sounded wrong.

Louisa stayed behind and looked up at the waitress's face. 'The poor thing.'

She turned to Borelli. Such a sight made her pensive, heavily so.

'In a street or at a bus stop we probably wouldn't notice,' he said. 'It's because she's here.'

But Mrs Cathcart respected Louisa's gaze. She would

have nodded but Louisa wouldn't have seen, so she assumed her grim determined expression. Things at least were not like this at home. The gnarled legs remained with them for a long time.

Trust Violet—to break the ice.

'My legs are killing me. Are we through?'

Only Garry gave a snort, appreciating Violet.

As usual, as if they were at the end of a long journey, they began sparking up and talking again, although they were tired. There were wisecracks: a sign of relief and expectation.

The director remained the same, lecturing them over his shoulder. He turned a corner.

'Do you still think he's so interesting?' Louisa asked Borelli. She touched his arm. 'My, you look pale. Are you alright?'

She looked concerned. Louisa: so oval, smooth and blue.

'It's homesickness,' he smiled weakly. 'The subsequent melancholy produces paleness. I find it is often mistaken for a disease. Gum trees and heat and an expanse of beach give me back the required colour. All this is too technical and gan-green.' He waved his walking stick: illustrations of artiodactyle freaks and plaster casts missed by the others.

'Don't be silly. What's the matter?'

Borelli leaned forward. He seemed to be in pain.

'Louisa, you're very nice.'

He touched her cheek.

Instead, Louisa shook her head. Her breasts moved.

'Why do you need that stick?'

She asked without looking down. The angle of his shoulder showed how he leaned on it now. In his faded jacket he could have been a Vietnam veteran convalescing on a verandah. He was the age.

'It's an affectation. I need sympathy from people, from women especially—like yourself—otherwise I'd come to a grinding halt. True.'

She looked away.

'You won't tell me.'

'Listen . . .'

'I don't want anything to happen.'

'Listen, everything I say is stupid. Don't take much notice of what I say. And it's the effect of this place, all these legs—they're parts of ourselves. It has made me consider things. But I think you're more interesting, really much more than all this. Come along.'

As Louisa stared at him the others stood before a map of the world showing the different 'legs of an air journey' and Gerald pointed to their next destination, north-east. 'Hooray,' cried Violet. Although tired they smiled. A few turned when Louisa and Borelli arrived and noticed how the pair looked thoughtful but perplexed; but it was more their obliviousness which struck Sasha and Shiela, and they openly gazed. They liked Lousia.

Hofmann had wandered ahead, the wittol, joined by Cathcart, the two not exchanging a word: Hofmann slender and straight, the other stubby and bow-legged. They glanced at a small library devoted to Museum Fatigue.

'Hang on,' Doug suddenly said, 'this is a bit rugged. I don't know about this.'

What were these in the tall preserving jars? Pale limbs suspended in a cloudy fluid. About twenty in all; each one labelled. All within sight of the front doors and daylight.

The director faced them.

He showed no interest in the ballerina's leg in its soggy shoe—such elegant muscles; leg of Kentucky coal-miner— mauve scarred and black-headed; the German racing driver's braking foot—donated by his widow.

There were more. (No two legs are the same.) A Catholic's left leg and an obese woman's of elephantiasis proportions. One labelled 'Jarred Leg' confused them— because all the legs were 'jarred'—until the small print explained it was taken from a parachutist. The real growth of museums occurred after the invention of glass.

Agostinelli had his arm resting on the last jars. Separated but positioned close together they invited comparison. The first was a Commercial Traveller's limb (tragic, alabaster); alongside it an Expatriate's Leg—distinctly fleshy and hairless; Exiled Leg was similar but careful inspection showed it to be a shade paler, thinner; and finally to summarize the entire museum, LEG OF TOURIST (ENG.). It was thin, boney and experienced. It was thick-skinned. It had corns. It was theirs but it could have belonged to an old man.

Bending down Hofmann read out the former owner's name: 'Lambe'!

At that Garry laughed and turned around.

'Recent donations,' the director said, staring briefly at Violet's ankles. Clearly this was the finale. Framed by the doorway his dark head was silhouetted inevitably against a volcano. What meaning would he attach to the tourist's leg? What angle?

'This Lambe,' Doug broke the spell. 'Still alive?'

'Tourists fly away, always.'

This led in nicely (but who was Lambe?).

Of all legs, the tourist's is the most interesting; by far. He, Agostinelli, oughta know. Not only *his* museum lived off them; *all* museums do. The draped legs bring in the bodies and the minds, of all shapes and sizes, all colours (smiles). The traveller's inquisitive—acquisitive?—drive is transmitted as a kind of half-running from one place to the next, relying largely on the legs. Compare: an everyday working leg with that of the tourist. Discuss. Aren't they one, yet not the same? What? Well, one comes before the other and then makes the other possible. Notice how a recently hard-working leg is unable to slow down, possesses a kind of inbuilt momentum, compelled by that inner force to march and fill in the minutes, accumulating, to do something—or rather, the sense of doing something. Some sense of achievement is apparently essential. Compare: the tourist with the sedentary holiday-maker. Different legs of.

What is a tourist?

By then a polite but distinct restlessness showed. Certain heads, especially those with a known aversion to speculations, swivelled more to the open door where clarity, rock solidarity, awaited them. The Italian had anticipated this. It was all to do (as was everything here) with legs.

Consider, he went on, the pressure. Feel it. More than

most the tourist is made aware of his limits, not only in mileage terms, but the limits of comprehension and tolerance. Tired? There you are, you see. It was a measure of something. And yet you don't stop. The tourist keeps going, one leg after the other, or stands waiting, queued. You embody the Human Condition. Stop. Keep going. Searching. For what? It is always a grand sight. You deserve medals.

Medals imply uniforms: trust a Latin.

Breathing heavily he pointed to Borelli leaning on his stick, and to Sasha, to still-dazed Louisa, Gerald, to Violet Hopper who had all assumed, without realizing, the monopede posture of African flamingoes, and held out his arms.

His short treatise on museum fatigue followed. Unlike most other major museums this one had been carefully modified not to reduce museum fatigue, but to increase it. To draw their thoughts down to their legs! Hidden gradients and featureless walls, monochrome colour and bare boards, had been carefully incorporated. It had taken him several years. The voice rose, exhorting: learn not only from the contents of museums and natural sceneries, but from your own two pins. They are you. They are a measure; have ways of speaking, even barking. Ha ha.

He laughed for a second.

'God bless!' he suddenly finished, dropping his arms over his crutches, the exhausted teacher.

Filing past they found they had a real affection for him. Bowing slightly, he shook their hands like the village curate farewelling his flock. They saw how his small head was moist from the sermonizing; perhaps that's why he bowed? They wouldn't forget. As they were leaving they realized they would never be returning.

And standing outside they were uncertain of direction. They stood for a second on the white steps, blinking.

The layabouts were still draped on either side, taking an interest, and the shoe-shine boys, although reduced in numbers, began banging their brushes, automatically. It was chilly.

Then Kaddok detached himself; but he couldn't have seen the perspective of the rooftops, the deeper shadows and the completely different pattern of the sparrows. Gwen watched, out of pride really, for he proceeded to hurry down backwards, unaided (one leg higher than the other, his legs and balancing arms almost forming a swastika side-on) to take their photograph: wide angle shot of squinters and handbag-holders which would reveal that patch of magenta behind them, Agostinelli, locking the doors.

'Well . . .' one of them offered, a bridging word.

What happened next?

The black-clothed swastika then turned towards the crowd on the steps and seemed to merge: the jumble of ponchoes, of taut emaciated faces, one fitted with a dusty bowler. Something wrong here. A flicker, an irritation. They rose to meet him—yanked up in unison by strings. Kaddok seemed to get tangled up. As Gwen stumbled towards him crying out Kaddok missed the spittle on his shoulders, sea-gull shaped, dripping, and all their arms. A brief look of surprise and he was multi-armed himself, cart-wheeling down the steps, one arm somehow always holding the camera.

He could have broken a leg.

Screaming, Gwen pushed back the men. The shoeshine boys began barracking, rattling their tins.

To the rest it had unfolded in a slow motion of disbelief. There was a gap. They had remained separated.

'That's nothing, when we were in South America . . .' they might say in years to come.

Shouting out Spanish words, Gerald took two steps at a time; wide steps which are tricky to run down. A little misunderstanding. *¡Basta! ¿Qué hay?* Gesticulating, appealing, he was joined by Garry Atlas and Borelli—Borelli, the interested.

Thrusting forward, Garry said something to the chief Indian.

'Shut up!' hissed Gerald, turning.

'Leave it to him,' said Borelli. 'Leave it to him.'

And Ken Hofmann sauntered down.

178

'This is a nasty place,' Violet commented, meaning Ecuador. 'He wasn't doing any harm.'

Nodding, nodding, Gerald listened to the sallow one in the front and turned to look back at Kaddock. He nodded again. He held up the palm of his hand and cocked his head: of course, of course. And again as if they were controlled by pulleys and wires the mob slowly subsided, back on the steps. 'What's eating them?' Garry demanded. Certain primitive peoples believe a camera paralyzes.

Bending over, Gwen kept dusting the photographer's coat, a form of visual loyalty, for he was still on all fours. The shoe-shine boys had begun laughing, the nasty little wretches: a dark window in one of Kaddok's eyes had shattered.

Getting to his feet he looked dazed. He had to be pointed in the right direction.

They heard him saying, 'As I fell I took shots of myself. Wait till you see them. They might well be unique in the history of photography.'

Oh yeah? Shiela had hidden her little Instamatic in her bag, as they all stepped down.

'They won't hurt us,' Doug reassured; how could they? 'I mean, we're only visitors.'

As Violet said again, 'You could feel it before. It's not a pleasant atmosphere. I don't think we're welcome.'

'I haven't felt sure about anything here,' she added.

There was group-nodding at that, natch. If this was South America it had been interesting but . . . no one could say it was exactly pleasant. A queerness pervaded, an edge. The arches; the formal geometry of the stone plazas; the impassive copper faces; unknown statues. It was so remote. The public clocks gave a different time. As for their friendly museum director: he'd shut the doors.

'We should go.'

'All walk slowly . . .'

Still breathing heavily Garry said, 'That bastard in front. Did you see him? If he took one more step I was going to poke him one.'

'Come on!'

Leon had lost his lens cap.

'I'd leave it,' North murmured to Gwen. 'There's no sense in staying; tell him.'

She took his elbow. She pulled. She almost had to drag him. First loyalty, now compensation. She said loudly, 'I should have thought these people would have liked their picture taken. They're not doing anything.'

They drifted away from the Museo and its plaza. Stubbornly, the façade was the last to go. When they turned it had suddenly gone, cut by a corner decorated with stately quoining. It would remain in the memory, a cavernous stain. It would grow larger and more deeply shadowed, it would be heavy and grey; yet strangely empty. Already it had saddened them. The procession could not go much faster. Limping badly Kaddok was supported first by Gwen, then by Garry while the others drifted on.

A city encircled by volcanoes, tall cones, and those cube houses tumbling down the slopes supplying an interesting analytical space and shape to the bowl. Ghost houses: a tremor either in the photography or the printing plates (Photogravure, Quito) had multiplied the images, including the steeples and belfries, the hands on the clock. Which part was real? Which edge? The many thousands of red roof tiles had multiplied three, four times, their blood-coloured ink seeping across the sky, spoiling the otherwise typical postcard blue—that perfectly clear, international over-blue. An arrow in biro pointing down to a roof in middle distance, and the words OUR HOTEL had found instead the Museo de Piernas.

> Hello All
> Having an interesting time here—2nd highest capital in the world—did you know?—shops—colourful blankets & people—lawns—Spanish is the spoken language—Catholics—do you know Spanish for *man*, boys?—you'd like the volcanoes!—quite an interesting party, I think I said—no word from you—anybody. Did you get my scarves?   S.

Mrs Cathcart also took the opportunity of writing postcards; sitting among their luggage stacked in the foyer there was little else to do. She scribbled the same fractured message to one and all. Having a good time, etc. Climatic conditions. Summary of cleanliness as related to skin pigment of the locals. Leaving today. At least these postcards would serve to pinpoint their location. The receiver could look at the picture on the front—the same as Shiela's—and try to imagine. Seated on a suit-case beside her, scarcely had Doug licked a stamp when another card was flung down ready; the two were like an economic unit, a cottage industry. In pale blue shorts and the knitted shirt with his sunglasses hooked over the pocket, Doug liked to be occupied.

The others ambled around; the men, hands in their pockets, testing at random the edges of cases and the carpet pattern with their shoes. It hardly mattered if the bus was running late. Wearing a demilune brooch Louisa struck a gay pose; her eyes and head moved like a child's. While Hofmann preferred to drift, allowing the residue of the shuttered-up alien place to recede, she chattered about this and that, not even expecting an answer. Strange how seemingly trivial images— section of a peeling wall, the pores of a stranger's nose—persisted in challenging the most obvious landmarks.

Violet, now she—

Violet smoked cigarettes not so much from habit, but with aggression or realism. She wore large sunglasses and smelt of powder. It generally happened in a group: she found herself isolated, to one side. Sasha had dragged North and Gerald Whitehead over to a display set up along the side wall. Approximately thirty one-litre jars of water had been placed on a long shelf. Beginning clearer than gin the liquid gradually darkened until the final jar was a pale brown with a good inch of silt on the bottom. Interestingly, this was Amazon water collected at evenly spaced, consecutive intervals along its entire course. Although no more than ten yards long here the graduation of the jars graphically demonstrated the length, and even the steady speed of the almighty river. The freshly painted banner running the full length listed in several languages statistics and wild life, signed by the Amazon Tourist Board.

'But it could be any river,' was Gerald's complaint. 'I don't see the point.'

'You're never satisfied!' Sasha laughed; but so excited by their company and the prospect of movement again she hugged his arm, squashing her breast. And the trouble with Phillip North: if you showed him anything, he took too much of an interest. Hands clasped behind his back he was peering closely now at the last jar.

Watching them Violet became angry at her own contempt. She stood to one side, a sharp rock, dark.

'Did you see your lavatory this morning?' she demanded of Hofmann. He had been standing a few feet away, facing her.

He wandered all over her face, keeping her waiting, but couldn't penetrate her sunglasses.

He began half-smiling.

'You're a bastard,' she said.

She blew out cigarette smoke.

'I wasn't listening. What did you say?'

'This morning in our room,' returning to the subject, 'the lavatory was boiling. I wondered . . .'

Hofmann remained looking at her, his smile spreading. She turned away slightly.

Cupping both hands over his mouth and imitating an airport voice . . . that Esperanto of steadiness which rises at the end . . . Garry Atlas announced the arrival of their bus. No one laughed at him, whereas early in the trip they might have out of politeness or caution.

They each had to lift their own luggage out: all that leaning and bumping of knees, striving forward; and Gwen there solemnly holding the shrunken head.

The bus had a dashing cream wave painted down its side and shivered as it waited for them. At the same time it stood boiling—one of those minor Latin American paradoxes. The driver seemed anxious, his foot stamped the accelerator, and as they got going he looked over his shoulder at them, scratching his moustache with a finger.

They were chattering as the bus went through the narrow streets, glancing at the familiar sights as the dogs of Quito began barking. The sky had darkened. Dogs barking, skidding around and around in streets and the open spaces behind them and one crazy mutt ahead, in front of the bus. Rabid roosters were crowing. The small zoo was in a turmoil. The air became still; but obscured, hidden, by the moving bus, its windows open; and such a noisy loose engine. Something hit the roof, more than likely a by-product of speed. But was it rain or was it steam stroking the cracked windscreen? Birds, wild squadrons, were yanked across the sky. The animals know. Beyond the town sheep reportedly huddled in the corners of paddocks. These, and the birds and the mad dogs, couldn't be seen from the bus; no one, not even Kaddok looked behind. They had entered the poor part of town, misery, stench, and the driver surely was speeding. His engine and juggernaut back-draught seemed to pull a tottering balcony away from a wall, tilting and dropping bits; dust, smoke, masonry behind. Metal shutters on shops clattered down. Shutters on first and second floors swung open, hit and cracked. In the bus they nodded, made comments, expressing interest. The southern walls of the archbishop's palace had come down largely intact. And long lines of washing fell from nails, from hooks and poles. Cooking pots cracked; many unscathed would later explode at a touch. At least a dozen road maps filed behind the driver's sunvisor cascaded on his head. And now he had to stop, reverse and go back. A load of jars and plaster virgins had scattered on the street, off a truck apparently. The heavy street lights on wires were swinging. Bronze bells throughout the city were ringing, terrible toll, causing Violet to glance involuntarily at her watch. The tiny minute hand had fallen off. Such a noisy engine, so many vibrations. Other walls had fallen. There was smoke elsewhere, behind, everywhere, and small running figures among the dogs, a quick-silver effect, like the fast-receding scenery of the streets and signs, memory erased. A fissure split a major intersection, a rip in a postcard, like an error of fact, and already a carbineer there shining a torch down it. The sewerage pipes had opened like the bank vaults hadn't, revealing riches, darkening the gutters. What a stench. Say, a light pole describing an arc, before held at an angle by its violin wires. Burst water mains; rolling oranges and bowls. Look, group of Indian women crying. Rubble and dust and steam. Almost out of town, the row of shacks on the left collapsed, erased by time and speed, on the edge of vision, part of the general blurring of impressions. The South American racing driver had been arrested lapping the Plaza San Francisco in a friend's Pontiac, scattering beggars and chooks, collecting a wild dog. Shrunken heads rolled off shelves; many shelves tilted. A flattened street market was quite a carpet of colour: peppers, cracked melons still hovering and rolling. Man lying face down. A crack ran up a wall like a rat. And behind them a motor scooter slipped through a bridge, one less in the mind. The distant faces melted. The hotel and the shape of the main plaza and the hulk of the black Buick were among the last to go. There were premature births and deaths, smiles unknown to them. The city was blurred by speed, and receding. It was all collapse. A tidal wave in the Amazon swept through the jars, flooding the carpet. The bus pulled up and they were ushered into the plane, the calm of the cabin, of split seats, leaving Quito under a cloud, on time.

4

There are two hemispheres, a Greater and a Lesser. The one above of tall rectangles and glass, andromeda dazzle and the landmass; the other with its oceans, of heat and tangle, raw materials.

One is congested, the other sparse.

All things imaginable spread or screech to the south in a curve filling the emptiness, for better or for worse. The heads of antipodeans glance upwards (shielding their eyes): multicoloured wires, tightly bound, possess magnetic powers. Moths to flames? With its museums and plethora of laws and words the Centre of Gravity lies in the Northern or Upper Hemisphere. It preserves.

There are two hemispheres, Left and a Right. One has words and equations stored like insects, hemisphere of engines and Armstrongs, one step at a time. Its partner is a map of manias, of blurred phrases, rhythms, shape, praise the Lord. The line dividing is properly blurred. The Left hemisphere constructed the right-angle; the other knows the Golden Rectangle. There are three sides to every story.

Blink, blink.

The Right is responsible for the recognition of faces and flags.

Heck, to the majority the city New York was an immediate religious experience! Always a shade prosaic, Gerald Whitehead thought their dizziness might be induced by the towering rectangles. They'd spent the first day walking and had aching necks, for the glass surfaces appeared to lean in and the reflected clouds swirled, slid slowly across the surfaces, giving the illusion their legs were not properly on the ground. Until they were accustomed it was necessary to check their perpendicular positions, hastily.

'Whoops! Ha ha!' They suddenly clutched at each others' elbows.

Still limping, his souvenir from Ecuador, Kaddok bumped into a parking meter where it hurts.

Interesting how the left or logical hemisphere is responsible for jerking the right arm up in fits of emotionalism—nationalism's puppet.

They were walking around Wall Street eating ham sandwiches, Garry a Hot Dorg. He had his right arm raised, a German salute at something high. Chins raised and following comments they took up most of the footpath. 'Look at that. Fantastic!' he pointed. However, the pedestrians here were all running. Narrow side lines had been reserved for cripples or tired people, although these were virtually empty. Among the runners a dark-suited President could be seen sprinting from a lunch or heading for an appointment, and there were bankers and brokers, dark horses and operators, chartists, and the inevitable programmers trailed by assistants, and many middlemen and hired consultants all after a slice of the apple pie. Even the cannon-fodder—the mail boys, messengers, recently married clerks—were carried along, although theirs was a variety of jogging.

—'Move your ass!'
—'Outta the way!'

The group had to spill out almost into a culvert. Sure enough, as they looked on, a silver-haired cambist in a Hathaway and the essential cuff links tripped and fell on his dial, spilling his Parker 51 and snapshot of the family. When Sasha moved to help him, he pushed her away. 'Then piss off yourself!' she hissed. It's easy to join in.

A hectic day on Wall Street. They quite understood—being visitors—when a cop asked them to move on. Another party, Japanese, was waiting.

The white clouds above were slotted into a narrow gap of blue and were triangular, surprisingly straight-edged, mysteriously erased at intervals like the revisions on a commodities graph. Framed by the tops of buildings the sky-scape was signed lower right 'Steinway' (advertisement for grand pianos). Elsewhere a perpetually rolling news flash consuming God knows how many watts demanded FREE ENTERPRISE! Yes, the nation's largest aircraft carrier had been seized by some tin-pot country, Asian, communist-ruled. 'Fantastic . . .' Garry craned, as a hand lifted his wallet.

And over all was the rattle of jackhammers. These alone managed to surpass the combined brouhaha of the teleprinters, the ticker-tape machines, the whirring photocopying machines, the banging carriages of thousands of electric typewriters. New York: aptly titled. Like that ship of the Argonauts each part was gradually changed, so that the citizens constantly had a new city without having to change its name or idea. Single rectangles or entire precincts were coming down. The materials of the city were light for this reason. Small museums at intersections showed how the neighbourhood once looked.

It was exhilarating. They felt at home, and yet it wasn't home. Since Ecuador, Gerald had again retreated to the background and Garry, Doug Cathcart and Hofmann entered the foreground.

'Howdy!' Doug stepped in front of a man, easy. 'We're looking for the Empire State Building.'

It was something he had always wanted to see.

'Can't help yerz. I'm from Australia.'

'Hey!' Doug cried out. So were they! There's a coincidence for you. But the man had kept walking and had already disappeared. He had sandy hair and a tanned neck.

'Perhaps he works for the UN?' Kaddok suggested.

The next man squeezed his eyes which were small anyway and looked around, and thought the Empire State had been pulled down—'Hadn't it?'—adding anyway he came from Melbourne. The city was full of Australians, including a complete archery team. There were exporters with heavy cuff-links and bulging fountain pens, the newspaper execs, diplomats—yes, and artists from Sydney trying to break into Abstract Expressionism, and a blackfellow out to licence the US manufacture and distribution of bullroarers and returning boomerangs. Only the other week the Prime Minister and his party had taken a suite at the Waldorf.

'Two bob,' Garry whispered to blinking Shiela, 'he's here.'

'Who? I beg—'

'Tall, dark and handsome. That drunk—you know who I mean. I'm kidding, Shiela. I'm kidding. He's alright.'

Her eyes had widened and she'd bitten her lip.

While the Cathcarts kept searching for an American, and met two ladies from Largs Bay, South Australia, Kaddok spoke up. The Empire State Building was *not* the tallest building in the world. It was some other new building. He mentioned the exact measurements. They nodded but it didn't matter; they still wanted to see the Empire State. As Kaddok spoke—dark glasses, dark suit—generous Americans dropped cents into his explaining outstretched hand.

In the Statue of Liberty twelve people can stand inside the torch held high in the right hand. First, climb the steps inside the radial artery. The arm is forty-two feet high. The vital statistics were reeled off by L. K.: a man could put both head and possibly shoulders inside her nostrils. The nose (Grecian) is five feet long. The distance between the eyes is three feet thereabouts, imagine that. She must have the world's biggest unsmiling mouth: a yard across. Ken Hofmann could give details about her teeth. No sizes are given for the breasts beneath the academic folds, but work it out. She'd sure need a *Büstenhalter*. Imagine the size of her—. In all, she weighed four hundred and fifty thousand pounds. The copper was in three hundred sections. 'That is worth a fortune today,' said Hofmann, thinking of the London Metal Exchange. From sandals to tip of the flame a hundred and fifty-two feet. A folly, and dull.

Only twelve could fit in the torch.

'It's alright,' said Violet. 'I'll stay here.' She had her arms folded. 'If I go another step higher I'll be sick.'

'Vi-olet!' Sasha laughed; because she was having a ball.

They were standing in the hollow forehead. As they moved up into the arm Violet rested her thin elbow on the ledge, their footsteps and chatter echoed behind her, dying away. The emptiness then became larger, a state of mind. There was the dappled deep sea far below and on it a red tanker; Manhattan rising from the water and mist, more a cluster of distant tombstones.

She heard or felt a movement behind her. As Violet turned, the hand already touched her waist; such a knowing hand.

'I thought I'd study the view,' Hofmann gazed past her. 'I may have missed something.'

'That'll be the day.'

'Well, what have you seen?'

'That's a boat. That's New York. Those there are seagulls.'

Looking past her Hofmann smiled. 'I see.'

Around her waist the grip tightened.

'They look like molars, those skyscrapers. Don't you think?'

Violet hunted for her cigarettes, as she did in these situations.

'I keep forgetting. You're the dentist.'

And she laughed.

She twisted away but the hand on the arm held. It pulled her in.

'Shouldn't you be upstairs,' said Violet flippantly, 'with your little woman?'

Hofmann gave no answer. Skidding past once, his mouth found hers. He pressed hard. She, against the parapet, cracked: her willowy back. His other hand felt its way along slowly, time and space were allowed, and found her loose breast; and a thick mist wreathed the city.

'You're taking liberties—' Violet joked from the back of her throat.

Now why does she—? Somehow flippancy can turn a man right off.

But after glancing over his shoulder Hofmann pressed on,

a kind of burrowing. He squeezed, flesh against flesh, too hard. She cried out.

'What?'

'It's alright,' she muttered. His knee pushed against her legs, invited; her legs parted. The Liberian oil tanker passed out of sight.

Now what: Hofmann whispered words, directed at her, there was no one else, obscenities, curses.

Well, Violet had tight lips, the tight surface.

She shoved him back, and for a second he kept blinking. Several times he ran his tongue over his teeth. It didn't suit the dentist, then.

'Enough,' she said, 'don't get carried away.'

She watched him.

'Run along upstairs,' she said again, 'to your little woman. She must be waiting.'

Her painted nails, her mocking sunglasses matched.

Staring at her Hofmann tugged his lapels, as if they controlled his facial muscles.

'They should be down,' he agreed, distant.

'A man of very few words,' Violet commented. 'Well, at least that's something.'

She gave a short laugh; Violet could even be hard on herself.

Hofmann's lips returned to thin and firm, though still without colour, and his face to cardboard.

Watching her casually now Hofmann smiled slightly.

'You assume too much,' she said, now defensive and unsteady. 'You're not so smart.' She began poking around for cigarettes. It looked wretched.

'In some things I'm not far out,' smiled Hofmann.

'Listen to him.'

But he was right. Violet found a cigarette, unhappily, as if he wasn't there. And when she looked across at Manhattan rising, and the struggles there (all those young actresses), it was made worse. For the first time Violet began smiling. She was almost crying.

But then he was looking down, elbows on the parapet. She reached out and touched his arm.

The others were returning: travellers descending stair-case. They were about to spill into the wide observation platform.

'It's what I've been saying,' Garry reverberated, 'a woman's head is completely empty. Nothing's there. We've just seen it with our bare eyes.'

'Ha! Hear that,' said Louisa.

'I'll clock him one where it hurts,' Sasha called out. 'You're no Rhodes scholar yourself.'

'What are you laughing at?' She peered at North from dark into sudden natural light; a tricky aperture problem for Kaddok.

But she pointed to Violet and Ken Hofmann: silhouetted against the sky, his arm outstretched lighting yet another cigarette. Both were so neatly attired; they were so New York.

'What was it again that made you come on this trip?' she had asked.

To Hofmann, lighting the cigarette was sufficient answer. It implied casualness.

Sasha held North's elbow. 'Now isn't that a lovely shot? They're like that cigarette commercial. What is it?'

'I don't have television,' he had to remind her; but obediently gazed at the pair.

'Stuyvesants,' Gwen offered.

'Right.'

Internation-al
passport . . .
to smoking pleash-ah!

'Violet starred in one of those commercials,' Sasha confided. 'Did you know that.'

'Did you all have a lovely time?' Violet turned. 'What was the view?'

Gerald was laughing. His face went wider with horizontal creases yet his head somehow bounced up and down; an odd laugh. 'Someone's written up there, GO HOME AUSSIES. That's a turn up.'

'I never thought I'd see that,' Doug frowned.

'It's somehow all senseless this,' Borelli murmured to Louisa. He had turned from looking down at the sea and Manhattan. 'We're doing something odd. Don't you feel it? Going to places like this, simply in order to . . .'

A feeling of futility: there at a great height, scrambling up and down inside a copper head. The sea was like a dirty mirror. But never one to remain despondent Borelli showed by his expression he had thought of something else.

'Next thrill!' Sasha cried out. She nudged Violet.

And Louisa turned to Borelli.

The float-bowl, its arm and point of pivot, the two valves, inlet-outlet, and the three or four split pins (mild steel) make up the efficient operation of the cistern. Include the length of chain and the wire lacing it to the external lever; these generally have a smooth penis-shaped wooden handle or a metal bracelet. Contemporary cisterns—now properly called water-closets—have the chrome-plated plunger which slides in a cylinder, an aesthetic breakthrough. When flushing, the floor of the cistern is opened, releasing a draught of water. The float (ball) then tilts in the void and so opens the valve, allowing fresh water to refill. Rising with the water, the float returns gradually to the horizontal where finally it turns the water off: from gush to bubble/hiss, faint high whistle, silence. The cistern is then ready to perform again. Only about the size of a grapefruit the floats were originally stamped out of discoloured copper—designed to last forever. But there have been many cases, especially lately, of hotels chiefly in Hungary, in Latin America and the Low Countries, and in the higher street numbers of Manhattan, where the *copper has punctured*. Summoned often in the dead of night the manager can only demonstrate a manual method of refilling, enough to get by. Stand on the seat; lift the cistern lid; raise the copper ball, reproducing the familiar gushing sound, until it is horizontal. In Southern Italy and certain cities of Russia other 'managers' have been known to arrive with a plastic pail of water and leave it at that. In under-developed countries with a large tourist inflow, chains have been known to come away in the hand. Scores of wooden and plastic lavatory seats crack under the almost hourly pressure. Even in some recently built hotels the push-buttons jam. Constant use wears the cylinder. The valves too become worn. They stick. After a day of wandering the bazaars and the endless parquetry of museums it is irritating to return to a leaking or 'whispering' cistern. The manager is called. And how many of the slick so-called 'low-boy' cisterns of plastic are spotted with cigarette burns, the colour of human ordure itself? The efficiency of the lavatory may not be affected, certainly it is not sufficient reason to call the manager, but the burns are an eyesore, a sign of traffic, the odour of statistics, like hairpins left in a drawer or the piece of smooth cuttlefish soap found in the shower recess.

Some of the picturesque countries of white stones and peasants in black have upwards of twelve million tourists per annum. Upwards—in other words—twenty-four million hands and heels of shoes scuffing the corridors; twelve million bowel movements, regular and irregular, to be catered for. The assortment of valves, copper floats and make-shift chains, the seats and the rusted but crucial internal split-pins take a hammering, night and day, no respite, not to mention the loading on the sewerage system, almost beyond the calculated diameter of the underground pipes. And where does all the muck—the weight and mass of it—go?

Crimson flowers in the carpets of foyers and stairs are trampled; cathedral steps worn down in the middle; bannisters are rubbed smooth, honed, eventually loosened from the walls: twelve million sliding hands, many with gold and sapphire rings. And next year there are always expected to be more. The sub-contractors in these centres make a killing more than usual, testing the cables holding lifts. Regularly replaced are the diving boards above pools, the backs of dining-room chairs, pillows and mattress (kneaded by many interlocking smooth bodies, holidaying), the ballpoints of desk clerks—thousands of them—and telephone cords frayed by idle fingers. The languid arms wear out tablecloths, and on the vertical façade of the reception counter a single season of North American, German and New Zealand knees can wear away the varnish in the shape of a heart. Requiring constant adjustment, regular replacement, is that pneumatic device with elbows which steadily closes the glass doors. Even mirrors used by so many tanned but anxious faces wear out.

Quires of paper, of oblong registration cards, are imported to handle the . . . the invasion. Tons of, or miles of; the same for biro fluid. Not to mention petroleum products (more foreign exchange), and the extra kilowatts of juice: additional underground shifts requested of distant coal-miners. And the tourist like anyone else has to eat. This can drive the price of food up. Twenty-three point four percent of the perishables trucked and railed into Manhattan is consumed by them; said to be more like 80% in that other island, Venice.

'God knows—I mean, really—why we chose this hole,' was Gerald's comment; but he was distinctly unsympathetic to the jackhammers of the New World. Granite, Carrara marble, bronze and oak were his substances: permanence, like the residue left by religion and history—and in the Old World it's so much part of the whole, so visible. As he spoke the tapered shadow of a yellow jib came in from across the street, and across the carpet like a draughtsman's compass, swinging an iron ball. The desk clerks wore yellow hard-hats. The chairs and carpet had a fine coating of demolition dust. A confident travel agent several oceans away wasn't to know. In the last decade the hotel had enjoyed tremendous traffic, an old favourite for the package tour, the seminar and sales convention. The carpets and even the floorboards underneath were now badly worn, and the janitor and several of the white-collar staff were over there all shoving, trying to open one of the sliding windows. A black woman vacuumed a corner and as Mrs Cathcart watched the old heavy-duty Hoover gave up the ghost: a declining whine, almost-human sigh. In its heyday the lift used to be the fastest in the western world. It still had the brass plaque. Festooned now with fingerprinted mirrors and advertisements for bistros, Rotary International and a dozen nearby museums and hair salons it seemed to be held by ropes of rubber, took its time, tired, with coloured lights flashing when they shouldn't have. After walking or waiting all day naturally they were impatient. Doug for one got irritable if he went too long without his shower. They all wanted showers and to put their feet up. Already Hofmann flipped the pages of the latest *Time* as he entered his room, looking forward.

Each had an end wall of tinted glass and they could step over and look down and across at the landscape of verticals and thrust, capital's example, the sections here and there being replaced, as in a child's building game. A pearly light refracted through petro-chemicals softened the edges and imbued the pastel canyons with high mercantile drama and a sensation of even greater—if that were possible—opportunities. Such a sense of complications and graduations. The various ELECTRIC WORDS could be gazed at for hours. In Rooms 104 and 109—Shiela's and the Hofmann's—soap worn smooth into cuttlefish had been found in the basins . . . disconcerting . . . and Gerald Whitehead found strands of hair on his pillow.

In Borelli's room the tan tip of a Florsheim shoe protruded from under his bed. He stepped back: anything can happen in New York. Poking it with his stick he found it empty. He sat on the edge of the bed. Such a piece of flotsam could make him rueful. He turned it over. The shoe, that of an American male, fitted a tall heavy man leaning to his left. It was his right foot. Nationalism and shoe styles: the American male prefers the soles protruding around the perimeter giving the appearance or the illusion of flat-footed, well-meaning eagerness. Across the ocean the Englishman's brogue with its serrated tongue and extravagantly punched bindings is a subtle yet loud counter to the quiet English architecture, the greens, and subdued speech patterns. Shoe styles and nationalism: they fit. Americans who readily buy classic Burberry raincoats are reluctant to step into those alien brogues.

'My lavatory's kapput,' he said aloud. In the corridor he asked, 'Do you have water?'

'We're next door to you,' Louisa leaned out. 'He can use ours—can't he, Ken?'

Squatting near the window Ken appeared to nod but didn't turn.

And here was the redeeming feature of their hotel—worth writing home about. Instead of Gideon Bibles each room had been given a powerful telescope. These were the 16-inch Japanese refracting type and not cheap. They were chained to the windowsills. Guests could study at close quarters the habits and appearance of the local inhabitants without embarrassment. Proposed amendments had been constantly rejected by Congress: the use of high-powered telescopes was a constitutional right of the individual.

Quickly getting the hang of it, members of the group focused on their preoccupations. Each one became chained to the window, some with their doors wide open. Both Hofmann and Garry Atlas had focused from slightly different angles on the cleavage of the platinum blonde wobbling below; but it was Hofmann who switched to the brown tenement building in the adjoining precinct, an unsavoury district, and slowly panning floor by floor found there, between fire escape and busted downpipe, fourth window along . . . telegram boy in kitchen seated on housewife's knee. A large woman, she was stroking the boy's head. And look now she began—. 'What have you found?' Louisa typically asked. 'Let me see.' 'Nothing.' But the window grew so large and so clear, revealing the woman's teeth and heaving bosom as she whispered in the poor boy's ear, leaning forward now to see his glazed open-mouthed expression, that Hofmann moved to another window, as if she could see him, before quickly returning. She wore only a slip. She stood up and sat down with the boy again . . .

Even Kaddok sat by a window directing Gwen as she focused and described. She began everything, 'There's an

American tying his shoelace . . . an American with parcels trying to get a taxi . . .' as if they were natives. And Kaddok running his tongue over his blue lips, nodding, nodding: make great natural shots, these, for sure. *City Life* or *The Big Smoke* or *Americans at Play.* Meanwhile Garry began following a policeman and couldn't help grinning as the magnified red index finger suddenly entered one nostril and worked around, pulling a variety of faces, as if he were tightening a screw inside his head. Searching behind for his Budweiser can he said aloud to himself, 'The filthy bastard . . .'

'Let me look,' Louisa asked Hofmann for the fifth time.

'Just a second.'

'I'll go next door!'

What else in the following hour or so did Garry see? What did the Cathcarts see? Black in open sports car scratching his crotch at traffic lights; grey-haired helicopter pilot perspiring and *running tongue over bottom lip* as he settled on top of a skyscraper; an aproned maid in black who stepped out onto posh balcony and threw out the orange contents of a fish bowl; firemen in a yard behind the station playing poker; the ballet class; chap in a checked suit having pistol practice on his penthouse roof—successive bulls; followed a blind beggar: who left his corner and in a diner opened the *Wall Street Journal.*

Gerald spent his time profitably. To his surprise he stumbled upon grimy caryatids and plaques and other folk-carvings set among the entablatures and portals of the brownstones, normally invisible or very difficult to see from the street.

'There's something wrong here,' Borelli frowned from his window, 'Wherever I turn I see a woman, ah, fitting herself into a brassière. Wherever I turn. Here's one in a hotel window now. Ah, she too is so beautiful. I don't think I should be looking. Put yourself,' he turned to her, 'in my position.'

Louisa met his eyes, laughing. She touched her throat, 'What can you be afraid of?'

'It must be the position of my room.'

Every room has its own view, its own angle.

'Let me look, I'll bet it doesn't happen with me.'

Silk shirt settled against denim; and Borelli asked, 'Now the way they pitch forward like that—with these brassières—is that standard practice?'

'Well I have to,' said Louisa, not exactly answering. She kept her eye on the telescope.

Mmmm: Borelli thought for a while.

'It doesn't suit you,' he said changing the subject. 'It really doesn't.'

She had gold ear-rings; hair pulled back; she had pale skin; she had sadness spreading in her forehead.

'What doesn't? What do you mean?'

But she returned quickly to the telescope where she was listening more than looking.

'I mean looking through that thing. It doesn't suit you. You don't have to do it.'

But Louisa had noticed something. The telescope pointed down almost vertical. 'That looks like our Shiela in the park. I think it is.'

In other rooms others had recognized her, and focused. Every room has the same view, but different angles. Shiela's paisley scarf and worried expression fluttered large. She was half-running.

'She doesn't have her handbag,' Louisa observed.

In 105, Sasha turned as North sauntered in through their open door. After knocking, of course. 'We've just seen a man and his wife mugged in Harlem!'

'Oh dear,' he said, 'and I wanted to show you some squirrels, a family in the park.'

'I'd like to see that! Show us.'

'Since when have you been a squirrel-freak?' Violet asked out of the side of her mouth.

Sasha took North's arm. 'Show us where.'

The zoologist easily found the tree and stepped aside.

'There you are,' he rubbed his hands.

In the time it took Violet to focus, a Central Park carriage-horse moved into the foreground, black and bulging, obliterating the tree; raising its tail it dropped a pad, a turd, a crap. It was just like Violet to snort through her nose: she could have died.

'Really, you can be so crude,' Sasha shoved her aside.

It was then that she joined the others observing Shiela.

Down there in her English shoes Shiela had left the path and veered across the grass. Reaching the copse she hesitated, expressing second thoughts. For a full minute she stood looking all around. Then she took the remaining few steps to the tree. There was no one near it. In her room while tracking the squirrels from her acute angle, a figure had appeared in the right circumference, busying itself. Focusing she saw a man, his back to her, cutting something into a trunk. COME DOWN AND—. She recognized the neck and shoulders of Frank Hammersly.

Not a soul around now, only the tree. The message, Hammersly's task, deep cut and still bleeding, was complete.

COME DOWN AND
SEE AUSTRALIA

Now that would urge and beckon for years. The others in their rooms read it and laughed. They saw Shiela shield her eyes and stare up at their hotel, almost as if she had heard. Garry quickly waved but she couldn't see. Moving away she sat for a while on a bench. A woman without a handbag can look desolate.

'She's a dear,' Sasha declared. 'I quite like Shiela. Don't you?'

'I've hardly said a word to her,' North admitted. 'I don't think we know her.'

'She's a bit bonkers,' said Violet. 'I can't get through to her. And what's more I can't be bothered.'

Remaining at their posts they witnessed a few traffic accidents and the cocktail hour until it became dark, and when they sat together for dinner were full of comparisons and anecdotes and conflicting opinions (points of view). All this was old hat to Doug: patting his binoculars hanging around his neck, 'Ha, you know, I've known about this for donkey's years. You see what I mean?'

Nodding sagely, Mrs Cathcart could confirm. Doug never offered much that wasn't solid.

Without knowing exactly why, they were all specially kind to Shiela, so much so she might have twigged. Animation and concern are certainly the advantages of group travel. Now only Louisa felt left out of things. During all this talk she stroked the edge of her plate. Seated directly opposite, James Borelli had his face averted, deliberately it seemed, listening to Hofmann and Violet Hopper, and there was laughter, nodding among them. Not once did he look at her. Louisa listened. Now he was trying to tell them one Giovanni Borelli, of Pisa, had invented the telescope, and Gerald not Kaddok this time weighed in with the facts.

So varied and many were the sights that the party took to their windows early, observing the wakening rites of the great city, and the majority elected to stay in their rooms all day.

The sun came through the tall glass and bathed their knees. It was warm and pleasant as the world unfolded before them.

At around ten interest shifted to the avenue below. An argument had broken out between a parking inspector wearing epaulets and a young hood in a lieutenant's uniform. They could see the neck muscles bulging in one, slight tic developing in the cheek of the other: signals of the species, said to be chemical. All telescopes paused as Hofmann entered, the casual onlooker, smooth-faced and mildly interested, and the telescopes described slow arcs in unison, as he went on heading for (he'd told Louisa) the large survey exhibition of stripe paintings assembled from all corners of the globe, at the Museum of Modern Art; he wasn't going to miss that. An erect figure of a man with one hand in the side pocket. Hell, could have passed for a successful American; a lawyer maybe. Alone in their room Louisa followed him and smiled slightly, but in a different way from Violet Hopper several windows along, at the way his head jerked at every—and there were many—

handsome woman. So Louisa witnessed the freak accident. It was when he entered the sunlight of a relatively open section, flanked by iron railings decorated with arrow heads. According to the *Post* the American flag had torn free of its aluminium pole and after gliding and dipping on the city's tremendous updraughts came down twenty blocks away upon a lone Australian pedestrian (Kenneth Hofmann, dentist, of Sydney), enveloping him. It was the loyal corporate or skyscraper flag, approximately five times larger and normal, and although woven from a silken synthetic fabric it weighed a ton. Hofmann was knocked flat to the ground. The telescopes magnified a momentary beauty—twisting lines and stars. So unexpected was it that a few began laughing until they realized he could suffocate or could be hurt underneath. Louisa had been the first to cry out. The struggle entered their own rooms.

A small crowd gathered but nobody lifted a finger.

'Get him out! Why don't they?'

'What some people do to attract attention,' Violet murmured.

Hofmann had to struggle with the monster alone.

It subsided and first Hofmann's head appeared, blinking, then his torso. He stood up casually dusting himself.

'Ah he's OK. He's broken his glasses, that's all,' Violet reported. 'He looks funny without glasses.'

The crowd on the footpath moved closer.

A man had called out, 'Is this a stunt?'

'Say what's the big idea?'

'Yeah, what are you trying to prove?'

Hofmann had taken out his lapel handkerchief to wrap his glasses. He looked down at the flag.

A yellow truck slowed down and double-parked. Three men in muddy boots jumped out.

'Awright, the funny-boy—who is he? Get it off the ground.'

Surprised, Hofmann pointed to the sky. Behind the telescopes they could see his lips moving.

'Get it offa the ground.'

'Goddammit.'

'It was some sort of stunt,' said one.

Quite a crowd now, ragged-circular around Ken Hofmann. It became increasingly harder to locate him in the telescopes. Of Kaddok's half dozen or more Ektachromes only one would reveal Hofmann—and then an elbow and the back of his head.

'They've got him trying to lift the flag,' Violet said.

It was too much for one man and when he held up an armful it began spilling like a mad fluid, the rest suddenly rising and flapping. An impatient American gave him a shove. As he fell—out of view from the windows—the police cars arrived; sirens, flashing lights, the men in blue.

One of those incidents or experiences of travel.

'It wouldn't have happened if you hadn't been here,' Borelli observed, saying the obvious but making a point.

'You know they asked me where I came from?' Hofmann laughed. ' "Godammit, not another one," they said. That was when I was about to get lynched.'

'We saw you! It made us hopping mad.'

Shiela turned to Louisa. 'Weren't you afraid? I think I would be.'

'It must have given him a fright,' Louisa answered.

'Anything can happen in New York.'

'I suddenly saw stripes,' Hofmann admitted, dry.

'And stars, surely,' Kaddok added, missing the point.

Violet opened her mouth and rolled her eyes. She made Louisa laugh.

'What were you doing,' Borelli turned to North, 'during the drama?'

'My little friend here dragged me all the way to the Bronx Zoo. Kicking and screaming, I might say.'

'Thank you very much!' Sasha turned away. 'You said you had a good time.'

'I did,' said North and waited for her to turn. He patted her knee.

'And I thought you'd given up the animal world,' Gerald joined in. He rocked on his heels. 'I thought you told me—wasn't it you?—you'd switched to Science. Disillusioned with it already? I'm not surprised. Never mind. We understand. I think this is another victory for the humanities. And is it a good zoo?'

Looking at Gerald, Phillip North simply blinked at the first question. He felt Sasha watching him.

'Oh yes. There's nothing much wrong with the Bronx.'

'Come off it,' Sasha returned, 'The kangaroos were awful; poor moth-eaten things. You said so yourself.'

'I could have been killed,' Hofmann shrugged. 'They were like animals.'

'That'll be the day,' muttered Violet, cutting.

Louisa gave another laugh; for her, surprisingly harsh.

It had enlivened their day. It stood out vivid, angular, among the everyday; it would for years. A flurry for the future. And since all had in a sense participated they rallied around, adding to it, rendering it theirs. It epitomized their sense of being away, and at the same time their distance from local events. It was a foreign experience.

Come to that: now that they'd grown accustomed to their hotel, as if their eyes had become used to the dark, they found it a veritable centre of gravity. Mass movements, messengers and energies crossed before their eyes. In the ornate banquet rooms were sales conventions of Caterpillar tractor reps, the Federation of Plastic Bucket Manufacturers, as well as the Private Eyes' Association of America. High up on the roof, apparently unaware of the hotel's fall-off in services, the British Caterpillar Club had chosen the revolving restaurant for its annual get-together. An Indian diplomat gave master classes in the sitar on the 23rd. Those sallow, wrinkled-skinned figures in the dark corners of the lobby and bars were fugitives from the symposium of world-wide speleologists. Singing, shouting could be heard after hours. And all along (meanwhile) it had been discovered by accident—Borelli strolling around back—that the entire rear wing of the hotel was being dismantled, and hanging and swinging in the breeze, had been hired out on an hourly basis to an amalgamation of rock-climbing clubs. This then accounted for the steady clink-clinking, like ice rattling in martinis, as dozens of alloy steel pitons were hammered into the perpendicular face. It sure was a centre—a hum, a hive—there could be no denying. At night the tall box-like structure flashed and radiated lights. In the elevator women were accosted by convention members with plastic name-tags pinned to their lapels, and other heavy-breathers: accosted in the nicest possible manner. A middle-aged rep with tired eyes actually tipped his hat to Violet and Sasha; was told smartly to 'Piss off!' by those two girls.

Recommended:
1. The Dog Show
2. Police Museum, East 20th Street, (Baseball bats with horse-shoes fitted at one end, etc. 'Graphically they illustrate the criminal potential of misguided youth.')
3. Institution of Marriage.
4. *Uniforms: the Psychology of Non-uniformity*; exhibition at the Metropolitan Museum.
5. Collection of Rare Blood Atlases, Morgan Library.
6. Walk across the Brooklyn Bridge!
7. Intercontinental Ballistic Missile display; foyer, IBM building, Fifth Avenue.

The Institution of Marriage. A slice of the bucolic wood of Westchester County has been set aside, near a village of white fences and neat zebra crossings (Pleasantville). Stripped of their leaves the silver-limbed trees had scattered a kind of confetti all over, russet and coquelicot, and there were untrodden paths, thorny moments and unexpected marshy parts, tiny creeks like running tears. The light timber stood still, like the legs of patient men. These were the proper grounds for marriage: idyllic, mysteriously fertile. A pair of geese passed overhead, creaking. It was wonderful.

The Institution was a fortress. From a distance it looked like a wedding cake—perhaps the architecture was intentional—what with its lavish use of stucco, its lily-white curtains and columns; but although it was fundamentally intact, they could see it had been allowed to deteriorate on the surface, not only by the prevailing climate—slakes of rust—but by time and bird-droppings. It was surrounded by a barbed wire fence. As they approached, they could see a clothes line and two women conversing over the fence. The fat one had her hair wrapped in a scarf and the friend wore an apron. The path went close by; again probably intentional. For when they were within a few yards those in front suddenly pointed: these women were extremely accurate models, a combination of wood and plastic, beautifully posed and painted. Reaching out Sasha fluttered the doll-like eye-lashes of one; instinctively Kaddok raised his camera.

They were still discussing the craftmanship of the models when they reached the Institution's entrance. A separate enclosure had been fenced off next to the wire gate and two arctic stags were locked in combat, the metallic clash of the antlers metronomic in regularity, supplemented by grunts, bulging thighs and steam, chips of antlers sometimes cartwheeling into the air on impact. Fascinated, they stood watching for a while.

'They're fighting over a female,' North coughed. 'Come along.'

But this only increased their interest. They rested on the fence.

'I want to see who wins,' Sasha cried. She turned to North.

'They could be going all day. It's a process. There has to be a loser. One of them might easily die.'

'Survival of the fittest,' Garry explained.

'*The Origin of the Species*,' Kaddok added mysteriously.

'Stupid bloody men!' said Violet. 'You can get some idea of the trouble they cause. Look at them, the fools.'

North laughed and pushed open the gate. 'They'll be still battling away when we come out.'

Following him, they glanced back at the colliding grunting males.

'I wish someone'd fight over me,' Sasha whispered.

'Shiela, what do you reckon? Say a sword fight. Something like that.'

'I suppose,' she glanced at Sasha. 'If no one was hurt.'

'Someone always is,' Violet came between them. 'I've always found. But that's only me.'

The Kaddoks were at the door bowing and scraping to the guardian of the Institution, a North American redhead, forty-odd, decked out in a tasselled mini-skirt, a white Stetson and a lasso. She had a freckled jelly-cleavage and blue knees.

'Why, hell-o there,' she beamed. 'Wel-come to the Institution.'

The men had to squeeze past her.

'Howdy,' nodded Doug, pulled past by his wife.

'What have you got this thing for?' Garry pointed to the lasso.

'Keep moving, please.'

They waited in a hall decorated with dried flower arrangements which met with Mrs Cathcart's approval. From another room came the pleasant hum of a domestic vacuum cleaner. Framed on the wall was HOME SWEET HOME in New England needlepoint.

'Boys and girls, I see. Any singles?'

Shiela involuntarily raised her hand.

'What does she want to know all this crap for?' Violet whispered.

But Louisa had raised her arm. Louisa was usually obedient. 'Oh I'm without husband.'

'I'm sorry,' said the woman. 'I am sorry to hear that.'

'He's only out looking at more stripe paintings. He's always been interested in that type of modern art. I don't mind,' Louisa smiled.

'Where's old Borelli then?' Garry asked, unthinking. They had become accustomed to seeing the two together, talking to one side.

'He doesn't believe in institutions. He said he wasn't interested. I asked him to come but he marched off somewhere else.' The vacuum clear hum was replaced now by light organ muzak. It sounded like a church warming up.

They waited for the redhead. She had both hands on her hips, like a predatory bird.

'Alright now, I won't chatter away. That would be nagging, and I think that's dreadful. It can drive even a good man away.' Slight laughter here and there, stopped short. 'I'll come along and keep you company, shall I? I think that's best. And hasn't it been a gorgeous day?'

As usual Gerald Whitehead remained at the edge cracking his red knuckles: those of a bachelor. To the Institution of Marriage and to America itself, Gerald had decided merely to tag along; hands in his pockets, so to speak. America hadn't been his idea, and the Institution represented its worst excesses. He would have preferred being somewhere else. Vienna, say; or cobbled Florence say: in Europe where the clocks show Roman time. It invited contemplation; he allowed himself to drift, separate.

He'd raised his hand to poke the glasses on his nose when *Swooooosh*: the whirring loop dropped and wriggled like a quoit around his wrist; and before he knew it, before he could prevent it, was dragged forward into the arms of the redhead.

'Gotcha!' said she.

And they were laughing and whistling, joining in, even Shiela in disbelief. Gerald reddened as she undid the lasso.

'There now . . .'

Gerald gripped his wrist.

'I didn't burn, did I?' she asked all solicitous.

But the others were still wiping their eyes, ho hee.

'It's nothing,' he said.

'So that's what it's for?' Sasha said. 'I never thought of that before. Isn't she clever?' Turning to Phillip North she had a mocking shine.

'There are also other ways,' her friend Violet reminded, 'you should know.'

'Say,' Doug was asking, 'where on earth did you learn to use that thing?'

'It's bloody lethal,' Garry Atlas shouted.

Ignoring them, or affecting to, she took Gerald's hand. 'So you're with me. OK? Everyone, this way.'

Again they couldn't help grinning and pointing. The back of Gerald's neck and ears had reddened. It was like a game.

The exhibits here were arranged as in any institution: small rooms and the usual étagère and glass cases (horizontal, vertical), wall fixtures and photographs.

First of all, there was nothing unusual about marriage. Ceremonies and subsequent suburbias had been observed even among colonies of *ants*. The redhead said nothing except a few moist whispers to Gerald. The point was driven home by photographs and scientific statements with arrows.

This put the subject into perspective.

Cabinets at easy intervals displayed the odds and ends employed in the courtship ritual—dead posies, lockets, examples of lavish compliments, theatre programmes and the like. Promises, promises! It was all very familiar and yet Mrs Cathcart and Shiela, and Louisa, why even Violet Hopper, appeared to take a close interest. The redhead here interrupted as Garry began telling everyone about the 'incredible bloody bucks' night' he'd been to at Bendigo, pissed as lords, and 'we got the groom and—.' It was easy, only too easy, to make a mockery of the Institution. 'Okay, okay,' he put up his hands, 'you're nagging me.' Between the furniture of western courtship—the floral sofa, walnut love-seats in the shape of S, the arctic back seat of secondhand cars—the path was so narrow it casually forced them to proceed in pairs. Most of them didn't suspect.

A suspended post office bag spilled a quantity of letters, many perfumed and one French. It demonstrated the desire to put difficult feelings into words. A few had been opened and ironed flat for easy perusal. Bundles were tied with pink ribbons. Take away the reams of business correspondence and a high proportion of all mail is love letters.

'I feel sure this is where the phrase "tons of love" originates,' the redhead said. She stared at Garry in case he tried to be funny. 'And I think that's just wonderful, don't you?'

Gwen bent over with Louisa to read some.

'You know,' said Kaddok at an inaccurate tangent, 'France is the only country that doesn't have the air-letter.'

Sasha asked Phillip North, 'Have you ever written poems to anyone?'

'Poems? Good God, by the mile. I've lost count.'

'No tell me,' said Sasha gently, 'I'd like to know.'

'They get embarrassed,' Mrs Cathcart said.

'Do you have any ruddy ball-and-chains here?' Doug laughed, embarrassed.

Marriage was a force. It was a subterranean, was light and dark, pink and white, grey, elemental, in its growth and hold. It was meant to be binding. That was its social function. In part it diminished and yet two could ripple outwards; the institution was circular in its shape and helplessness. One Californian couple wrote rhyming letters to each other every day for thirty-three years from the same house. A regular diet of lies is needed.

'You've all heard the term "fabric of society" bandied about? Well here it is. You can touch it.'

And temporarily dropping Gerald's moist hand the redhead took the hem of a wedding gown and felt it between her fingers, sperm-like in its viscosity. About a dozen gowns were fitted to blonde mannequins, demonstrating the slow almost negligible change in fashions.

Opposite stood an equal number of poker-faced grooms. A guard of honour; visually quite effective. The women clustered around uttering cries and wearing solemn expressions, as they mentioned comparisons with their own ceremonies. The redhead began telling them about her own. They all seemed to like her. There were no distinctions between them.

'I fear this was a mistake,' North commented to Gerald. To one side Gerald gazed at the ceiling, scratching his throat.

Making a move Garry put out his hand and touched a nylon train—and yanked back.

'Yeow! I got a boot then!'

It made them laugh. 'It serves him right,' said Sasha. She turned to the redhead, 'You were saying?'

'No kidding!' Garry kept yelling and pointing.

'Static electricity,' Kaddok naturally explained. He hadn't taken a photograph yet.

In this institution, labels were printed in a cursive hand in the style of invitations.

Black and white, the colours of marriage, represent the shared twenty-four hours a day, split night and day. Wearing black the husband has been designated (genetically?) the earlier death. It has been established since Adam that white represents propagation, future tense, flights of fancy, hope, a clean slate. But it stains easily. In a rare reversal of the designated colours the white sperm swims into the night-black womb. Between the two poles lie the grey tones of every day: gentle acquired knowledge, tolerance, shades of meaning. Hence the colours of marriage, black and white.

'What do you make of all this?' nodded Doug. Whenever his spouse showed involvement Doug beamed.

'We could well be here for the day,' North sighed. At least he showed patience.

Doug beamed and glanced back. 'Ah, but you know, it doesn't do them any harm.' And he rocked on his soles, 'Yup . . .'

Gerald made the point, 'If it's so "elemental" and "subterranean" how is it we feel segregated?'

'Oh I of course recently had a wife,' murmured North vaguely.

The women now faced them. With their florals, holding their handbags, they looked formidable but for their serene, almost lofty, expressions, as if they possessed inner secrets. They were in agreement.

'Come on. Don't stand there on one foot,' said Sasha to North. The others could hear. 'Show an interest.'

She was on the point of saying more.

And Violet and Shiela were talking. Answering Violet's question Shiela looked back, 'I've never thought—I mean, yes. I suppose so. If anyone would have me,' she added without mockery. 'I know myself. I am not the easiest person . . .'

Marriages of convenience, marriages between dynasties, arranged marriages (legalized prostitution?). Mixed marriages and shotgun marriages, marriages of couples who had never been married before; some who dreaded it, others who couldn't wait (for it). There were marriages between in-laws. A marriage of killer and victim's wife. Photographic evidence of child marriages, of giants and dwarfs, yeah, and Siamese twins, nudists and octogenarians, communist marriages. There were marriages at sea.

The redhead lifted a flyproof dome on a silver tray. A coal-like substance made them crane with curiosity.

'One of our most treasured possessions,' she said to help.

Still they didn't know.

'Gerald, please read those words.'

Bending close he fogged the sterling silver with his breath.

He read,

'The Queen's Bridal Cake, Buckingham Palace
Feby. 10, 1840.'

He straightened up.

'Queen Victoria,' Mr History spelt it out, and decided to take a photograph.

Hooray!

Anyway, Mrs Cathcart had a piece of wedding cake locked away in a side-board. Sometimes she has a look at it. A practice not followed these days by the young.

The redhead had been listening, interested. She closed one eye.

'Average age of marriage, 23.6 years. Twenty-two percent of your marriages are Roman Catholic. Divorce in Australia is on a terrible increase. Already it approaches the United States. It is ahead of England. In the past decade there has been a large swing from gold rings to silver. The man wears the pants.'

The way Kaddok moved his lips showed he was memorizing it. 'Very interesting,' he said.

The ritual offering of food in the wedding ceremony is another universal. Yes, our anthropologists find it practised in the most primitive societies. Always cooked and usually a delicacy the mouthful acts as a social cement. There is an audience (auditors), watchful, almost serious. And isn't it a reward for a job well done; sustenance also for the journey ahead? The symbol is accepted by the couple and verified by the elders. That same orifice—close-up of chewing mouth—soon bears the initial transports of passion.

Unlike other institutions the interior surfaces here were painted in domestic hues: pinks from the bedroom, pale blue of the veins, lilac and such. Casual and pleasant, the rooms were full of interest. It was like walking through a life.

Pinned like butterflies in a spotless showcase an array of stained and torn marriage certificates folded into wings provided just a hint of the world-wide army of printers employed to keep the institution going. But of course they don't prevent the unscrupulous person, nearly always male, abusing the carefully worked-out system. For this same cabinet acted as a kind of transparent arrow to an adjoining rogue's gallery of *bigamists*—mug shots, case histories, from the floor to the ceiling. It was dimly lit and frowned upon, and the redhead began tapping her high-heeled shoes, Gerald stationed at her side; at least he was no bigamist. But the snapshots exerted a fascination. What sort of man becomes a bigamist? Garry held up his cigarette lighter, like those entrepreneur herdsmen who point to prehistoric cave paintings with flaming torches.

Look, the majority were men in their forties, early fifties, with ballpoints protruding from their coats: they openly gazed, all of them. One smoked a pipe. Like the rest he had small eyes. It was almost enough to dispel suspicions. They had regular features, uncongested, nothing to hide. One who smiled stood out (by the door). He was bald and wore a propeller-shaped bow tie, an exception, perhaps even a bit soft in the head. Aside from the smooth foreheads, remarkable for men of their years, the only telling sign was in fact the very absence of 'signs', as if a hand had passed over their features—although a surprising percentage had shaving nicks around the chins.

As the senior married person Mrs Cathcart assumed the natural mantle of leader or spokesman and was the first to break the curious silence, first by sucking spit and air through her teeth, then muttering 'blighters' and 'the beggars!' As the others kept studying the photographs she could no longer contain herself: 'Rotten pigs! I'd shoot the lot of them, every one of them. The misery they cause.'

'You tell 'em,' Garry clapped: at this stage he liked to pronounce his bachelorhood. 'I reckon, Christ, they deserve medals—the Victoria Cross. To have two or three women on the go: one's trouble enough.' He turned to Phillip North. 'How do they do it?'

'The voice of experience,' Sasha jeered, almost including North.

'Another ruddy feminist! They're everywhere,' he answered.

The redhead went over to him. 'Why don't you,' she twanged in his ear, 'shut your face. You're not funny.' To Mrs Cathcart she said, 'I agree with you. Completely.'

A few smiled good-naturedly, to lighten the mood; and drifted around the walls. Hardly anyone heard Violet Hopper, 'I knew a bigamist once . . .'

It caught only Shiela's interest. She gazed sideways at the floor. 'That must have been—.' But she changed it to a characteristic dead question: 'What was his name?'

What did it matter?

'I think these men are essentially weak when you consider it,' Louisa said.

And since she had scarcely spoken, and walked alone, they turned, remembering her. 'Anyone who can't make up his mind, or has to lie like that. I wonder what they think of themselves?'

It was almost worth another look. Garry felt for his cigarette lighter.

'Come along,' the hostess called out, cracking the whip.

She took Gerald's arm as an example. From behind they looked a natural couple.

A welcome change appeared through the door: set into the long side wall a brightly lit replica of a shop window. It could have been Tiffany's: only these velvet trays and turntables were crowded with rings of every description, almost indiscriminately. Unlucky opals rubbed shoulders with 40-carat diamonds which lay alongside mirror rings from the Punjab, and ultra-marine lapis taken from Afghanistan. One slowly turning wheel, a ferris-wheel in miniature, scooped up wedding rings from a pile, raining them down again as it turned, a kind of perpetual motion.

Ingeniously, the window allowed up to a dozen or more to look over the merchandise, though again it was the women who had their noses and fingers to the glass. The slipping on of a ring symbolizes the sacred sexual act. Hemmed in, Kaddok could only look back over the coiffured heads.

'They're having a good time,' Doug beamed, standing back; so was he. Folding his arms he winked at North.

'It's all they ever think about,' said Garry walking away. 'I don't know what this place is driving at. It must have cost a fortune. What's the point? Say, does anyone know the time?'

Phillip North seemed to attract a response merely by his presence. Some liked to stand near to bounce off or soak in. He listened and so he seemed always interesting.

Violet Hopper came away from the window. Although softened somewhat, her face was not lit up like the others.

North nodded politely. They'd scarcely spoken before.

'Very little surprises you,' he observed, nodding at the window. Such observations were possible with Violet Hopper.

'If you mean this, it's old hat to me. Once or twice at the time it was nice; even then not always. It becomes irrelevant. You've been married, haven't you?' She looked at the window, at the crush. 'Sasha,' she turned to him, 'is a close friend . . . I like Sasha.'

North thought about this and looked at the window. 'I know.'

'Yes, you're not blind,' said Violet sharply.

Kaddok had brushed past, pulled by his wife. Turning to North again Violet opened her eyes wide. 'I've put my foot in it again. Have I?'

Sasha had arrived. She stood with them quietly.

'Not at all,' said North.

Marriage is big business, bigger than tourism. Is only marginally affected by economic, political, climatic downturns; if at all. Not only is there the outlay on the gold and diamonds: consider the wedding cars and uniformed chauffeurs, ribbons, and the fuel they burn; remember the cost of new clothing, the wedding haircut, the tons of scattered rice and confetti; feast food, jugs of beer and bubbly; the stenographers, photographers (film emulsion, the price of silver); there must be shoe repairs of waitresses and priests; above all, the shower of gifts, usually consumer durables, often electrical in nature; cutlery or sheets don't come cheap; and without honeymoons, the motel and leathergoods industries would collapse. These out-goings filter through all sectors of the economy. The institution of marriage is fuel to the capitalist engine.

Are there any questions ?

Marriage brokers, marriage guidance counsellors, private detectives and legal costs.

Following their leader, Sasha marched ahead with North, taking his arm in full view, and her breast squashed against him as she leaned; so Sasha then took an even greater interest in the exhibits. In allowing it Phillip North could merely have been urbane, giftedly so; could have been: but Mrs Cathcart apparently still fuming at the idea of bigamy, and recalling her position of seniority, made the clicking sound with her tongue (in her lifetime these had often been effective) and to those around her, shook her head: 'And I believe he's recently bereaved. I don't understand it.'

The androgynous zones of . . . marriage.

They surrounded the redhead. Both she and Gerald were

handing out printed sheets: a glossary of terms, of endearment. A kind of love dictionary. It could be folded and kept in a pocket (or under a pillow: extraordinary the partners who find trouble expressing themselves). The nouns and adjectives were printed in an ornate style but were easy to read. Non-words and harmless white lies and whispered obscenities are essential—aren't they?—for the successful marriage. New words, including nicknames and adhesive pet-nouns which were demonstrably inaccurate and yet perfectly apt were listed in alphabetical order. A penetrating new language is required, solely for the requirements of love. It can be as private as you like.

Holding the paper close to her eyes Sasha tried a few out on North. This was no time for jokes. 'Kinsey's Twentieth-Century Dictionary,' he'd begun to crack, to dismiss. 'Good God, they might have crossed some of those out.'

'Don't be a prude,' said Sasha; and she held onto his arm as she read out more words. 'Listen . . .'

And in the half-dark, in a corner, Shiela trembled as Violet still held her hand, as warm as a sparrow's now, and touched her cheek, so understanding. It had been all of a sudden: almost all engulfing. Shiela could have cried, could have cried out. A glance showed Violet's experience. She was unsmiling.

Brass beds, water beds, electrically driven models (circular; Made in Germany), and the inevitable sturdy four-poster, and a bed of roses. There were double sleeping-bags and camp-stretchers; and a small but hypnotic collection of stained mattresses. Bloody sheets from Sicily had been randomly selected the morning after and were preserved between sheets of glass; enough to make Atlas flinch; factual and historical to the others.

Sasha wanted to know all. She wanted to participate. 'Where did you meet one another?' she asked. The question flew with the spirit of things and like the lasso settled on Mrs Cathcart. For the first time they heard her laugh. It was generous and unexpectedly high—a girl's.

'Oh I saw him at a friend's wedding. He came with friends on a filthy motor bike. I said to myself, what a silly little man, and he kept blowing his nose. I wouldn't care if I never saw *him* again.'

'You were proved right there,' Doug had to nudge. He winked at Sasha and Louisa, enjoying himself. All listened in an interested congratulatory way.

'He's been good to me,' Mrs Cathcart returned to firmness. 'We have a family,' she said simply. Her mouth and jaw suggested early economic hardships. Sasha and Louisa had their heads inclined, measuring Mrs Cathcart's echo. All Doug could do was keep glancing at the others vaguely grinning, 'There you are . . . so . . . Well!'

They had to find Gerald and the redhead. These two had turned not one corner but several. Broken with irregular, spaced doors and alcoves the corridor resembled an out-of-the-way hotel: purple carpet lay underfoot. Glancing over his shoulder—at the passage, empty—Gerald cleared his throat. With an ease which suggested she had done this before the North American put Gerald's hand down her front and onto her powdered breast.

'There now. That'll keep you warm.'

And yet that part of the building was definitely over-heated, perhaps deliberately. Not only to Gerald: others had complained.

She had large rough nipples and five minutes passed before the others came.

'Gotcha! There you are!' Garry shouted. 'Here they are.'

'We have an annual congress,' the redhead resumed quickly taking the handle of a door, 'where every aspect of marriage is thrashed out.'

They followed as she pushed open the door.

It was a small motel room. It had a green TV set, drawn curtains and two horizontal suitcases by the mirror with their lids raised. A lamp in the corner illuminated a champagne bucket and—

HEY!

Rapid twisting movement on the bed.

'Oh excuse us. I am sorry.'

A young man with his bride had turned, glazed. The pale legs around his waist froze.

Kaddok stepped back onto Gerald's foot. Retreating backwards the others fell into the corridor, a pack of cards.

'What's up?' Garry demanded. He wanted to see.

'My mistake,' murmured the redhead, gently closing the door. 'Ask one of the others,' she smiled.

It was then difficult to know whether it was real or merely an accident planned by the institution.

His smirk spreading, adding two and two, Garry wanted to hear it. Nothing—nothing is sacred any more.

'Never mind,' Louisa told him. She was pensive for the woman disturbed. In the dark she had glimpsed the young man's moustache.

Garry kept on. He wanted it all.

'It was someone's room' Louisa sighed. 'They were making love,' she murmured, and frowned, 'when we barged in.'

Ah. Garry smacked his forehead. 'The poor bastard!' Then he turned over her choice of words. 'They were making . . . love . . .'

'God,' Sasha wheeled around, 'you're crass. When will you grow up?'

Scientists are saying we are essentially machines for the propagation of our genes. Nothing more or less. So it is said. The institution of marriage implies there is more.

Dust sheets in the next room were removed; Gerald gave a hand. Gradually, they revealed a classic nuclear family at leisure: kneeling in front of a gas-fire, playing Monopoly. The smooth-faced mother and father with their offspring (boy and a girl), were the equal of anything by Madame Tussaud. It looked like a Sunday night. Dad in a real cardigan held a pipe. So convincing was the setting they felt compelled like all good travellers to stand a while, searching for inaccuracies.

'The living room is a cave,' Phillip North pointed out. 'There's the fire. Take away the decorations which seem anyway faintly self-conscious.'

The hearth fire held the family in a circle of approximately four yards diameter. Central heating, said to be a sign of civilization, has been largely responsible for the disintegration of marriages, of traditional family life. It encourages each member to sit in distant rooms, alone. The subsequent fall in communion, communication, *family warmth*, is a cause for concern. Consider this before installing C.H.

'We don't have that as a problem,' Doug laughed. 'Where we come from it's as hot as blazes. You need fans.'

As hot as Hades.

'We had a fire in the lounge,' his spouse cried out. She looked at the other women, telling them.

'The Parsees,' Kaddok threw in for no apparent reason; and kept searching. In fact he didn't finish it.

Under perspex on an unstable pedestal a gum-pink toothbrush lay horizontal, like an avant garde sculptural object. The institution rightly saw it as a valuable trophy, one possessing vague sexual undertones; it summarized the act of sharing, important in any Western marriage. This toothbrush had been shared by a married couple for seventeen years (donated by the Knudsens, 31 Dakota Ave, Algonquin Is., Toronto). It spoke of intimacy, barriers finally down. There was nothing more to say.

In another room the wraps were ripped off without ceremony

Several wheelchairs (at first glance, the first horseless carriages) established the point that—ideally—the healthy partner too becomes geared to the chair: and so there was some embarrassment here, side glances at Gwen Kaddok. She certainly seemed a shade more solemn, even quieter than usual.

Joint cigarettes, joint bank accounts, joint interest in sports, hobbies and magazine subscriptions: of little interest.

Shiela and Violet stayed outside.

Then came a group of crudely carved stones, about knee-high, a dozen or more in rows. Compelling in their simplicity or in their lonely arrangement they radiated a kind of . . . demanding silence. Again certain modern sculptures sprang to mind: what was that art museum on West 53rd Street? Such comparisons however were superficial. Lifted from the outskirts of villages in Northern India these were monuments to those faithful and virtuous Hindu widows who'd thrown themselves on their husbands' funeral pyres, were suttee stones. The ultimate testimony to marriage.

Opinions and objections broke out.

'I can't believe that!'

Moving among them they touched the stones. Each one—representing a life—provoked violent images in full colour; and Violet yawned.

'They must have loved their husbands . . .'

'It was their tradition.'

'It's ridiculous. Degrading.'

Banned in India from the days of the Raj, sutteeism is still practised today. Yes: on good authority. Paragraphs occasionally appear in the *Times of India*, Bombay. Whatever one may think, they stand as the supreme monuments to uxorial devotion; interesting word uxorial.

'What does the institution feel?' North asked. 'Is it right?'

'Of course, yes and no,' the redhead replied. 'Some of the older, more traditional members approve.'

'How silly,' said Gwen.

'Anyway, you're asking a moral question,' Gerald interrupted.

'We're pleased to have them here,' the redhead insisted, patting his arm. 'They make a wonderful valid general point.'

Outside the last door but one: they were checked by a rotting stench, and the few who ventured in pressed handkerchiefs to their mouths. In the middle of the floor stood a standard garbage bin. It had its lid slightly askew. The banal object had assumed a queer ominous power.

Now the point was, the point was—

Who puts the garbage bin out at night? A pedestrian question, to be sure, yet it lies at the heart of the institution. The unpleasant, regularly spaced chores can suddenly crack the finest relationship asunder. Here the rotting scraps which included fish had been randomly collected on a regular basis to demonstrate the problem.

'It can cut both ways,' the redhead told them. 'Some folks find this a lyrical task, epitomizing their devotion to their partner. They come to adore the filthy lid and handles.' She beamed like a Chinese cadre. 'I always carried it out for my husband.'

'That's a man's job,' Mrs Cathcart insisted. 'I never have, unless Doug was sick.'

The redhead glanced at the others and turned to the last door.

About to turn the handle she stopped. Voices could be heard: single syllables, from a man. A woman's jagged sentences entered rising. Straining outside they had difficulty decyphering the words. The woman began crying. The man shouted: impotence. They were yelling, both of them now, and Louisa turned away.

'I can't bear this,' she said. She confided to Gwen. 'I stopped arguing long ago, I give in. Otherwise it can be too much.'

'It doesn't get us anywhere,' said Gwen understanding. 'They're difficult; stubborn is the word. I sometimes feel sorry for them.'

'Yes . . .' Louisa glanced at her. 'Yes . . .'

'We had our arguments,' North answered Sasha, 'Not many; I think we were too lazy.'

Sasha wanted to know more.

Caricatures of mothers-in-law. Haw, haw: the interfering old war-horse is evidently another universal. Four rusty chastity belts, c. 1460. One had the key jammed.

Leaning on Phillip North's elbow as they entered a large light-filled room Sasha kept pointing and whispering at things, in many cases unnecessarily. Virtually unnoticed Violet and Shiela brought up the rear.

To Gerald's dismay—his grimace at North—the walls were lined with small photographs. They had been collected from all over the world. Beginning along the top were newly marrieds and descending in the rows below marriages which broke up after One Year, Five Years and Ten—so the far edges formed a jagged hypotenuse.

At intervals a small printed card interrupted the photographs:

OF THE ESTIMATED 100 BILLION PHOTOGRAPHS IN
EXISTENCE A GREAT PROPORTION ARE — NOT
UNNATURALLY — RECORDS OF MARRIED LIFE. IT IS THE
NICEST THING TO RECORD THOUGH NOT ALWAYS.

'Only a selection,' the redhead piped up. She had to yell for they were dispersed around the long walls. 'We have the rest on microfilm. We believe we have just about every marriage in the world after 1950.'

A Honeywell computer link-up would locate a name among the four walls and mark it with a flashing light. It could retrieve a broken marriage from the many thousands in 'storage' and in no time at all place the victim's photograph in the appropriate row, marking it with a flashing light. Film stars were much in demand. Hidden among the statistics were many famous names. Only the United States with its resources and resolve could have pulled all this together: land of so many promises.

The redhead stood behind a special hooded keyboard and arched her eyebrows. 'Alright now, gang. Who's been divorced?'

Violet Hopper raised her hand and watched amused as the freckled fingers typed out her name: flashing lights appeared in two, three, *four* separate places around the room. It drew whistles and cat-calls.

'Violet,' Sasha laughed, 'you should be ashamed.' Violet had joined them to inspect her own photographs; Sasha could have hugged her friend, she was having such a good time. Only Mrs Cathcart remained in the middle, holding Doug's sleeve when he made a move, and let out two tremendous sighs.

The photographs showed Violet cheek-to-cheek with her former husbands, and in the first—the light indicating Married Five Years—she must have been scarcely nineteen. At that time Violet was taut-faced, already rueful. The husband gazed straight at the camera, but she turned to one side slightly, looking away. Oddly enough, as Shiela remarked, three of her four men had moustaches and were fleshy-faced. Her husbands looked remarkably the same.

'I suppose I'll be up there soon,' Louisa remarked, though the one who heard, Gwen Kaddok, earnestly shook her head.

'Anyone else?' this redhead called out on one foot. 'No? Well, give us another name. A friend or relation. Anyone want any dirt on a politician?'

Standing beside her Shiela whispered, 'Hammersly, Frank Hammersly.'

Instantly two lights appeared.

'What are you bothering with him for?' Violet asked. 'Listen to me.'

But Shiela had gone up and squinted at Hammersly and his first mistake, a pleasant face with a crooked front tooth. As a young man, Frank Hammersly had a country boy's jug-ears.

'He's no good. I know it. Believe me.'

'But Violet, he has been nice to me. I can't imagine how I seemed to him. What must he be thinking?'

The walls lit up with the busted marriages of Australian architects, secretive aunts, randy male friends of some, and Hofmann's father. A good half hour passed before the redhead closed the 'switchboard', saying for their benefit, 'That was fun. That was fun.'

All along there had been nothing new; though perhaps something had been set in order, confirmed, or set in motion even. The institution would always remain. 'I didn't see much to photograph,' Kaddok complained. 'There are no surprises in the institution of marriage,' said Mrs Cathcart satisfied. 'What did you expect?'

At the exit a small portable chapel had been installed. Ceremonies can be quickly performed for couples overcome. Sliding screens guarantee the ambiance of each denomination. But on the other side, a walnut confessional with purple curtain and scratched step had been placed for marriage counselling, thereby harshly balancing the overall favourable impression provided by the institution.

But the redhead didn't seem to notice. 'Come again!' she said to each one as they shook her hand. She planted a kiss on the side of Gerald's neck, sending colour up to his ears. One of the stags was on its knees, but still fighting back. And Sasha held onto North's arm.

This was the time of the Primaries and rejoicing at the freeing of 'Enterprise' in South East Asia; wild rejoicing; crash landing of that lazy Jumbo at Kennedy International Airport (13 survivors); concern expressed by the committee of crack metallurgists at the hairline fissures around the ears—around the ears of the Statue of Liberty ('that's perlooshun'); world bantam-weight title fight at Madison Square Garden (the boy from Ghana, on points); snow, sleet and slush. Monday. This day was proclaimed national holiday. Strange how the streets and the tremendous straight avenues of Manhattan had been drained of vertical figures, collisions and purpose: then little left to stockade the razor wind off the Hudson. Shadow slabs, tall silence, that stretch of distant avenue blocked by a slow hump. Violet Hopper mused, as if on stage: the city made a person aware of time, of its slow white volume, and how they were loose particles briefly within it. The gradual accumulation of confusions was now revealed, there temporarily being no other confusions to distract. The congestion had gone. It felt similar to jet-lag.

They turned to each other.

'We don't speak very well. Have you noticed how the Americans are so descriptive and confident? Our sentences are shorter. Our thoughts break off. We don't seem comfortable talking, I don't know why. Have you noticed we make silly quips, even when someone asks the time? I caught myself with the bus driver yesterday.'

'You mean us, Australians?'

Borelli agreed. 'We're embarrassed. We're not as confident as we look. We speak in jerks, or we're over-familiar. The quips you mention I think might be connected to our geographical location, and our land emptiness.'

Louisa laughed. He could talk, yet he so rarely remained at the table.

'Possibly,' said North looking at Borelli, Sasha seated beside him.

'We're not bad,' Doug called out. 'I've known a few who could talk the leg off a chair.' He turned to his wife. 'You've met Clem McCagney at work.'

'But I think quips keep us going. Being so far removed and relatively alone,' Borelli went on, 'we seem to need encouragement. Quips help us along; things aren't all that bad. It's as if, in Australia, we're all in hospital. There's a lot of quipping in hospitals.'

And they all laughed and glanced down at their clothing.

Mrs Cathcart had to correct the impression: 'Sir Robert Menzies was a fine speaker.'

'The Australian Prime Minister,' Kaddok put in.

North turned to Borelli. 'The explanation might merely be habit. Why, for example, do men and women in Paris talk with cigarettes hanging from their bottom lips? In India people slowly shake their heads when they mean "yes".'

'The French. Aren't they piggy to foreigners?' Sasha asked.

Gerald leaned forward. 'I'm not 100% sure about the Americans. I must say I've always had my doubts. As you say, they can talk.'

'They've had television for a long time . . .'

'The Yanks are alright. They're generous. That you would have to admit. And great artists, great scientists . . . .'

'You mean they're clever.'

'What about Canadians? Have you ever met an interesting Canadian?'

The comparisons, their anecdotes. Gerald pursed his lips.

'Yes, I'm not crazy about the Canadians.'

'I don't remember any,' Violet mysteriously cracked.

'I've never been one for the Germans,' Shiela confessed. 'I don't know why.'

'The Second World War,' Kaddok chipped in.

'What about the English?'

The English . . . What about the English?

'Ar, the old Poms are alright,' said Doug. 'Let em go.'

'They're miles better than the Irish.'

'You don't find the English have their nose in the air, perhaps a trifle superior?'

'No more than the French,' said North.

'The English are on a plateau,' said Borelli, 'It's green and cultivated, and they're resting. They're having a good time.'

'The Scots don't have a sense of humour,' someone said.

'Mind you, I've heard the Poles keep to themselves. It's not on our ticket, is it?'

No. Poland was off.

'I don't like the shoes they always wear,' Sasha laughed.

The Poles wear peculiar-looking shoes. The Russians wear socks with sandals. The Dutch wear clogs.

'Europeans.'

The intricate pull of hyperborea prevailed, assisted by the magnetic pole. Towards . . . cold metals, the ornate railings of boulevards, verglas, and gutterals.

Gerald thought the Spanish were a marvellous people but could be better.

'The Italians and the Greeks—'

'I don't mind the Italians.'

'We've got them at home all over the place. They've got their own newspapers. No skin off your nose!' Doug suddenly turned to Borelli.

'He's not Italian,' Louisa insisted.

'They were piss-weak in the war,' said Garry.

Mrs Cathcart mentioned the Dutch: 'They're very clean.'

'Like the Swiss,' Kaddok agreed.

'What about the Swedes then?'

'They're a cold people!'

Socialism and suicides. Blue eyes. Volvos.

'Hasseblad cameras,' Kaddok told them, though they hardly listened to him.

What about Einstein's tram at Berne? Did you ever see reindeer racing in Finland?

'Indians,' Shiela recalled now, 'are sometimes oily. Perhaps it is the tropics: I had trouble communicating. They all have moustaches.'

'I think of those blacks in Africa.'

'What about the Japs? What makes them tick? I'm darned if I know,' said Doug.

'They're like the Chinese, aren't they?'

'You should see them in Singapore.' North went over to the window and Ken Hofmann moved to go to an exhibition. When he tapped Louisa's shoulder she nodded without turning, letting him go.

Japan's GNP figures and the village structure in corporations were supplied by Kaddok. He mentioned Mr Honda, their Nikons and Canons.

'I think everyone has been rudely disappointed,' Gwen was saying, 'in the Arabs.'

The Cathcarts had both heard they were dirty.

'Yes, I must say I don't like the look of them.'

'Egypt was interesting . . .' Shiela said.

Here Garry arrived from the Automobile Show, something he had been looking forward to. He plomped himself down in Hofmann's chair.

'But friends of ours were robbed of everything, in full view of the Pyramids.'

In Russia they say you've got to carry your own plugs for the basins. It's hard to get a hot shower in Italy, France. The Japanese in their wisdom don't believe in street names.

Doug slapped his knee. 'I keep saying, we're not bad the more you look around.'

'I think we're very lucky,' added his spouse. 'There's too much talk.'

Fair enough! General consensus at that; pursing of lips.

'We've got ourselves,' said Gwen simply. She told the truth. It was vaguely understood: a kind of refuge, always there.

More nodding. Silence. It was hard to hold on to the subject.

'Well, we've seen a few countries . . .' said Doug. Then catching sight of Garry he cried, 'Howdy, stranger!'

Slumped in the chair, Garry waved.

'I say,' Gerald smiled, 'you look as if you've had a good time.'

'I say, thanks.'

A snicker from Violet, second on the left.

Leaning across the table, Borelli whispered to Louisa: 'In London I'll get you a postcard I think you'll like.' A single postcard: but he alone seemed to understand what she would enjoy.

'What is it? Tell me.'

'It is a drawing by Blake, "The Builder of the Pyramids." That's all. I was reminded before when someone was talking. The builder has the most extraordinary nose. And isn't that a good title?'

Louisa nodded. 'I'll remind you.'

'Old Garry's peeved about something,' Doug turned to his wife.

'It was a real bloody let-down.'

What was? The Auto Show. Not everyone listened anymore.

'They had the engines running and you could hardly see the machines for the bloody smoke. I was coughing like a bastard. Have a whiff of my coat. I saw an immaculate FJ though, at the back, and they had an original Hartnett, alongside an Edsel. That was worth seeing. The rest were all big Yankee Jobs.'

'What, Duesenbergs, Packards, Bearcats with the circular windshield, and so on?'

'Right.'

'And quite a crowd?'

Garry held his hand horizontal below the eyes, like a water level.

'I'm glad we didn't go,' Sasha turned to Violet.

'Then I got bloody bushed in the subway on the way back. I thought for a while I'd get done over by a bunch of negroes. You've got to watch them.'

'Ah well . . .' Doug consoled through his nose.

Leaving the table Borelli joined North at the window. The doctor folded his arms nodding. Sasha went over, making three.

A few days remained in America. 'How time flies,' Shiela sighed, somehow causing Violet to splutter-laugh.

Sunlight crossed the floor and mounted the linen table.

Several times Borelli glanced back at Louisa while he was talking, but after opening her bag for some private reason she went up to her room. When Borelli turned he saw an empty chair.

Among her new friends Shiela released a most beautiful smile. The way it unfolded like a large bird leaving a cage: mouth and nostrils stretched to tremendous widths, and her eyebrows arched, her ears angled back. It had never been refined, Shiela's smile. Now it sometimes grew when no one spoke, as they remained sitting there; and then others would begin smiling, looking at her.

That peculiar interior perspective of hotels: the quiet corridor and blank doors. As James Borelli trod towards his room, three of the crumpled table-napkins left behind slowly unfolded of their own accord. The corridors were empty of staff pushing trolleys loaded with sheets and soap. Quality of light: goldish, thick. To the left and right a prime function of the hotel, of any hotel, operated smoothly: scattered personal effects of travellers remained as they were, waiting for the sudden light.

Paraphernalia and the personality of travellers: another doctoral thesis could be written. In 113 a nomad's razor and brush lay alongside the bed, while the man's habitual 'Spirex' notebook and ballpoint were in the bathroom. A spare khaki jacket—now said to be rare—and a clean shirt (blue) spilled out of a canvas bag squashed on the floor. Little more. No camera, for instance. Engrossed in a range of things, Borelli travelled, unlike Phillip North, without a library. And with the curtains pulled wide open the room looked unnaturally bare, distinctly a transition point. The telescope dangled, ignored. Two along Violet and Shiela looked at a forties musical on afternoon television, their curtains drawn. After pacing with his hands behind his back Borelli went outside to the next door.

He knocked.

'Louisa? . . .'

For the door had swung with his touch. It had been slightly ajar.

'I'm sorry! Excuse . . .'

She must have been tip-toeing, rushing forward, for she slapped her arms across her breasts, a white X. Yet this left all that was below exposed, a focal point. Louisa was naked.

Twisting his head, protecting her, Borelli had to leave. In mid-twist he stopped. He tried then to look only at her eyes, normally natural for him, normally so easy, but his eyes wanted to wander down, and so they did. Such rise and fall, slope and fullness, soft alabaster possessing its own warmth and illumination. Her suprisingly wide hips he hadn't noticed before. It was all there and before him.

Louisa smiled slightly, nervous now.

'Close the door.'

'What? Uh . . .'

She had lowered her arms. Borelli put one hand near his chin. He closed the door.

Louisa laughed. She stepped forward. She placed her hands around his neck; he rested his unnaturally on her hips. All over, her body was warm and frail, perfumed from a bath.

'Why are you trembling?'

'Well I shouldn't be here,' he said hoarse. 'I shouldn't be, should I?'

'We're nervous,' she laughed. And in a sing-song voice, 'But we shouldn't be.'

It was ten minutes to four, New York.

'Let me see you again,' he said.

Louisa stepped back. He shielded his eyes: joy and despair.

'I am nice?'

'Oh yes,' he added. 'Stripped of your jewelry.'

As he slowly shook his head Louisa half turned and laughed from the back of her throat, 'Just like you.'

She was so bold now in her nakedness. It surprised him: it began to flood him. She did a fancy pirouette but he couldn't smile. When she came back to him, he frowned.

'I can't stay. And you know, I shouldn't be here.'

But he drew her to him and into his clothing. Near his wide-open eye a tiny vertical vein vibrated in her neck, the silver balance-wheel in a watch, fuel-line to an engine. It was hers; Borelli kissed it.

Louisa whispered, she tried to look at him. 'This is better, this is better.'

But there was the spreading expanse of what she had offered, of what was natural now. He couldn't quite understand, he frowned, but lifted her. On the point then of shaking his head he stopped: someone outside in the corridor.

Louisa didn't notice.

'Better put something on,' he whispered. 'Sweet one. Go on.'

Louisa didn't appear to listen.

'Do you have any brothers and sisters?' she wanted to know.

Borelli looked at her. These were the questions of a married woman. He glanced at the door and the corridor.

'Do you?'

'No.'

'Are your parents alive?'

'My mother is.'

'Poor boy . . .'

'Why, what's the matter? But go on, quickly. Get dressed. Louisa? Or I'll have to go.'

Louisa wanted to dawdle though.

Gazing away she pronounced his name several times. She tried it in broad Northern Strine. It was so unlike her it made him shake his head. This Borelli was dark-haired, yet pale; so serious and watchful to her. There was a density of his she wanted to dismantle. Louisa kissed him quickly several times and then rested her chin on his shoulder.

At a right angle to them, Room 315, Hofmann balanced on one foot removing his socks. Violet had left poor Shiela to her postcards; and while Hofmann went through the exhibition he had just seen—hop-hopping—Violet unhooked her brassière, glancing at herself in the tall hotel mirror. She was only half listening. Upright and horizontal lay perfume bottles and puffs, paper towel products, brushes and oval pink lids, and in the air remained the vague scented humidity of talc. In this way the room resembled a dressing room of a theatre; and those who used the mirror here were replaced with similar regularity, in short repertory.

'Where's your little girlfriend?' Hofmann suddenly asked.

Violet blew out smoke. 'Sasha's traipsed off with her doctor friend, again.'

'Old North?' Hofmann folded his shirt. 'I haven't spoken much to him.'

'He's alright,' said Violet pausing—although naked, she had nothing else to do. 'He's not exactly old. No, I wouldn't say that.'

Hofmann didn't answer; he didn't want her getting thoughtful.

But when Violet turned, thin in her nakedness, she began laughing. 'My, I've got me a coloured boy.'

The smooth sides and back of him were striped with red and blue bruises from the flag.

She was still laughing when he grabbed her wrist. They fell on the bed, on top of the clothing. 'Ere, not so fast,' she gasped, always the star of stage or screen. She leaned over to stub out her cigarette. But with Hofmann already at work she let out a cry.

The same soothing muzak was piped into every room. When it changed Hofmann sauntered back to his room, a few along. He passed Borelli and they nodded slightly.

Divided more or less into two: there were those who frowned in silence trying to hold and separate the constellation of impressions, mainly useless impressions; and those who cluttered it with words, any words, shattering the approximate form of things. The first were easily recognizable. In the foyer they pondered the carpet with their toes, as if they'd found a fleeting impression underfoot. The rest, comprising the hub, stood as a group distinguished by skipping head movements and voice, and light-coloured clothing. A surprising number stamped in the one spot, rubbing their hands. It wasn't cold. To fill in time they offered cracks, quips, comments and isolated adverbs. Yes. For example, Garry: 'Did everyone bring their mosquito nets?' They received only casual acknowledgement, but were still appreciated. It was considered normal: mortar between the bricks.

They were finishing mugs of instant coffee—'good old nylon coffee'—a crack—and two or three, the ladies, had trouble fitting their mouths around the huge hero sandwiches. Many wore coats, furs, mufflers and whatnot; and the early tea certainly added to the atmosphere. It was almost dark outside. The traffic had more of a distant night sound. Abruptly Doug Cathcart breathed on the pale blue eyes of his binoculars and felt for his handkerchief; Kaddok there had the leather-hooded telephoto lens protruding ready from his abdomen.

The tour organizer from the hotel hurried over. Natty, natty.

'Alright, gang,' he said looking at his watch, 'you're on. Good luck.'

Good luck? What does he mean?

But the entrepreneur clapped Gerald on the back, smiling. Americans can do that: easy.

The Landrovers, long wheelbase models, were fitted with metal spades and spare cans of juice, spotlights and winches. Driving the front one a barrel-chested American had a scraggy silver beard, a scar on his forehead and whisky on his breath. When he spoke he either swore or grunted in some Indian lingo—a nasty bastard. He was the Park Ranger. The second driver, his partner, never left the vehicle and only afterwards when the party compared notes did they discover he was the Ranger's exact double. Both men also wore the same crumpled safari jacket equipped with sheath knife, a cartridge clip and a water bottle. In this respect they were similar to their specially equipped Landrovers.

A practised forward-arching motion of his arm out the window; the Ranger then shoved into whining four-wheel drive and the convoy got going.

The Game Park was located in the central most un-expected part of New York, uneven terrain of abandoned benches, of bushes, rock formations and small ravines.

The Ranger wasn't answering questions.

So Phillip North said to Sasha, 'Well I'm told they have foxes, jack-rabbits, skunks and owls. And of course the squirrels.'

At that the Ranger let out a roar of a laugh and shouted over his shoulder: 'You hear that, Charo? That's rich.'

'Yes, bwana.'

A black man in khaki shorts and bare feet crouched in the back; had to uncoil slightly to answer.

Muttering to himself the Ranger laughed again or rather hissed through his teeth. It sounded remarkably like the Landrover engine.

Wedged against him, Sasha glanced at North. He shrugged. Better leave him alone.

Turning into the Park the headlights were switched off and Violet in the back was told to douse her cigarette. The Ranger drove carefully. Many of the trees had lost their leaves. The track wandered in and out; edges of dark branches tried to scratch and sprang back. Black bushes bulged like boulders, yet ordinary footpaths and stone benches were glimpsed at the sides. Before long the pet-roleum hum and horns of Detroit faded, the lights of the surrounding tall buildings almost all blotted out. The Landrover swung into a large bush; they were enveloped unexpectedly in leaves.

He switched the engine off.

All quiet then: the leaves rustled when anyone moved.

Quickly, they followed the Ranger out some thirty paces, all but Kaddok stumbling and tripping, the virtually invisible black man taking up the rear, lugging two wicker hampers under his arm like suitcases.

The Ranger shinned up a large Black Oak—remarkably agile for a man of his size and age. The pleat in his safari jacket opened to reveal a Colt .45 in its tan holster. Violet and Gerald were giggling and whispering, but a sharp word came from above among the vibrating bending branches. Gwen, the first to follow, found a wooden ladder. Doug began pushing his wife up. Heh, heh. The life of the party, Garry, bunted Sasha with his head, and she told him to stop; the others were glancing around furtively instead of laughing.

So subtle and naturally camouflaged was the panelled treehouse that they were inside it before they fully realized. In the moonlight they made out an upholstered bench around three sides, and sat down automatically, shoulder-to-shoulder.

The bearer too finally made the climb with the hampers, and after giving him a playful punch in the stomach the Ranger closed the door.

'You can speak normally,' he said in his twang, 'if you whisper.'

They could hear him breathing heavily as he made space for himself by the slot which they now noticed opened like a window behind their necks. It explained the draught, the cold.

Staring outside into the dark the Ranger moved his hand and found the special switch.

'You've got to hand it to the Yanks,' Garry whispered, the first words spoken.

Directly below, an ordinary-looking street lamp coruscated then lit up with unexpected vividness a typical intersection of footpaths which are found in the park. A bench and a casually placed trash bin set the scene, and the surrounding grass was pale green. A newspaper blew across and clutched the base of the lamp. Inside the specially constructed blind the same light illuminated their faces and shadowed the walls.

They looked around, interested. For some reason Gwen

235

Kaddok and Atlas both smiled.

'I'm not liking this,' Sasha whispered.

'They can't see us,' the Ranger breathed. And he looked around at them, settled on Violet, then Louisa, before returning to the window. Those with cameras and binoculars set them up and waited.

The effectiveness of .357 magnum rifles cropped up in a polite and professional conversation with Phillip North. On this the Ranger proved to be extremely knowledgeable. Elephant and aardvark entered the conversation. Single syllable impressions of Africa.

'My heroes,' Violet yawned. 'How boring.'

'Quiet, woman.'

The Ranger glanced at his watch and took a swig from his hip flask. Soon after, the bearer opened the hampers for the others. It was good eating the ham sandwiches and coffee, steaming black. It all came in the price.

'Ever shot a red roo?' Garry leaned across. That reminded him. Ha, ha. Friend of his, Bill Smallacombe, last year—

'Bwana!'

The Ranger held up his hand to the others.

'Is that our decoy?' Garry enquired. He gave a low whistle.

'It should be an old man on crutches.' The Ranger looked at his watch. 'I knew he was late.'

So they looked down at the woman in the fur coat. She was young and paced up and down as if she waited for someone. They could see her white face.

'She shouldn't be there,' the Ranger went on. He was being earnest. 'She could get hurt.'

'Not a bad decoy though,' Garry laughed, a bit nervous.

The others were silent.

'A mob was sighted at dusk farther along. About five; all males. She's going to frighten them off or she'll get hurt. She'd better move on.'

He took another swig and scanned the undergrowth behind and on either side of the woman. The street lamp formed a yellow canopy blurred at the edges, hundreds of moths circling the centre as the woman paced up and down.

'She's going to spoil everything.'

'It is finished,' said Charo. He stood up.

'No. Wait.'

No one spoke. Experienced travellers, they made allowances. In the poor light Ken Hofmann could move his hand to touch the neck of Violet Hopper. Louisa had squeezed Borelli's hand.

'Capitalism,' Borelli was saying to Gerald, 'free enterprise, is by nature violent. It's structured on power, speed and visibility. It relies on them. Visual differences and selfishness are promoted—'

'There has to be a winner,' said Kaddok.

'No wonder those who are flung out to the edges feel the recourse is simply to grab.'

'Survival of the fittest, the law of the jungle?' Kaddok threw in. Another platitude.

'But you're not political, are you?' Louisa whispered.

'Not especially, no. I've just been thinking.'

Phillip North tapped the Ranger's arm. 'Shouldn't we warn her, call out or something?'

'No, that would frighten them.'

This being their last night in America, the Cathcarts took the opportunity to scribble messages on a pile of postcards.

'Bwana,' whispered the bearer.

The woman had stopped walking. She swung around.

'No!' cried Sasha.

'Shut up,' the Ranger hissed.

Puerto Ricans in leather, one white face among them, stepped out from the shadows, nonchalant-like, as dark and as silent as the shadows, surrounding her. The woman glanced one way, then the other. She held the neck of her coat.

'They're big,' the Ranger breathed.

North shook the Ranger's arm. Leaning forward, watching intently, he didn't seem to feel it.

The woman tried running. She pushed against one and fell. They closed in around her, the circle. Rolling on her back she tried kicking, and lost a shoe. First, her handbag was pulled off her. She began sobbing.

'Somebody stop them!' Sasha cried. 'The animals!'

The Ranger pulled her back from the window.

'You wanted to come. Now stay. The woman has committed an error in life. Nature takes its course. That's life.' He turned to North, 'You too, sit!'

Poor woman, her white thighs parted in the moonlight. The fur was pulled open, her dress torn up and sideways. Others pinned her arms. And the shadows multiplied the union in all the angles, violent, interlocking blackness.

None if any noticed Shiela, her mouth and eyes wide, and the tremor which spread through from her warmth, electrical at the nerve-ends, which suddenly, violently, splayed her feet. Shiela stifled a cry. But then while a few tried to preserve some detachment the majority were breathing in and shaking their heads at the spectacle, or making that perplexed clicking sound with their tongues. 'Chhhhrist!' Garry let out hoarsely. He spoke for the majority. 'They're animals, look at that.'

The Cathcarts had addressed all the postcards and began licking the stamps.

Sasha had settled to the floor, her head in her arms, comforted by North. And Louisa with Borelli was crying, shaking her head.

But their own position was felt to be precarious, preventing intervention. Directly below were five armed with freedom of excitement and assorted flick-knives. At least up in the tree they were downwind.

She lay, an exhausted animal, the woman, a crippled furry thing, split and torn. She moved her foot as the last two fought over their turn. The tall white one fell on top of her.

Sudden darkness. The light was cut. They felt the bulk of the Ranger quickly swing around. 'Who did that? Where are you?'

'We've seen enough,' said Borelli.

The voices in the street rose and fell. Then there was quiet.

'This is not your country, boy. This is my business.'

'You're wrong there.'

'That's right,' said North.

'It wasn't what we thought,' Gerald explained.

'It wasn't what you thought? Oh you're rich.' Fumbling around for the switch. 'I'll find this and punch you in the face.'

'This doesn't happen in our country.'

'I'm going to punch you in the face.'

Borelli's walking stick hit the window ledge. 'The light can go on in a minute. Then you can do what you like.'

'Very well done. Splendid,' said Kaddok who had followed it through Gwen's whisper. 'Well worth the trip. Thank you very much.'

Gwen pulled him down. 'We're not going just yet.'

Muttering obscenities the Ranger shoved against one or two. Lunging forward he switched on the street lamp. It swam before them. They blinked. A white handkerchief fluttered on the ground, nothing more. They listened, and decided it was safe to go down. Hofmann and others quickly inspected the site before returning to the hotel.

5

What is known about the problem:
1) loss of appetite
2) statesmen and businessmen discover: intricate ne-
   gotiations can be upset. Decision-making processes
   suffer
3) air hostesses complain: it upsets the menstrual cycle
4) it is unnatural to break the body's arcadian rhythm.
   It is going against the spin of the earth, not to
   mention the other planets. Never happened with
   propellers: remember the Pan Am Clippers, slow
   boats to China, zeppelins, flying boats, upholstered
   saloon carriages?
5) interference with natural biological cycles has been
   shown to reduce the life-span of animals.

The city appeared to be the same, the mass as remembered,
yet it was different. It was they who had changed, if only
slightly, a shade. They waited in line for the double-decker
at Heathrow. Taking for granted now the solid long objects,
the city proper, they followed the contributing details, the
ever-changing parts, small and brightly coloured, people
here and there sliding across, the movement, the words and
the gradual lights.

It all passed in a blur, stroking their eyes. They had to
pull themselves up. Tourists, just returned by jet; gazing
through glass; distanced, out of step and place. It had been
a late last night in New York. That city of verticals already
receded, rose up again, receded. Nobody felt like talking.

Old Marble Arch—still standing. It made them feel at
home.

Their vagueness showed in the simple grey of the Arch,
the outline of which was imprecise and not worth the effort;

irritation showed when they returned to the British Museum, to their hotel in the dead wing, for it had been Gerald's sensible idea to stick to what they knew. In their previous stay it had grown familiar, informally so, and all had agreed: they had become part of the place. Now beginning with the formerly jovial moustached desk clerk who once explained with diagrams how he and Gwen Kaddok could well have been related, onto the West Indian porters horsing around and sitting on their luggage, no one recognized or greeted them, or if they did, they chose to hide it, and yet they'd been chatting and joking, seeking directions, only what, three or four weeks ago. A slap in the face, in effect. It put them in place, with all the rest. While the feeling of irrelevance didn't appear to worry Borelli and Gerald, the others grew by turn quiet, indignant, increasingly critical and crabby led by Sasha and Mrs Cathcart. And now that they looked at the place the cream corridors and the cold rooms were down at the heel (not even genteel), like the long thread hanging from the stained cuff of the lift attendant they'd before learned to call 'Guvnor'. The hotel in New York, even with its jackhammers and tenacious mountaineers, was preferable to this.

After the flight a hot shower would have helped; it was only natural: but they remembered as they unpacked and ran their tongues over their teeth this hotel was equipped with nothing but vitreous enamel baths. Each one noticed however they had been given the same room.

Louisa remembered the *Hair Salon* and homed in across the street taking the other women: such a determined group, fast in its gaiety. Well, they were removing themselves from the lives of men for several hours, and planned on keeping them waiting. It made Borelli for one ask aloud whether being groomed by fellow members was an underlying ceremony, organized by and indeed essential to the tribe. Did it occur in all cultures?

Desultory drift of male travellers.

'It is like a wedding rehearsal?' North suggested.

Well, absence and formality play their part in both.

'During it,' Borelli tried, 'the woman also projects and imagines herself. Is that what you mean?'

'Grooming', snickered Hofmann; no apparent reason.

'What about,' Kaddok floundered, but kept going, 'the animal kingdom? I'd look there if I were you.' Turning to where he expected North, the zoologist, he faced an empty chair. Without Gwen he was tentative; or it could have been the jet lag.

'Now listen, comparisons with animals are useless. Next minute you'll trundle out the peacock.'

'I'm not sure that animals help each other anyway,' North said to Kaddok. 'Generally speaking, animals don't rely on anyone. They're already decorated.'

With Gwen missing they could look Kaddok in the eye. He was brooding, impervious. He was hunched; never said anything funny: a leaning shouldered rock holding his place, not wanting to let go. Over the years he had accumulated and clung onto hundreds of scraps and well-established facts like barnacles. These he bartered, removing them from his mind. Without them he imagined he was lost.

'There's a reason for everything,' Borelli stretched his arms. 'But I don't know . . .'

'Nothing is as it seems,' Hofmann smiled.

Some of them laughed. Borelli laughed. (They didn't know what they were talking about.)

'Of course, it could be our fault,' North shifted. 'They say today it's a male-dominated world. I must say I haven't thought about it much.'

'Our fault?' Garry echoed. He'd been arguing with Doug Cathcart about something else. 'Listen, they love getting dolled up.'

And they themselves swung in their seats and made the right noises, changed their way of talking, when the women swept in just before lunch, shining from the outdoors with news to tell. Well-practised—after more than thirty years—Doug let out a whistle from across the room; quite a distance. 'Whacko! Say, that looks better . . .' Get in early and be positive. It saved a lot.

Phillip North and Gerald of the old school, stood up.

'You look fine,' Garry told them. 'I'm not kidding.'

'What did I tell you?' Mrs Cathcart said to Louisa.

'What do you expect from this lot?' said Violet.

'Hey, what's up?' Doug looked pained; and Garry scratched his neck.

The faces of stupid men looking up from their chairs.

'Someone tell him!'

'You're a rotten hopeless lot,' said Sasha. She looked at Phillip North. 'It just goes to show.'

'We've been,' Shiela laughed, 'but we haven't had our hair done.'

'They're as blind as—' said Violet.

'Listen,' Garry shouted, 'we've been talking about you all the time. Haven't we?'

'It's not serious,' said Gerald. He wasn't much interested.

Mrs Cathcart plomped herself down near Doug. 'It was a queer place, and who would have known?'

Doug still pulled faces at her hair, trying to see what he had missed.

'And you didn't know?' Sasha asked North. 'What does *Salon* mean?'

'French,' Kaddok declared.

'It used to be where they had an annual exhibition of paintings in Paris,' said Hofmann.

'Well it means large reception room, I think,' said North. 'I suppose it's been bastardized now.'

'Our *Salon* over the road is full of special hair. It's a museum.'

Even Gerald became interested.

'My feet are killing me,' Mrs Cathcart said, while the others were all talking at once.

'We paid a small admission,' said Shiela, 'and really quite enjoyed it. The word "hair" comes from "air"— because it's slightly heavier than air. We were told.'

'But that's rubbish,' Gerald laughed.

'There is a scientific reason for having hair, for body warmth and so forth,' Louisa entered in her smooth voice, 'yet it is the most easily alterable part of the body. In most societies the length and style of hair are an indication of a person's religious and political beliefs.'

She patted the back of her head.

Borelli glanced at North.

'And what were we talking about before? But why didn't you come and get us? We were sitting here scratching our heads.'

'They had hair,' said Violet looking at them, 'from a man's and a gorilla's armpit; we couldn't tell the difference. That made us girls sit up.'

'Come off it!'

But they all thought that was good; seismic hiccups for once entered the shoulders of Kaddok.

'Did old Sampson get a guernsey?'

'So did Lady Godiva, poor thing.'

'Violet, what was that proverb strung across the wall, from wherever it was?'

'No, we decided not to mention that.'

'The Persian proverb,' said Shiela. ' "Women have more hair than brains." '

Haw, haw. Horse laughs.

'Shiela!'

And Garry slapped Violet on the back.

'People are afraid of hair,' said Gwen quietly. 'The hair of others is difficult to brush off.'

A little snippet; it made Borelli slap his forehead.

'That's not bad. That's alright.'

'Why are you so interested in hair?' Louisa quietly asked.

'We all are. It's constantly on our minds!'

Gerald leaned between them, his elbows on their chairs, 'Freud, you know, was supposed to have said about weaving that it was a woman braiding her ah, pubic hairs to form an absent . . . an absent penis. That was what Freud said.'

'How silly,' said Louisa. 'All his ridiculous theories.'

'Of course he was bald,' put in North.

'We don't seem to require all these theories,' said Louisa meaning the women.

'They had a diagram,' Gwen went on, largely for Leon's

benefit, 'which showed that if the hair from one day's cutting from the world's hairdressers was swept up into a pile it would be bigger—imagine—than Mount Kanchenjunga. On Fridays they say it is higher still. The disposal of hair is a little known but serious problem.'

'It's a growth industry,' Kaddok nodded pursing his lips. His sideburns were thin and greying.

Hair in cushions, in horse collars, glued on dolls heads; the extremely lucrative toupee industry in Hong Kong. These were some of the solutions offered by the *Hair Salon*.

The 'blonde myth', the problem of women with hormone moustaches were exhaustively discussed by means of closed-circuit video equipment. The *Salon*'s trichologists had assembled extremely good examples of superfluous hairs, of short and curlies, locks of royal hair and other bigwigs, tonsures of certain religious freaks, bits of mysteriously singed hair; lanugo and an oily film star's quiff had made the ladies shiver. A small room with flesh-coloured walls was filled with nothing but eyebrows ('supraorbital ridge hair'). Whose eyebrows are these? *a*) Karl Marx's. *b*) Sir Robert Menzies'. *c*) Rasputin's.

'Guess how many hairs are estimated in the head of a typical thirty-year-old Englishman?'

Gwen turned to her husband; Mister History didn't know.

'Eight hundred thousand, three hundred and twenty-odd.'

Terrible photographs showed how the head is forcibly shaved—by fellow members of the tribe—as punishment, a sign of disgrace.

'They didn't have only hair,' Sasha said.

There were secondhand combs, shaving gear through the ages, disgusting hair-powders, many nickel-plated depilators, a hair-trigger from a .303 rifle and examples of dangerous hairpin bends. An ingenious skull had been rigged up on a table to show at the flick of a switch how hair stands up with an electric shock.

'Any turbans?' Kaddok enquired. 'You'd expect them to have turbans.'

Yes, a good cross-section: the East African and Indian types were both represented.

Glancing at North, Violet whispered to Sasha, 'Never trust a man with beard. My mother always said.'

Hair continues to grow for several hours after death, the last to get the message.

'I had no idea hair was so important,' said Louisa. 'We had a marvellous time, didn't we?'

Sasha and the women laughed.

'You should have come,' Shiela said to them. 'It was very interesting.'

The social factors behind the left-hand part. Bottles of seban: transluscent, secretive. The world's longest recorded moustache (that Punjabi rice merchant).

The real truth about crabs; brief history and estimated daily tonnage of dandruff. In the dandruff stakes England was the world leader.

'Very interesting,' Kaddok moved his lips to commit it to memory.

'Yeah, but what conclusions if any did it draw?'

That hair is symbolic, a visual measure in more ways than one; that hair has its own history and power.

Reproductions of hair paintings included 'Woman Combing Her Hair'.

'What's-his-name?' Louisa clicked her fingers at her husband, looking at him for the first time. 'The modern French artist . . .'

'You always forget,' was Hofmann's comment—not a hair out of place. 'Pablo Picasso.'

'Was that all?' Borelli looked around at them.

'I love cutting men's hair,' Sasha was saying to North. 'I don't know why. I'll cut yours. It is getting long.'

Collection of early shampoo bottles. Clippers. The stigma endured by albinoes and redheads. The extra length of male hair between world wars.

They glanced at each other. 'That was all, wasn't it?'

'Who would have thought?' Shiela said, brimming with the extra knowledge.

The high incidence of hairy wrists in English and Australian literature.

'Everywhere's a museum,' Sasha now complained.

'The whole world is a museum,' Gerald agreed.

North, and others, nodded. An interested glaze entered their eyes: reflexion and extension. The spectator is forced back onto himself.

'Museums are a microcosm,' Kaddok added significantly.

'That's right.'

'Yes, I wish I'd been,' said Borelli.

'It's only across the street.'

It brought Mrs Cathcart back to earth. 'It was unexpected.' She bent over to put on her shoes. 'I need a rinse and a perm.'

The world itself is a museum; and within its circumference the many small museums, the natural and the man-built, represent the whole. The rocks of Sicily, the Uffizi, the corner of a garden, each are miniatures of the world at large. Look, the sky at night: the most brilliantly displayed and ever-changing museum of harmonic mathematics and insects, of gods and mythological figures, agricultural machinery. The catalogue is endless.

There was the man in a Derbyshire village, Freddy Russell by reg. trade name, who lost his job with the adjoining pottery concern (commemorative and musical mugs), made up for it during the summer months, conducting tours around his nose, chiefly interested Australasian parties, occasional wide-ranging North Americans. Performance and conceptual artists tried to claim Russell. Art historians sporting the crumpled bow-tie published formalist essays placing him—catapulting him—at the forefront of the vanguard; Manhattan dealers and three of the world's great modern museums had all offered him prestigious One Man Shows, as they are called; to no avail. Russell would remain the humble retiring sort, 'Fred' to shopkeepers, neighbours and friends.

247

His small house in dreary mock-Tudor behind the village main street was distinguished by a yellow no-parking zone outside, the length of several tourist buses, although at the time the only vehicle was a motor bike and hooded sidecar at the twilight end of the street.

Formal behaviour for the first minutes: Mrs Russell in the lounge room rubbing her hands, commented at length about the weather with a fluidity which suggested more rain; they, all bowing somewhat, listened intently, conscious of the personal ornaments and smell of someone else's home. Mrs Cathcart warmed to her at once.

A dun-coloured curtain divided the lounge room. The vinyl sofa, the worn armchair and assorted dining room chairs and nick-nacks had been arranged facing the curtain in two rows. 'Please make yourselves comfortable,' she indicated.

The alert photographer in the front touched the curtain with his knees. Doug could sit at the back with the calm skeptics, elbow on the telly. He had his binoculars.

'Fred, are you ready?' Mrs Russell put one ear to the curtain.

No answer.

'He always does that,' she smiled back at them, 'the blighter. Coming ready or not!'

She pulled the curtain aside.

On a camp-stretcher, Russell lay face-up within arm's reach of the front row. Neatly dressed, in his fifties, and lean, he had sandy eyebrows and several days' growth the colour of saltbush; but all their attention centred on his nose. Side-on it was uncanny. It rose out of the red skin and stubble with a monolithic force . . . instantly recognizable. In slope and proportion, down to the smallest detail, it was a replica (in miniature) of Ayers Rock. The grey tufts in the nostrils matched the dry vegetation choking the two much-photographed caves at the windswept north-eastern tip. And because it looked so heavy, almost false on Russell's ruddy face, it drew a response similar to the first sight of Ayers Rock in the flat Australian desert: murmurs of appreciation, disbelief. A flicker of a smile altered Russell's cheeks like a faint wind in the desert. The wall behind had been painted suitable azure—classic cloudless sky of the Dead Centre.

Breathing heavily Kaddok quickly switched from a telephoto to wide-angle lens. The others leaned forward on their seats.

By a series of body or 'weather' changes Russell, lying motionless, successfully duplicated the world-famous colour changes of the Rock.

It began as a cold startling presence, factual and grand, of grey weathered stone. Ayers Rock is like this in the mornings.

As they watched and drew nearer it changed by degrees, deepening to heliotrope, majestic carbuncular purple, extraordinary for a rock. Russell achieved this by holding his breath—hence the mirage-like shimmer in the last ten seconds. Any similar change in the rest of his face was hidden by the surrounding stubble.

Next, the glowing brick-red, another aspect of Ayers Rock, much depicted in travel posters, was fairly easily reproduced by swigging in quick succession three cans of beer, quietly belching. The nose reached a bright almost transparent red, and held: Ayers Rock, late afternoon.

They applauded spontaneously and waited for the next change.

Russell now settled down, appeared to brace himself, and with a barely perceptible movement of his hand lowered the lights. The nose immediately registered a different hue. It threw a tremendous shadow.

A long pause, building up the suspense. They were all staring at the nose! It darkened even further.

Suddenly Russell made a sound in his throat like thunder and a cardiganned hand from behind the curtain—that of Russell's wife—poured water from a plastic can onto his nose and face: the cloudburst which flooded Ayers Rock in the mid-1960s, flooding the surrounding mulga and sand, filling the water courses and holes; and Russell's nose duplicated exactly the cascading spray in detail, nostrils leaking, the pitted walls now all grey and defensive, steaming like a great stranded whale.

It was remarkably effective. Again they applauded. At the back Doug passed the binoculars to Gerald who leaned forward squinting; Doug could have sworn he had seen steps cut into the Rock there to the left and a euro trying to escape the deluge. Most of them recalled the dramatic colour photographs published world-wide at the time, which was probably where Russell himself had seen it.

They were still nodding and whispering when the lights came on—much brighter it seemed.

Again Mrs Russell's well-rehearsed hand entered, this time for Russell to blow his nose.

Ten, fifteen minutes passed. The light definitely was brighter. They found it necessary to shade their eyes. At the same time concealed radiators and an electric blanket stoked up the small room, and before long those seated in front loosened their coats and waved at non-existent flies. Russell's nose was now bone-dry. And like some geophysical litmus, like Ayers Rock itself, it measured the degrees of heat in a series of pastels, culminating in matt ochre as the surface under the glare became almost too hot to touch— baked, aboriginal ochre. Outlined against the azure walls this had a tremendous impact. The colours could belong only to an ancient hot continent—theirs. Several minutes passed before anyone could speak. Even Gerald had a small lump in his throat.

Now for the first time Russell raised himself on an elbow and smiled wanly. He looked exhausted as if he had suffered fevers in a tent. It had lasted less than an hour.

Clapping and smiling to encourage him they asked for a repeat performance. It had made them homesick.

However, Mrs Russell entered with tea and lamingtons; perhaps unintentionally the green knitted cosy resembled the shape of Ayers Rock. Russell sat on the edge of the camp-stretcher.

'I have never been to your country,' he said—a quivering voice. 'But I should very much like to.'

'Oh you must,' said Louisa.

He shifted his weight and took a sip of tea.

Garry gave a shout: 'What, and see Ayers Rock?'

'Oh no. No, that would be unwise. It would be an anti-climax. It's all in the mind, you see. All up here. I'd come away disappointed.'

He chose another lamington.

'We've never left England,' Mrs Russell explained. She adjusted her hem, placed her cup and saucer on the plastic antimacassar. 'We're perfectly happy in Buxton. Fred enjoys the imagining.'

'I have a pretty fair idea what the Eiffel Tower looks like,' Russell nodded.

'For that matter,' North admitted, 'few of us have seen Ayers Rock. Has anyone here?'

They all looked down at the carpet. Only Shiela had.

Russell raised his nose. 'And you've come all the way here? All we've got,' he said self-deprecating, 'is Brighton Rock.'

They laughed in their cups.

'He always says that,' said his wife pulling a face. 'Every time he says that.'

Nodding, Mrs Cathcart sank her teeth into a lamington. This served to confirm her relationship with the other, a woman of her own age. Russell looked at his wife and smiled.

According to Hofmann, breathing on Violet's ear-ring, Russell's wife had been asked to lie alongside, bare-breasted throughout each performance. This would have simulated the Olgas which lie twenty miles to the west of Ayers Rock. She had the properly large breasts, but she had refused. She had a family, three children, all married.

Violet almost spilt her dregs. She had to hold both hands onto the cup.

'We destroy the very things we go to see,' said North. 'I sometimes think.' He seemed to be asking Russell.

'He's a zoologist,' Sasha explained.

'It's not a rock,' Kaddok reminded. 'You'll find it's called a monolith.'

No one listened to him now but Russell pointed a finger:

'So I believe!' Then he stared at Kaddok and looked at the others. He frowned.

'Eleven hundred feet above sea-level; pre-Cambrian; named after the Premier of South Australia.'

'You've got a valuable property there in your nose,' someone nodded. That was Hofmann from the back. 'I'd have it insured if I were you. It was a fine performance. Very good. Some call it Body Art.'

'What?'

Meanwhile Doug had finished his tea. 'It's something to be proud of, Ayers Rock. It's a plus in Australia's favour.'

Borelli was still thinking about the function of travelling, of seeing sights, but Gerald began laughing.

'What with the Great Barrier Reef . . .'

'Yes,' said Gerald, 'and what else?'

'There's more tea here, if anyone wants some.'

But North and Sasha stood up to leave; Mrs Cathcart offered to help clear away. The men each shook Russell's hand, staring for the last time at his nose. It had been a great success.

'Well worth the trip out.'

'Keep it up.'

'I suspect it's better than the real thing,' said Gerald.

Doug breathed in.

'Come on,' said Garry.

At the door Mrs Russell folded her arms. 'Yesterday, we had an Australian gentleman here. Fred, what did he want you to try? For films and television, he said it was for.'

'The Hamersley Ranges, Western Australia,' Russell smiled. 'I couldn't help him. He offered the world.'

'Is that bastard here again?' Garry nudged at Shiela.

'I don't know,' she fumbled.

The Russells stood waving from the porch.

It prompted Mrs Cathcart: 'I could have stayed there all day!'

'They were a corker couple,' Doug agreed. 'He hasn't let it go to his head. And he's got a really nice little set-up there.'

The spectacle had certainly made them reflective. They

thought of the remaining sights they planned to see; and their thoughts returned to home.

'I must say, for a while I thought I was seeing things!' Louisa laughed.

It implied—

'Don't believe all you see. It just goes to show.'

'None of us have seen Ayers Rock!'

'Shiela has,' Violet reminded.

'I don't think,' Kaddock declared as if their trip would go on forever, 'there's any point now. We all know what it's like.'

'But we had an inkling before, if that's what you mean. There's no reason to see anything then. We've all seen pictures.'

Shiela said she no longer knew what was 'real', what with all the sights; and she laughed, nervously.

'It was a man making a quid; and good for him.'

'At least we're asking questions . . .' Borelli sighed.

They were driving slowly back to London.

Sasha had been silent, spoke up. 'I'm sick of travelling. I want to go home.'

'Don't say that, Sasha,' Shiela cried.

Gerald gave a kindly smile, 'Well, you're almost there. It won't be long.'

But they fell silent for a while, for many miles. The Cathcarts' expressions showed they were thinking of their street in Drummoyne with its honest bleached telegraph poles, the embedded solid shapes, weathered colours and glare, the family grown up. They passed neat pastures and the fixed spaces of England, the British Isles, the cultivation of centuries. So neat and ordered, so tame, it was slightly depressing.

In the 1930s, Douglas William Gumbley, CBE, ISO, invented and designed the airletter or *aerogramme* while he was employed in Iraq as Inspector General of Posts and Telegraphs. Gumbley was one of those Englishmen who labour(ed) tomato-magenta under a blazing foreign sun:

bazaar hum, servants with sliding eyes, the evening nimbu pani, a game at the club, dirty messengers in strange garments, drumming efficiency into them and what-not. So forth. Some favoured the pith helmet. Some formed a path by swinging a silver-tipped cane. They set an example which in itself kept them going. Not many went native. Out there, Gumbley ran a tight shop. Had to.

In Iraq he realized the need for a 'lightweight missive of specific size and weight.' International air services were growing by the day. For this purpose he designed and printed an air mail letter card which was issued by the Iraqis on 15 July 1933. These soon became accepted and relied upon by travellers the world over.

Douglas Gumbley had been in India in 1898 and was responsible for the construction of the telegraph line from Karachi to Tehran . . .

He died on the Isle of Wight in 1973, the ripe age of ninety-two.

The airletters (*aerogramme*: 'by air mail', 'par avion') of countries such as India and Pakistan are smaller than others, the paper and gum are noticeably poor in quality. And not all air letters are blue. For reasons known to themselves, the Danes chose spotless white. America's air letter is oblong, suitably large, efficiently laid out. France now has an *aerogramme*; ether blue. Britain's which is small but long when fathomed out naturally has the most powerful blue (best to use red biro on theirs!), an attempt at regal, near-royal, historical blue.

Walking with Borelli, Louisa looked as if any second she would grab his hand. Gaiety (spontaneity) inflected her flying coat tails. Leaning forward she kept glancing at him, shaking her head with a type of mock sadness: well, at his hare-brained theories and the observations he made. And it was as if they were against the world, the two of them: forcing their way through the surge of oncoming words and soldier faces. Borelli was discussing the social implications of toast, Anglo-Saxon toast, when he crouched wombat-shaped to tie a shoelace, and she turned and stood over him, and out of the blue demanded to know about the walking stick, 'and no monkey business, please.'

'Silly bitch!' He fell backwards onto his flat palms. 'What a time to ask.'

This wasn't like Louisa.

Several people stopped or at least turned.

'Never mind,' he called out, 'she's crackers.'

'Tell me! I am not letting go!' Louisa laughed. Never had she acted so carefree, one foot planted on Borelli's jacket. A few seconds before he'd been strolling like a drum-major.

Waving the stick Borelli called out, 'Help me. I'm a cripple. This woman—' To her he said, 'Wait till I tell my Uncle. Help!' he croaked aloud.

'Stop it!' she cupped her mouth. They wouldn't have done it in their own city; certainly Louisa wouldn't have. It was because they were away and felt anonymous. 'It's all your fault.'

'What?' He took her arm. 'Seeing you've embarrassed me, I'll have to tell you. And keep it to yourself.'

They were walking and she looked at the ground.

'It has nothing to do with my leg. I have legs that are in perfect shape. It's an affectation. A way of getting sympathy, attention. Some people have their arm in a sling. I need the sympathy.'

He went on, 'It's a swordstick as well . . .'

'You've told me all that before, and I never know whether to believe you or not,' she walked on ahead.

'This uncle told me the way we behave before women reveals our selves. He was right. I've been telling lies because—you've confused me. I think we're lost.'

Borelli pulled out a street directory.

Back, turn left, right, left again, cross Dean street. Women pushing wicker prams had them filled with cauliflower heads (nothing more). Street musicians; one a former pug. A balding groovoid leaped out of a cab in tan platforms, silver film cans glittering under his arm.

Borelli tried to answer Louisa's questions about his uncle: his age, his women and appearance, physical and geographical history, why he chose to live alone—not only in London, but in Soho. He held Louisa's hand. A bearded man vomited in the gutter.

'In Soho alone because he sees himself as a specimen in a glass case. He examines himself minutely. He told me last time it accounted for his stooped back; I believe him. He said his room is almost the precise geographical centre of London. It is like a small museum. The angles and lines from elsewhere press in on him, as does the entire population. It forces him further into himself. In any case, we are all specimens, he says.'

'Then he's where you get all your silly ideas from. Hey?' Borelli glanced away and frowned.

'I promised I'd see him again. He's from my mother's side.'

'I think I'll like him' said Louisa swinging her bag.

A crane lowered artificial clouds onto the outside of a cinema for a display.

As usual Borelli couldn't contain himself. He stopped. 'Isn't it interesting how the normality . . or the actuality of things goes on without our descriptions? Our time is spent cataloguing the description of objects and animals, and explaining, even though they exist solidly in the first place. I find that increasingly odd. We like to classify and describe. We want to understand; I certainly do. But it only adds to the nature of things, it doesn't alter.'

Louisa was shaking her head. 'No, I didn't mean it like that! I love being with you!'

Borelli looked up. 'After you . . .'

They climbed the stairs over the sandwich shop. Bending down on the landing he read the sign opposite

FREDDIES * * * This Is The Show!

'I didn't notice that before . . .'

He continued, his voice sounding loud.

'You see what I'm saying. Everything continues without descriptions, and yet descriptions are all that we are doing – it seems to me. I find it strange. Museums, for example –.'

He tapped on the door with his walking stick.

It was opened by an aging redhead in a pink dressing gown. Borelli smiled and glanced past her. She put one arm across the door and the folds of her gown fell open.

The woman glanced at Louisa.

'Who are you looking for?'

Borelli looked around the landing.

'This is 7. This is it. I came here some weeks ago.'

The woman folded her arms.

'No you didn't. I'd have remembered.' Again she looked at Louisa.

'No no! My uncle's place,' Borelli corrected. 'He lives here.'

The woman laughed.

'I've been here for four years April. There's no one else who lives here. No man. I have a name. It's Flora Burton.'

'I remember,' Borelli frowned, 'that banister there is very loose, right?'

'It's always been like that as long as I remember.' She added, tired 'I've never in my life touched a banister that isn't loose.'

'Did you say your name is Burton?'

'That's not who you're looking for, is it? Well I'm here any time,' she smiled. Then she began coughing.

'Come along, James,' Louisa tugged.

'But I was here only a few weeks ago,' Borelli said loudly. 'He was in there!'

'He must have moved,' Louisa whispered.

Borelli went over and touched the wall and the banister. The entire building seemed unstable.

'Now you listen,' she called down from her door. 'I've been here for years. I don't like people imagining. You're worrying me.' A high, thinly pitched voice, a worn violin.

'Come on,' said Louisa, 'we've made a mistake.'

He looked through the window at FREDDIES and back up again. The first floor landing was empty. There was silence.

'Poor woman,' said Louisa.

The flash of chrome and plate glass struck them from all angles. The stairs had been dark, the walls finger-marked and torn, as remembered: a building condemned. The essential interior colour was brown. Even the traffic patiently banked in the street looked like the other day. Brightly lit clarity: always deceptive. Beware.

Louisa had to take his sleeve. 'Now come along.'

Her gentle way implied a mistake.

'But I wrote to my mother about him. He asked me to come back. We had things in common. And this is the street. I remember the stairs; that's the building.'

'If you walk along, we might see him in the street,' Louisa suggested.

She had to lead him away.

'I couldn't have been imagining . . .'

'Even if you were,' Louisa half answered. She was looking left and right for a nice restaurant. She'd steer him away from his mistakes.

As mechanical as the trumpets, strippers were performing behind the walls, weary in the bones; business as usual. It was a bright morning in London.

Over the door in wooden serifs (soaked in printer's ink):

ZOELLNER & ROY G. BIV
* Definitions, Maps *

'This is the place,' said Gerald.

A tiny brass bell shivering on a spring shaped like a comma sprang into action when they entered, at odds with the sedentary calm of the shop, and remained shaking there long afterwards, like a salmon dying on a line. Undoubtedly it indicated the turbulence beneath the marmoreal calm of both Zoellner, the dying bibliophile, and his junior partner, the repressed Biv (one given to daydreaming). Still waters, so it is said, can run very deep: even these scholarly backwaters. Otherwise, wouldn't the harsh little bugger— the bell—get on their nerves? Perhaps, as North pondered afterwards, it punctured the parchment-yellow steadiness of their day, reminding of the world outside—only a few feet away through mullioned glass—of words spoken and deeds, the real action, so making their lives more tolerable. Much has already been written on Zoellner in technical journals around the world. Roy Biv out the back, handling the maps, glanced up. Not old Zoellner. Behind the desk where books tilted like laminations of slate he kept his head down, annotating a pamphlet on Swahili phonemes. An electric waistcoat (for warmth) restricted his movements to a tight circle: a badly frayed maroon cord fell from the light socket, into his collar. In Clarendon Bold on the wall a small sign announced: NO BAD LANGUAGE. 'This is the place,' Gerald rubbed his hands. He was evidently pleased with his find.

Words had been collected from all corners of the globe and stored in bound volumes, singly or in sets. The air was grey, teeming in effect with phosphenes—an appearance of rings of light produced by pressure on the eyeball, due to irritation of the retina. Zoellner & Biv retailed every dictionary and word-binge imaginable; every Harrap's, Larousses from way back, old Grimms' and a Littré, and the latest Langenscheidt; the Oxford blues with Supplements alongside Chambers Twentieth Century—preferred by the crossword-puzzlers; Webster's Internationals, American Heritage, and all the other Yankee upstarts, illustrated and non. Zoellner & Biv stocked glossologies, language maps, semantic atlases on Gleek, Anglish, Jappish, East Indian, Ptydepe and Jarman, Double Deutsch, and an indispensable phrase book on Swiss; all kinds of cocky argot, Strine and Partridges: a low shelf of Dirty Words or 'rudery' made browsers bend down or squat. [*Wowser. n.* (Aust.) Fanatical puritan; spoilsport, killjoy; teetotaler.]

The varnished steps placed to reach the higher shelves— Astronomical Definitions, Scientific Terms—were opened like the arrow A, the rope stays forming a taut X. There were words and articles lying on the floor. They stumbled over certain words. Zoellner & Biv had one of the finest collections of Collective Nouns to be seen anywhere. A regular Scriptorum; polyglot's trove.

Dictionaries of Surnames, of 'Misunderstood, Misused, Mispronounced Words,' long shelves bending under the weight of Historical Principles. 'Ghost' words made their occasional appearances. And in a dimly lit corner languished those languages suffering from entropy, gathering dust and mould: Old Norse, Celtic and Wild Boer, Latin, boring Olde English, Volapük, Zend and Tasmanian Aborigine, Navajo and Mandarin. Et cetera.

The gargantuan cash register, an antique Remington, resembled a Japanese typewriter or a small lino machine: so tall and wide, so black and scratched, so appropriate. On either side stood the virile new tongues in glossy rows. They included Canadianisms, Afro-French, West-Indian and Anglo-Indian, stubborn Esperanto, and the rejuvenating neologisms from America, e.g. jeep, coke, napalm, apartment, typewriter and skunk. Lingua franca! As a sideline Zoellner & Biv sold letterboxes.

Unable to concentrate on any one shelf, Gerald crouched and darted left and right. In this way—for the first time— he resembled and understood Kaddok's clutching and tripping with his camera before an exceptionally rare motif.

'What was it we came in for?' North scratched his head. He remained on the apex of the steps, turning the pages of the *Scientist's Bible* (1973).

'We just don't have this back home,' Gerald complained. 'It's a part of the infrastructure missing. A major lacuna.'

Zoellner at his desk cleared his throat.

The storage of words, like the lines on a map, records and fixes the existence of things. Inside the shop, the repository, a feeling of serenity pervaded, as if the four walls contained the entire world and even what lay beyond, each part isolated, identified and filed. It was based upon facts, upon known quantities. Exactitude reigned. It contrasted casually with the chaos of forest impressions suffered by the travellers. It was a haven.

Ho-hum: on the slippery leather stool Sasha crossed and uncrossed her legs. So very boring. A few minutes before she said airily she had always assumed etymology to be some sort of skin disease, and so produced from North some attention: an indulgent cheek-squeeze. Sasha turned to fidgeting Biv.

Reversing heavily down the steps North wore a satisfied expression.

'We need a phrase-book and a strong map, if you can tear yourself away for a second.'

Gerald had his nose in a *Dictionary of Architectural Terms* (Unabridged). They opened a phrase book with a red and white cover. Running his finger down North looked up *blat*: 'Getting what you want through friends and influence.'

'This'll do. It seems up to date.'

'My friend,' said Sasha to Roy Biv, 'loves a good map. If I wasn't here he'd stay all day. D'you have trouble folding maps? I don't s'pose you do.'

Biv squinted past her. She was about his size and age.

'Say, don't you find it terribly musty in here? I mean all day. Why don't you open a window? I'd want to get out.'

Leaning over his desk Sasha picked up a 45° set-square, opaque with scratches, and a new handbook, *The Walls of Peking*. Unconsciously she pressed her thighs against the desk, beside him. Oh boy! So Biv launched into the old argument for maps, including memory maps, cartography in general; in case she was interested. Maps make visible verifiable truths. Maps don't change the physical world; the drawing or even the manufacture of maps is one of the few worthwhile professions left. 'Maps of course are . . . metaphors. They can do no harm.' He said it again. 'They're designed to help people.' He also began raving on about the mystery of maps, even of street directories. 'Oh well that's better,' Sasha agreed. 'Now you're talking, because I find facts incredibly boring.' She ran her painted nail along the hypothenuse. 'My life,' suddenly dropping the set-square, 'is one big confusion. I think I'm experiencing too much. But funnily enough, nothing much happens.'

Biv had orange hair and a hairy houndstooth coat. He didn't know what to say about that. He picked up some French Curves; he put them straight back.

Gerald Whitehead and North, wise old men looking pleased with themselves, joined them and showed a keen interest, the way travellers do.

Biv became conscious of his blue nose, and to participate let out a laugh for no reason at all.

'What is the nicest word you have here?' she asked, to help Biv. 'What's your favourite, frinstance?'

Creaking back in his chair Biv didn't hesitate: 'Pavement! Pavement! I often dwell on that word. It has a smooth sound. And it's related to maps.'

Pave-ment . . .

Zoellner in the corner snorted.

'I think I've heard that choice before,' Gerald said.

'I love verandah and boomerang,' Sasha said.

Gerald nodded. 'Boomerang has a pleasant ring. It's a traveller's word.'

The bookworm fished in his side pocket and pulled out a paperback. 'Listen to this.'

'Here he goes again,' Sasha complained to Biv.

North elbowed her gently. 'No, listen. A Russian finds us mysterious. "Whenever one sees Australia on a map,"' North read out, '"one's heart leaps with pleasure: Kangaroo, boomerang!" There, page 151.'

'Hip hip,' said Sasha.

Gerald angled the book to see its cover: Andrei Sinyavsky, *alias* Abram Tertz.

'Not bad, what?'

'Of course,' said Gerald, 'he wrote that in a labour camp. So he was writing from a zoo.'

'You mustn't be too harsh on your country,' a voice called out. And they turned: Zoellner was looking at them between two piles. 'Other writers have been hypnotized by "kangaroo". "Boomerang," to a lesser extent. Those words represent the mystery of Australia—its distance and large shape.'

'You mean in particular D. H. Lawrence?' Gerald asked respectfully.

'Not only him. It is quite a pronounced, if minor, trend in world literature.'

Really? Go on?

Roos along with other marsupials were Dr North's field. Many of his papers in the zoological journals began with an apt quotation, from the north.

In particular, French novelists have long been attracted

to kangaroos. The beast is biologically and visually surreal. The word itself is histrionic: a series of rhythmic loops. 'Implacable kangaroos of laughter,' wrote young Lautréamont—a fine metaphor. Very fine. Young Alfred Jarry had his supermale box with not one but several kangaroos. You find the noun leaping like a verb from the hallowed pages of Louis Aragon, Malraux in China, and Goncourt's *Journal*—yes, he reported eating authentic kangaroo meat during the seige of Paris. Another naturalist is Gide. He described in his journal a monument in some little French village square, peopled with 'familiar kangaroos'. To Proust, an acquaintance ravaged by time looked unexpectedly strange, 'like a kangaroo'. There is Tiffauges, the ogre, astride his 'kangaroo-like horse'. (But then Michel Tournier can also throw a boomerang. It is said.) It appears in Boswell's *Life*, in *The Mill on the Floss* and 'Dear Kangaroo' is the nickname in Virginia Woolf's letters—ha ha. And who was that sad Irish clown who spent pages confusing the kangaroo with women and shirt-tails? The frequency of the word increases the farther north the writer is from Australia. Distance = novelty and a desire to conquer. Writing in Zurich, James Joyce recommended the Kangarooschwanzsuppe. 'Kangaroo-shaped' is a common metaphor. See Isak Dinesen's description of hares, or the young philosopher in the Thomas Mann story, 'At the Prophet's'. Chekhov in his notebooks used it to describe a pregnant woman with a long neck; and in Ehrenburg's novel he has a vintage car hopping like one. The great Osip Mandlestam questioned the logic of kangaroos in Armenia. And when discussing the cosmos in his autobiography Vladimir Nabokov writes, 'a kangaroo's pouch wouldn't hold it.' Not bad? Very good. In a thunder-storm Henry Miller stripped naked and 'hopped around like a kangaroo,' the damn fool.

'Sinyavsky,' Zoellner put his head down, 'is part of a northern tradition.'

'And "boomerang"?' North wanted to take notes.

'I agree, the word is splendid. So far as I can see it doesn't crop up as much as "kangaroo." I imagine this is because the boomerang is merely—strictly speaking—an inanimate object. It's a clever piece of wood. But used in northern literature ·it's as if the Europeans are encircling your country, to bring it into the field, like the lasso-flight of a boomerang. You become a member State:

> . . . *L'amour revient en boumerang*
> *L'amour revient à en vomir le revenant.*

North, the zoologist bookworm, nodded. 'Apollinaire.'

'Then you know Samuel Beckett has used "boomerang",' said Zoellner seeing his interest. 'It describes a nomadic character of his who always returns to the point of departure. "Ding Dong" I believe the story is called.'

'He doesn't usually talk like this,' Biv frowned. 'You're very lucky.'

'I think he's nice,' Sasha decided. She had her head to one side.

'There's a very evocative story by Nabokov,' North exchanged, 'which has a real dingo in it—"A Guide to Berlin." And if I'm not mistaken, in one of his last novels, a character sees the shape of Australia during a heart attack.'

Gerald laughed and Zoellner smiled.

'Conrad,' Biv here called out. 'He wrote of its shape on the map.'

The visitors glanced at the walls of books, at the definitions stacked from the floor to the ceiling. There was an answer to everything here. Zoellner had returned to his work.

'We've heard a lot about you,' Gerald ventured. His neck reddened out of respect. 'I'm pleased to meet you.'

'My name has travelled? I imagine it has. I've slaved my guts out. Now I'm busy.'

He put his head back down.

Sasha laughed. 'Why is he suddenly so grumpy?'

'He tells me,' Biv whispered, 'the future is tense. But I think he occasionally likes the sound of words. He likes hearing them after seeing them so much.'

North paid for a 1913 Russian Baedeker, a street directory of Moscow, and a Russian phrase book.

It was raining outside: European rain. And it multiplied the images yet again, complicating the most simple memories; and their taxi driver happened to have the foulest Cockney tongue they had come across in their travels.

'I'll tell you . . .' Kaddok had to speak up, 'we saw excellent newspaper photographs of English teams standing on top of Mount Everest, and weight-lifters breaking heavy world records. They can lift a small English sedan over their heads. On display too were the world's fastest car and motor bike. These were—'

'Where's this?' Garry looked up.

'And spaghetti,' said Gwen. 'They had spaghetti because it's long. It's unpredictable.'

'The Exhibition of Extremities,' Kaddok wheeled around trying to find Garry. 'Government-sponsored. Very interesting; I recommend it.'

'No thanks.'

'It sounds like an Exhibition of Simplicities,' Hofmann drawled.

'Did they show examples of Extreme Moderation?' Violet chipped in. 'They're the world champions at that.'

'The English are alright,' said Gerald gently.

'I can see it now,' said Hofmann. 'Abstract paintings and two-tone music scores mixed in with Molotov cocktails. I don't know which they'd find more extreme.'

'They did,' Gwen looked disappointed. 'How did you know? We thought it was good.'

'Oh come on!' said Hofmann. 'We're not stupid.'

Borelli had become subdued again, so Louisa pinched his elbow.

'I could keep travelling,' Shiela sat up, 'every day of my life. There's so much to see.'

'Well, I'm sick of it. Always stop-go, stop-go,' Sasha cried. 'I'm not used to this life. I really am not. I don't think anyone is.'

'It's a bit hard to know what's happening,' Borelli frowned. 'No, I'm serious!' he said when North laughed. 'Something very funny happened today.'

'How long have we been on the road?'

'Lummy, let's see.'

They couldn't work it out.

'But it's interesting. Sasha, listen to me. Don't you think?' Shiela leaned forward. Her earnestness resembled love. 'We've seen things you couldn't have imagined. I think everything's interesting. I thought of being an air hostess once. I even made the necessary enquiries.'

Experienced air travellers, they turned to her: sadly enlarged eyes, her bedroom pallor, cardigan with opal brooch—a badge from a different age. And strange pale veins on her throat and forehead stood out, tributaries of a remote, rarely visited country.

'And don't we have a nice group? Above average, believe me it is. We couldn't wish for better. It can make such a difference.'

She glanced—without meaning to—at Sasha's hand resting on North's wrist.

'How many marvellous people have you seen again after one of your innumerable trips?' Hofmann asked and returned to his magazine.

'Ken!' said Louisa. She touched Shiela. 'You must excuse him. He's not very nice.'

'But this happens,' said Shiela brightly, 'when a group gets to know each other. People start telling the truth.'

But she began blinking, glancing around.

Turning to Violet, Sasha asked, 'You're very quiet. What have you been up to?'

'I'm having an okay time,' said Violet, 'It could be worse.'

'Hey, cheer up,' someone said.

'What?' Gerald looked up. 'Oh I'm thinking of the things we missed.'

'But you're never happy,' said Sasha. 'I don't mean that nastily.'

'I suppose not. I tend to take things too seriously.'

Garry began whistling a nationalistic ditty, though not loudly, absentmindedly. In mid-verse he zyvatiated, raising his glass. Then he forgot the words.

'Well, look who's here?' Cathcart shouted. 'Howdy, stranger!'

Doug stood up bow-legged, leather-faced, for the vaguely familiar figure.

'Hey, buggerlugs,' Garry put out his hand, 'I thought you were in the States?'

'So I was,' said Hammersly nodding to the others, easily. 'I thought I heard the old national anthem here. I thought: hell-o!'

'Take a pew.'

'Sit down, for Christ's sake!'

Hammersly found a space beside Shiela and unbuttoned his suit coat. He stood out in the group: was not one of them, tourists, something else. The natural rhythms of time, like sleep, had washed or softened the faces of the others. Problems of purpose and deadlines showed in the straight lines of Hammersly's face, the angles of his suit and the stripe of his shirt, a silk tie with the Windsor knot. Clearly, he travelled for a purpose.

'So how's it going, Shiela?'

'Watch him,' they yelled, not caring. 'Watch out, Shiela.'

'Fair go!' Hammersly laughed.

Give a bloke a chance.

'I think perhaps I might retire,' said Gerald Whitehead standing up.

'He's a dark horse,' Violet muttered.

'We leave England shortly,' Shiela said to Hammersly.

'You've only just arrived.'

'It's what's called a Cook's tour,' Borelli chipped in. 'But we're all having a good time.'

Louisa touched Borelli's hand. He was slouched in the chair. 'Ah, there, Mrs Cathcart: you're back. How are you?'

Her glance showed she had noticed Louisa was more talkative than usual.

'Doug and I have had a pig of a day.'

It was the sameness of things: being channelled by the

worn avenues of London, the familiar façades, the humidity and the dirt.

'I think we've done the UK.'

'Hang on a sec,' Hammersly said to Shiela. 'Don't shoot through.'

Desulatory conversation. Fragments.

'What's our next thrill?' Garry shouted. 'Another glass.'

Borelli took Louisa's hand under the table; and North and Sasha retired upstairs.

On all fours, the night shift made its way along Number 3 shaft, a helmet occasionally scraping the roof. Bert, Wal, Eddy-boy, Ezra, Clarry, Mick n' Les, small men, cracking jokes. Arrrrh, yairs. (So that's where the accent comes from?) Another gang laid the line for the trucks, each man giving the other a hand. Creaking wainscotting gave a dim direction to the mine. Electric globes had been strung up at economic intervals. On the work-face though it would be lit up brighter than a Greek afternoon. Above their heads a polythene pipe the diameter of a man's waist supplied a steady cool wind and through its rips and perforations a labial *phssss*, as pronounced in the words photo or philosophy, or footslogging. And water which rapidly and constantly dripped met the floor with another sound: the way a bed-ridden old man stumbles over moist food and words. Obscenities had been scratched into the walls with pick axes.

Beginning at a former tube station in ECI the mine followed a seventeen foot seam of pure anthracite running in a straight north-easterly direction: supporting the City while undermining it. The mine had been operating for seven years. At Threadneedle Street and the Bank of England it followed a short-lived shoot at right-angles. It then took a westerly direction, the transom tunnel known as Two Shaft, very rich, under Queen Victoria Street and the Embankment, burrowing under the Thames at Waterloo Bridge, stopping four hundred yards beyond hallowed Festival Hall. Here another shoot looked promising. An unexpected cave-in (14 March 197—) forced a retreat, left a cadaveric cul-de-sac (3.1 casualities). This exploratory shoot and the one beneath the Bank of England were coffered and converted to ventilation and service shafts, respectively. Blasting and shovelling, retreating, advancing, wrestling and installing rails and then the rubber conveyor belt and amenities, the men worked Shaft Number 3 night and day, due north, slightly by-passing Covent Garden (orders from above) because their blasting would upset the imported sopranoes. Reaching the British Museum and the hotel, the tunnels duplicated on a grand scale, invisible to the naked eye, the shape of its own cross-section: π

London itself in the early hours lay emptied and dark. It too had confusing distant lights in the air-sea of blackness. The slowly approaching car (shift-worker returning) and its solitary roar could have been the narrow-gauge loco on its way back for the last load. Water too ran down many of London's gutters, reflected the overhead bulbs. Working men wearing caps assembled at intersections the way the day shift below waited for the cage.

But inside the mine it was a different night, the density of centuries. It had its own space and proximity of things. The darkness was solid. And the coal had to be removed like time itself, piece by piece. The city slept: oyez, mouths and hands in the hotel rooms remained open, fingers apart, body temperatures and breathing down to a minimum in the quiet. Some men lay on their backs to remove the coal. Others scratched with the pick in the foetal position, crawling, blackened and grimacing. They were in the lower intestines, beyond the womb. A colony, another life down there: with its leather ledgers, artificial light, the grimy tea-urn and first-aid boxes marked with the thick cross. They had their rosters and hierarchies. There were subtle mockeries. Where the mine widened, at level 4, a class of troglodyte timekeepers wore the blue shirt and neckties, sat at desks in a glassed-in 'office'. The mine had its own momentum, its own laws and rules of time. It had its own narrow-gauge railway, and a system of bell signals known to all. In 207, two were commingled in drift and descent, one suddenly crying out. Hammersly turned her over. Others under their blankets lay as if they'd been flung down after an explosion: mouths, hands and legs apart. Gerald Whitehead had gone to sleep with his reading light on, his bags already packed. Violet lay nude. Phillip North in his dressing gown stood looking out the window: the city, the vast machine, beginning to stir, rejuvenating. Light trucks shadowed like the zebras were radiating through the open tunnels. Beneath his slippered feet, a mile down, the men squatted over their bread and pies. Their mugs of tea held a black brew. Elbows resting on knees, they considered the fusain sandwiched in the rock behind them, the job ahead, their intention being to blast. Great tonnages were shifted, great movements unbeknown.

6

Yes, I went to Russia late February 19—. I was in a group. I was in the party. Fifteen thereabouts in all, well-educateds, in woollen tweed jackets, mainly British. The American schoolteacher—something wrong with him—his plaited Southern wife and kid were always the last to board the bus. Something wrong with him—built into his forehead. I remember that tall thin Englishman from Norwich who had almost no lips, very small eyes, forever looking over everyone's heads, complaining about the absence of tea. The lecturer in Russian from St Andrews University was pale, bald and boney: a living example of how a Slavic language can enter the convert's features. A plucky bulldog surgeon very neat in silken scarves and royal blue: she had a glued-on nose, stout rubber-capped walking stick, result of a car crash. I forget her name too. For the first few days she and her husband who was taciturn and from Hampstead, I seem to remember, sat at a separate table with the Professor and his French wife—it was she who told me he was a Mallarmé specialist and a friend of J-P Sartre. Such behavioural patterns emerged after the first sit-down meals and excursions. A natural sorting process took place. Initially our group sat dispersed in the plane, concealed from the other passengers and even from itself.

The cold exhilarated us all. So did the expanse. Both sharpened our sense of proportions, of what things are or can be, as the Ilyushin crossed the northern border of Germany.

The land below became wide open, bare, all grey ice, emptiness, the same colour as our accompanying clouds and the dripping alloy of the wing. The jet went on and on labouring and labouring, as if it worked against a head-wind. It was hard to know if we were making progress. It was the sensation of endlessness . . . that this extraordinary, barely coloured expanse can never end . . . which gave the impression. The ice and snow barely changed; villages were few and far between; forests were eaten into, clogged up with snow; the occasional long empty road looked like a line scratched into the metal wing; and so the simple fact of Russia's expanse and harshness signed itself into our minds. I thought of the madness of Napoleon and Hitler, the tail of long armies. How many boots and weapons must be buried under the snow? Other examples of platitudes (obvious truths?) abounded.

I remember the landing. I was taken to one side by a stone-faced officer. His long-coat was grey. He didn't mind the Penguin *Secret Agent*. He was concerned about my hardback on their revolution picked up secondhand. Curiously empty of colours and airport movement, the bare terminal caused the passengers to go quiet, more obedient than usual, a kind of confusion. He kept turning the pages and reading a paragraph at random, turning back, then forward. Trying to determine . . . I don't know. He saw the photograph of Trotsky in uniform and stared at me. Speckled green eyes: I saw the forests of Russia there. Eyes of a similar fractured perspective belonged to the guard in the buttoned overcoat checking each face—and mine—in the line at Lenin's tomb, close to the wall and the ashes of Reed and the cosmonauts.

This was Leningrad. Our hotel was that modern one alongside the Neva. Each floor had its samovar and an officious woman at a small table. She held a pencil over papers, keeping track of our keys. The ground floor had a purple carpet and a long enquiry counter. A row of wide-cheeked women there spoke patient English. A strange enquiry counter, looking back. The staff remained seated and since the counter stood almost chin-high we had to stretch on tiptoe and look down, while they looked up. I suppose it's still there. The Professor of French demanded to know if our freedom was being inhibited by the itinerary of the tour. He seemed to be making a point, insisting. I had to interject and tell him not to worry. In Leningrad you are free to go anywhere. Silver-haired and transparent-skinned he moved his lips as if he was chewing something small; not out of nervousness, I confirmed later—out of age. First impressions can be very interesting but are often misleading. He was a gentle, reflective man; impressive the way he had fun travelling with his wife. They were forever laughing. And delegations from Mongolia stood around, looking lost.

We, tourists, must have been conspicuous for being bareheaded. The Russian men and women and their children wore the same fur hat; and taxi-drivers and truck-drivers did so while driving. I seem to recall the sparse traffic consisted almost entirely of trucks. Green, grey or khaki their bonnets and radiators were fitted with quilted canvas flaps, rather like ear muffs. The lecturer from St Andrews wore a fur hat like the locals and appeared only at breakfasts. He'd been a student at Moscow University and went about visiting friends.

The Neva—like so many pieces of jigsaw on the map— was dramatically clogged up with broken ice, small icebergs, most of all under the bridges, and Peter's canals were frozen solid. Downpipes on many buildings had their water suspended a foot or more out, frozen in mid-air. Taking a stroll by the river I noticed condoms evidently flushed from various hotel rooms preserved in the ice like bloated toad fish, for all to see. A small unnecessary detail. The cold, not soggy like London's or Dublin's, was the true biting cold of insects swarming around the mouth and ears, especially as I walked along by the river. And the Russians kept saying how warm it was, much warmer than usual. Leningrad has more than forty bridges.

A loaf of bread cost forty cents. Taxis could be hailed only at designated ranks. Rent for an apartment was nine dollars a month, approx. Five cents on a bus can take you anywhere in the city. The streets were clean. Women were seen repairing the bridges. Others were climbing along steel scaffolds—plasterers. A sense of cleanliness, of emptiness, made some in the party complain it was drab. Few bright colours in the clothing, and no advertising signs. I was told

273

that in Old Russian 'red' is the same word as 'beautiful.' Was it the lecturer in Russian? The three single English-women travelling together, led by a particularly loud-voiced slide photographer reported how they were each fined ten roubles for jay-walking. In Leningrad it was oddly gratifying to see people crossing casually against the red light.

Leningrad's splendour had little to do with precision, spreading the way it did under the immense sky. Leningrad is in harmony with the land expanse. The town planners were instinctively easy with space. That was my impression. Such wide streets and squares—so many squares—and crescents and columns; and the architecture seemed deliberately, 'unnecessarily' baroque, as if to busy the emptiness. Held low and broad the skyline accentuated the feeling. Even underground in the smart subways casual lavishness with space was evident, as in a Malevich suprematist canvas, or in the page numbers of a Russian novel or Herzen's autobiography.

There was scarcely a green leaf, a single shaft of grass, not even in the parks. Yet I remember the parks. Many times I think back to them. The trees were bare, the benches had couples resting after pushing a pram, and the floor of the parks was all ice, grey and streaked ice, like a river in flood among trees. Through it all people walked: figures in dark coats. Those strange frozen parks remain—Leningrad's beauty. In dramatic grandeur it was unlike any city I had seen.

I can tell you, the Russians were very pleasant, polite, except for the officer at the airport and the guards outside public places. Often I observed, however, a peasant stubbornness, a kind of moody irrationality. For example, in officials at desks, waiters at restaurants, in some taxi drivers. This has been reported by other travellers. It can be irritating to some.

As in any foreign country there was the instant impact of the local people's faces. For several days these were as constantly curious as the windows on the buildings which all had deep double-glazing to keep out the cold. I found myself staring at them: at the tundra hairlines of the men, their cheekbones, eye-sockets and pallor. Being surrounded by such faces underlined my visitor's status. That is, in the streets I felt conscious of my foreignness, of that definite separation from the nearby faces. As a further reminder they seemed to take no notice of me or the group. We didn't exist. I remember sensing that in a crowded bus.

Our guide supplied by Intourist was a student— Natasha. She was slender and had her hair tied in a pony tail, yet she was somehow disorganized. Natasha was pensive, slightly sad even. She spoke always with her lips pursed. Her mother had been a ballet dancer. It was quite sad when we came to leave. (The Professor of French gave her a present on our behalf.)

'Natasha,' that English bluestocking slide photographer would call out through her nose, insistent, 'Natasha, what is that there? No, no, Natasha. Over there.'

There is no doubt being in a foreign country rejuvenates the powers of observation and sense of wonder. In Russia I felt that wherever I turned my 'experience' was being broadened. I think Russia, especially, does that. It gives that impression. I said to the American school-teacher . . .

I noticed among couples a conspicuous amount of arm-holding: wives with their husbands, and pairs of men too. Someone in the group merely put it down to habit, a result of the cold. I don't think so. I sent an inordinate number of postcards to show friends ('Dear Comrade') that I was there in Russia, and they were not. The best was a colour photograph of Lenin's blue Rolls Royce, a Silver Ghost in a Moscow Museum. Skis had been fitted under its front wheels, and a caterpillar-track grotesque but no doubt practical replaced the elegant back wheels.

Many reasons can be given for visiting the Soviet Union. The dark-haired Brazilian (in our group; I forgot about him), always laughing, wanted to see Communism for himself. He wasn't impressed. I think we all wanted to 'see Communism', a Communist country. Certainly that was a large reason for going. Outside an enormous shop for children the tall Englishman nudged me, 'You know what that building is next door? The Lubyanka.' He nodded significantly. Next to a toy shop: ironical, you see. But there are other reasons for Russia. The Professor of French was interested in the art collections and early Russian architecture. 'My husband,' his wife said, 'knows much about Manet.' He kept asking to see a wooden church. Churches I was told are called *Pokrov*, meaning 'covering' or 'protection.' Again this must have come from the lecturer from St Andrews. He asked questions for us in Russian and sat up front with the drivers enjoying conversations.

For anyone interested in the history of the Revolution, Leningrad has many landmarks. It can feel eerie standing at these places. In Russia you can sense the force of history: the spot opposite the old Singer Sewing Machine building where the Czar was assassinated; the terrible open space before the Winter Palace; the Finland Station and Lenin's preserved locomotive; and so on. Russia. Doesn't expanse and tragedy exist in the word?

Yes, there is much evidence, remaining from the Second World War, traces of the siege of Leningrad. Shrapnel-marked walls and chipped corners, and German bunkers near bus-stops, the cemetery and the reconstructed villas, have a profound impact. Such marks must mean something or have a constant effect. I found myself searching the faces and again noticed the wives holding the arms of the men. No city in Australia, none in America for that matter, possesses such scars. Two pudgy New York girls (in the group; I clean forgot them) went to the ballet and the renowned theatre for children. The language, the climate, the foreignness, the sense of drama, of past events: quite a panorama. Absurdly, too, I think many of us had the vaguely thrilling feeling of being in forbidden territory. And there was the food: the different soups, borscht, their smoked fish and so forth. Vodka, not Smirnoff's either. In a foreign country there is always the cuisine.

Interesting how in a group certain figures stand out for some reason or other while others remain level, or recede. The group began as complete strangers. I'd clean forgotten about that Brazilian doctor. He had a wife, beautiful face, who rarely spoke, only nodded and smiled. Some in a group like the tall Englishman remain clear through their complaints. I remember he was the only one who wore gloves (yellow suede and wool-lined). There was another woman in the group in her mid-forties—I only vaguely see her face. She latched onto the baritone spinster (with the camera) and friends. Others created a presence by their very silence, attracting questions and glances. It was interesting how certain people gravitated to one another, first in conversation, followed by regular seating positions at tables and in transport, then walking together towards the next spectacle, a building or a museum. The group subdivides into smaller groups. How in the space of a week most of us became silently irritated at the frowning American, his wife and kid, when they kept the bus or the meal waiting yet again. Travelling makes us tired, perhaps due to the constant state of heightened awareness. It is a series of anecdotes, visual and personal. Towards the end the tall Englishman told me his wife had left him a few months before, so he decided to take a package holiday. Those two New York girls were fun. One was an actress; imagine forgetting her.

Standing at the front of the travelling bus Natasha bent down to point out the statues of famous men and their preserved houses. I saw Gogol's nose dripping with snow. In Russia you hand your overcoats to an attendant, an old man, immediately on entering a public building. Dreaming of Russia I often see the coats, heavy overcoats, whole racks of them and the old men who take them, or the distant dark coats in the frozen parks.

At Heathrow we shook hands and departed. A few such as the Professor and the actress exchanged addresses. I wonder if they ever met again?

Sometimes I think of the group, but no one person stands out. Perhaps that is only natural. I have more the view of wide buildings standing back in the frost, the dirty snow and ice, and the way my curiosity in all things was lifted to a proper alert pitch. Scraps of general knowledge and images are inter-connected by great spaces and the wide sky. The cold and foreignness in that sense acted as preservatives. Individual faces in the group have faded, their names forgotten.

7

They were met at the airport by their guide—moon-faced, tub—who introduced herself as 'Anna'. When she smiled which she did at every question and before each designated monument she showed a set of stainless steel teeth, a legacy of the thirties. But nice! Nice woman! The other day she had become a grandmother, she confided to Mrs Cathcart. She smiled. And for Gerald she went patiently through the long Russian alphabet, lighting up at each and every letter. As for Doug, whatever Anna or other Russians were like, he went deliberately out of his way to say hello to them, ponderously, showing there were no hard feelings, that communists were there and had to be recognized—a form of condescension.

In the parks and on the streets, Muscovites went about in singlets, trousers, sandals with dark socks: recent communist custom. Many of their women wore peasant blouses from the Ukraine which were all the rage then in Moscow. Long queues shuffled forward to buy ice creams and the beer stalls on the footpaths were surrounded, almost hidden from view. In the parks grandparents sat on benches fanning themselves with faded newspapers. And unexplained bands played dented trumpets.

'Before going to Red Square and our Kremlin,' Anna announced, after clicking her fingers, 'we will try in here.'

They were standing outside the imposing ochre walls of a mansion in Botkinskaya Street. It could have been a Rome suburb: similar metal shutters and stately proportions. Pre-1917 it had been a well-known ballroom.

'We have more to show,' Anna went on, 'than what is printed on the calendars and postcards. What is it you say? "There is more than meets the eye." This is correct.' She showed those teeth again and her eyes almost disappeared.

'One of our countrymen has equated museums with forests, which is nice. Our Red Square and Kremlin will always be there tomorrow.'

'Don't bet on it!' Garry cracked. Some of them turned; God, he could be boorish. Kaddok though had the information at his fingertips. 'The Kremlin has been burnt down several times by marauding tribes.'

Doug slapped his forehead: 'Postcards!'

'I've made a note,' Mrs Cathcart nodded. To Anna she turned, 'We intend sending friends postcards showing your country.'

It was an early reward; Mrs Cathcart made this clear by not smiling.

It was here that Shiela noticed the man across the street behind the broadsheet *Pravda*, like the man who leaned out from behind the fluted pillar in the hotel foyer. Staring, she said nothing. She went in with the group.

Gerald and Phillip North had been trying to translate the sign tacked up at a slight angle above the entrance:

ЦЕНТР ТЯГОТЕНИЯ

'Centre . . .' Gerald managed, moving his lips.

An ingenious slot device, working on an incline and requiring a copek, got them past the turnstiles. It had glass sides and they could see the copper disc rolling and tripping steel levers as it fell through a trapdoor, releasing springs, a horizontal ratchet lock and flashing lights.

Inside it was dark and cool, a relief. It was a Government hall.

Anna sat down and wiped her neck. She handed them over to the Ministry's permanent head who'd been standing there all the time. The two were so familiar they didn't bother to greet each other.

Appropriately slant-eyed this Slav had a pale blue eyeball rolling loose in one sloping socket, evidently out of control. Otherwise his face was immobile, distinguished for its large sadness. So many things in the world appear, recede! This one's nose leaked, sometimes corrected with the back of his hand, and his coat and black trousers were versts too short. On the other hand he was clearly devoted to his role. It had become his obsession, an end in itself. The Centre was an area of knowledge with clear perimeters—in that sense, a province. As Anna had smiled, 'like our guides at the Museum of Atheism, the Museum of Curiosities, and of the Revolution. They think of nothing else. They're all the same.'

'I was going to say,' said Borelli to North, 'all museums amount to the same.'

Ha! This one had already launched into his spiel as they removed their shoes and put on the special felt slippers to protect the ballroom parquetry. But then, of course, so highly polished were the first corridors they found it difficult to walk. Brass rails had been fitted along strategic parts of the walls to assist the gingerly treading laughing ones, the girls; but the rails themselves were highly polished. To both Sasha who had taken North's hand, and Violet, it was like a child's game. Others began smiling and shuddering as they slithered behind the Russian bear. Joining in, Garry gave Shiela a small shove. Well, they were on holidays. Apparently the Russian was used to all this. He went on mournfully, easily, and told them the Centre of Gravity had been started during the Cold War.

He spoke excellent guttural English, considering. And they found his angle interesting.

'Gravity is central to existence. Superficially'—pronounced with Slavic fluidity—'the health of nations is dependant on it. Without it, the walls of our lungs would collapse; our blood pressure is set to balance it. We are all conscious of that. Nails would fall out from timbers. Beams fall on citizen's heads. Gravity is an experience. We feel. We are conscious. What is death but a loss of gravitation; a collapse. Back to the grave.'

'Thirty-two feet per second, per second!' Kaddok said for no apparent reason.

'We, in the Soviet Union, are infected with gravity. We are constantly investigating . . . ways of improving it, how to respect it. Hence the Centre.'

Kaddok wouldn't have seen the Russian's eyeball oscillating like the pale bubble in a builder's spirit level.

Evidently he tried hard to fix his gaze upon them. He stood alongside a crude cartoon of a red-haired man dropping cannonballs from a leaning tower; but still his pupil kept rolling up and down. Next to it an etching showed an ancient Englishman holding an apple with a surprised expression, slightly foxed.

As Borelli and Louisa suddenly clutched at each other to avoid slipping on the floor the Russian sketched in Khlebnikov's correlation between gravity and time.

'Have you ever considered,' said the rasping voice, 'the peculiar relationship between gravity and perspective, between gravity and coincidence, and gravity and rainbows?'

The world and its multifarious objects! Its many laws and items to consider; the relationships to inter-relate.

Gravity and coinc—

Garry Atlas thought he knew. 'Right!' He nodded. 'I'm with you.'

Lines of chance, trajectory of bombs, slapstick films. History's nagging central question: if a falling tile had killed Lenin in Zurich would the Revolution still have taken place? If yes, tick. No, place a cross. Moving bodies and nations attract, collide.

This guide's pronouncements combined with his enormous grave head, locally mobile with the dissident eye, held them in a new reflective mood. To Louisa, whispering to Borelli and touching his hand, he was among the saddest men she had ever seen. At any rate the idea was to take it slowly, one slipper after the other, gingerly, at the same time listening, keeping an eye on him. Most things were worth a pause; and they soon forgot about the outside world.

'Several other examples of gravity have been classified,' he was saying.

The sinking foundations of the mansion had given the far end of the room a glistening declivity, similar to some of the decrepit ballrooms said to be still operating in Vienna. A row of heavy chandeliers increased the stately feeling, as did the gold leaf, and the wallpapers in chevronian tatters.

Here were specific examples of gravity, including Specific Gravity. They were propped against or tacked onto the walls; some were suspended from the ceiling. Other things stood in the middle—isolated objects. Ambling over, their Russian leaned forward with an interested air as if he had never seen them before.

A sequence of photographs demonstrated in black-and-white the rise and fall of the German empire. Standing in rubble a Russian private pointed to the fallen statue of the Third Reich, the fierce eagle still clutching the wreathed swastika. From the very beginning the emblem had been encircled by a wreath.

The guide almost smiled; it didn't suit him.

'Gravity makes everything eventually come back to earth,' he said.

Other exhibits made Sasha and Louisa frown and turn away.

The trajectory of shrapnel, of rockets; the flight path of heavy bombs. Photographs. Those taken at night could have been displays of fireworks. Destroyed in Russia during the war were 89,500 bridges, 4,100 railway stations, and 427 museums.

Mrs Cathcart here slipped over, her thick legs tucking under, and muttering had to be helped up. 'Where were you?' she hissed at Doug.

The guide took no notice.

The clear correlation between gravity and time was demonstrated, perhaps rather obviously, by a line of synchronized hour glasses. Detecting their interest the guide again almost smiled.

'A central image,' said he. 'It never fails. Is gravity therefore connected to magnetism? We have a fascination watching time running out before our very eyes.'

Sasha yawned.

A common household tap had been pressed into service. All but Sasha and Mrs Cathcart squatted with the guide and studied the Pavlovian drip. The crystalline stretch grew, hovered swollen, pulled by gravity, and burst into tears. Pause. It began again.

Born the diplomat, Garry had to gurgle and cross his eyes. 'I can't stand it! Chinese water torture! I'm going crazy!'

'Oh dry up.' That was Violet. But she stopped smiling when Hofmann laughed.

The Russian carelessly observed, 'Water is woman.'

'What does he mean?' Louisa whispered.

Borelli pursed his lips. 'He means rivers; that they are always beautiful. Rivers are subtle but strong, and have no sharp corners. They also flow one with nature, are life-giving.' (He was wracking his brains; glancing at Louisa who was smiling. She wasn't properly listening.) 'And men are always wanting to conquer rivers and discover their source. Treacherous undercurrents.'

She squeezed his arm. 'You're making that up.'

'I think your husband's watching.'

'Certain cities suddenly become centres of gravity,' the Russian bellowed. Certain people gravitate. 'It used to be Vienna, Paris, Berlin. Now they tell me it is New York and Sydney.'

'Sydney?'

Gerald gave such a laugh the Russian looked surprised. 'So I am told.'

'What about Moscow?'

'The Olympic Games'll put you on the map,' said Doug.

The Russian said in a low voice. 'Not Moscow. Not yet. I don't think so yet.'

'Hey!' Doug stared down at his thigh and everyone began laughing.

His car-keys on their silver chain began climbing out of his pocket. A small but powerful red wall magnet had been mounted at waist level to demonstrate the similarity between gravity and magnetism.

Other movements then caught the eye.

In the middle of the room an angled pink blurr signalled by a perpendicular waving arm as Sasha slid down an ordinary slippery-dip or children's slide. At its base Mrs Cathcart stood firm, an overseer.

'Go on, Mrs C. Have a go!' Garry called as they went

over; but then Ken Hofmann, a satellite as usual, slipped and grappled with the nearest, Borelli holding Louisa, bringing them down, Gerald too, his spectacles bumping off his nose, and Kaddok in the midst accustomed to trips and spills, cupping his camera and held his other hand out to the floor. And the writhing heap of five slowly began sliding, as in a dream, towards the end wall—such was the polish and angle of the Moscow floor—until Hofmann amid the high laughter of Sasha and Violet, both on top of the ladder, grabbed at and held the first rung of the steps.

First to extricate, Gerald began savagely cursing.

The ursine Russian had kept ambling unconcerned back to the side wall, a proven path, pointing with his crumpled arm at the laziness of nature—a basic truth which, according to him, passes unobserved by most people.

'Look at waterfalls,' he suggested, as the others eventually made their way back. Excellent photographs of seven great waterfalls. 'And the course of every river in the world. They go only where they can, naturally, without fuss.'

The interest shown here by Borelli seemed to be excessive. To Phillip North, the guide seemed to be stating the obvious. He and most of the others drifted away.

'The law of nature,' the Russian quoted, 'is to act with the minimum of labour . . . avoiding, so far as it is possible, inconveniences. It doesn't fight.'

An excellent illustration was the catenary droop of the ordinary clothesline; the one rigged up close to the wall had been completely missed by the others. With Borelli and Louisa, and Shiela remaining, the guide stood back admiring it.

'You understand, it has reached a state of equilibrium with respect to gravity. What is called the principle of least action.' Shaking his head he seemed lost in admiration.

'That's me,' Borelli breathed.

'It is close to poetry,' the Russian agreed.

Louisa looked at Shiela and slowly rolled her eyes. Turning to her, Borelli took Louisa's necklace in his hand. He let it drop.

'The principle is everywhere.'

'Everyone can see that.'

'But we haven't properly considered it before; when you think about it.'

'One could say that about everything,' Louisa shrugged.

The stocky Russian meanwhile was busily removing his coat and shirt. Hairily bare-chested he stood waiting as the others returned. With his coarse weather-tanned throat he suddenly looked old. On his stomach he had a few bullet and shrapnel scars.

'We were talking about the laziness of nature, its line of least resistance.'

His enormous grave face; its poorly shaved folds. Holding his arms out horizontally he used his chin to point to the pale flesh under his arms which had dropped, pulled earthwards by gravity. 'I am not a young man,' he said.

His breasts were sagging.

'I can hold twenty-cent pieces under mine,' Sasha told North airily. 'I believe that's the test. I don't like this museum anyway.'

'Shhh, you'll learn something.'

Gravity had ravaged the man's cheeks, pulling them to earth along with the flesh underneath his chin, letting air into his eyelids: the line of least resistance. As he put on his shirt again some found themselves frowning as they pinched their own chins.

'Anything,' the Russian quoted, 'becomes interesting if you look at it long enough.'

Remembering his job he suddenly mentioned neckties, although he himself was not wearing one. Well, their performance depends on gravity. He pointed to Gerald's. Borelli nodded, 'Almost entirely.'

'Ha ha!' shouted Garry.

'He's a real weirdo,' Sasha whispered. 'What difference does it make? Darling, come along.'

Russians can be so bloody morbid.

'Stay around,' said North, 'and listen. Stop fidgetting.'

Gerald nodded. 'It's becoming interesting. Much of what he says we've simply overlooked. It's a new slant.'

Reconstructions: a brown boulder poised on a papier

mâché hill, and towards the middle of the room a superb scale model of a shot-tower. However, these were abruptly overshadowed, as was everything they had previously seen, by the gallows a few paces to the right: standing black and waiting.

'History and gravity.'

'Wow!'

Who said that? Garry Atlas.

They could see it was not a replica, not a reconstruction. The wooden steps were worn. Gerald poked around underneath the trapdoor, the black space for the kicking into *Ewigkeit*. Bumping into people, Kaddok manoeuvred to take a picture. How many people had ever seen real gallows? He called out for someone to stand on the platform.

'I will!' Garry volunteered, and for effect protruded his tongue and bulged his eyes.

'I wouldn't if I were you.' Hofmann advised.

The guide was watching them. 'You are like Americans and Canadians. You know very little. Nothing.'

'We can sometimes be shrill,' said North alongside.

'We often seem corny,' Borelli agreed.

'Do you still have capital punishment in the Soviet Union?' Hofmann called out, turning it back onto Russia.

'Come on,' said Sasha, upset. 'It's an awful thing.'

'Where's our Anna?' Mrs Cathcart asked. She went off labouring and elbowing up the slope.

'This is Russia alright, eh?' Garry grinned.

'Shut up,' said Violet.

'We should all listen to him,' Gerald nodded. 'There's nothing wrong.'

The Centre must have known the effect produced by the gallows. The section following dealt briefly with Sport.

'You realize, most games are a play with gravity; I draw your attention to gymnastics and ballsport especially. Proficiency is simply being best at counteracting gravity.'

He passed onto the various ways of 'beating gravity'. In pride of place of course stood a bust of Igor Sikorsky and a pair of tremendous grey blades from one of his choppers.

Both the inevitable Sputnik and the mug-shots of the first Soviet cosmonauts failed to interest them, which in itself was an interesting question, although according to Kaddok the dates given were wrong. Instead, a vaguely familiar lever trailing a piece of broken cable, lying in a glass case, caught their eye. They turned to the guide.

'Hah! Handbrake taken from a Moskvich.'

For some reason Borelli burst out laughing. He apologized.

'I am sorry. It's unexpected there.'

The Russian stared at him but could see he was enjoying himself, learning.

Visually intriguing in their way was the assortment of lift-pumps; a vodka-still of intricate elegance; the fearsome stomach pump; a passenger lift in art nouveau style from one of the grand old St Petersburg hotels—soberly they 'tested' it, standing in facing out, until Atlas began calling imaginary floors, as in a Myer emporium. In Russia it seemed Garry Atlas joked more than usual to show his independence. There was also a trapeze artist's stained tights.

All these were examples of man's attempts at defying, with varying degrees of success, the law of gravity.

Tatlin's resurrected glider was suspended from the ceiling, and a row of parachutes (history of) wafted in the breeze like anemones. A pleasure to stroll among these silken cords with the transluscent carapace above; gradually they forgot the gallows.

Sasha leaned on North's shoulder.

The guide now began searching his pockets, announcing: 'This arrived only yesterday.'

He muttered a few words in Russian as they waited. That can be the trouble with museum guides. There was no way of knowing it was not, rather, part of a well-rehearsed act. For when he found the cable he held it at exaggerated arm's length.

'Who reads English?'

'Violet,' Sasha pointed. 'She's an actress. Use your best voice, darling.'

GRAVITY [she read]:
Palmeira dos Indios, Brazil, June 9, REUTER

Violet cleared her throat.

> *The Mayor of this north-eastern Brazil city has desisted*
> *from his intent of mustering a majority in the city council*
> *to repeal the law of gravity, according to press reports.*
> *Mayor Minervo Pimentel was annoyed at the law of*
> *gravity because city engineers told him it prevented their*
> *building a water tank on the sloping main square of the*
> *city.*
> *When he called on the Council's majority leader Jaime*
> *Guimareas to muster the councilmen to repeal the law, he*
> *was told it was better to leave it alone.*
> *'We do not know whether this is a municipal or state*
> *law and it might even be a federal law,' Guimareas said.*
> *'It is better not to get mixed up in this business so as not*
> *to create any problems,' he added.*

Violet handed back the cable.

'Yes, we went to Latin America,' Kaddok told him over the racket, the horse laughter. Slapping himself so much Garry had lost his footing on the floor and fell, keeping his cigarette in his mouth.

'Very interesting place. At the Equator we—'

The Russian nodded without listening. Even he had to concentrate along this stretch of the floor.

Slowly raising his arm, to preserve balance, he shouted over Kaddok: 'The machinery which has sprung up around gravity. We have the hydrometer and the gravimeter . . .'

Some like old Doug and Shiela, and Gwen Kaddok, tried squinting expressions, denoting interest and concentration, but once a person began grinning it seemed impossible to stop it. Residue from the telegramme remained, and always would; contributing was the fun-park angle of the floor. Holding onto North's trouser belt, Sasha just couldn't stop giggling.

Stactometers (various sizes); and they slid past a village-built tribometer not noticing the ingenious system of greasy ratchets, the leaf-spring off a German army truck and the ballast drums of gravel suspended on frayed cables, attached to the face of an alarm clock. Leaning in the corner, a primitive janker—what's that got to do with gravity?—and a collection of stuffed birds put to one side for the time being.

'I think they find such absurd things fascinating because their lives are grey,' said Violet in a clear voice.

'Violet, I think I agree with you,' said Gwen hanging onto Kaddok.

But they were subdued by the grave expression of the Russian. That large worn-out head; his unspeakable sadness. And he had a job to do. They were at the corner of the ballroom.

'The purpose of the Centre,' said he tying it in a knot, 'is to show gravity from every angle. The history of mankind is one of grave situations strung together like beads on a necklace'—he attempted to smile at the simile. 'Gravity is the common thread. It can be observed both on the national and personal levels. We manage to keep going, nevertheless.'

The 'grave situations' were illustrated rather pedantically by photographs of war graves. Those in French soil, at Verdun, appeared like freshly planted geometric vineyards—order restored after chaos, as if to say it was all worth it; quite a contrast to the austere mounds like brown snow from the siege of Leningrad.

Disasters on a grand scale illustrated the 'national level', mentioned next: scenery after earthquakes, eruptions, plane crashes; the emaciated figures of famines and African plagues. Finally, the 'personal level' was shown by photographs of people with long faces, grave expressions, chins resting on hands, widows weeping: culminating in an enlarged shot of a young woman, mouth open, arms high, leaping from a bridge.

'That's Brunel's bridge at Bristol,' Gerald broke the silence. He turned to Phillip North. 'Remember we saw that? One of the most important bridges in England.'

Remember too the high tide in the harbour; the Bristol zoo; the cold sausage rolls for afternoon tea?

'People are sometimes awful,' Shiela bit her lip. 'I don't know . . .'

Putting her arm around her, Louisa moved her from the photographs. 'Never mind. I always think it happens only to other people. We read the papers and we never seem to know the unfortunates.'

'I suppose so.'

'Our present theory,' the Russian rasped, 'is that we dream in order to break away from gravity. In every dream, gravity is defied. Without such relief the pressure would be intolerable. I'—he added a queer personal note—'sleep badly.'

'It must be awful,' Sasha murmured. She too had a vast surplus of sympathy.

'Ah, but it's not worth losing any sleep over!' Louisa cried unexpectedly. Her husband laughed so harshly people turned.

'You should leave her alone,' Borelli turned, staring at him.

Evidently such troubles were common in the museum, a by-product of the grave atmosphere, the concentrated force of the exhibits and the tiring slant of the floor, for the guide simply veered to the penultimate exhibit, the obligatory Soviet graph depicting the grave downward path of capitalism. Various economic measures were used. About to elaborate he stopped and craned towards the wall. He turned to them with a sigh, 'Which one of you?'

'What?'

Garry Atlas went over: he should not have laughed. 'Someone's written here "Down Under". There's a small map of Australia drawn.'

'Hurray!' cried Sasha, but was elbowed by North.

Garry turned back to the wall. 'This someone's really been busy. There's "Down with Gravity" and . . . "Down with Communism".'

The laughter fluttered, fell short.

The Russian stared.

'Which one of you.'

'Ay, come on. Fair go!'

'What's he saying?'

'You're from down there . . .'

'He can read English,' Violet declared, 'when he wants to.'

'I think it's perfectly alright,' said Gwen. 'It's freedom of speech. We believe in freedom of speech, where we come from.'

'Don't say anything,' Hofmann advised. 'Everyone shut up.'

'Listen,' Garry faced the Russian, 'we didn't do this, if that's what you mean.'

'One of you is missing.'

They looked around. They turned to Doug. 'Hey, just a minute!' he laughed. 'She toddled back to the entrance. Anyway, she wouldn't dream of—' He made a second embarrassed laugh, looking at the Russian. 'You don't know my wife . . .'

'It's in biro,' Gerald reported.

'It doesn't matter,' said Borelli. 'These things unfortunately happen.' To show his nonchalance he practised a golf swing with his walking stick, and almost fell over.

'Incorporate it in the Centre's collection. What's wrong with that?'

'It will be reported,' said the Russian. And they didn't fell sorry for him anymore. Moving quickly—for a bear of a man—he slid to the right preventing Kaddok photographing the defiled corner. Remaining there he pointed to the door.

So no one noticed the last exhibit, the attempt on the Russians' part to finish on a light note. Tilted above a false door a bucket of white-wash hung in the balance: the old silent film joke, akin to falling down the open manhole; depends entirely on gravity. No one noticed. And in all likelihood they would have enjoyed that. It would have relaxed the strained atmosphere. The guide seemed to remember. He half-turned, programmed, but went on without another word.

'They're a strange people,' Hofmann was saying. 'They're definitely paranoid.'

Garry nodded. 'A bit of bloody graffiti never hurt anyone.'

They made their way carefully up the narrow slope, the Russian taking up the rear.

Mrs Cathcart was seated at the entrance, watching Anna knitting. She scarcely looked up.

'A spot of bother,' Doug reported, and hitched up his trousers. 'Silly business. We've got to watch our Ps and Qs.'

'It's still hot as blazes outside,' Mrs Cathcart observed. 'Anna and I have been sitting here.'

When Shiela asked the guide if the Centre had any postcards he didn't answer.

'Let's go,' several suggested. 'Come on.'

They pushed open the door. Garry stopped and looked back.

'Say, where's Smiley, our bag of laughs?'

'I think he's gone to report us.'

'We could be shot, all of us.'

'He could be, more like it.'

Anna was gathering up her knitting.

By sticking together they could come to no harm. That was the feeling: it showed in the way they barged out into the open air, and for several minutes stood around, squinting, a form of carelessness.

Coughing, exaggeratedly slapping himself, Garry made Russian cigarettes briefly the centre of attention: trying them was part of the overseas experience. Back home before recalling the curiosities of the Kremlin or even the Centre of Gravity he'd say, 'Ever tried a Russian cigarette? Chrrrist! In Moscow . . .'

Opposite at the table sat their guide, the moon on embroidered cotton.

'Don't take any notice of him.' Sasha advised. 'We all hope he chokes.'

Nodding and smiling Anna wiped her mouth with her handkerchief.

They were picking at the pink salmon. The white wine was sweet.

'There aren't many lights at night,' Shiela observed, and they twisted in their seats to check. 'It's black as pitch outside.'

'Compared to Europe and New York, it is.'

'There were more lights in Africa, I feel,' Shiela persisted. 'Remember?'

'I don't suppose here they're allowed out on the streets.'

'Louisa, you always exaggerate,' said Sasha.

When Hofmann joined in, his windows glittered. 'Not in this case, she doesn't. You're in Russia, don't forget.'

The dentist suddenly coughed and quickly picked inside his back teeth: almost another fishbone incident.

Further comparisons were made here and there around the table.

'Don't we talk so much rubbish?' Borelli turned to Phillip North. 'We expect you to lift the standard and you haven't said a word.'

North pointed with his index finger. 'With this ring through my nose I'm a trifle inhibited.'

'So we've noticed. It must be terrible—difficult to breathe?'

Sasha who had been listening to Violet swung around. 'Thankyou-very-much!' But the toss of the head and distant glance showed she was pleased. While Borelli and Louisa watched, she leaned against North and whispered, 'You don't feel inhibited, do you?'

Gerald was talking to Hofmann. 'It should be interesting seeing the Kremlin; I'm looking forward to that.'

'The fifteenth century,' Kaddok volunteered.

Those fragments; comparisons: distant memories of the skirting travellers.

Gerald reversed, having doubts. 'What can be seen in two days? Russia is too enormous. But even if it wasn't—'

'Anything is better than nothing, I always think.'

'I'm not so sure,' said Gerald.

'But you're never satisfied,' Gwen turned. 'You can be a very negative person. What is it you like?'

Reddening, Gerald looked down at his plate. Towards the end of their tour people were speaking freely.

This was the hotel, Anna mentioned, where the Provisional Government first met in 1917. 'Red Square is directly behind us.'

Violet suddenly turned and smiled tightly. 'You never ask us about our country. Aren't you interested?'

'Ah yes. You have told me. And I have your passports—' She smiled.

'They're not interested,' Hofmann shook his head. 'Everyone's got to understand that.'

Anna smoothed her skirt. 'We don't travel as much as you.'

'Because you can't.' Hofmann again.

'I couldn't stand that, Anna.' Violet lit a cigarette. 'I'd go right out of my mind.'

'Why can't you travel?' Hofmann asked. 'Why don't you tell us that?'

'Don't be harsh,' Louisa turned to him. 'Let her be.'

'We have no need,' said Anna. 'Oh I would like one day to go to Egypt.'

'Egypt?' Garry yelled.

Anna remained smiling. 'You can take trips all your life, but there's always death. Don't you think?'

The others were listening, leaning forward. Anna turned and said something in Russian to the waiter.

'She always wears that lovely smile,' Violet muttered.

'Fair go, Anna's alright.'

'We're supposed to be on holidays,' Mrs Cathcart reminded. 'We're their guests, in a strange country.'

Only Borelli seemed to consider Anna's statement. Tapping his lips with his fingers he glanced at Hofmann.

'We come from a country,' Louisa turned to Anna, 'of nothing really, or at least nothing substantial yet. We can appear quite heartless at times. I don't know why. We sometimes don't know any better.' All smiles; to help Anna. 'Even before we travel we're wandering in circles. There isn't much we understand. I should say, there isn't much we believe in. We have rather empty feelings. I think we even find love difficult. And when we travel we demand even the confusions to be simple. It is all confusing, isn't it? I don't know why we expect all answers to be simple, but we do. We expect it to be straight forward. In some ways, in your country, you are lucky.' Louisa slowly flushed, noticing everyone looking at her. 'At least that's what I think.'

Sitting away from her, Hofmann snorted.

'Speech! Speech!' Garry banged; a form of reduction, of fragmentation. And the Cathcarts stared at their plates and solemnly up at the cornice.

'We are an odd lot,' admitted North, and suddenly began laughing.

Louisa was biting her lip; Borelli had touched her arm.

Of little or no concern to Gerald: gazing through the dark window at nothing in particular, trying not to be negative. And North at the far end bent towards Sasha to hear better.

Uncertainties may have increased as they stood in the queue outside the tomb of Lenin. The mausoleum was invisible, uphill. The flagstones of Red Square rose before them, a solid wave, and darkened in the heat, produced a kind of undertow. The queue of several versts moved slowly forward, dragging: inevitable tourism.

They were sandwiched between a delegation of jabbering bookbinders from Kiev and a clan of ginger-faced Highland flingers in kilts and all, red knees, said to be ballet devotees. With Gerald at the point the group cast Japanese shadows, a source of idle interest. All but Anna had turned somewhat reflective, little being said. A sense of loss spread as they stood now in the open, within sight of the tomb; a sense of sliding time and place. Apart from the long queue Red Square was empty. And what: those tattered trumpets could be heard somewhere producing unexplained exhortatory tunes, reminding them. It didn't make sense. It was hard to hold the moment; and yet time and the surrounding solid objects passed slowly. It all slipped through their bodies.

At intervals—as if pulled by wires—a buxom or a bow-legged figure, usually elderly, would fall out of the line, a quadrant collapse to the eye, left or to the right, immediately clustered with crouching next of kin or friends, and carried into the shade. It caused Mrs Cathcart to wonder aloud if they, poor beggars, were given enough to eat.

Astride a rise, hemmed in by ancient dark walls, Red Square had a bulging orthodox church at each end. It was so vast it remained continually empty; how could it ever be filled? At its church ends it leaked air and people, and there was that dramatic fall away from the approximate centre. The low mausoleum had been slotted in there on one long side, against the Kremlin wall. They were now less than fifty paces from its entrance. Violet who'd undone a few buttons stood with her eyes closed, catching the sun.

Remembering her job Anna turned from the nodding bookbinders and with a raised finger made these points:
The mausoleum is
   a) of red granite
   b) bullet-proof and bomb-proof
   c) the sole remaining example in the Soviet
      Union of pure Constructivism
   d) upwards 7 million respectful visitors per—
Something had caught their eye.

'Yoo-hoo!' Mrs Cathcart waved. 'Excuse me, Anna,' she said. She elbowed Garry like a son, 'Here we are, tell them.'

The Kaddoks came towards them in the heat, Leon holding Gwen's elbow and sloping forward as if trip-tripping into a wind. Gwen was hurrying, anxiously scanning the line. Festooned with his leather-hooded equipment, similar to the blackened trophies on primitive necklaces, he cut a powerful figure, ultra-modern and complacent, unable of course to see Gwen biting her lip. The party smiled when relief suddenly smoothed her features.

'You almost missed the boat,' Doug slapped by way of a welcome.

Kaddok immediately began telling them about the Party

Machine he had gone to photograph, housed in the longest building in the Eastern bloc, 'Kouznetski Street, a stone's throw from here.' Of immense proportions; it actually covered several blocks: yet apparently it could apply itself to the smallest, seemingly trivial detail.

Having spent several hours in the queue, the scenery of Red Square had become progressively mundane, like the shoulders and back of the neck of the person directly in front, and so the group turned to Kaddok's story with an interest perhaps out of all proportion. The Scotties leaned forward to listen too.

Yes, it is off the beaten track—Kaddok told them—more the obligatory mecca for travellers from the Eastern bloc; but well worth a visit, well worth a trip. The glass megastructure allowed the Machine to be viewed from the street. But it was much better inside. Parallel catwalks had been fitted for visitors to follow the workings in close-up. It consisted, in the main, of rigid maroon pipes and drums attached to shivering copper feedlines. The drums revolved, see, setting forth a chain-reaction further down the line. Ratchets and sprockets interconnected to pulleys and lazy S-shaped wheels, vigorous elbows as in a steam engine, then activated the machine in various parts and in all directions, and yet somehow prevented the whole from disintegration, heavy flywheels, governors, ironed out the contradictions, the slight discrepancies. The rocking chassis with its esoteric standards and cesspools of grease held her steady; sideways movements were at once activated and yet kept to a minimum by *rubber* connecting rods and torsion bars, all wired to warning gauges. It had been working for years. The maintenance supervisor, the zealot with the oil can, said many decades. This man's name, Kaddok declared, was Axelrod.

'Do you know what?' North asked over the smiles.

'What?' Kaddok hated being interrupted.

One of the Scots jumped in. 'It must have set up a God-awful racket.'

'It was relatively quiet, in fact. It was hard, in fact, to know if it was working. I was impressed.'

Gwen nodded.

It was a machine of words, largely.

'The interesting thing,' Kaddok tried to continue, 'was at the finish, it reproduced replicas of itself. They were quite something, like transistors. They were only an inch or so long, of the whole machine.'

The ironical cheering and shouts from the wild Scots were cut short by the guards in grey. They also pointed to Violet: she had to button herself up. Cameras were allowed but—hang on—just a minute!—Doug had his binoculars confiscated. They had reached Lenin's tomb.

Touching the granite walls Hofmann and the Cathcarts had already descended a few steps when a scuffle broke out behind. There was shouting, swearing in English. One of the Scots, big man, struggled with the guards. His hat and sunglasses dropped onto the floor.

'That looks like Hammersly,' Garry pointed. 'It's not, is it?'

'I don't know,' Shiela squinted. 'It could be.'

It was hard to tell.

'I'm sure I saw him,' said Violet, 'his shape in the foyer.'

It was Hammersly.

'Hey, he's alright,' Garry went forward.

'He's not with us,' said the Scots.

And Shiela and Garry Atlas who tried to help were pushed back. The mausoleum's metal door was slammed shut.

'Hey, that's the last we'll see of him.'

Then they noticed: the bookbinders in front had gone. They were alone in the mausoleum.

'What's going on?'

'Anna?' Mrs Cathcart called. It echoed. 'Where is she? Anna!'

It wasn't entirely dark. Subtle wall fixtures gave the granite a rosy religious glow.

Anna had all along been at Mrs Cathcart's elbow. She shrugged. 'There's nothing to worry about. I wasn't told,' she added, perplexed.

'Let's go back,' said Sasha.

'We can't,' North murmured. 'The door is bolted.'

'Yoo-hoo!' Mrs Cathcart called out. She could be a pillar of strength.

Following Anna they slowly completed the remaining steps and turned right into the sepulchre itself, a bare room of grave sumrak, with the precise angles of a bank vault. A thick-legged worker wearing a flannel bathing costume (as worn in Black Sea resorts) was hosing the floor and walls. There Lenin lay facing the ceiling like Oblomov, lit by a spotlight. His beard glistened like the wet walls. A rope fence prevented them from going closer.

A group of dolichocephalic party bosses in their loose suits and pierced cream-coloured shoes stepped out from the shadows. They motioned Anna over. Listening intently, she glanced back at her group. She nodded.

'Hey, you sarmations,' a member of this nomenclatura called.

'We're from Australia,' Garry corrected. 'And what's the big idea?'

'Yes, I'd like to know,' said Mrs Cathcart.

'But it is a great privilege,' Anna beamed. 'You are very lucky. You must listen to him.'

'I wouldn't trust them,' Hofmann was heard. 'As I said all along. We shouldn't have come here.' Shuffling, some scratching of themselves.

The Russians remained partly in shadow, impassive and patient, and the worker kept tugging at the hose to wash the end wall. After again conferring among themselves a spokesman moved forward and, pushing Anna aside, ducked under the velvet rope. He was a heavy man with bushy eyebrows and long ears. His hand rested on the transparent lid near Lenin's head. Two others followed, skinny and coatless Russians. One had a movie camera resting on his shoulder; the other gripped an old Speed Graflex and managed to whisper to Sasha his name was 'Ivan'.

The frontman was accustomed to audiences of several thousand. He gestured easily with one hand: a brief panegyric on the dead leader.

'For Christ's sake,' Hofmann groaned. 'Did we come to hear this garbage?'

Shuffling eagerly around the edges Kaddok photographed the photographers of the State.

'Excuse me—' Borelli raised his hand; but was cut short by the Russian.

'Now we get down to—you say?—talking turkey.'

'They think we're Americans,' Violet sniggered.

Making a sign to the photographers he paused, then lifted the lid of the bevelled sarcophagus. A murmur ran through the party, the tourists. Lenin was exposed. This was altogether different.

Slowly, ponderously the Russian chose his words:

'We understand you have travelled. There is nothing like travel, eh? You must have seen wonderful sights, those cities and towns with their empty cafe tables, local customs and colour, the innumerable objects fascinating for their detail, the different sunsets. You've been to many countries. Africa too, I'm told. Very good. It makes you feel experienced, *nyet*? It gives one the added perspective, a means of comparison. Naturally by now you have sorted out the . . . wheat from the chaff, the real from the nylon. Your eye has sharpened. As in war, travel has heightened your senses. That is good; very good. Perhaps you are less naive?' He looked at each one of them, taking his time. 'But appearances, of events and things seen around, are deceptive. What can we believe anymore? What is real? Appearances are not necessarily exact. The appearance of things is generally a lie. That has become a problem of life, wouldn't you say? You were in Moscow yesterday and now today. But how can you prove it? *Chuzhaya*! Where is the truth, the real existence of things? Increasingly the edges are blurred.'

Borelli and Gerald Whitehead nodded.

The Russian now glanced at Lenin's exposed face.

'What do you accept, what do you choose to believe? That which is before you? You came to see Lenin. In your country you have your embalmed Holy Men and Royals. There is the Roman Pope—a man who can lift both arms.

301

And movement, someone has written, is the basic characteristic of reality. Okay. To you Lenin is a curiosity, a shape; to us he is both the living Idea and the Ideal, example and reminder. So in certain quarters abroad scurrilous rumours are regularly let out that Vladimir Ilyich here is a dummy, a fake. Such is his central importance and the persistence of attacks we are compelled every five years to show the world it really is . . . Lenin. Understand? That is our plan. A simple test . . . randomly selected independent observers.'

Slowly he looked at each one. Most of them still didn't understand.

'Step forward, please. Mind the rope. Of course, ladies first.'

The Cathcarts glanced at Shiela, at Phillip North. Holding North's arm Sasha shrugged.

'Well I'm game,' said Doug as Hofmann ducked under. For some reason Hofmann was more than usually keen.

Lenin lay waist-high on a kind of podium. He wore the familiar three-piece suit, the baggy trousers steam-pressed, sporting the polka-dot tie and the gold tie-pin. His face seemed to be real, though it had a distinct cadaveric pallor and the beard glistened as if treated with preservatives. From behind the ropes Lenin had certainly looked more natural, as if he was dozing.

'Madam . . .'

Smiling, the Russian gave Shiela a small hand mirror.

'Go on,' he urged, gently.

The movie camera with the surging hips whirred; and Ivan from *Pravda* squatted and waited.

'But we've seen too much!' Shiela cried. 'It's been hard to digest. There were so many things. We are the least qualified.'

'Shiela's right,' Borelli said. 'It's been confusing. We're still in the dark.'

'Come on. We can form an opinion,' Hofmann said. 'This is simple enough.'

The Russian took Shiela's trembling hand and guided the mirror to Lenin's slightly opened yellow mouth.

'He's dead. Yes?'

Shiela turned. 'I can't look!'

But Hofmann leaned forward. 'He's dead.'

The Russian nodded to Violet. She got into the spirit of things.

Leaning over she tweaked the nose.

'It feels real enough. It didn't come away in my hand.'

'Very good,' the Russian nodded. 'That's the spirit.'

Doug Cathcart tapped the bald head with his knuckles and turning to the zooming movie camera reported, 'Fair enough.'

Then Hofmann, impatient, offered his services: 'I'm a dentist.'

The Russian nodded.

Hofmann bent close to the face.

Signs of ecchymosis, several shaving snicks. Professionally prising open the mouth he squinted in. He clicked his fingers for Garry's Ronson. Lenin's teeth reflected the food of exile, prisons, the Russian cigarettes and borscht.

'Gold fillings,' Anna observed. She grinned at everybody.

Hofmann frowned. 'Some are missing.'

'What?' the Russian leaned forward.

Hofmann shook his head. 'He didn't look after himself.' He tried to close the mouth.

'Lenin never had enough time,' the Russian answered. 'And he liked to dine not with tourists, but with the chauffeurs and workmen.'

Then seeing both photographers staring open-mouthed—only Kaddok aimed a camera—he elbowed Ivan then the other. '*Bolkan!*'

After Hofmann closed the mouth Gwen Kaddok at the other end dipped into the reliquary and grappled with a leg. It was stiff but she managed to lift it up. The black shoelace was undone and he had no socks.

Mrs Cathcart shook her head. Nothing would make her touch him.

Gwen struggled to put the leg back. 'He's alive—I mean he's not false. I can see it's not wooden or anything,' she frowned at the cameras. 'It's a leg.'

Hofmann stared at Louisa. 'My wife has a great passion for truth. So go on.'

Tentatively she touched the necktie. The others would have laughed at Gwen and Lenin's leg if it weren't so serious; and easily embarrassed Gwen crossed and rolled her eyes.

'We ask,' the Russian interrupted Louisa, 'that you prove the existence of him, of his solid body, and not his decorations. Of course his clothing is authentic! Clothing is clothing.'

But the tie abruptly came away from the waistcoat. It had been cut short—was only a few inches long. In the strict analytical sense it was not a real necktie.

'Oh dear. That was so unexpected.'

'See what you've done?' Borelli joked.

'Enough!' said the Russian harshly.

The cameras were lowered as the tie was gingerly tucked back into place.

The incident, so human in its unexpectedness, lightened their mood and they chatted among themselves. Anything is possible after a time.

Returning them to the task the Russian had to speak loudly.

'Some say revolutionaries are basically lazy. For example, that is the English view. But it has been estimated that Lenin wrote ten million words.' He pointed to Borelli. 'Now you, why not see if that is true?'

Borelli thought for a second, then bent over the coffin: fresh outburst of camera whirring and clickings. He lifted the writer's finger and twisted it back and forth under the lights.

'Careful,' murmured North.

'Is it worn?'

Borelli nodded. 'Where his fountain pen must have rested. There is a distinct flat spot—'

'Speak up,' the Russian smiled at the cameras.

'A distinct flat spot, shiny, almost a callous. The finger has formed a lot of words. Dirty fingernails.'

'Did you know,' Kaddok boomed out from Lenin's feet,

'Soviet nail-polish is the longest-lasting in the world? It's made from old films.'

The Russian looked surprised and Borelli stepped back, wiping his hand on his jacket.

'It was quite waxy to touch,' he told Louisa and Shiela, 'and stiff but it was a finger alright, just as it looks. My uncle I was telling you about would have appreciated this.'

Because Phillip North wore a grey beard he was elected to test Lenin's: suddenly the expert, Auditor of Beards, to the world at large. It was important. The beard was one of Lenin's most conspicuous features, and all along comments had been made of its false appearance. It was ginger and glistened too much.

All North had to do was touch it, tug at it. This he did several times to everybody's satisfaction: the physical aspects corrected the visual.

'I think we believe he's the real McCoy,' said Doug slipping into argot. 'I'd say he's genuine enough. I'm convinced.'

'I haven't had a go yet.'

Stepping forward Garry Atlas raised Lenin's right arm to 45°. He let it go with a satisfied expression. But it remained in salute. The other Russians shouted and moved forward, ducking under the rope. They pushed Atlas away. International incident at——. It took two heavily built Russians cursing and perspiring, and Ivan who gave Gerald his camera to hold, to press the arm back.

'You're a silly bugger,' Hofmann snapped. 'You could have had us all shot. Do you know what you did?'

'What d'you mean? That wasn't my fault.'

'It doesn't matter,' North soothed.

The Russians had returned to their corner, glowering; and Ivan took his camera back. Their spokesman straightened his lapels and cleared his throat. 'Ladies and gentlemen, we very much thank you. It was unfortunately a brief, necessary task. You will understand. It should convince'—his voice rose—'the most hardened reactionary lackey. Some things have a force of their own, are a statement of fact. Lenin lives!'

The glass lid was carefully replaced, fitting beautifully, and a snap of his fingers produced two bottles of Stolichnaya and glasses on a hexagon-shaped tray. Setting it down near Lenin's head he poured them each a nip.

'Vodka straight?' Garry turned to the others.

'We are not monsters,' the host joked.

'What about the others waiting to come in?' Shiela asked. She looked up at ground-level but there were no windows. The Russian waved his hand.

The chilled glasses left moist overlapping circles on the lid. A party atmosphere naturally prevailed, and small circles developed. Violet and Sasha found cigarettes, and the Russian rushed over with matches.

'Well, that was an eye-opener,' said Doug rocking with his glass. 'That's what I call an experience.'

'Aren't you glad you came?' Shiela asked Gerald. To Shiela it epitomized travel.

'You have been honoured,' Anna smiled. 'It is not every day . . .'

'I found it instructive,' Gerald admitted. 'Very Russian, it seems.'

'What did you try?' Sasha asked.

'The leg. Remember?' Gwen cupped her mouth. 'I nearly died.'

Sasha and Violet laughed. The Russian glanced at his watch and nodded to the others. He opened a second bottle.

Shiela wondered again about the people waiting in the queue.

'Let them be,' he waved. 'Our people are patient.'

'I'm more concerned about the Scots,' said North.

'At least it's nice and cool down here,' Mrs Cathcart observed, 'and clean.'

Doug glanced around. She was right as usual.

Garry Atlas who had asked Ivan, 'So what's it like being a communist?' (well, because they didn't look any different), broke off: 'I bet old Hammersly's fuming!' He threw his head back. 'If only he knew. Drink up! How long have we been down here?'

Taken for granted now, the shape of the tomb had

blurred. The walls had gradually fallen away; tired walls. It was as if they were alone. There was nothing unusual—nothing novel—in the shape of the grey claque in the corner, backs turned, and the cleaner with the dribbling hose gaping at them. The body of Lenin lay alongside them but behind, for they had turned, and anyway it was difficult now to distinguish his embalmed features, so many glasses and marks left by moisture, and palms of hands, as well as Violet's handbag were on the lid.

The Russian proposed a toast.

Repeating his gratitude and their wide experience ('men and women of the world') he added a few statistics on tourism in the Soviet Union and a dubious plug for the safety record of Aeroflot. He bowed graciously. 'Tell your people what you saw.'

In reply Phillip North reddened.

'We too are grateful. I like to think that in realizing something for the first time we come close to ecstasy. Is it possible? At any rate, that should be the essence of observations. I'd say it is. Um—all things—I mean the inanimate as well as the mobile—have a life of their own. Every experience is a journey.' (Hear, hear!) 'What we have seen today I don't suppose we shall ever forget. But time is needed to sort out impressions.' Always the zoologist North closed with some obscure lines from Vvedensky, and an appreciative word on the overwhelming proof of the vodka (joke, joke).

Laughter mingled with the clapping and genial smiles from their hosts. Returning to his place Sasha squeezed North's arm.

Both Shiela and Mrs Cathcart would write postcards that evening, their last:

'Hello, everybody. You'll never guess what happened to us today—'

But now they congregated behind the dead leader, holding the empty glasses in their hands like trophies. Each one formed a previously decided, tested facial expression for Kaddok's tilted composition. Louisa and Sasha smiled.

307

'This is a rotten place. It's awful; empty.'

They could hear Sasha being homesick in the basin. These rooms were nothing but partitions jerry-built in the second five-year plan, the sloping ceilings plastered with varnished travel posters: the metal products of Tula and the wonders of Samarkand.

'Never mind,' North soothing, 'cover yourself up.'

'The waiter was rude. I hate the food.'

After shouting their orders to the kitchen in his thick tongue he'd leaned on the servery window watching them. And the Soviet cutlery had felt queer to handle. The rest of the dining room was empty. Borelli had said the world was speeding by, separate from them. They were flung out at the edges; it felt as if it would be hard to get back.

'I can think of worse,' North assured her. 'We're just being left alone, that's all. It's educational.'

To comfort her, he sat on a tabouret which revealed his short woollen socks. Violet had gone off to another room. He stroked Sasha's hand which fluttered and fidgeted. The swallows had migrated south weeks ago.

'You don't care,' Sasha pouted.

From her bed Shiela heard:

'But I do care. 'Course I do.'

'Do you wear pyjamas?' the voice as transparent as vodka-and-ice.

North coughed. 'Beg your pardon?'

Although she was sick a few minutes before Sasha gave a rattle-laugh and came to life under the eiderdown, finally resting with her cheek on her hand. That was the creaking.

'Cover yourself,' North advised: traces of anxiety. 'Sasha? You'll get cold!'

'He's embarrassed! I think he is!'

'Shhhh,' whispered North, 'you're being silly.' But the way he spoke showed he was smiling, looking at her. Shiela could tell.

The acoustics were activated by the angle of the ceilings and the varnish. The layers of tourist posters also contributed.

'Do you know eiderdown,' North changed the topic,

though not quite, 'comes from the Icelandic: *Eider*, being a species of duck; *dunn*, if I'm not mistaken, is Old Norse for the soft underplumage of fowls and so forth.'

'Chooks,' Sasha inspected her elbow. She wasn't interested.

He coughed again.

'You like to educate us,' she said. 'You can't resist, can you?'

'I imagined you'd be interested.'

'Eiderdown—what difference does it make? I suppose that's why you came here. You find every little thing interesting.'

'Nothing much happens to us. It's all happened before, at some other time. We can see it in the museums or the libraries. It's been stored for us to see. There are almost too many things.'

'There he goes again,' Sasha yawned. 'How boring. Youch! I'm going to get rid of that beard. Now don't be such a prude. Listen'—her voice descended to that of a child's. Shiela couldn't quite hear.

Gerald also lay in his room, trying to read.

'There's only this one night.' That was Borelli's voice: cramped, as if he was lifting something. 'You don't like it much either?'

On his bed sat Louisa Hofmann, the married woman.

'You know; I told you why. The places make very little difference.' She clicked her tongue. 'Look at all the washing you've got to do.'

Borelli didn't seem to hear. Standing on his bed he was peeling from the ceiling a lime-green shot of the Volga, revealing now a corner, and finally the whole of Riefenstahl's 1936 Games. 'A-ha! I thought it was.' It was one of the original posters. The ceilings were decorated with them.

'Where's old Gerald? He'd be interested in this.'

'I'm trying to read!' the voice shouted. An aerial view would show where.

Borelli pulled a face and Louisa laughed.

She leaned back on her elbows, her legs vaulting into the

shadows of her skirt; above her the planks and congested angles of a wooden church seemed to crown her head. Gold hung on Louisa's wrists and curled on her lobes; a fine chain fell like wheat down inside her blouse. She'd been watching Borelli. At the same time she seemed to look past him and into herself; or in the near future. Borelli sat beside her.

'What is it?'

Louisa smiled. 'I didn't say a word.'

Shiela, for one, listened.

Borelli's voice of understanding: 'But what though? What were you thinking?'

'But you always ask me that.' She added, quite mysteriously, 'But it's nice. . .'

'Has Ken gone somewhere else?' Borelli asked. 'Where is he?'

'I don't care where he is.'

She touched the edge of the eiderdown.

Borelli hesitated but now leaned towards her, and kissed Louisa. They could hear Gerald somewhere clattering the pages of Pevsner; Shiela heard Louisa sigh as if turning in her sleep. 'Doug, what's the name of Jean's eldest?' came Mrs C's voice, polishing off the postcards. They heard Louisa: 'What's going to happen now?' Fumbling, Borelli undid the French buttons of her blouse. Louisa began murmuring something (inaudible); her young man put his finger to her lips. Her blouse opened like a coat. He kissed her throat, her breasts, pressed his cheek between them. Louisa held onto his hair. She began crying, but so softly. 'What for? . . .' Borelli asked. 'Nothing!' Louisa cried. Gerald loudly coughed and blew his nose.

No one ever knew what the Kaddoks spoke about. The tidal murmuring could be heard, mainly Kaddok's monotone as he changed a film, using a device like a black coat turned inside out; but now they were shouting. Gwen was shrill. Kaddok preferred single, curt words, patient spitting—both in a foreign tongue, a private language. Soon they were quiet.

Sasha and North were laughing, and he was old enough to be her father.

Shiela heard the interruption. Slamming the door Violet shook all the other partitions. Her voice was high.

'Violet, wait a sec,' said Sasha.

She took no notice of them. 'He's a pig, and I know them. He's disgusting.'

'What?' said North.

Sasha held his arm. Tipping out her bag Violet searched for cigarettes.

'Sit down. Tell us. They're on the dressing table.'

'Smoothie-chops. I could clip him one. I pity her, poor girl.'

'I'll toddle off,' said North.

'Stay! Violet, you sit down. Now calm yourself. It doesn't matter.'

Violet laughed. 'Listen to her.'

'Nothing much matters,' North offered. 'What can we do about many things?'

His hands rested on his knees.

'What do you know?' Violet turned. 'I'm talking about myself.'

'At least we're together,' said Sasha. 'We're supposed to be on a holiday. I've been sick.'

'So I heard. Shit.'

The relentless snoring of Cathcart could be heard, yards of gravel raised then rolling down a tin slope. Sleep: a form of death rattle.

Someone banged on the wall. Everyone could hear everyone else.

Shiela had to laugh.

There was Hofmann's voice, 'Where the hell have you been?'

'Never mind,' Louisa said. She began whistling.

'I asked a question.'

'Then I can ask: where have you been?'

'Shut up.'

'You weren't very successful? You poor man.'

And Violet nearby began crying. 'She's so nice, from the beginning I always thought.'

'I'm tired,' Louisa told him. 'I'm retiring.'

Sitting up Shiela buttoned her pyjamas. In the midst of a group, among friends, the world was so intensely and constantly changing: even alone there was so much to see. The door unexpectedly rattled, then opened. It was Garry Atlas: almost falling in.

'Whoopsie! Fuck, where's the light?'

Shiela covered herself as Garry sat heavily on the bed.

'There we are . . .' said he.

Looking around the room he smacked his lips. Almost neat, on the sharp side, in his new Simpson's coat, the knitted shirt and flaired trousers, Garry's bibacious face had rushed infra-red in places, blown slightly off its axis, and breathed heavily. Below the eyes, around the nose: flesh had shifted away. Someone staring like Shiela could glimpse the bone contour and sunken expression of twenty years' time. Already his mouth was crimped as if he had lost his teeth. From the lapel pocket protruded the uncircumcized tip of a Cuban cigar.

'Well, Shiel,' he sighed. 'How's it going?'

He was tired.

'I met some really interesting people downstairs, Shiel. Really interesting, good people. But I couldn't speak their language.'

Clutching at her shoulder, the eiderdown slid off.

'I've been meaning to ask, Shiel. Are you having a good time?'

But Shiela tried to straighten the covers.

'For Christ's sake, Shiela. Live dangerously! I've been meaning to tell you. That's your problem. You're cooped up.'

Garry belched.

'Listen, Shiela. Are you having a good time?'

She stopped pulling the eiderdown.

'I see interesting sights and customs; I like people. I think everything can be interesting.'

'Fuck!' Garry leaned forward. 'What sort of angle is that?' A perplexed solemnity entered his face, and held. 'I feel we're the odd ones out.' He was breathing heavily, looking at her. 'We're the dark horses, you and I. They know fuck-all about us.'

Someone coughed.

'I had never thought . . .' Shiela started.

Garry nodded significantly. 'Think about it.'

He sat up and raised his chin like a rooster. 'And you know the other dark horse?'

'Who?'

'Old Gerald . . .'

'I think that's unkind. He's very nice.'

She had hardly spoken to Gerald but knew his way of trailing, of holding back.

Garry laughed, slapping his knee. 'We understand each other, you and I. We're in this together.'

Shiela frowned as he kept nodding his head.

'Please don't smoke now. I won't get to sleep. These narrow cubby-holes . . .'

'Fair enough, fair enough.'

'Some of us are trying to sleep'—voice next door; Gerald's. Others too lay awake, storing each others' secrets.

Shiela whispered to Garry. 'You'd better go.'

Sitting up, the white surface of one of her breasts appeared, a partial eclipse of the moon.

Lurching towards her, Garry changed his mind in mid-air.

'To sleep!' he shouted instead. 'To sleep!' Struggling to his feet he swayed: shooting his arms out horizontally, he tried to hold. His sunglasses struck the dressing table, scattering tinted shards over Shiela's little handkerchiefs and postcards; and he fell against the jerry-built partitions, enough to punch in the lower panel.

'For goodness' sake,' Mrs Cathcart called out. 'Doug? What's going on?'

He could sleep through an earthquake, the end of the world.

'For Christ's sake,' Garry argued, but muffled. Most of his head and shoulders were in the next room.

'You could be hurt!'

'Give us a hand, Shiela. Fuck!'

Gerald had switched on the light. Someone came to Shiela's door.

'Is everything alright?'

'You're a pack of dull bastards!' Garry shouted. 'Watch it, watch it.'

Kaddok had arrived with his camera and flash.

'It's alright,' said Gerald in his dressing gown. Bending down he tried to fit back the partition.

'I think he's unhappy,' said Shiela trying to help.

'Probably,' said Gerald. 'I can't imagine why. I'll get him to his room.'

It began raining slightly and then steadily, as if the locals were throwing stones on the roof. To Shiela, as she relaxed, it was like it was back home.

This museum stood with its back to a wall as if it had been squeezed into the town. It was the tail of a broken church or a small cathedral (which?) renowned for its Dutch bell. In 1943 the nave had been blasted to smithereens and the streets showered with slate and parables in stained glass.

The Australians were talking loudly, lounging by the wall. The sunlight made them squint. A wife had to pull a husband back from a reversing vegetable truck. Beetroots were under tarpaulins like soldiers. The local people passing took no notice of them.

The keeper arrived swinging a tan spleuchan bulging with change. Pear-shaped, he looked like a priest in civvies; of course they had to pay.

There were no turnstyles, no divisions inside, no corridors. So the museum echoed.

Any movement on the formerly sacred floor was translated into sharp clatter. Any noise in this hall could only be theirs. They remained in the middle rubbing shoulders as they had so often before, a group.

'Oy!' It multiplied something terrible.

'For goodness' sake.'

Even in the dark some liked to express themselves.

Some are strict. Others remain quiet but fidget. There was a blind man.

A fluorescent tube lit up and ran in a line towards them, igniting a second parallel row, a third, and a fourth. Several strategically placed searchlights (war surplus) were the last to come on; when it rains, it pours. The hall was rectangular, short and bare. This didn't stop them radiating in all directions.

'It said museum in the book, definitely.'

They soon returned to the centre.

'He charged us. Where is the bastard?'

'They must be renovating.'

The walls and the beamed ceilings were white.

'It could be a Wind Museum; something invisible like that.'

An Electric Light Museum?

There is one in The Netherlands.

The harsh unnatural light threw perfect shadows on the white, and because they expected or demanded more, they shifted about swinging their arms, sometimes pausing, followed by their shadows. A certain worldliness showed in the way they sauntered. Their remarks, isolated laughter, their cracks and expectations instantly showed on the wall; and magnified or isolated here were the Lantern Jaws of some. The apparition of a quiet one was characterisitically weighed down on one side by the foreign phrases in his left pocket, although he had his back to the wall like the rest. The breasts of women, young and old, suggested experiences and future possibilities. Some shadows had already joined at the elbow, or merged into one with two arms, two heads but four legs. Optimism and years, gentleness, intolerance could be confirmed here by shape, posture and movement. Not everyone had noticed. They were burdened with equipment, notably the straight angles of the manufactured bag, large and small, with handles, the arm held horizontal for that purpose; impedimenta of nomads. Strange how women have been made to walk on tip-toe. Those binoculars showed as an irruption of the man's lower intestine. There was a beard; possibly a wise man. The shadows pointed back to them.

They'd returned to the centre again.

One had his feet planted apart, arms dangling at his sides, and one leg vibrating like a high-jumper about to begin his run. There was no hurry, there never was, and yet impatience showed in the foot, arm and jaw movements, and a scratching of the side of the neck, now increasing.

As so often happens someone away from the centre called out and they went over, still talking, a reflex action.

Near the entrance, which is also the exit, words had been

found along the wall, possibly a work abandoned by a muralist. By watching, by contemplating, they could fill in and fit the details. Gradually, standing quietly, they began to see themselves. Possibilities included the past and the near future: it was possible to consider a sense of place, of their shape and long time. Strange sensation then. The words were being read aloud by one, and they followed remaining squashed together before disintegrating: shoulder-blades, ear, pelvis, heart, movement, elbow, nose, eyes, air, rib cage, bladder, cigarette, trees, thorax, shoes, penis, shadow, postcards, memory, mountain.